Under the Acacia Trees

A Novel of Colonial Australia

Elinor De Wire

© 2023 Elinor DeWire

All rights reserved: No part of this book may be copied, re-sold without the cover, or reproduced without written permission from the publisher and author, except by a reviewer, special promotion, or distributor who may quote brief passages. Nor may any part of this book be reproduced, stored in a retrieval system, or transmitted in any form or by any means (electronic, mechanical, photocopied, recorded, or other) without written permission from the publisher and author.

This book is a work of historical fiction and alternative history. While some characters are based on real historical persons, the majority are fictional. The author and publisher disclaim any liability in connection with characters and information contained within the book.

Cover design by Jessica DeWire.

Cat in the Window Press
lightkeeper0803@gmail.com

Dedication

To my mother, Ruth Rebecca Keeney, who taught me to love books and reading and to regularly exercise my imagination.

And to the friendly, fun, and welcoming people of Australia who have given me a love for all things "Down Under."

Elinor DeWire and Cat in the Window Press pay respect and acknowledge the traditional custodians of the land on which this story takes place. We also pay respect to their Elders both past and present.

Author's Note

Under the Acacia Trees is set during Australia's Colonial Period in a rural place called Wahroonga. (Pronounce it Wah-**roon**-ga, accenting the middle syllable.) It's a real place, a small town in New South Wales about a half-hour north of Sydney. I heard it mentioned in a television interview a few years ago and loved the sound of it, the way it rolled off my tongue and paid tribute to the Aboriginals of Australia—believed to be the oldest humans on earth.

When I discovered "our home" is the meaning of Wahroonga in Dharug—the language of the Aboriginals of the region—I knew I'd found the setting for my story. I researched, researched, and researched, as this is what consumes 90% of historical fiction writers, then I rolled the fictional time machine back to the early 1800s, had my Writer's Passport to Imagination stamped, and crafted a tale that could easily have taken place in Wahroonga in the burgeoning colony of New South Wales. Call it an <u>alternative</u> history.

According to historical records, emancipated convict and Sydney timber merchant, Thomas Pinnick Hyndes (1778-1855), was the first white man to own land in Wahroonga, beginning in 1822. He never lived there but operated a timber business in the area. The convict timber-getters he hired and sent to Wahroonga were its first white settlers, though I could find no names for any of them or a description of exactly how or where they lived.

Thus, I believe Mr. Hyndes and his convict workers will forgive my impertinence in replacing them with more interesting players in *Under the Acacia Trees,* an alternative fictional account of the founding of Wahroonga.

My main characters, Dr. Thaddeus Bennett and Vicar Gregory Mayhew, as well as nurse Ella Fielding, arrive in 1806 and 1818 respectively. All three are suffering from loss and heartache. The novel follows their lives from 1818 until the 1880s and details the many challenges they face becoming Australians. Along the way, I showcase the delights they encounter, too, in a place completely upside-down and different from their homelands in England and Canada.

The Epilogue of my story is fictional too, jumping forward to modern-day Wahroonga, but I'll avoid any spoilers. You'll have to read to the end to find out what happens. I hope you enjoy my tale.

Elinor DeWire
Canterbury, Connecticut
July 2023

One

**October 1818
Wahroonga, New South Wales**

Whenever it was that God made this corner of the globe, He used a different template.

Stephen Donovan
Morgan's Run

The spire of a little wooden church came into view in the distance. Ella Fielding sighed and straightened her sore back. She was weary after so many months of travelling to reach the British colony of New South Wales and the small place called Wahroonga. Her hands held fast to the wooden seat of the heavily loaded wagon as its driver guided the horses slowly uphill. They were almost to her new home. The two brawny Belgians high-stepped in anticipation. Every horse knows when it's near to the barn, especially after a hard day of work, and this pair were no exception.

The rough dirt road ahead passed in front of the church and seemed to narrow by perspective and disappear into a hazy-gray eucalypt forest so thick as to allow only thin threads of sunlight to filter to the ground. Surrounding the church on one side, a large green parcel of weedy lawn appeared, flanked by flowering trees, their vivid yellow blossoms flying in the warm spring wind like so much confetti. Pastoral, Ella thought, but in a strange way so unlike rural scenes she had grown up with in Canada and England.

She tucked a few loose tendrils of her honey-blonde hair under her straw hat and smothered a yawn. After spending most of the day on the hard seat of the wagon, watching the Belgians' ample, beige, and betailed backsides waggle from side-to-side, and hearing their giant hooves *clop-de-clop-de-clop*, her journey finally was at an end. She was here at last! Acacia House and its sprawling farm lay just ahead through the trees.

A sandy-haired man appeared at the back of the little church. He was dressed in a clerical robe, its black folds undulating in the spring air. Behind him a gaggle of children followed, bolting into a run the moment they reached an open space where a simple play area had been built with swings, seesaws, a whirling wagon wheel mounted on a large stump, and a ramshackle treehouse perched high in a tall spotted gum. Several children clambered up a board ladder nailed on the gum to access the treehouse.

The children's liberation from what Ella supposed was school, and the unfettered joy they exhibited, made her smile. She loved children and suddenly realized these were the orphans she would help to supervise. She had come to Wahroonga not only to assist the wealthy Dr. Thaddeus Bennett in his busy medical practice at Acacia House, but to see to the health and education of some two dozen foundling children in an orphanage behind the church. She would teach them to read, write, do arithmetic, and know the world around them through science, history, and geography, all the while working alongside Anglican vicar, Father Gregory Mayhew, whose distant, reedy form she now watched as he walked back inside his church.

The property was well-groomed and had a tidy scattering of purposeful wooden buildings, including the church. At first glance, it seemed as bucolic as a Wordsworth lyrical ballad, a patch of Eden set down in the midst of endless fragrant forest and the music of birds and insects. It was a fine opening look, for sure, Ella thought. But she also knew first impressions sometimes were false, or at the very least misleading. Mayhap, this pleasant glimpse was authentic.

As the wagon neared its destination, the horses grew more eager and instinctively picked up their pace. The dray was loaded with Ella's trunks of belongings and a crate filled with medical supplies the doctor had asked her to buy in London before she sailed for New South Wales. Additionally, there were numerous items the driver, Henry Douglas, had purchased in Sydney for the orphanage and Dr. Bennett's household— miniature bottles of exotic spices; wooden boxes of sugar cones; bags of flour, oats, and cornmeal from the mill in Henrietta Town; expensive oolong tea imported from Jakarta; several large blocks of beef tallow for candle-making; a new halter for the doctor's favorite horse; a half dozen bolts of cotton fabric to make clothes for the children; books both the doctor and the vicar had ordered; and bottles of wine and whiskey.

"De doktor no like rum," Henry Douglas had told Ella as he stowed the liquor. "It mead on de becks a' sleaves in Wes' Indie. Doktor heat sleavry."

Henry had detailed all the purchases, speaking in his curious, cobbled-together Aboriginal English, as he and Ella traveled the dusty, red-brown roads north of Sydney. Beyond the settlement at Parramatta, the track was little more than an animal path widened by the clearing of trees and rocks and the subsequent traffic of wagons and the occasional carriage. Heavy rains from winter had gouged and rutted it, forcing Henry and the horses to zigzag around the hazards.

"Ho'ses' foot so big git rock stucked in hoof…pry off shoo. Muss be-uh cayful."

Mrs. Mildred Hughes, the doctor's chief housekeeper, had written in her last letter to Ella—and she had written many letters—that the doctor's half-caste assistant, Henry Douglas, would fetch Ella from the convict ship *Isabella* after it anchored at Sydney Cove.[1] Hours earlier, Ella had been more than glad to greet Henry as she disembarked the stinking, overcrowded vessel and stood wobbling on firm ground, feeling nauseous and a bit light-headed. Henry had smiled with a set of fine, straight teeth—one tooth missing in the front—and taken her arm to steady her. He offered a chunk of ginger to chew, saying it would ease her post-voyage vertigo.

Seeing the taboo exchange, a crewman from the *Isabella* leaned over the rails and cursed at Henry, reminding him to keep his "bloody black hands off white women." Ella frowned and yelled to the crewman to mind his own affairs. She knew racism was rampant in the colony and had already resolved not to be a part of it.

Along the twenty-five-kilometer route to Wahroonga, Ella had asked Henry many questions, for everything around her was new and strange, even a little worrisome. Where were the convicts imprisoned? Where did the Governor live? To whom was she to present her immigration papers? Were there highwaymen on the roads who might attack them? Was the weather always this clement? What were the curious green capsules on nearly all the trees?

Despite her concerns, the wagon trip had been pleasant, though at this moment Ella was sure her backside could not endure another kilometer of travel, what with all the bumping and jostling on the unyielding wagon seat.

"Almoss der, ma-laydee!" Henry said. "Dr. Benna hows' jus' ova der."

He pointed to a stand of small, shrubby trees with lovely golden blooms, the same flower-laden trees Ella had been seeing for hours. The dust cleared, and the shape of a large, light-green house materialized amid the blossoms and greenery. Behind it were several other buildings, including two barns and a carriage house. How odd to see an English carriage house here, in such an unfamiliar setting.

"I am so glad to arrive!" Ella replied to Henry, smiling and clasping her hands with joy.

She sighed again, suddenly realizing she had been traveling since December, almost ten months, first from Canada to England on a mail steamer and then on a convict ship on the long voyage from London to the notorious penal colony at New South Wales. She had been told hers was the longest trip one could make on earth, all the way to the other side of the globe.

---

[1] The term half-caste is considered derogatory today, but in the early 1800s it was used with impunity.

Where, exactly, the other side of the globe might be she had little idea. She only knew it was far, a weathery, exhausting trip of many months over seemingly endless seas that allowed her little sense of direction or progress but kept her stomach in a near-constant state of distress. No matter. This was Australia, as Governor Lachlan Macquarie wanted it to be called—the curious, Antipodean place where Ella Fielding would find purposeful employment, a welcome home, and likely spend the remainder of her life. She also would live among the natives, some like Henry, born of two worlds.

Ella had decided Henry was strangely handsome, almost exotic. He appeared well into his thirties and more Aboriginal than white. Soft, crinkly strands of dark, reddish-brown hair, sprinkled with a few white ones, covered his head. His nose and lips were full and finely formed. He had caramel skin and light brown eyes, almost the color of nutmeg. Though he was sparingly built, he had shown himself to be sturdy and strong by his easy handling of the wagon's bulky contents and his control of the two powerful draught horses.

His only physical flaw, as far as Ella could see, were the smallpox scars on his face. Ella felt sure these were from the 1789 *galla galla*, as the Aboriginals called the contagion that had decimated half of their population the year after the First Fleet arrived in Sydney. Henry had been a small boy then. It was a wonder he had survived. From what Ella had been told by the *Isabella's* crew, the horrific epidemic was hardest on the sick, the very young, and the very old.

Many of the soldiers and even the convicts in New South Wales had been vaccinated against smallpox or were possessed of a hardy Anglo-gumption that resisted the illness or reduced it to a minor malaise. The Aboriginals, however, were neither inoculated nor robust where European disease was concerned. They died by the hundreds. People were still questioning whether smallpox had arrived in the colony by accident or by intention, since vials of pustule scrapings had been shipped with the First Fleet in anticipation of being needed for vaccinations. How easy it would have been for the British to infect the native population, who they considered more aggravating than accommodating.

At the top of the hill the horses had been climbing, an entrance appeared to the long Acacia House driveway. To the side of it a sign read, "Dr. Thaddeus Bennett, Physician & Chemist." That's him, Ella thought, the doctor she had agreed to assist. She had committed bravely to work for this man sight unseen, having answered an advert in a London newspaper mailed to a priest who gave last rites at the Canadian hospital where she worked.

Henry slowed the horses and turned to look behind the wagon. There was a commotion and a curtain of dust. Ella heard him mutter something unintelligible and possibly profane in his native, Aboriginal language—

Abruptly, a group of burly, roughneck men on horseback emerged from the dust cloud and sprinted by the wagon, shouting, gesturing, and stirring up more dust. Henry shuddered and held tight to the Belgians' reins. The ruffians cursed Henry as they passed, gesturing rudely, and whistled and hooted at Ella. One man stood up over his saddle and jerked his hips back and forth provocatively, whooping and catcalling.

Ella immediately turned away, paying them no mind. A waste of masculine theatrics, it was. Travel on a convict ship had made her immune to men's heckling and vulgar body language. There had been plenty of felons and soldiers on the *Isabella* lewdly admiring her and wishing, albeit hopelessly, for her favors. Fortunately, the captain and his officers had kept her safe.

"Timba cuttas…frum up Colah weay!" Henry shouted, shaking his head with disgust. He clenched his jaw in frustration. "Deys no betta 'n animas."

Ella nodded, noticing Henry fingering the pistol tucked in his waistband. They had traveled undisturbed for hours. Trouble could not possibly happen at the end of the driveway to Acacia House. The hecklers passed. Henry eased his hand away from his pistol and turned to Ella with a smile.

"We uh here, Missy Fieldin'!!"

Seeing the doctor's big house through the trees, Ella thought back to her decision to come to New South Wales. Dr. Bennett's correspondence before she sailed for the colony had been infrequent but demonstrative. The doctor said he was desperate for a good nurse to assist him in his practice, which turned out to be mostly caring for the six-and-twenty orphans at St. Andrew's Anglican Church and seeing to the needs of the small communities around Wahroonga. These included the timber-getters to the west near Mt. Colah, the orchard pickers to the southwest near Toongabbie, a few hardy free settlers along the Eastern Road and at Bungaroo in the Dundas District, and a group of uprooted Bidjigal natives who camped on the western border of Dr. Bennett's lands. He had befriended them soon after his July 1806 arrival in Wahroonga and had no desire to see them harmed or run out of the area.

The doctor's housekeeper, Mrs. Hughes, had shared some of his history in one of her letters, telling Ella how Dr. Bennett and Father Mayhew had sailed together from England in 1806 aboard the convict ship *Fortune* on its first voyage to Port Jackson. *Fortune* was under the command of Captain Henry Moore. There were 245 male convicts aboard, along with tons of food and clothing for the penal colony. The repulsive smell of the men's over-crowded confinement below deck permeated the *Fortune*. After tending to ailments among the shackled convicts and seeing their grim and filthy living space below deck, Dr. Bennett discovered the ship's surgeon, William Price, had no medical training at all and relied on a first aid pamphlet to treat the sick. The doctor stepped up and quickly proved himself indispensable.

The filthy convict hold was cleaned up; the felons' clothes were washed. The shackled men were made to bathe in a barrel of soapy seawater once a week and come on deck each Sunday to be treated for lice and sores, all the while hearing Father Gregory preach his self-styled, liberal version of the Gospel. The fresh sea air and the extra portion of porridge given to the prisoners during the sermon was a sure incentive.

After disembarking the *Fortune* at Sydney on July 19, 1806, Dr. Bennett took title to a large parcel of mostly cleared land in the north section of an unsettled area called Wahroonga. The land had been abandoned inexplicably by its original claimant, a freed convict, possibly due to crop failure or a skirmish with the natives. Phillip Gidney King, who had only two months remaining as governor, was anxious that the colony be infused with educated, wealthy men like Dr. Bennett. Thus, acquiring the land at Wahroonga was easy for the doctor. The governor simply gifted it to him.

Dr. Bennett and his large entourage of servants and trade workers, and his close friend, the vicar, Father Gregory Mayhew, spent only a few nights in the rowdy, congested settlement at Port Jackson before several waggoneers and drift boats were hired to take them northwest to their new home. For some of Bennett's employees, it was daunting to see the appalling conditions and treatment of the convicts and accept the harsh, untidy, wrong-side-up land of New South Wales. But the doctor and priest assured them this was their paradise waiting to be embraced…if only they would work and persevere for a few years.

As Henry and Ella finally arrived at the front of Dr. Bennett's big house, the verbose Mrs. Hughes appeared on the spacious front porch, waving a greeting with her handkerchief. Henry murmured unhappily to himself, remembering a recent flogging from Mrs. Hughes with a broom. He didn't know what he had done to upset her. He would not tell the doctor about her anger either, for this would surely cause an uncomfortable confrontation between the doctor and housekeeper. It was well-known amongst his peers that Henry despised disagreements.

Ella combed her loose curls with her fingers, adjusted her straw bonnet, and slipped on a pair of worn lace gloves. She carried a reticule containing a few personal items. Henry helped her down from the wagon and looped her arm through his to lead her properly over the white, crushed-shell path to the porch stairs and front door. She was smiling with anticipation.

"Here uh be da butte-ti-ful Missy Fieldin'," Henry announced. He turned to Ella and motioned to the housekeeper. "Dis here uh be Missy Huez. She kip an' rule da howse. We all obehs her."

At the sight of Ella, Mrs. Hughes appeared speechless, lifting her handkerchief to the side of her mouth and slowly smiling. Ella quickly learned, however, that the housekeeper was never at a loss for words.

"You are here at last, Miss Fielding! How lovely you are! How wonderful to meet you! We expected you might be a spinster, or a matron…but you are young and beautiful. How was your voyage and the trip from Port Jackson? I have been counting the days, my dear. It is such a pleasure to welcome an educated and refined young woman to our staff. I know you will be happy with us. The work here is truly gratifying."

Her greeting was said with alacrity and amazing rapidity…in one big breath. She held a hand over her heart. The fresh southwest breeze ruffled the hem of her light blue dress and starched white apron and teased a few gray hairs that had escaped from her bun.

Ella immediately noticed how inviting the porch was, with its bamboo-framed settees and chairs dressed in plush cushions, its tables made from odd-shaped, lacquered tree stumps, its colorful fringed rugs hooked together from scraps of material, and the numerous hanging pots of flowers and ferns. The air coursing through the ornate railings had a subtle minty fragrance and nudged a wooden swing at one end of the porch.

Ella eyed the comfortable furnishings and thought she might collapse, without invitation or hesitation, on one of the settees for a nap.

"I believe I wrote to you that Dr. Bennett named this Acacia House," Mrs. Hughes announced, not waiting for Ella's greeting.

The housekeeper swung her arms wide, indicating the numerous and diverse blossom-laden acacia trees standing on the property. Their yellow flowers exuded some of the scent that pleased Ella's nose.

"They are enchanting, Miss Fielding. So many blossoms this time of year, and into summer. Thorns on some types, yes, but we seldom think of that. All things must protect themselves, yes? Oh, spring is such a wonderful season in New South Wales!"

Spring? Ella had difficulty regarding October as spring. She supposed everything she had learned in Canada and England was the opposite here. Reversed and foreign. Inverted. Uncomfortably overturned. Her senses suddenly were barraged with the unfamiliar. Even an opaque, third-quarter moon hung backwards in the vivid blue northern sky.

"Some people call these flowering trees wattles," Mrs. Hughes continued. "I believe wattle refers to the use of acacia branches to form lattice-type walls for the crude houses the convicts build down in Sydney town. We prefer the name acacia. It is Greek for *honorable*. The fragrance of the acacia flower is so complex you must whiff it yourself and decide what perfumes have commingled to produce such an irresistible fragrance."

Did Mrs. Hughes not hear Ella's weary sighs of exhaustion? Her stifled yawns? She desperately needed to relieve herself and rest. She had been traveling for such a long time.

Unexpectedly, Ella perked up when, to the west, she recognized a blue-gray mist suspended over the faraway mountaintops. She had seen it in a London gallery in a painting of New South Wales.

"Those must be the tops of the Blue Mountains of which I have read so much," Ella said, excited to identify something in this strange place. "Is it true the bluish color comes from the gum trees?"

Mrs. Hughes chuckled: "Dr. Bennett will tell you the science behind it, but yes, the gum trees emit a minty, citrusy, miasma that hangs over the peaks and looks blue when the sun hits it."

Acacia House did not resemble any of the great homes of England, but Ella decided it had a certain, new-found charm representative of its far-flung, austral location. It was built of the area's hardwoods, part of its exterior painted light green, the doctor's favorite color she would later learn. The roof was shingled with slate from the distant Slate Quarry Creek in Gundagai. The simple exterior trim was white☐white sashes, white shutters, white Doric columns holding up the roof of the northwest-facing, wrap-around porch, now gilded in spring-time light.

They entered the house through magnificent sandalwood double doors thrown wide by Henry before he bowed and departed for the barn. The horses were tired. Henry was tired. Ella watched him go with envy, knowing he and the big Belgians would get some much-deserved rest.

The foyer was not large, as were those of aristocratic homes, but was modestly furnished; yet it was welcoming and charming. A large bouquet of brushy pink blooms and bizarre-looking, candle-shaped yellow cones was arranged on a marble table near the entrance. Next to it was a miniature sandstone model of Stonehenge, a nod to the doctor's possible homesickness. A rich brown floor with an intricate pattern of woodgrain greeted Ella's dusty shoes.

"An acacia wood floor is beautiful, is it not?" Mrs. Hughes said, not really asking. "It is used sparingly in this house, due to its expense in milling. Acacia is an extremely hard wood that dulls a saw quickly. But do look at the lovely grain and knots. It is like a tapestry spread over the floor!"

They studied the floor together for a few seconds. Ella suppressed another yawn. She realized there was no getting around Mrs. Hughes. The woman clearly was overcome with enormous joy at Ella's arrival and intended to give her a detailed tour of the seemingly misplaced, elegant house.

"Dr. Bennett was glad to receive a large order of acacia lumber from the sawmill in Waitara," Mrs. Hughes went on, "enough to floor the formal rooms downstairs and his bedchamber on the second floor. I believe the trees were felled in the Pennant Hills somewhat west of here. Other wood floors in the house are mostly soft cypress pine. But the dining room has a lovely rosewood floor, the lumber of which was brought down from the Hawkesbury River area."

Ella knew nothing of the names the housekeeper used—Waitara, Pennant Hills, Hawkesbury. However, she thought it appropriate that part of Acacia House had acacia wood floors. She liked the name and its meaning, *honorable*. Her work here would be honorable, she was sure.

The furniture in the drawing room was lavish, yet functional. The décor lacked the usual snobbery of English manor homes. There were no statues of naked cherubs, no busts or paintings of King George III, or likenesses of any other monarch. No celestial vases with scenes of the Orient, no wallpaper with out-of-context designs, no opulent ceilings painted with mythical gods and goddesses, clouds and stars, or biblical scenes.

There were only watercolor landscapes on the softly colored walls, paintings of flowers and animals and the majestic mountains to the west. The high ceilings possessed modest ornamentation, though, with gold-leaf crown moldings and carved medallions for suspending candelabras. A portrait of Dr. Bennett's mother, looking sage and severe, hung in an ornate frame over the drawing room hearth. She was as close to a monarch as Ella could find.

"Is Mrs. Bennett living?" Ella asked.

"Oh no! She passed when Dr. Bennett was a boy," Mrs. Hughes replied. "I remember that day as if it was yesterday. My little boy, Thad, cried and cried."

"You were with the family when he was a boy, then?"

Mrs. Hughes straightened and smiled.

"Miss Fielding, I was with the family when Dr. Bennett was born."

After touring the front rooms, Ella was escorted up the acacia stairway. It curved gently to the second floor, each step a marvelous artwork of nature. A marble bust of the doctor's father sat on a table at the top of the stairway, with a painting of a grand Northampton house on the wall over it. Mrs. Hughes informed Ella that Dr. Bennett adored his late father, the elder Dr. Thomas Bennett, a man who had transformed medicine through his experimental remedies and procedures. Dr. Thaddeus Bennett had grown up in the English house pictured in the painting and occasionally waxed nostalgic about it.

Mrs. Hughes pointed to a door a short distance from the top of the second floor. It was slightly ajar and had a kangaroo carved into it, a large one sitting on his long, thick tail and looking straight-on at whoever dared to knock or enter.

Ella had read about this peculiar animal, the unofficial emblem of Australia. There were several sizes of the oddly constructed beast. This one was large and appeared to be a male, as it had no marsupial pouch with an inquisitive joey. It was a buck, sometimes called a jack or a boomer or even a *bounder*, for its penchant for jumping…not a tendency to behave badly, as some men did. Ella recalled reading that the British explorer, Captain James Cook, coined the word kangaroo in 1774 after hearing the Aboriginals at Botany Bay call the animal a *gangurru*. The oddest fact she knew about this native animal was that it could not walk backwards, a sure disadvantage.

"The doctor's quarters," Mrs. Hughes said in a quiet voice, pushing the kangaroo door fully open. "I shall take you here briefly, as I do not expect Dr. Bennett home for a few hours. He has ridden Wanyuwa on a call to Warrawee. Sick old man there. It is just a few kilometers from here."

Wanyuwa? Warrawee? Gibberish, Ella decided. How was she ever to learn such names?

"Wanyuwa, is that his horse, Mrs. Hughes?"

"Why, yes! Dr. Bennett loves that old horse. Had him brought here from England in 1806, along with several others. The little herd has since increased to nineteen, I believe. Wanyuwa was a gift from the doctor's father. The elder Dr. Bennett wanted his son to have a fine horse to accompany him to New South Wales. The horse had no name, so the doctor called him Wanyuwa. It means 'horse' in Dharug…the language most of the local native people speak."

Ella was confused, as she would be time and again over the coming weeks.

"The Aboriginals do not have horses, do they?"

"No," Mrs. Hughes flatly stated, "but they have learned about them and have a word for *horse*. The doctor tells me horses are not native to this land."

Dr. Bennett's private space had a perceptible masculine smell. Ella presumed from Mrs. Hughes' hesitant demeanor that neither of them should be in his rooms. But since they were, she would look around.

A mongrel dog lay on the floor beside the bed. His tail thumped, and he lifted his head at the sight of Ella and Mrs. Hughes, then he went back to sleep.

"He is good company for the doctor," Mrs. Hughes said, patting the dog's head. "He is old, though, and sleeps most of the day. Dr. Bennett believes he has gone deaf."

Ella saw that the dog's face was grey and white, and his eyes were glassy. An old dog, yes.

The bedchamber was expansive, taking up the entire front part of the second floor of the house. Fine Turkish rugs overspread most of the floor, acacia floor. Dark green drapes cascaded around the windows, separated by white sheers. The bed, with its green-striped counterpane and matching bolster pillows, was large. Ella thought it much too large for one person; yet she knew the doctor was unmarried.

There was a maroon, almost brown, chaise—Ella's mother always called this a headache couch—to one side of the room. It was complemented by several chairs and a small table on which some half-dozen books were stacked, along with paper, a feather pen, and an ink bottle.

"He sometimes takes his meals here," Mrs. Hughes explained, pointing to a larger table and chairs. A sketchpad lay on the table with a charcoal drawing of a little girl. "And he is a prolific reader, writer, *and* artist," she added.

Ella lingered by the bookshelves, themselves an artistic touch with their various colors and patterns of bindings. She estimated there were well over one-hundred books.

Over the large four-poster bed was a painting of a sweet-faced young woman with red-gold hair and bright blue eyes. Ella wondered who she was.

"His betrothed, Edith Fullerton," Mrs. Hughes whispered, as if reading Ella's mind. "She died of consumption in 1804, two years before the doctor brought all of us here. Everything you see at Acacia House and its surroundings, my dear girl, was built to assuage Dr. Bennett's grief over her death."

It was a sobering discovery. Ella realized she had much to learn about the man for whom she would work.

Three large armoires sat along one wall in a separate room, with a wide bureau and a tall rectangular mirror propped against the wall opposite them. There was a separate bath as well, which Ella was keen to see, but Mrs. Hughes seemed harried, anxious to go. They left the doctor's quarters, leaving the sleeping dog and heavy kangaroo door ajar behind them.

The housekeeper led Ella downstairs again, toward the back, where a large kitchen stretched widthwise across the house. Maids were busy chopping, kneading, mashing, and stirring. One was carrying China to the dining room. Another was washing pots. Ella could smell the beginnings of a delicious dinner.

Mrs. Hughes continued her seemingly endless commentary—

"There is no 'below stairs' in this house, as in English aristocratic houses. Only a basement for storing foodstuff and seasonal items. All the meals are prepared here on the first floor and taken forward to the dining room, unless the doctor orders otherwise. We, the staff I mean, eat at one end of this large kitchen table. And we are housed upstairs opposite the doctor's chambers. All of us are treated with great kindness. It is quite a contrast to an English estate, Miss Fielding. I believe it is because the doctor despises snobbery and arrogance. He is not pompous or prideful in the least."

Ella nodded her weary head, glad to hear these platitudes about her employer.

Behind the big kitchen was the doctor's large medical clinic, rooms with medicine cabinets and examining tables, shelves stacked with white sheets and towels, bottles and vials, and instruments. A well-equipped surgery was the centerpiece. Everything was sparkling clean and in its proper place.

In the first room of the clinic, Ella stepped on the weight scale and adjusted its balance. It read in pounds, 109 pounds to be exact. Ella calculated the amount as a little under eight stone. Looking up, she saw, to her chagrin, that a handwritten table of pound-to-stone conversion had been posted.

"I am an under-nourished waif," she thought to herself.

She knew she had lost weight on the voyage. How could she not, what with the horrid food and continuous vomiting from *mal de mer*.

A young woman occupied one of the beds in the clinic. She waved hello and gave Ella a bright smile.

"Ye mus' be dee doctor's new nurse!" the woman called through her open door, reaching a hand toward Ella. "We hurd ye arrived. I be Bessie Holme, wife o' one dee timba gettas in dee hills no'west o' here at Colah. I be bone in Syd-nee ta uh sold-jer an' hez wife. I wed me uh convic' name uh Sam Holme. He be a free man nowl."

Ella took the woman's hand, smiling: "Hello. I am Ella Fielding, come all the way from Canada via England. I look forward to working with Dr. Bennett."

She wondered if the woman knew where Canada or England was.

"Oh, miss, he be dee kind-ess, sweet-ess man! He tend ta me wit' dee gent-less, best-ess hans, big hans dat cans do so minna tings. Has Missa Huez tol' ye he play-ees dee organ in dee church?"

Ella raised her eyebrows. Big hands? Organist?

"She has not, but I am not surprised, as I saw a fine piano in the drawing room."

She paused a moment.

"Mrs. Holme, what is the treatment you are receiving?"

The young woman sighed and rubbed one hand over her lower belly.

"Me chil' inside me woom were dead, ma'am," she answered matter-of-factly. "Dr. Benna taked it a week 'go, me womb, babe an' all. He spur me see it, fo' wich I be tankful. He be keepin' me here fo' few dayes rest."

Ella was nodding sympathetically. She lifted Bessie's bedsheet and studied the bandaged place on her belly.

"I am sorry about your baby, Mrs. Holme. May I assume you have a big family that requires your constant attention, and that is why you would get no rest at home?"

"Aye," Bessie said giggling, showing off a row of rotting teeth. "I be gla' me woom be gone. I be mutta o' fo'teen chil'rens, enuf fo' enna wo-man."

An understatement, Ella thought. The woman could not be more than five-and-thirty.

She had learned more about Dr. Bennett from his patient, Mrs. Holme. He *was* an excellent surgeon, one willing to open the human body when necessary to prevent death.

Most of the surgeons Ella had assisted in her nursing career had eschewed working inside the body. One doctor in Canada had told Ella that the interior of the human body was possessed of a revolting smell, and that God forbade meddling with its workings.

After bidding the patient good-bye, Mrs. Hughes and Ella went back upstairs to the rear of the house where the housekeeper showed Ella the housemaids' quarters. Ella was not much interested, but she knew it was useless to object.

"Dr. Bennett really does surgery inside the body?" Ella asked as they moved from room to room, all identical in furnishings but differentiated by colors of walls, rugs, and quilts.

"Indeed, Miss Fielding. His father was one of the first in England to do so, a medical pioneer. Thad…er, I mean Dr. Bennett, learned from the best."

Mrs. Hughes swung around a corner in the hallway.

"I have saved this part of the tour for last," she said smiling. "I am sure you will want to rest in your room until dinner, so that is the last place we will visit."

Saints and angels, yes! Ella was *so* ready to rest.

Mrs. Hughes breezed by a larger maid's room at the corner of the upstairs, quickly noting:

"My room."

"Where are the men's quarters?" Ella asked.

"They have a large bunkroom over the horse barn, a clean, well-appointed place. The doctor scolds anyone who suggests they are livestock kept in stalls."

She laughed, her face wrinkling gleefully. Ella laughed too, picturing Henry Douglas in a stall with the horses, eating grain.

"How many servants are there in all, Mrs. Hughes?"

The housekeeper thought for a moment.

"Nine here in the house and let me see"—she was counting on her fingers—"I believe two-and-twenty for the gardens and barns and other outdoor work. Dr. Bennett does not call them servants. They, including me, are paid *staff*."

Ella smiled as a portrait of Dr. Thaddeus Bennett began to take shape. He was an alternative thinker for certain, and a man who had discarded the pompous ceremony and frippery of the aristocratic class. Much of his wealth was directed at improving people's lives and the burgeoning society of Australia. Even more, he was willing to try new things, like cutting into the interior of a living human body.

Ella liked the idea of working for a philanthropic maverick.

"Miss Fielding, I think you may wish to wash up after your long journey, even take a nap. I will show you to your room now. Dr. Bennett had the carpenters combine two rooms for you so that you would have more space."

Ella's bed chamber was on the sunny west side of the upstairs, capturing the afternoon and evening light. As Mrs. Hughes opened the door to the room, Ella noticed the acacia stairway to the left and a large door diagonal from hers. It had a big kangaroo on it—the doctor's chambers, which she had already seen.

Did he want her near him? Was she to be more than a servant, more than staff?

Though suddenly worried about the doctor's intent, she gasped with delight when the door to her own room opened. It was a large space with a big bed and more furniture than the maids' rooms contained. And it was far more luxurious than her rooming house quarters in Canada or her cramped cabin on the smelly *Isabella*.

Unlike the other staff rooms, Ella's had two windows, both open a few inches, their lace curtains fluttering cheerfully in the sweet spring air. A floral counterpane matched the green wool rug. There were numerous styles of pillows on the bed and several chairs placed around the room. A vanity sat along one wall with a mirror and a tufted velvet chair. On top were brushes and combs, glass dishes for keeping hairpins and lotions and powder, and pots of rouge and lip color. Beautiful landscapes and watercolors of New South Wales' wildflowers hung on the walls. A fern potted in a wicker stand stood under one window.

Most unexpected was a bath all to herself, furnished with a copper tub, a sink with functioning spigots, and—the biggest surprise of all—a flush toilet.

"The doctor has running water in this house?" Ella asked, putting her hands to her cheeks in surprise. "I have never lived in a place where there was indoor plumbing. In fact, I did not know it was even possible here!"

"I felt the same until just a few months ago," Mrs. Hughes replied with a giggle. "It is truly a newfangled but convenient invention. Dr. Bennett spent a long time researching it and making drawings of the design. The challenge was to get water up to the second floor, which he solved with a large tank installed in the attic. The Barn Boys—oh, that is what I call the men who work outside—fetch buckets of water to a pump outside that pipes it to the attic to replenish the tank regularly, unless it rains, of course, in which case water is collected off the roof. The Barn Boys use an outside stairway and door into the attic, so no one inside is disturbed. It is such a skillful design. I do not think indoor plumbing is much in use yet elsewhere, even in England. Experimental, I am told."

Mrs. Hughes rubbed her hands along the edge of the copper tub in Ella's bath and thumped one side. It uttered a bell-like bong. Her eyebrows playfully went up and down a few times. She explained that Ella could have hot water from the kitchen to fill the tub, and that she need only ask her maid for it.

A maid? I shall have my own maid?

"You are a lucky woman, Miss Fielding. I think Dr. Bennett had indoor plumbing installed in anticipation of your arrival. It serves his bath, yours, the large staff bath, and the kitchen and surgery, plus an outside spigot so the maids can do the washing and the men can clean up and water the gardens. But he hopes to have it extended to other places, even the bunkroom and barn, next year."

Only those places? Surely, there was plumbing enough, a useful novelty in this emergent colony.

Ella's trunks sat under a tall bookshelf. A servant had already brought them to the room. She perused the many titles on the bookshelf and then looked closely at a watercolor on the wall next to it. The wildflowers of the painting were multicolored and wispy, with the face and front paws of a little wallaby peering from behind them.

"How delicate and whimsical!" Ella observed.

"Yes. Those flowers are pink-fingered orchids. The doctor is as capable with a paintbrush as with a scalpel," Mrs. Hughes said, smiling. "And he loves the plants and animals here in New South Wales. Wait until you see his glasshouse, built three years ago. He will want to give you a tour. He absolutely adores taking people through it and teaching about all the plants."

Dr. Thaddeus Bennett appeared to be a fascinating man. Ella hoped he would be easy to get along with. Doctors in Canada were not. Her unpleasant treatment by the medical staff at the small hospital in the Ontario settlement of Bytown[2] had led her to believe she was done with nursing. But then, the hospital priest from the town's St. Alban's Church left her a London newspaper, with an advert urgently requesting a nurse and teacher.

The opportunity sounded utterly romantic to a lonely, jaded woman of six-and-twenty. Ella's mother had died four years earlier, and she had no siblings, no family. The doctor's home in Australia seemed romantic, perhaps only by its name, Wahroonga, a small place about which she had been able to learn nothing. It was not even marked on the few maps she had found of New South Wales in a London library. But she loved the name—*Wah-roon'-ga*. She only knew it was northwest of Port Jackson in a sparsely populated area of the colony. She thought she would live like a pioneer!

In Canada and England, people had warned Ella what a terrible choice she was making, going to live in an insect and reptile infested place that was scorching hot part of the year and home to naked, spear-wielding natives, black as coal. Then, there were the many convicts living in the colony, mostly men. But there were women convicts too, many of them prostitutes.

"It is a den of iniquity!" one of her peers had told her. Another had stated: "You will surely die of snakebite within a month!"

Mrs. Hughes left Ella in her bedchamber to rest before dinner. It would be served at 6:30 p.m., and Ella would meet not only the doctor but Father Gregory too.

---

2 Bytown later became Ottawa.

After the housekeeper had departed, Ella rummaged through one of her trunks for a suitable dress for dinner. On top was the light blue silk-satin that fell slightly off her shoulders and had a wide sash under her bosom to emphasize her figure. It would make a good first impression, a dress that exhibited fashionable taste but also revealed Ella's adventurous side.

She shook out the wrinkles as best she could and hung the dress by one of the open windows. Let the balmy breeze iron out the remaining wrinkles. She desperately needed to relieve herself, wash up, and then lie down and rest. It had been a long journey from the other side of the world.

Two

Ella woke with a start. The sun was angling low across the end of the bed, and the breeze wafting through the windows was cooler. She sat up, sleepy and momentarily unaware of her surroundings. Her wits returned quickly—

Australia! New South Wales! Wahroonga! Dinner at 6:30, Mrs. Hughes had said!

She searched through her reticule on the bedside table for the tiny locket-watch her mother had given her on the occasion of her eighteenth birthday. The time was 6:20 p.m. She was going to be late for dinner, and on her first night in Wahroonga!

She jumped to her feet and quickly flung off her traveling dress, then shimmied into the blue gown, pulled a puffy petticoat under the skirt, and slid into her white, kid, kitten-heeled shoes. Unable to do up the buttons on the back of the dress, she opened her door and peered into the hallway. Fortunately, a maid was coming down the hall.

"Oh, Missy Fieldin', dinner be ready," announced the maid. "Mrs. Hughes send me ta fetch ye."

"Heaven-sent, you are! I overslept my nap. Please, do up the buttons on my gown and help me with my hair and jewelry. Quickly now!"

Within five minutes Ella's dress was buttoned and her hair was done up in an attractive chignon with her natural, blonde-streaked curls cascading down along her ears and a pearl comb holding the rest in place atop her head. Her mother's pearl necklace hung around her slender neck with matching earrings dangling from her earlobes. She looked at herself in the Cheval mirror and pinched her cheeks to rouge them. Satisfied with her appearance, she took off to the formal dining room, calling a thank you to the maid as she went.

She was sure she made her appearance precisely at 6:30 p.m. As if to affirm the fact, the tall clock in the adjoining drawing room chimed the time.

"Miss Fielding," said Mrs. Hughes, as Ella appeared in the dining room doorway, "you are indeed punctual—not a minute early, not a minute late."

The two men seated at the table with Mrs. Hughes leaped to their feet, the taller, broad-shouldered one nearly knocking his chair to the floor. Ella looked at the two in astonishment. They were young and good-looking, both of them! Ella had expected two grizzled old men. She had never seen *young* doctors and priests.

The shorter one, dressed in a cassock and wearing spectacles, was obviously Father Gregory. Though he was not the handsomer or younger of the two, he had gobs of thick sandy hair, hazel eyes, and a friendly countenance. He gave Ella a look of reassurance. She smiled at him, then turned to the doctor.

He was taller, much taller than the vicar, somewhat willowy, and strangely beautiful for a man. Ella's mouth went agape.

His dark hair, with glints of silver here and there, rolled across his head in gentle waves and fell to his collar. He had a perfectly sculpted nose but an uneven mouth, with his upper lip thinner than the lower one. An uneven mouth, yes…but an attractive one.

His dusky brown eyes might have passed for those of a fallow fawn, if only deer resided in New South Wales. His hands were large enough to render a song on a piano, or paint with uncommon dexterity, even relieve terrible pain and sickness in a human body. Lanky, but dressed in fine, well-fitting clothes, he shyly pushed a couple of fingers on one of his big hands into his waistcoat pocket, as if fishing for something.

He was, without question, the handsomest man Ella Fielding had ever seen.

"Miss Fielding," Mrs. Hughes announced, "We are so delighted you are here. As you already know, I normally dine with the kitchen staff, but tonight I am invited here to do introductions."

The housekeeper, chatty as she was and garbed in a nice dress for dinner, suddenly reminded Ella of her rather plump and rosy-cheeked, Aunt Minnie, who had been likeable but could never stop talking. Widowed trice, she had died in an influenza outbreak in Canada eight years earlier. Mrs. Hughes even smelled of the lavender perfumed talc Aunt Minnie had used.

"Please meet Father Gregory," Mrs. Hughes said, referring to the older of the two men, "our dear vicar who runs the orphanage and capably ministers to our small parish."

The priest smiled, snickered with embarrassment, and reached a hand across the table to Ella. He bowed his head shyly. His hair looked as if he had forgotten to comb it before dinner, if he ever combed it. His hazel eyes were bright but tired. Ella knew he was a man devoted to his work.

"My lady, I am delighted you have arrived. I am sure we shall put your myriad talents to great use here. We have much need of a nurse and a teacher. I am told you are capable at both endeavors."

Ella nodded. Though she was not formally trained as a teacher, she had spent a great part of her time in Bytown, Canada teaching the young, novice nurses. No doubt, she could teach children.

"Father Gregory, I am happy to make your acquaintance at last. Mrs. Hughes and Dr. Bennett have sung your praises in their letters."

The cleric chuckled again and wrung his hands slowly with embarrassment.

"And do allow me to introduce our dear Dr. Bennett!" Mrs. Hughes fairly sang, a pink color rising up her neck and cheeks to match her rose-print muslin dress. "This wild, unruly place would go wanting without his splendid guidance and good work."

Ella turned her eyes to the doctor again, a bit wary of looking upon his strikingly stunning face. How was she to work with such a distracting man? She had imagined him old, pot-bellied, and balding, with foul breath and perhaps bushy eyebrows and whiskers growing out his nose and ears.

Dr. Bennett extended his unpocketed hand and grasped Ella's hand lightly. She looked into his large liquescent eyes and wondered if he found her startling too. Had he been expecting a matron for a nurse, pudgy and plain with a double chin and pillowy, pendulous breasts that tested the seams of her bodice?

He had, but Ella could not tell from his expression that he thought her surprisingly beautiful, a jewel on the necklace of young womanhood. The doctor, fairly stunned with surprise, tried not to stare at her.

"It is with most earnest pleasure and gratitude that I welcome you to Acacia House, Miss Fielding. Trust that I will do everything within my power to see to your comfort and happiness here."

His voice was low but soft.

Ella hesitated a few moments, bedazzled by the collective attractiveness of the two men. How could they be unmarried? Were there so few highborn women in New South Wales that these gentlemen could not find suitable matches?

"Dr. Bennett and Father Gregory," Ella finally replied, "I am so thankful to have arrived and look forward to meeting the people here, especially the children. There are more than twenty orphans, if I recall correctly from Mrs. Hughes' letters."

Father Gregory chortled again, sounding like an amused owl. It was obvious he had not seen a young woman from his homeland in quite some time, and surely not one so lovely as Ella Fielding. He surreptitiously glanced at her soft décolletage and her luscious full lips.

"Yes! Five-and-twenty sweet children," he replied. "Most of them are half-Aboriginal, their parents dead or not desirous of keeping them. We cannot seem to place them in local homes, so we are rearing them at the church orphanage."

No one wants them, Ella thought. Outcast children. And these two men were generous and compassionate for raising them in a proper way.

The four of them took their seats at the table as a lovely, caramel-complected Aboriginal maid brought in soup. Mrs. Hughes introduced the woman as Mabarra, meaning *eyes*, "for her magnificent blue-green eyes."

Ella had been under the impression that the Aboriginals were ugly. Yet, Henry and this one, the girl with pretty eyes, were truly striking. They were half-castes, both endowed with the best of their parents.

Dr. Bennett cleared his throat and fiddled with the flatware around his place setting.

"Mabarra grew up in our orphanage, Miss Fielding. She works here now but returns to the Bidjigal *wolli*, their camp, from time to time. I do not want her to lose the traditions and language of her people, so I encourage her to embrace her heritage."

Mabarra smiled fetchingly at Ella and nodded. Father Gregory added that Mabarra would teach Ella to speak some of the Dharug language if Ella wished.

"Feelings between the native people and the settlers remain tetchy," the doctor resumed. "The settlers refuse to consider how they have trespassed and usurped native lands, even demanded the natives live as we transplanted Europeans do. Aboriginal hunting grounds in New South Wales are nearly gone, and some of their sacred sites are destroyed. I am sad to tell you many of the natives have been killed, either by disease or deliberate gunfire."

"Yes," Father Gregory affirmed, "and were it not for Thad's…er, uh, Dr. Bennett's large parcel of land here, many of the Dharug people would be gone. He allows a few of the remaining clans, mainly the Bidjigal and Wangal, to camp on his lands and sees to their well-being. I am fortunate that many of them return his kindness by attending church. I do not force Christianity on them but attempt to merge Christian beliefs with theirs. We give them food when they come to our Sunday services. They enjoy the singing."

Ella nodded and looked out the windows of the dining room, thinking.

"The Bidjigal and Wangal people…are they clans of the Dharug family of Aboriginals?"

Father Gregory nodded: "Exactly. Dharug is the language shared by the clans here. Some are Eora too, but they also speak Dharug. Though there are some differences clan to clan, they understand each other. The Wangal people are on the southeast end of the property, the Bidjigal are closer, and sometimes the Wiradjiri camp on Bennett land."

Dishes of food began appearing on the table, and both water and wine were poured. There was ale as well. Everything smelled wonderful. Ella hoped they were not dining on local fauna. No loin of wombat or fried dingo! She did not feel ready for such delicacies.

"You need not worry about the water, Miss Fielding," Dr. Bennett assured her. "The kitchen boils any water we drink."

Ella was confused. Why would they need to boil the water? She would learn later that Dr. Bennett's father, the elder Dr. Bennett, believed boiling removed whatever was in water that might make a person sick.

"And who watches over the children when you cannot, Father Gregory?" Ella asked.

"I have several adult helpers, and there are five orphan children in their teens. The young ones are well looked after. They are probably hearing stories now, saying thankful prayers, and preparing for bed. Jiemba and Yarran likely will have helped the little ones dress for bed and given them a little milk and sugar bread. Wandya, one of the boys of the Wiradjuri people, is a wonderful storyteller."

Ella cocked her head to one side, smiling—

"Perhaps I will need tongue exercises so that I might be able to pronounce their names!"

Dinner was delicious, a roast pork and sides that Mrs. Hughes said had come from the livestock and gardens on the doctor's land. Besides the pork, there were roasted potatoes, mushy peas, fried onions with bacon, and sliced beets, plus several sauces and condiments. The oatmeal bread was still warm and stuffed with butter, ready for slicing. For dessert, creamy and sweet English syllabub, a favorite of the doctor and the vicar, was brought to the table, flavored with local chocolate pudding fruit.

Dr. Bennett put down his knife and fork—

"Root vegetables thrive here, Miss Fielding, thanks to manure from the livestock and the guidance given us by Henry Douglas, who has taught us about the soil."

He smiled, showing off his mouthful of fine-looking teeth. The conversation continued, light and convivial, then Father Gregory announced he needed to return to the church.

"I have considerable correspondence to read, as the *Isabella* brought not only you, Miss Fielding, but also much mail. I bid you a pleasant evening. Do come by the church and orphanage whenever you wish tomorrow. The children are anxious to meet you."

Mrs. Hughes, who had said she normally did not dine with the men, promptly excused herself too: "I shall go to the kitchen to help Old Betty. She cooked us such a fine meal, did she not?"

Ella wondered if Old Betty was part Aboriginal too. When she stood up and gathered her plate and flatware to carry to the kitchen, Mrs. Hughes frowned.

"Miss Fielding, Mabarra will clear the table and help clean up the meal. It is one of her duties. Please, join Dr. Bennett for conversation in the drawing room. I will send tea and biscuits."

Ella had been told by the officers of the *Isabella* that tea was a luxury in New South Wales. Colonists paid dearly for it. But Dr. Bennett served tea, exotic oolong tea from the Dutch East Indies. Surely, he was as wealthy a man as she'd been told.

The doctor offered Ella his arm and led her to the drawing room. The old dog of unidentified pedigree she had seen in the doctor's bed chamber suddenly appeared and followed them. Dr. Bennett pointed to a place in front of a high-backed, blue, velvet settee.

"Warrigul, lay down, boy."

The doctor pointed to the floor. The dog obeyed, then his generous tail thumped on the floor for a few seconds. Ella grinned, thinking Warrigal was not a typical dog name. It probably was Dharug, the language she'd been told the Aboriginals spoke.

"He followed Gregory and me up from Port Jackson when we first arrived here," Dr. Bennett said, "just a pup at the time. Silly mutt jumped into the Parramatta River and began swimming after us. I pulled him aboard the towboat, and he has not let me out of his sight since."

Dr. Bennett patted the dog's head, which caused Warrigul's tail-thumping to resume with renewed energy.

"May I assume Warrigul means *dog*?" Ella asked.

"That's correct, Miss Fielding. It is from the local Dharug clans and means "tame dingo." I believe you are catching on to native names already!"

His laugh was a low rumble, almost like a cougar's purr. Ella had seen cougars in Canada, prowling the outskirts of Bytown. Surely, there were none of the big cats here, if there were any cats at all. The fauna in Australia, she had read, was of its own making, peculiar making.

She took a seat on a Chippendale chair with green, striped upholstery. There was another chair just like it a few steps away. Just the name Chippendale meant the chairs were ridiculously expensive. They probably had been brought from England.

Dr. Bennett crossed his long legs and leaned back comfortably on the velvet settee. Ella looked at her lap, embarrassed to have been ogling the doctor's slim physique.

"You should rest for a few days, Miss Fielding, unpack and make a list of things you need and give it to Mrs. Hughes. Surely, your trunk does not contain everything."

"Thank you, doctor. I have few needs beyond the essentials, maybe some extra hairpins and handkerchiefs, but mostly I desire books. I consume books like I breathe air. I was able to bring only a few, most of which I read on the ship."

Dr. Bennett smiled. Here was a woman who read, an intellectual. He was delighted. Other than Gregory, there was no one with whom to satisfyingly converse. He had taught the Welsh housekeeper, Mildred Hughes, the fundamentals of reading, but she did not take to it. He had taught Henry Douglas to read as well, but the man found conversations about books intimidating, as he lacked the cultural background to understand them.

"Take some time to get to know people around here," Dr. Bennett continued. "Tour the property. If there is a medical emergency that requires your help, then I will find you."

He smiled at Ella, causing her to shiver slightly and inhale deeply.

"I left some books in your bedchamber about the animals and plants here," he resumed, "and the native people. There is also a very thin booklet published in England a few years ago about the settling of Wahroonga. My family was responsible for the booklet. Few copies were made, and most were given to family members or sold in London."

He looked embarrassed.

"It is mostly about Acacia House and my medical and social work, as well as Father Gregory's efforts with the parishioners and the orphanage. Please forgive my boastfulness, Miss Fielding, but Gregory and I are the first permanent free men here in Wahroonga, the only educated residents for miles. I am told another man, a freed convict, has received a land grant to the south of my land below the high sandstone cliffs, a Mr. Thomas Hyndes. He plans to timber the land, I think, probably using convict labor. There is a great need for timber in the colony and in England."

Ella relaxed into her comfortable chair and crossed her legs, a somewhat forbidden posture for a young woman. She doubted the doctor would object to this misstep. He appeared to accept alternate ways of living and behaving.

"Tell me about the people in New South Wales, Dr. Bennett. I know there are many types, from soldiers to convicts to free men like yourself, and the natives, of course. It seems like a mixed society."

The doctor uncrossed his legs and re-crossed them in the opposite direction.

"We have Governor Macquarie, the fifth man to oversee the colony. I am fond of Macquarie and his wife. They have worked hard to gentrify New South Wales and direct it toward democratic self-governance. As you may have guessed or even read, we are at present a quasi-military autocracy. There are numerous garrisoned soldiers, some British regulars who serve the administration of the colony, but mostly there are soldiers of the New South Wales Corporation. They have a great deal of control and influence. The governor has been at odds with NSWC, particularly over sales of rum and their treatment of convicts and natives. He is disbanding them this year, as too many of them are shiftless alcoholics."

"Convict life is difficult," he continued. "Only in recent years have the felons been better housed and fed than when the colony was first established. I am reminded of the black slaves in the West Indies and America when I see how our convicts travel here and are forced to live. They are assigned to daily work-details and harshly treated for the smallest infractions, sometimes flogged until unconscious. Most of them were transported here on ludicrous charges such as pick-pocketing, scavenging garbage piles, or offending the aristocracy. I met one convict who was jailed in London's Newgate Prison and then transported here for stepping on a duchess' flowers."

"But why send them here at all. Is it not expensive?"

Dr. Bennett sipped the cup of tea Mrs. Hughes had brought to the drawing room. He sighed, appreciating the delicate fragrance and flavor of oolong.

"Expensive, yes. But after the American Revolution, England could no longer transport its criminals to America. Parliament decided to ship them here instead, likely not caring if they lived or died," he stated, raising his bushy, black eyebrows. "New South Wales has free settlers, like Gregory and me. We are called *exclusives*. Convicts who gain their freedom after a period of good behavior are *emancipists*. The convicts are mostly English, but there are Scots and Welsh too, and the much-despised Irish. The Irish have revolted on several occasions. Hatred of English rule still goes down hard with them, even here, halfway around the world."

Across the room was a collection of Aboriginal artifacts. Ella recognized some of them from a book she had read about the natives. There were throwing sticks and clubs, as well as *womeras* for launching spears and *wo-mur-angs,* those funny crook-shaped objects that could knock a kangaroo dead with just one hit or come flying back to the thrower. Some were plain and polished, while others had lovely designs painted or carved on them. Especially pretty were the shell mosaics, which Dr. Bennett said were gifted too him by the native Bidjigal women.

"Tell me more about our local natives," Ella requested.

Dr. Bennett grinned. He was sure Ella had read or heard all sorts of false information about the Aboriginals.

"I believe you will be surprised at what you learn about them...from them. Let me just say they are not much different than we are, Miss Fielding. Of course, they dress differently, if they dress at all, and they celebrate their own beliefs and customs and follow their own laws and code of conduct. Yet, they venerate family life. Men and women marry, have children, and try to raise them wisely, just as we do."

"They are not all one nation either," the doctor added, "though the way we speak of them presumes so. They are composed of many, many clans and larger groups, all speaking their own languages and with their own customs—not unlike the many ethnicities we know from our lives in Europe and North America."

He paused a moment, searching for the profound truths he had learned in Australia. Ella caught herself staring at his mesmerizing eyes.

"One thing I have realized is that the Aboriginals are not savages. They know this land and how to successfully live on it. I believe they have been here for millennia, a fact which contradicts biblical time, I know. You will quickly learn that I put little stock in the Bible as a source of scientific fact. It is much better used as a groundwork of stories to teach morality. Father Gregory likely agrees with me, though I doubt he would admit it. One of his reasons for coming to New South Wales was to teach about God gently, indulgently...and to embrace and honor all spiritual beliefs. He has always disliked Christianity's arrogant insistence that all people must accept religious dogma verbatim...and live as Christians do. This attitude is one of the things I like about Father Gregory."

So, Ella thought, the vicar is an alternative thinker too.

"I know," the doctor continued, "you have been told the Aboriginals are dangerous, that they are murderous. But you will learn they can be neighborly, even good friends, if their way of life is not greatly disturbed. They have already shown themselves more accepting and forgiving than the colonists. I have set aside a portion of my land for them near the Baulkham Hills border and south of here. I try to assure they are not disturbed. I want to be a good neighbor, a good steward of the land. Yet I know, my land is really their land, taken forcibly from them before I arrived."

"You see, Miss Fielding, The First Fleet considered Australia to be *terra nullius*, no man's land, or perhaps they feigned such a belief. The first governors gave much of the Gadigal, Gamaragal, Bidjigal, Wiradjuri, and Wangal lands in these parts to farmers. This land was already ruined for the Aboriginals before I came here. Now, I simply try to live in harmony with them and help them preserve what they have left in this part of New South Wales."

Ella was conflicted, for everything she had been taught in church and by the society where she grew up said the native people in places like Africa, the Americas, the West Indies, New Zealand, the Spice Islands, and now Australia were dangerous and ignorant, even subhuman, that they should be forced to give up their beliefs, learn God's word, and live civilly as whites do.

"I have much to learn, Dr. Bennett, or should I say unlearn and then relearn. Almost everything I was taught about the Aboriginals appears to be false. I shall be your obedient student on these matters, I promise."

He liked her statement about unlearning her mistaken attitudes and relearning new ones. He had always felt that unlearning and relearning were the hardest, yet the most laudable learning tasks. He admired anyone who not only could do them but wished to do them.

"The best way to accomplish your goal, Miss Fielding, is to ease yourself into friendship with the half-castes here. You will learn a great deal from them, and they will help you prepare to meet the full-caste natives."

He leaned down and opened a drawer in the table beside his chair. Ella feared he might be getting smokes, maybe a pipe, but instead he pulled out a leather album and handed it to her.

"I enjoy sketching in my free time, and sometimes painting. Perhaps you paint as well."

Ella nodded, relieved, and undid the ribbon on the album.

"I have seen your watercolors throughout the house, Sir. The one in my bedchamber of the wildflowers and wallaby is very sweet, calling to mind their shyness. Will I see any wallabies here at Acacia House?"

"Yes. They wander out of the bush to the north of the cleared property at dawn and dusk to feed on the grasses and, in late summer and autumn, to eat the fallen fruits from the plum, apple, and peach trees. Some have tiny joeys now but will force them out of their pouches this summer to make room for the next little occupants."

Ella flipped through the doctor's art album. There were pencil and charcoal drawings of flowers, animals, and people. Acacia House was rendered across two adjoining pages. A handsome horse appeared on another page, and then a small animal that resembled a bear. The strange flowers Ella had seen in the foyer vase, the ones shaped like candles, were beautifully done in color. The artwork was quite good, reflecting the keen eyes and able hands of a surgeon.

There were sketches of the natives too. One was an elder, a spear leaning against his shoulder and one of his feet drawn up and propped against the inside of his other leg. He was practically nude, with only a thin animal skin wrapped around his crotch.

"His name was Wugan," the doctor said, seeing Ella's interest in the drawing. "It means *raven*. He haunted my property for more than a year before I met him. I think he found me interesting but benign, since I had no issues with his people and gifted him food whenever he visited. He died a few years ago, but not before he brought his grandson to me for an introduction. You will meet his grandson, Medang."

Near the back of the album, a portrait of Henry Douglas was depicted with extraordinary accuracy, though it was obvious he was much younger in the sketch. Dr. Bennett provided some background:

"I rescued Henry from a Burramattagal camp near Parramatta only months after Gregory and I arrived here. His mother had died giving birth to a younger half-sibling. Henry was being ill-treated by the clan because he is half-caste, maybe a quarter-caste. It is hard to know. The clans that live closest to Sydney are the least tolerant of the half-castes."

"Rain was falling hard that night, and I found Henry sleeping in a ditch along the road, naked and cold. He had been beaten by his mother's new husband and blamed for her death. He was despised, too, because he had survived the smallpox epidemic...had the scars as a reminder. I hauled him up on my horse, wrapped him in my camp blanket, and brought him home. Gregory made him a bed in the makeshift rectory, a rather large tent. None of the buildings here were completed at that time. We slept in tents."

Dr. Bennett sighed and rubbed his forehead. Ella sensed the story of Henry was difficult for the doctor to recount.

"We named him Henry, because we didn't like his native name, Bamulguwiya. It was too difficult for us to say, and it means "dirty," which we felt disgraced him. He did not know his age. I judged him to be in his early twenties."

Ella was wide-eyed listening to the doctor. She had grown fond of Henry on their wagon trip from Port Jackson to Wahroonga. He had been so gentle and kind.

"What a horrible early life," she whispered. "But he seems happy here. He is quite cheerful and generous. I am sure I will become accustomed to his broken English."

The doctor chuckled: "You will. And you will find him helpful and devoted in many ways. He likes to think he is my *aid-de-camp*. He was the reason Gregory and I started the orphanage. We knew there were many cast-out children like him who needed love, guidance, and proper care."

They were quiet for a few minutes as Ella leafed through the album.

"I noticed he is missing an upper incisor tooth. Did that happen when he was beaten?" she asked.

Dr. Bennett chuckled again. There was so much to teach Miss Fielding.

"It is a custom among the Aboriginal people of this region to knock out that front tooth as part of a male initiation ceremony, called *Yoolong Erabaddjang*. It signifies that a young man has been trained in survival skills, spiritual beliefs, and clan customs. I do not know the origin of the tradition or how old it is. Very old, I believe. Should you chance to see Henry's bare chest, you will notice another initiation custom—a series of scarifications made by a sharp rock. They, too, are a rite of passage into manhood."

Ella shrugged: "I see. But why put him through the initiation customs if he is only to be beaten and cast out?"

Dr. Bennett began petting Warrigal again, carefully gauging what he would say.

"Henry's mother was taken against her will by a white man, a *whitefella* as the natives say. She was sullied, the Burramattagal believed, by white intruders. It is known that the soldiers and convicts creep into the native camps at night and kidnap and rape women. Perhaps some of the free men do as well. Sadly, many of the resulting half-caste babies are unwanted, even abused. They are reminders of all that the native people have lost to the British, as well as the bittersweet relationship some of our British men have with native women. They desire the women but do not acknowledge the resulting children."

Twilight had come and gone rapidly, as it did this time of year near the date of the Southern Hemisphere's spring equinox. Ella was wary of the darkness outside Acacia House. The drawing room had grown dusky, despite a maid having lit the candles. It was becoming difficult to see the doctor's sketches.

At the very back of the sketchbook were drawings of a beautiful young woman. Ella held the album closer to a candle to see more clearly.

"She is lovely," Ella whispered.

Then, looking up at the doctor, she asked who the woman was, though she already knew.

He stared out the window into the night, long enough that Ella thought she had re-opened a barely closed wound in his heart. But then he smiled and spoke.

"I had plans to marry her. Miss Edith Fullerton, the daughter of a Liverpool shipbuilder. I am sad to say she died of consumption...the pervasive and abysmal disease of our time."

It was a horrible way to die, Ella knew. A person literally wasted away, choked to death. She suddenly felt enormous sympathy for Dr. Bennett.

"I was stricken," he admitted. "Gregory, wishing to assuage my grief, told me of the call for doctors and men of God in this new colony. He thought it would heal my heart. We resolved to sail here together and start a new life."

Ella smiled and handed back the album.

"And has your heart healed in this place, Dr. Bennett?"

He regarded her with slight apprehension but answered her question truthfully.

"It has, Miss Fielding. It has."

Three

Ella was a long time falling asleep the first night in her new home. She had no qualms about her room or its comfortable furnishings. She thought she would be happy here and was anxious to begin her work. Still, the place felt strange, shadowy, shrouded in mystery, rife with secrets.

She read by the light of a candle for a short time, the booklet the doctor had suggested about Wahroonga. She was pleased to read on the very first page that Wahroonga meant *our home* in Dharug. This was an ironic fact after Mrs. Hughes effusive welcome and socializing with the doctor and the cleric that evening. It helped banish her disquietude.

"Our home."

How reassuring after all she had experienced coming here. She vowed she would think of it as *home* from now on.

As Dr. Bennett had said, much of the pamphlet about Wahroonga concerned his arrival and putting down roots. The author, who he had said was one of his family members back in England, glibly recounted:

Dr. Thaddeus Bennett brought such a large contingent of domestic workers, skilled tradesmen, and farm workers, not to mention the benevolent vicar, Father Gregory Mayhew, that their habitation of northern Wahroonga in and of itself could be considered an instant town.

The pamphlet slid out of Ella's hands and onto the comfortable bed. She yawned, warm and drowsy. Just as her eyelids fell shut and she entered the dreamy limbo between wakefulness and sleep, a loud bellowing sounded outside.

She sat bolt upright.

"Dear God! What is that?" she said out loud.

Going to the window nearest her bed, she peeked around the curtain. After a few seconds, the sound came again, a combination grunt, growl, and roar.

Whatever it was, she believed herself safe in the upstairs of the house. Someone would see about it. She needed to alert no one. The men housed in the dormitory over the barn would hear the dreadful noise.

Then came a call like a cat meowing. It ended with a stranger sound, a guttural grind. There was another meow followed by the original grunt, growl, roar.

Ella crawled back in bed, pulling the covers up to her chin. Again, she wondered if she ought to wake someone.

No. No one else seemed worried. She should not appear silly and frightened on her first night at Acacia House.

The uproar outside continued for the better part of a quarter hour, or so Ella thought. She wasn't sure, because at some point she slipped under the blankets and returned to her much-needed slumbers.

———

Tantalizing smells drifted up to Ella's snug bed chamber. Breakfast! She had been so nervous and enamored with the vicar and the doctor at dinner the night before, and bound so tight in a whalebone corset, she had not eaten much.

She resolved to make up for it this morning.

Right away, she noticed her trunk and the medicine crate were gone from her room. When had that happened? As she got out of bed, she spied a lovely satin robe lying across the chair nearest her bed. She slipped lithely into it, luxuriating in its softness.

The day before, Mrs. Hughes had shown her a call bell hanging by her bed. She gently yanked on the cord. Within a minute, a maid arrived, garbed in a clean, ironed uniform.

"May I assist ye, Miss Fieldin'?"

That was easy! She had never had a personal maid before now. It was an unexpected luxury.

"I am wondering…uh…Emily, is it?"

The maid nodded and giggled, her hands clasped in front of her apron.

"Where has my trunk gone?"

Emily giggled again and went to one of the armoires. She flung open the door to reveal all of Ella's fancy dresses. In the other armoire were her everyday dresses.

"I see. Thank you, Emily. May I assume my personal clothing is in the dresser drawers?"

Emily nodded and giggled even more.

This giggling was going to wear on Ella, the same as Mrs. Hughes' chattiness. Perhaps Ella could cure Emily of the habit...but then it was not so bad. Just the girl's way of showing happiness. Everyone at Acacia House seemed happy she had arrived.

"I put yer bath things away, ma'am, an' yer jewelry in thee little chest on yer dresser. Shoes be in thee bottom of the armoires, according ta they dressiness. An', Mrs. Hughes give me sum pers'nal items fer ye, soaps an' oils fer ye skin, pa'fumes, hair pins an' combs, an' hats. We seen ye brought jus' thee one straw sun hat."

Emily reached to an armoire shelf above the dresses where several nice hats rested, including a pretty woven one for everyday use.

"The sun, ma'am...it be fierce here, ev'n in winter. It burn ye skin quick. Thee doctor warn'd us to cover ou'selfs, else we gets dark moles. There be insects too."

Emily pulled a gossamer piece of material from a drawer and demonstrated how to secure it over the straw hat so that it covered the face of the wearer.

"This keep insects frum ye face, ma'am. There gonna be hordes of 'em soon."

The maid went to the everyday armoire—

"Will this be a workday, ma'am? Do ye wants a day dress? Mrs. Hughes had half-doz'n of them made fer ye."

Ella remembered the housekeeper, in one of her letters, asking for detailed body measurements.

"Why not choose one for me, Emily? I trust your good taste."

Excitedly, the maid pulled out a lavender cotton dress with a button front, pleated skirt, swirls of deep purple fabric sewn to the hem, and a lovely floral mauve sash. Emily added a purple shawl. Ella stared at the outfit in surprise.

"Goodness! This is a day outfit? It is so fine and pretty. Thank you, Emily."

"A corse, ma'am. Oh, an' thee crate wit' all thee medicines were taken down ta Dr. Bennett office. He be delighted ta have it."

Ella smiled with appreciation.

Wondering about the time, she reached for her watch locket. It was a little past seven.

"What time does the doctor take his breakfast," she asked.

"'Round 'bout dis time, ma'am. I thinks he wish ye ta join him ta-day, when ye feels ready. I were given orders not ta wakes ye or rush ye downstairs."

Ella found this amusing. Was she going to work here, or have a leisurely existence? Would she—Sleep late? Have a fine room with indoor plumbing? Wear exquisite blueblood dresses? Dine on the best foods and delicacies? Read whenever she wished? Do as she pleased?

Was she to be treated like an aristocratic lady? Perhaps these two men, the doctor and the cleric, just wanted an elegant, educated woman in their midst.

She decided she could indulge in a quick bath. Emily fetched hot water and gave her a sponge and floral-scented soap and a brush for washing her back. The maid helped her dress afterwards and coiffed her hair fetchingly in a braided bun near top of her head. A few curly tendrils fell in front of her ears. A quick glance in the Cheval mirror confirmed that she looked lovely. Emily could do up a fine hairstyle!

Dr. Bennett was seated at the dining room table drinking tea and reading a three-day-old *Sydney Gazette* as Ella entered. She noticed that Warrigal lay under the table.

The doctor was even more handsome this morning than last night! The most beautiful man she had ever seen…and hidden away on this side of the world in a most unusual and remote place. She took note of the silk waistcoat her wore and his fashionable, neatly tied cravat. Was it a Barrel Knot or an Osbaldeston Knot?

"Good morning, Sir! Any good news in the paper?"

She noticed the masthead of the newspaper read: *Thus We Hope to Prosper.*

"Hardly," he replied. "The infernal thing is heavily censored by the colonial government. Governor Macquarie is fighting that."

"Oh, and you need not call me 'sir,' Miss Fielding," he softly added.

But he did not say what she *should* call him.

She took a seat and noticed how oddly the doctor was looking at her. He put down his newspaper and sighed, half-smiling.

"It has been years since I shared my breakfast table with such a lovely woman."

Ella blushed: "Thank you, Sir…uh…I mean Doctor. I apologize for not joining you earlier. Apparently, Emily was told not to wake me. I slept until seven, well past the expected beginning of the workday."

"Workday? Not today, Miss Fielding. Your only assigned duties today are to get to know your new home and get some rest. No doubt your body is weary from traveling and your brain is addled from so much newness."

He poured her some tea and passed her the sugar cone and cream. If she didn't know better, she could almost imagine she was still back in England waiting to sail, except that the dining room was less ostentatious.

"I have asked Mabarra to escort you around the property. She lives in both worlds here, Acacia House and the Bidjigal encampment."

Breakfast was leisurely. Father Gregory came to the table after a time, having finished his morning chores at the orphanage. He smiled happily and asked Ella if she had slept well her first night in Wahroonga.

"I did, Father Gregory. My room is more comfortable than any place I have ever slept."

The conversation was lively and fun. Old Betty, the cook, who Ella learned was an emancipist female convict, transported to New South Wales for stealing a live chicken and then promptly given her ticket of leave, had made amazing scones with native bunya nuts and gooseberries chopped into them. Butter melted into all the nooks and crannies of the scones. Mabarra brought out eggs and ham and a dish of large, juicy plums. Ella groaned with delight over the taste of everything.

"Miss Fielding," Father Gregory declared in an animated voice, "you have not fully lived until you eat your toasts smeared with butter and *quandong* jam."

He held up a small glass jam pot, then offered it to Ella. She studied it a moment, seeing red chunks in it.

"*Quondong*, you call it?"

As she spread her toasts with butter and the jam, the two men watched. They seemed sinfully curious, as if *quondong* was too spicy or possessed a revolting taste. Quite the opposite, it was delicious.

"Oh, divine!" Ella crowed. "I adore the tart peachy flavor!"

Father Gregory smiled in triumph.

"*Quandong* is harvested in late spring from a tree that grows in the cool foothills of the Blue Mountains," the doctor said. "The drupes are red on the outside, and inside is a tasty, brown, wrinkled nut. Our cooks make jars and jars of the delicious jam when the fruit comes ripe. The nuts are dried and stored downstairs. If I recall, Old Betty puts out a bowl of *Quandong* nuts, roasted and salted, at Christmas. They taste a bit like almonds."

"I am so glad you slept well last night," Father Gregory said. "I must admit we did not sleep well for many months after we arrived, what with all the odd noises in the night and the unpredictable weather. Of course, we were in tents at the time, almost like sleeping outside."

Ella thought back to the previous night and the strange roaring sounds she had heard.

"I did sleep well, but it is coincidental you mention odd noises. I wonder if you might know what animal—assuming it was an animal—I heard last night. It made such a guttural roar and growl, and then I heard a sound like squealing. I was a bit frightened."

The two men looked at each other and grinned.

"It was nothing to be frightened about, Miss Fielding," the doctor assured her. "Koala breeding season is in session. It comes with much clamor as the males bellow, chase, and assault the females. The act is almost like…well, I suppose you could call it violation. The females resist the males, fight, and cry out. But the males are larger and stronger and have their way. After the breeding season is over, koalas are quite docile and quiet."

Father Gregory was blushing. Talk of mating, especially the violent kind, embarrassed him.

Ella had read about koalas, those cute, bear-like marsupials that seemed to laze away their days chewing eucalyptus leaves and sleeping. Something in the leaves had a sedative effect on them, she'd been told; thus, they slept most of the time.

But male animals raping females! What sort of place was this?

Mrs. Hughes interrupted the three to tell them a visitor had come.

"Madang is out back, Dr. Bennett. I asked Mabarra to make up a food bag for him, but I believe he wishes to speak with you."

Dr. Bennett nodded and motioned to Father Gregory and Ella to accompany him.

"I shall introduce you, Ella. It seems you are to meet one of the natives this morning, an important one. Madang is the leader of our clan of Bidjigal people."

The man was black as ink and terribly thin, with an unruly hedge of dark hair. He wore a loincloth made from some sort of furry animal. A decorated stick was held in its folds. His chest had the scarifications Dr. Bennett said Henry had, and one of his front teeth was missing. Ella thought she had never seen such large, milky, brown eyes as this man possessed. His expression was almost frightening if not haunting.

The doctor spoke in Dharug, greeting Madang and shaking his hand. The Bidjigal leader looked at Ella with great interest, then turned back to Dr. Bennett.

"*Dyin garungarung.*"

Both the doctor and the vicar smiled and glanced at Ella.

"*Giyara*, Ella. *Garadji dyin.*"

Ella knew Dr. Bennett had told Madang her name.

"Ella this is Madang. I told him you are a woman healer."

She held out her hand, and Madang hesitantly took it and studied it. Carefully, he turned it about, examining her clean, well-groomed fingernails, the iridescent opal ring she wore, and her soft creamy skin. He looked into Ella's ice-blue eyes. She smiled her best smile, but his frightening countenance did not change.

"*Garungarung,*" he repeated.

"He is saying you are beautiful, Ella," Father Gregory said.

Mabarra appeared with a bag of food for Madang. She handed it to him and spoke rapidly in their shared tongue. She gesticulated with her hands and arms, seeming to grow annoyed with what Madang was saying. Dr. Bennett raised his eyebrows in question. Though he spoke Dharug, he could not completely understand when it was spoken so rapidly.

"He is not willing to share the food equally," Mabarra said. "There are several visiting Wiradjuri, and he has argued with them about burning the land southwest of the camp. Madang has told them the burn-off is unnecessary, since it is spring and there is clear, grassy land to the south and west. Plenty of grazing for wallabies and kangaroos. He says the Wiradjuri know this, and that they only wish to argue."

Burn the land? Ella did not understand.

Dr. Bennett spoke with Madang at length in Dharug. A second bag of food was brought, with fewer delectables, just some cheese, dried plums, chunks of possum meat, and a soda bread called damper. The natives, Ella had been told, loved bread.

Dr. Bennett instructed Madang to give the smaller bag to the Wiradjuri and tell them to go home. There would be no burning of the land until later in the season. There was plenty of grass and grazing game to hunt.

"Ah...so they burn the land to encourage new grass that attracts the animals they hunt," Ella said in a quiet voice. "Land management by supposed ignorant savages. Who would have thought?"

Father Gregory had heard: "They are neither stupid nor ignorant, Miss Fielding. Thad and I have learned much from them."

As Madang turned to leave, Dr. Bennett walked with him a few steps and then took a moment to inquire about Keira, Madang's daughter-in-law. She was *bindiwurra*, pregnant, quite far along, and with the baby still upside-down. She was also a tiny woman, a teenager really. Dr. Bennett judged her to be not more than thirteen.

After Madang left, the doctor asked Ella how she felt about the encounter.

"He was fascinating," Ella admitted. "But such a mean face."

"He was fascinated with you, Miss Fielding," Dr. Bennett said. "A beautiful white woman like you is a rare sight in this part of New South Wales."

It was Father Gregory who spoke next—

"That mean face is a trademark of the Aboriginals. They never want you to know what they are truly thinking."

"His eyes," Ella stated. "Was that milky glaze over his eyes cataracts?"

Dr. Bennett grinned: "You know about cataracts, Miss Fielding?"

'Well, yes," Ella confessed. "I have read about them and seen older patients with cataracts. I believe there is an experimental surgery in England to replace cataracts with good lenses. The lenses would be cut from cadavers, of course, and people are against that. And, how would we do surgery on eyes? The pain would be insufferable."

Dr. Bennett raised his eyebrows at Father Gregory.

"We may have a young polymath in Ella," he joked. "She seems to have much knowledge." He turned to Ella: "We have so many topics to discuss, Miss Fielding…but plenty of time."

He continued with another subject—

"I spoke with Madang about his pregnant daughter-in-law, Keira. She is married to Madang's son, Dural, who is the next man in line to be the leader of the clan. Keira seems too young and physically too small to give birth safely. I have suggested to Dural that I attend the birth, but he does not commit."

Ella was surprised. The doctor delivered Aboriginal babies?

"Madang said he would speak to Dural. That is the best I can do for now," Dr. Bennett said.

He shrugged and said he had letters to reply to from the large pile of mail that had arrived on the *Isabella*. Would Ella mind if he worked for an hour or so?

Of course not. She watched him go, unsure what she was supposed to do. Mabarra took her by one elbow.

"Shall we accompany Father Gregory to the church and introduce you to the children?"

———

As the three of them walked one of the garden paths between Acacia House and the open field leading to the church, Father Gregory proudly pointed out the native flowers and trees he and the doctor had carefully cultivated on the property. One was a tall bunya pine, elegantly shaped with cascading branches and rippled bark. Father Gregory grinned, telling Ella that after enjoying *quandong*, she now knew what a bunya tree looked like.

"You must be careful of the pretty leaves," he warned. "They can stab you. This is a female tree, but she will not produce nuts for many years, perhaps one-hundred years. Then, so long as a male tree is available for pollination, she will produce large cones with edible nuts inside. Her man tree grows just beyond the church."

He chuckled, and Ella childishly imagined the two trees being married, like people.

"But where do you get your bunya nuts if this tree is too young to produce them?"

"Ah, you are a keen listener, Miss Fielding! Our bunya nuts are brought to us by a man who travels miles north of here to a place called Toowoomba where he likes to hunt. There is a forest there with many bunyas. He knows when to harvest the nuts and pays Dr. Bennett with them for treatment of his itchy skin rashes. Thad…I mean Dr. Bennett, learned a couple of years back that the condition is called eczema, and it can be treated with a dilute coating of tar."

"Fascinating. The doctor accepts barter as payment then?"

"Indeed, he does. We are given all manner of things as payment."

They walked on as a colorful assemblage of lorikeets and parrots shrieked from the many trees along the path, their vibrant hues contrasting with the green foliage.

A crimson rosella stared down at Ella as if to say, "You are a stranger here."

"They are so pretty," she said, "but do birds here only screech and squawk? What happened to the sweet little chirp?"

Mabarra laughed and said—

"I think the spirits of the land gave them a choice, be beautiful or have lovely songs. Most chose beauty."

Bottle bushes were bursting with red sprigs of bushy flowers. Banksia, a commonplace family of shrubs, were everywhere along the edges of the property, their emerging blooms quite diverse and striking. Some of the gum trees were in bud too and were equally as various in form and color as the banksia.

The loveliest for Ella were the acacias, with their dense yellow blooms, some like small puffballs and others with petals. Sundry birds called from their branches. A tiny bluish bird chirped from an acacia branch.

"Oh, how adorable! What is that little bird?"

"A fairy wren," Father Gregory said. "We have many of them, and their songs are sweet."

The trail was kept groomed but was well-worn, hinting at the many footsteps that had been laid down between Acacia House and the church. Paper daisies in white, pink, and yellow bloomed along the sides of the path, along with purple fringe-lilies. Ella passed a patch of golden canola blooms and then waratah shrubs, some of them just beginning to display bright red buds.

"The racy red flowers are so seductive," the vicar said, "we sometimes call waratah the Shady Lady."

Ella giggled, more at Father Gregory's blush than the suggestive waratah blooms. He was so easily mortified.

Geckos scattered hurriedly as the vibrations of footfall and tenor of voices alerted them. Ella was charmed by the small lizards. Even more charming was the sight of a Sulphur-crested cockatoo. The bird's elaborate headgear fanned out as it studied Ella. She was an outsider to this intelligent avian, yet an enchanting one in her flowing lavender dress and elegant hairstyle.

Erected at the backside of the church, Ella could see an addition, a simple but long wooden building of considerable size, painted white to match the wooden church. Waxflowers formed a pink hem around it. Here and there near the building, a frangipani tree bloomed, its flowers heady with sweet fragrance.

"The building serves as a schoolhouse and a dormitory, Miss Fielding," said Father Gregory. "The children are skilled at converting it back and forth each day. Come, I will show you."

Ella followed Father Gregory onto an open wooden porch connecting to the back door of the church and also to the door of the large wooden building. Ella could hear laughter and thumping inside the building. When the door opened, calm descended. Ella peeked in and saw more than two dozen people, children and helpers. Father Gregory stepped inside, leading Ella by one hand.

A collective sigh of surprise mingled with appreciation passed among the orphans and helpers.

"Children! I am excited to have you meet Miss Fielding, who will be your nurse and part time teacher."

Oh, such beautiful children, Ella thought! Henry and Mabarra must have looked like this as children.

Pillows, blankets, and mattresses had been rolled and stuffed into open, compartment-like spaces in the rafters. Everyone was quiet as the children looked at Ella in disbelief. Father Gregory leaned close and whispered that the children had not expected her to be young and pretty…nor had he.

Ella stepped forward and faced all the children, her large blue eyes moving from one sweet face to another. After a moment, she smiled and greeted them.

"Hello!"

Suddenly, the room came alive with waving, jumping, clapping, and cheering. A few seconds of pandemonium, and then Father Gregory held up one hand to quiet the children.

"One by one, you may come up to meet Miss Fielding. Please, line up. All of you will get a chance."

Ella sat in a well-worn chair at the teaching desk. She offered a greeting as each child came forward. She learned his or her name and tried to pronounce it. There was some giggling at this effort.

Illuka said he was a rescued Bandjalung whose mother had tried to drown him because he had been born with two missing fingers. As he held up his three-fingered hand for Ella to see, Father Gregory explained that the Aboriginals did not understand human defects, thinking such children were incomplete and should be given back to the land to reform and be reborn.

Illuka took both of Ella's hands and said he loved Father Gregory and Dr. Bennett and would love Miss Fielding too.

Bindju held open one of his hands and showed Ella a small lizard he had caught—"It a baybee skink!" he snickered.

The boy looked to be about ten. He told Ella that Dr. Bennett had found him at a timber camp, being taunted and thrown about like a tucker sack.

"Me mayba two, tree year old den. Me seven now!"

Ella felt tears prickling in her eyes.

How could a mother drown her baby for having missing fingers? How could anyone treat a three-year-old in such a manner?

Duru, whose full name was Durunanang, came forward slowly, behaving as if someone preceded her, someone invisible. Her name, she said, meant "daughter."

"She lost her twin brother, Babana, to the Long Cough when he was only four," Father Gregory said. "Yet, his spirit remains with her, walks with her ...as you now see."

Duru, who was maybe ten, nudged the air in front of her as if it was her twin brother, and walked on.

Ella turned to Father Gregory.

"The 'Long Cough'?"

"Whooping Cough," Father Gregory whispered. "It ravaged Port Jackson a few years ago. Likely brought by a ship. Illnesses that white children survive the Aboriginals often cannot."

When the children finished their greetings, Father Gregory herded them across the wooden porch and into the back of the church.

"Yindi, go fetch Dr. Bennett. The rest of you sit down in the choir loft until he arrives."

Turning to Ella he grinned and said: "We have a surprise for you."

Minutes later the doctor arrived. He smiled beguilingly at Ella, or so she thought, and seated himself at the church organ. The children had lined up in the choir loft and seemed eager to sing.

Jiemba, one of the older girls whose name meant *Star of Heaven*, waited for the doctor's signal and note on the organ before beginning a beautiful solo. It praised all of those who devote their lives to healing, healing of the body and the soul.

As she sang, the others joined in one-by-one until an entire choir of Aboriginal, half-caste, orphans sang together, to Dr. Bennett's accompaniment. Ella was charmed. They were all so adorable.

She noticed one small white girl in the group. The little girl had not been in the orphanage earlier. Father Gregory told Ella that the child's parents, a British soldier and his wife, had died aboard a ship on its way to New South Wales. Dr. Bennett happened to be in Sydney when the ship's passengers disembarked. He was told about the parentless child and immediately offered to take her to the orphanage.

After the tribute was over, Ella wiped a tear from the corner of one eye, stood, and applauded.

"Such a wonderful welcome you have given me. Thank you, everyone!"

Yet, she could easily see how much she was needed. All of them were bereft of a woman's care.

Ella told Dr. Bennett she wished to examine each of the children. He had anticipated her request and brought along his medical bag when he arrived to accompany the children on the organ.

"If you need anything else, Miss Fielding, send one of the children to my office," he said, smiling at her.

His eyes were unusual, she thought as he turned to leave. They seemed to change color depending on the light, sometimes darker, sometimes lighter. Today, they were like fiery topaz.

Ella opened a notebook and recorded each child's name and age. She listened to hearts and lungs, pressed on bellies, looked in ears and at posture and sores. She examined the children's dirty teeth and grinned, knowing she had brought toothbrushes, gadgets that no doubt would be new to the children. She wiped snot from under their noses and checked their hair for lice. Nearly all of them had vermin.

"We have tried numerous concoctions to rid them of the aggravating pests, but to no avail," Father Gregory sighed. "Seawater helped the convicts on the *Fortune* when we sailed here in 1806. But we are a distance from the sea here in Wahroonga."

"No worries, Father. I have a formula that works."

She paused for a moment, seeing dirt behind ears and in the creases of necks and joints.

"How often do they bathe, Father? Cleanliness is so helpful in preventing sickness. They must learn to care for their bodies, the temples God gave them."

Father Gregory was chagrined.

"Well, Miss Fielding, they do not bathe as often as they should. If we are lucky, we find time to bathe them once a month."

He looked embarrassed.

"We will try to bathe them more often," Ella whispered, not wishing to offend the priest, "and we will be thorough about it. Their beds, are they washable?"

The vicar nodded.

"Perhaps this week I can set some of the maids to work washing the bedding, and all their soiled clothes. I have vinegar mixed with a little coal oil to kill the lice and then a good soap to wash it out. Shall I make my first goal one of cleaning everything, including our sweet children?"

"Of course, Miss Fielding. I am so grateful for your help. Jiemba and Yarran will be happy to assist you, as will I."

Three days later, the children and their dormitory-classroom were spotless.

Ella had made bathing a game, having the children jump from washtub to washtub as their hair and bodies were washed. Finally, they were taught to use a pinch of salt on the toothbrushes, donated by a London ladies aid society, to clean their teeth. Almost all of them made faces at the experience.

They had no cares about nakedness. Clothing and bedding had been laundered and pinned on a long rope strung from the orphanage dormitory to the tall spotted gum tree that held their treehouse. Each child sat cross-legged on the porch after their invigorating bath, letting their skin and hair dry. The spring breeze sweetened everything.

A wet and happy Ella stood with her hands on her hips and her hair and dress soaked when the sudsy undertaking was done. Father Gregory had promised each child a sugar cookie at the end of the ordeal, which had proven less of an ordeal and more of an orderly circus performance. Dr. Bennett was elected to fetch the cookies and returned with one in his mouth.

"Did you like the bath, children?" he asked.

Mani, intelligent and outspoken for an eight-year-old, complained that all the "goo' stuff" had been scrubbed from his body.

"Missy Fieldin', oily dirt on skin pro-tec me frum mozzie and bush mite. No bird land in hair now an' eat lice. Dog need bath too! Get rid of flea. I no wan' flea bite me."

Mozzies? Bush mites? Birds eating lice? Fleas? The place truly was insect-infested!

Father Gregory chuckled and called to the mongrel dog that was a pet for the children.

"Wibung, come!"

Wibung? Heaven above, another Aboriginal name, Ella giggled.

The dog seemed like a patchwork of many pedigrees. His mismatched blue and green eyes suggested a cattle dog, while his long legs and lanky body might have come from a wolfhound. Like the biblical Joseph, Wibung's coat of many colors was soft and long.

"We have cat fleas, Miss Fielding," Father Gregory said. "Cat fleas on our dog, ha! I hope the vinegar, coal tar, and hot water bath will kill them."

Wibung obeyed Father Gregory but put his head down when he saw the wash tubs. Ella patted him affectionately and lifted him into the first tub. Its water had been mixed with the formula to kill vermin. The oil would suffocate the fleas and destroy their eggs.

The children laughed at Miss Fielding and Father Gregory vigorously scrubbing Wibung, even his face where the fleas fled to escape drowning. The dog was mostly black with a few white patches and other colors. Hence, his name, Wibung, meant *magpie* in Dharug.

Pretending Wibung was in a race, the avid washers rushed him to the next tub for a soapy scrub and then to the rinsing tubs. When he was released, clean and happy, Wibung did a wild, shaking dance that flung clean water everywhere. Then he began running around the grassy churchyard and down to the barnyard area to dry himself. The children cheered.

"Wibung on fire!" Mani shouted. "Look 'im run fas'."

Mani then looked at the three adults and shrugged.

"You t'ree take baff now?"

Ella laughed nervously. No way would she undress and get in the tubs of dirty, dead-bug water.

"We bathe in the house, Mani."

Mani, as he usually did when confused, screwed up his face.

"In hows?? Dat no' fun. Outsi' betta. No towl. Can run an' get dry in sun."

The doctor chuckled.

"He is probably correct. Yet, I am still too shy to bathe publicly."

"As am I," Father Gregory put in. "The entire place would be laughing at my saggy, old body. And, just so you know, I can no longer run. My legs are too stiff."

Ella covered her mouth with one hand and giggled.

"Mani," the doctor tried to explain, "*whitefella* ways discourage being naked in front of others."

The boy looked even more perplexed.

"Dat silly. We all look same. Jus' differ colors."

A few evenings later, after dinner, Dr. Bennett invited Ella for a walk out the lane and down the road toward the spot where a crude wooden bridge crossed Cockle Creek. Ella and Henry had driven over the bridge a week earlier, on their way from Sydney to Acacia House. What was so special about it that the doctor wanted her to see it again?

"Perhaps we will see some new animals along the road. Besides that, walking is good for the body and mind," Dr. Bennett said, "especially after dinner. I believe it stimulates digestion."

Mabarra had given Ella a pair of sensible shoes, replacing a pair Ella had worn out before she arrived in Australia. Ella was grateful, as the road was rocky and rutted from the torrential winter rains the area had received earlier. She tried to walk on the side of the road where its surface was flat.

Dense stands of gum trees and cypress pines flanked the road. No wonder timber getters were at work near Acacia House. The area was plentiful with good building materials. Dr. Bennett pointed out different kinds of gum trees as they walked, but most looked the same to Ella. The doctor assured her she would learn to differentiate them by their lavish, firecracker blooms, the pods of which were just beginning to show.

"There are no deciduous trees here as in Canada and England," he told her. "I have been told there is a deciduous type of tree in Tasmania though, but I know little about it. The landscape here is vastly different from where we grew up, Miss Fielding, as are the plants and animals. I am sure you feel confused no matter which direction you go. I was bewildered, too, after first arriving here. But I know you will grow fond of this place."

Ella smiled to reassure him of her acceptance of her new home. She was determined to try her best to like Wahroonga and New South Wales. But there were just so many new, surprising things, sometimes frightening things. Her brain felt overloaded with information. At least everyone at Acacia House, the orphanage, and the farm was kind to her.

The Cockle Creek bridge appeared. It was constructed of long poles that stretched from bank to bank with a plank roadway nailed across them. It had wooden posts at its opposite ends, primarily for night travel so that horses or carriage drivers did not accidentally go into the creek. Dr. Bennett said that he had plans to build a railing across each side of the bridge.

He pointed into the creek from the center of the bridge.

"There is a peculiar animal that lives along the creek. We often see it from this bridge."

He took Ella's arm to steady her as they peered down into the clear water of Cockle Creek. Some fish swam by and a small eel-like creature. Ella noted what a pleasant song the water sang as it trickled over rocks under the bridge.

A moment later, she saw the odd creature the doctor wanted her to meet. It was like a shadow swimming out from under the bridge, something akin to a North American beaver, but with…with…webbed feet and a duck's bill.

"Doctor, what is that? Such a strange animal!"

He chuckled, watching Ella's amazement.

"It may be the colony's *strangest* animal, for it has the body of a beaver, including a broad, flat tail, but the bill of a duck. The feet are webbed like a duck's feet. It is covered in fur; yet—and this is the unbelievable part—it is thought to reproduce by laying eggs as a duck would."

"Half beaver and half duck? Impossible!"

"We might think so, but you see it before you now, Miss Fielding. It is called a platypus. The name comes from the Greek for 'flat foot.'"

She watched the curious animal swimming about, eating worms, small fish, and *yabbies*, the little crayfish in New South Wales' streams. Its webbed feet propelled it along as it wiggled from side to side.

"Platypus…what a baffling name. Tell me what purpose this creature serves in nature?"

Dr. Bennett paused, wondering about this himself.

"Well, I know it is hunted for its soft, warm fur. I saw a platypus shawl in a garment store in Sydney a few years back, a novelty. The Bidjigal eat the meat and use the fur. I am amused by the curious animal, especially its duck-like beak. Some people in these parts call it a Duck-Bill."

Ella watched the platypus for several minutes, until the doctor announced that it would be dark soon.

"We should head back to the house, Miss Fielding. I did not bring a lantern to show us the way in the dark."

They left the bridge and walked arm-in-arm back toward Acacia House. They had not gone far when Henry Douglas appeared, bringing two lanterns. He was, indeed, the doctor's *aid-de-camp*, Ella thought. Such a good man, not at all what she had thought an Aboriginal would be.

"Dowk com' fas' dis time uh year," he said, handing Dr. Bennett one of the lanterns. He took up a position on the other side of Ella with the second lantern. "*Marragawan* com' ot, lay on woom road. *Djirrabidi* too. Nut seaf."

The doctor nodded. He was grateful for the lanterns. Ella tugged on his sleeve—

"What is he saying? What lays on the warm road?"

Dr. Bennett patted Ella's hand in reassurance.

"He is worried you might stumble, what with the many rocks and ruts in the road."

Ella made a face. She was sure this was not Henry's concern.

Dr. Bennett preferred not to tell her the *marraguwan* and *djirrabidi* were the Dharug names for venomous snakes, the large brown snake and the red bellied black snake. He knew Ella was terrified of snakes.

―❦―

The following morning, Ella joined Mabarra and several other girls in the kitchen. A pile of mending lay on the large kitchen table. They were hard at work wending needles and thread. Cora, the laundry maid, was singing a version of the popular ballad, "I Love Thee Still."

> *Do you ever dream of me, love*
> *When the cold world is at rest*
> *Oft, my heart vibrates to thee, love;*
> *Like some chord thy hand hath prest…*
> *Could one thought of thee awaken,*
> *In my soul a deeper thrill,*

'Twould be thus to live forsaken
Yet to feel I love thee still…

"Is there someone you sing for, Cora? Someone you love?" Ella asked.

The girl nodded and stepped away from the table, pretending to need a drink of water. Mabarra leaned close to Ella and whispered that Cora's beloved had died on the voyage to New South Wales in 1806. Dr. Bennett had employed the man, named Joseph March, as an ostler to care for the half-dozen horses being transported on the ship. Somehow, Joseph picked up a lung infection while bunking next to the horses. The doctor did all he could to save him, but the damp, cold conditions on the ship exacerbated the illness. Joseph March died of sepsis on the final leg of the voyage and was given a burial at sea in the Southern Ocean.

Ella felt a lump form in her throat. She rose from the table and went to Cora, putting her arms around the woman.

"Please forgive me for broaching such a painful subject, Cora. I had no idea. I am sorry. Truly."

The gesture astonished the women, and most of all Cora. None of them knew any lady of the house who apologized to staff, much less hugged them. This woman, though educated and refined, appeared to possess a soft heart.

Ella turned to Mabarra and waved her hand over the table of mending, questioning why the women were so busy with mending.

"We do our best to keep up with this," Mabarra told Ella, "but with so many active children and workers, along with the doctor and vicar, well…it is a frequent chore."

Ella studied the pile of mending for a moment before grabbing a needle and thread.

"I will help. Give me something to mend."

Mabarra smiled and handed Ella a shirt with buttons missing. It was a fine shirt, the sort a well-dressed man would wear. Ella knew immediately it belonged to Dr. Bennett. The women giggled when Ella put her nose against the shirt and inhaled deeply, smiling.

"It has a wonderful manly fragrance," Ella whispered to herself, though all the women heard. She smiled mischievously.

"Here are the missing buttons, ma'am," Mabarra snickered, handing three of them to Ella. "Mind you do not pierce your nose with the needle trying to smell the shirt and mend it at the same time."

Ella giggled, which caused laughter to freely fill the kitchen.

Unexpectedly, Dr. Bennett appeared, carrying an empty teacup and saucer. The room grew quiet, though an occasional snicker could be heard.

"Ella?" he said in surprise. "You are sewing? How thoughtful of you."

"Yes, there is so much mending to be done I felt I should help. After all, I am good at suturing."

The doctor grinned at her wit. Already, he was growing fond of her. She was no laggard. In fact, she looked quite lovely sitting amongst his staff, mending…mending a shirt…his shirt! He relished the idea of her pretty hands on his clothes.

"I apologize for those missing buttons. They popped off while I was wrestling with Henry."

"Really?" Ella said, turning to look squarely at the doctor.

"Yes. And, I should add that Henry split the backside of his trousers in the tussle. I believe said pants may be somewhere in the mending pile."

Cora, who had returned to the table, held up Henry's trousers, grinning.

"Do you wish for more tea, Dr. Bennett?" Old Betty offered.

The doctor looked down at his teacup for a few seconds.

"Yes, thank you. And also bring one of those cinnamon biscuits we had at breakfast. Have Miss Fielding bring me the tea and biscuit when she has finished sewing on buttons. I have some clerical tasks I need to share with her."

He smiled, turned abruptly, and returned to his office in the clinic.

Old Betty watched him go, then looked at Ella.

"My lady…he does enjoy your company," she teased.

Ella blushed and changed the subject.

"I have no wish to be a bother," she began, "but I find myself in need of something for my skin. It turns red almost every time I step outside. Might any of you have a suggestion?"

Again, they were surprised. This fine woman was asking them for advice?

Mabarra, whose skin was the color of *mullumbimby* nuts, offered her advice—

"Ma'am, propolis helps. Bees make it. I can get you some from my people, the Bidjigal."

Four

Ella began teaching the children the week following the Bathing Revue, as Father Gregory had named the wash day. The orphans' sketches of the fun and productive day were now fastened to a string hung across the front wall of their dormitory classroom. Almost all the pictures featured Wibung being washed and rushed from tub to tub, with Ella and the priest doing the job.

It gratified Ella to see the gaggle of sweet-faced kids so clean and happy, even after she told them they would bathe one day a week. She justified it saying—

"It pleases God and all of us who love you that you are clean and dressed in fresh clothing."

They sat in the schoolroom on the floor, legs crossed, each with a writing board, pencil, and paper. Henry Douglas had made the writing boards from a long piece of pine, cutting them to size and sanding them smooth with a flat limestone rock. A coat of varnish made from pine resin and oil put a smooth finish on the boards. He had also sharpened the pencils with a small knife.

Ella wiped her damp forehead with a handkerchief. It was now late October, almost All Souls Day. The days were growing warmer with no cooling breeze. Henry had walked her from Acacia House to the schoolroom that morning.

"We ge' hot seas-son soon, Missy Fieldin'. Summa. I mick dis."

He held out a lovely fan he had constructed from reeds and stiff paper. On it he had drawn a beautiful Aboriginal scene of the night sky.

"Dees be de Ice Womens," he explained pointing to seven stars. "Ye cawls dem Pleiades. Dey tells win de eels swim up riva."

Ella was awestruck.

"Mr. Douglas, this is a most beautiful gift and one so needed too! Thank you...thank you so much! You must show me these Ice Women in the sky. I could see them up north but in the winter. Northern Hemisphere seasons are opposite from here."

Henry made a face, not understanding how it could be winter in Canada when it was almost summer in New South Wales. Ella grinned, not willing to launch into a difficult lesson about the earth's tilt causing the seasons.

She waved the fan in front of her face, and the cooling effect was immediate. She turned to Henry and smiled, extending her hand. He took it hesitantly.

"Would you like to attend school today, Mr. Douglas? I am sure the children would welcome you, as would I. That is if Dr. Bennett can spare you a few hours."

Henry's eyes brightened. He nodded and followed Ella into the classroom. He found a place on the floor at the back of the class. Ella gave him a writing board, pencil, and paper.

She walked to the front of the class, greeted the children, and began to sketch the world as she knew it on the slate board. She asked the children to follow her lead.

"I wish to show you where I was born and how far I traveled to get here by ship. I think this will be a fun geography lesson for you."

She drew a large circle to represent half of the world, then sketched the western continents in the circle to represent North America, South America, and the western part of Europe. She labeled the continents in view. She drew another circle and marked the Pacific Ocean, adding Australia and New Zealand.

On the east side of Australia, she outlined New South Wales and labeled it, along with a dot where Wahroonga was situated.

"We live here," she announced, pointing to the Wahroonga dot.

She drew a line replicating her voyage on the mail packet *Anna Maxwell*, from Canada to England, and then the *Isabella*, from England to Australia.

"Such a long way," Lucy whispered to Mani.

"Yeah, Missy Fielding' sea woman," the boy replied. "Mayba hab fish fin."

Lucy snickered.

"Mani, she is a normal woman, no fins. She came on a ship, just as I did."

"I neva seen ship. It lik' reala big canoe Fafha' Greg'ry say."

On Ella's rendering of the Australian continent, New South Wales appeared to be attached to a rather nondescript land extending north and west. She pointed to the land and ran her hand all over it.

"This is the continent where we live. Governor Macquarie says we should call it Australia, which means *southern*. We are not sure how big Australia is, but we know it stretches west, north, and south of New South Wales," she said, moving her hand in each direction.

Henry raised his hand and stood up, well-mannered.

"Missy Fieldin', dose uh lan' nort an' wes' uh here call Never-Never. Vera dry. Vera hot. No *badu*. Mina danger. Never-Never go der."

"*Badu* means water," Lucy translated.

Ella was delighted. She would learn from Henry and the children too.

"Have you been to Never-Never, Henry?" Ella asked.

He shook his head no.

"I tiks my own ad-viz!"

The children laughed. Ella too. Henry had quite the sense of humor.

But he had more to say.

"Missy Fieldin', Doctur say de wud be uh like big *djarduk*—bush apple—an' sun seem go uh 'round it. He say wud spin."

Ella smiled. She imagined this concept to be hard for Henry, as it was for her as a child.

"Yes, Mr. Douglas, that is correct! We cannot feel the earth spinning because it is so big, and we are small upon it. This spinning causes day and night. Sometimes we spin toward the sun. That causes daytime. And sometimes we spin away from it…"

"That nigh' time!" Mani shouted, joyfully.

"Yes!" Ella said, clapping her hands.

"And gravy kip us do'n on earf!" Mani crossed his arms as if he was the king of answers.

Ella laughed and clapped her hands again.

Henry leaned toward Mani and whispered: "It uh no' gravy *dinbin*! Missy Fieldin' tell ye now."

"Good thinking, Mani!" Ella said. "The force that holds us down on earth is called gravity. Children, let us all say it. *Gravity!*"

A murmur of "grav…uh…tee" went around the room.

"Very good! Very good!" Ella repeated.

She turned back to her large drawing board. She pointed to the dot on New South Wales where Wahroonga was labeled. Above it she trickled a ripply line and wrote Cockle Creek, then said it aloud. She paused then, allowing the children to imitate her sketch.

"I go swim Cocka Creek, Missy Fieldin'!"

It was Mani again. He stood up and made swimming motions with his arms. The children laughed boisterously until Ella held up her hand to indicate they should be quiet.

"Wahroonga means 'our home.' It is from the language of the Dharug clans," she said. "I believe all of you were born here, in or around Wahroonga. Most of you speak Dharug or Eora."

"I was not born here," said a high-pitched little voice.

It came from the lone white child Dr. Bennett had brought to the orphanage from Sydney. Blonde little Lucy. Ella had been told he named her Lucy for his deceased younger sister. Ella judged Lucy to be about eight years old.

"Oh, yes, Lucy. I forgot that you came here on a ship. Do you know where you were born?"

"Yes, ma'am. Dr. Bennett told me I was born in Ireland. I do not remember that place, but I can show it to you on your map."

Lucy came forward and took Ella's pointer. She laid the tip on the place where she judged Ireland to be. Ella again clapped her hands with delight.

"Why Missy Fieldin' clap han' so mush?" Mani whispered.

"Shhh!," Henry warned. "She uh happa we so smirt."

Ella had not heard the whispers. She was too intent on Lucy's knowledge of the world.

"Lucy, that is the correct place for Ireland! It is so far away from Australia, is it not?"

Ella drew and labeled Ireland and then filled in some lines delineating Ireland from Wales, Scotland, and England. Lucy quickly identified these other three.

"Dr. Bennett taught me to remember these places with the word 'WISE.' Wales, Ireland, Scotland, England."

Mani, who seemed to be the most talkative of the children, again piped up.

"Lucy be Dr. Benna subatoot dotter. He odop her. He mick her lern. Some time she eat wit' doc-tor. Sum night she sleep in big house…Acacia House."

Ella was a bit surprised. Dr. Bennett had not told her he had adopted Lucy, only that he had rescued her after her parents died on their voyage to New South Wales.

What was his intent in adopting the child? Surely it made Lucy feel separate, even favored above the others.

Lucy smiled at Ella and handed her the pointer.

"Dr. Bennett tells me I am just like all the other children," Lucy whispered. "He says people should not see others by color or status but by what is in their hearts. He allows all of us, one-by-one, to eat and sleep in the big house on occasion. It is not just me, ma'am."

Ella nodded slowly and followed Lucy's delicate form as she returned to her place on the floor. The child was quite pretty…and intelligent too.

No sooner had Lucy seated herself than Mani stood again and pointed to the door. Ella had propped the door open to let in the pleasant morning breeze and the perfume of the frangipani flowers.

"*Bulada!!*…she viz-it," Mani said in a low voice. "She wan' mitt Missy Fieldin'!"

The children softly giggled at Mani's announcement and waited for Ella's reaction. Ella looked toward the open door. A large colorful snake with a distinct triangular head and thick body had crawled through the doorway and lay inert, looking at Ella.

"Dat *fella* no hert," Mani said. "She jus curyus, Missy Fieldin'. She com viz-it all de time. *Bulada* be 'snake', Car-pet Pyfon. Fafha Greg'ry call her *Wiyanga*, 'Mufher.' One time she lay egg unda fall'd tree. Menna, menna babie' craw' ot."

Ella was frozen in place. She was frightened of snakes, and this one was huge—much longer than Ella was tall and bigger around than a man's upper arm. The python was staring at her as if she was an interloper. Ella thought of the many, many baby snakes Mani had mentioned. All of them would grow up as big as their mother! Had she brought them with her?

Wiyanga, Mani had said. Mother. Gooseflesh rose on Ella's skin.

Mani approached the snake and began to sing in his native language, gesticulating slowly with his hands. The snake turned to look at him. Ella could swear the snake was listening. She wanted to warn Mani he would be bitten, but she was unable to speak.

Henry Douglas motioned to everyone.

"Be uh still…be sigh-lent. *Wiyanga* 'onor uts wit' her viz-it. She dotter of Rainbow Serpent dat mick de mou'tain."

The room grew quiet. When Mani finished his song, he spoke again.

"Ye go now, *Wiyanga*. Missy Fieldin' scare o' ye. Soon, she not scare no mo'. We titch her like ye vera mush."

The boy quietly returned to his seat.

The snake, moving only her head, looked at Ella one last time. Then, as if obeying Mani, she turned and departed out the open door, the small tip of her tail flicking slightly as she disappeared.

The children watched her go. When the nether end of her long body disappeared over the door sill, they cheered…but a loud thump sounded.

Missy Fieldin' had fainted.

When Dr. Bennett got to the classroom, Father Gregory was on his knees fanning Miss Fielding's face with the pretty fan Henry had made. She was pale, almost lifeless. A few of the children had never seen someone faint and were terribly worried.

"Missy Fieldin' be dead?" one of them bravely asked.

"Oh, no," Father Gregory assured. "She was so afraid of *Wiyanga* her heart skipped a few beats. It made her feel light-headed. She will wake up soon."

Henry confirmed the Father's reassurance.

"She uh wuk up enna mow-ment," he said.

Mani told the class, "Missy Fieldin' no' eva see *bulada* like *Wiyanga*, vera big snake. Reala' big!"

"Why she scare a' *Wiyanga*?" Illuka asked, puzzled by Miss Fielding's reaction.

Father Gregory smiled. Snakes were a welcome presence in the Aboriginal world. Fear of them made no sense to the orphans.

"We all have fears," Father began. "I fear spiders, as you know. You remember I was bitten a few years ago and my arm swelled up and pained me badly. Miss Fielding is afraid of snakes. Perhaps she was bitten as a child in Canada."

After a minute, Miss Fielding's eyelashes fluttered. She woke to many pairs of eyes looking down on her.

"Ah, there you are, Miss Fielding," Father Gregory said. "You took a little nap after seeing our big python."

Ella inhaled a deep breath and shivered.

"It was horrifying! Tell me she is gone!"

Dr. Bennett nodded, chuckling. He had come running from the house when one of the children was sent to tell him what had happened.

"I suppose it was horrifying for someone who fears snakes, but you were in no real danger, Miss Fielding," the doctor said. "She would not hurt you unless you provoked her. She comes around here quite often. I think she feels safe among us."

Ella tried to sit up, but Dr. Bennett told her to lie still and recover. The children stared at her, worried.

After a few minutes, the doctor scooped her up in his strong arms, as if she were no heavier than a ragdoll, and began walking back to Acacia House.

The children cheered.

"Docta carra Missy Fieldin'!" Mani shouted. "She litta, not heavie. We need feed her mo'."

Ella's eyes were fixed on Dr. Bennett's handsome face. His eyes were like amber this morning, his black hair tumbling forward over one eye. One of his arms was wrapped around her back, hand clasped just beneath her left breast. He glanced at her briefly.

"You have had plenty of excitement for one day, Miss Fielding. I will take you to your room and let you rest until lunchtime. Gregory will take over in the classroom."

Ella did not refuse the doctor's orders. For one thing, she liked being held in his strong arms, so close she could smell his shaving soap and feel the hard muscles on his chest. And another thing, she *was* a little undone. A rest would improve her physical state and her spirits.

Dr. Bennett carried Ella into the house and up to her bedchamber, where he placed her on a chair. He rolled back the bedding and fluffed her pillows.

Emily was suddenly at Ella's side asking if she needed tea or a headache powder or a pictorial book of flowers to distract herself. Ella asked for a glass of water, to which the doctor added an order of claret.

Emily dashed away, as if water and wine were lifesaving tonics.

Dr. Bennett removed Ella's shoes, pausing to admire her small, narrow, silk-stockinged feet. He lifted her in his arms again and carried her to the bed. He paused before laying her on the soft sheets. His striking eyes locked on Ella's. She could see his pupils dilate and a tiny smile appear on his lips.

Was he enjoying this, laying her on a bed?

"Please forgive my familiarity, Miss Fielding. Know that I am acting as your doctor, else I would never enter your bedchamber unbidden or touch you so intimately."

Gently, he laid her down and pulled the bedcovers over her, making a neat fold of them across her chest.

"Rest, my dear. I am sorry you were frightened. There are many creatures here we have learned to live alongside. Most are harmless. *Wiyanga* was only curious."

Ella gave a small, surprised intake of breath.

"You call her *Wiyanga* too?"

Dr. Bennett uttered his low throaty laugh and sat down on the side of Ella's bed.

"Of course. I have encountered her many times, Miss Fielding. At first, I was wary of her too. But I quickly learned she means no harm. She seems to like it here; even left us a brood of babies once; hence her name. Maybe twenty cute little pythons. Sadly, they were all eaten by osprey chicks whose mother picked up the baby snakes one-by-one as they hatched, flew to her nest, and served them to her brood for dinner. Such is the way of nature…and the world."

Emily arrived with a tray bearing the glass of water and a small glass of claret. She placed these on the bedside table and curtsied politely. Dr. Bennett nodded, a signal that the maid should leave the room.

He wants to be alone with me, Ella thought, acting as my doctor, of course.

"The friendly boy, Mani," Ella began. "He sang to that snake…and…and it…she…seemed to listen to him. It was horrifying to watch. I was sure she would hurt him!"

Dr. Bennett offered Ella the wine. She lifted her head with the help of his free hand and sipped the claret.

"I find claret has a calming effect," he said. "I consider it a medicine, a pleasant one."

"Of course, wine and other libations can be considered medicinal," she agreed.

He waited until she had sipped all the wine.

"Mani…he is special," the doctor declared, "a child of both worlds. He asks endless questions and often comes up with answers we could never imagine. Need I say he is among my favorites of the children?"

Ella was grinning, fully agreeing with the doctor.

"I believe *Wiyanga* knows Mani does not fear her," Dr. Bennett continued, "nor would he harm her. She probably decided on her own it was wise to leave the busy school room. Her curiosity was satisfied."

He smoothed the bedcovers again and gave Ella's hand a soft squeeze.

"Now, you must rest until Emily comes to get you for tiffin."

That night, Ella dreamed that a great, colorful snake wrapped itself around her from ankles to neck and whispered in her ear the story of how its innocent babies were eaten by birds. Ella could not move and began to cry, telling the snake how sad she was about the lost reptilian children. Just as Ella woke, the python was slithering away into the grey mists of impending consciousness.

When Emily came to help Ella get dressed for the day, the maid found her standing at the window and noticed her sleepy eyes.

"Did ye no' sleep well, ma'am?"

Ella took Emily's arm affectionately.

"A nightmare woke me. But I am fine now, thank you."

Emily helped Ella into her dress, a confection of pink silk with light blue ruffles at the scooped neckline and hem. The sash was cerulean, bringing out her blue eyes.

Dr. Bennett and Father Gregory jumped to their feet the moment Ella entered the dining room for breakfast. The doctor pulled out her chair and complimented her on her dress, while Father Gregory quickly poured tea for her. He seemed unhappy.

"I so regret yesterday's terrifying incident, Miss Fielding…and on your first day teaching the children," he said apologetically. "I wish I had been there when *Wiyanga* appeared. As it was, Mani knew what to do. He has a magical way with animals. And Henry, well, he understands our British fears. Australia is a strange but wonderful place, my dear."

Ella nodded, chewing on a piece of rasher. In Canada, they called it bacon. It was her favorite breakfast food.

"Thank you, Father Gregory. I am sorry I was so frightened of that snake; I thought she would attack Mani and the other children!"

"She would not have," Dr. Bennett chimed in. "Did you see how quiet and still the children became in her presence? They know to do so. Henry reminded them of her virtue as a daughter of the Rainbow Serpent. Mani moved slowly and sang to her. For some unknown reason, snakes like music."

"Rainbow Serpent? I recall Henry talking about that."

Father Gregory tried to explain the Aboriginal connection to the land.

"The Bidjigal and other Dharug clans revere the animals as sacred descendants of the animal spirits that created the landscape. Henry's people believe the Rainbow Serpent spirit crawled over the land, creating creeks and rivers, and then she came to rest to form mountains."

Ella shook her head in amazement. How could a giant snake become a mountain range?

"I have never witnessed anything like it," she said. "I must admit, *Wiyanga*, as you call her, is a pretty snake. The yellow and black patterns over those brown scales and the undulating way she moved...remarkable now that I think about it. But I was afraid she would hurt someone. Reptiles are not very intelligent."

"True," Father Gregory said, "yet, this was not the first time she has come to visit the children. When we leave doors open, she feels free to enter. She has eaten some of our small livestock—chickens and ducks, piglets in the snuggery. I suppose she feels entitled to eat our animals, since we have taken over much of her territory."

Dr. Bennett chimed in—

"She has never caught Ngana, though. That cat is lightning fast, almost feral. And Wibung, he avoids both the cat and the snake."

Ngana? There was a cat on the premises? Ella was surprised. She loved kittens and cats.

Spurred by Ella's puzzled expression, Dr. Bennett explained—

"Ngana is secretive. You will not often see her. She wandered here from some other place, probably a timber camp or orchard, maybe Fiddens Wharf. Cats are travelers. They are not native to this place but have escaped from ships ever since the First Fleet came in 1788. Ngana may even have stowed away in one of our supply wagons returning from Sydney. She is wild though. She hangs around here only for the food she receives."

"I am fond of cats," Ella said, "tame ones that is. I had a little moggy in Bytown named Scamper. I left him with a friend when I traveled here. He was a sweet pet."

Dr. Bennett made a mental note of this. Perhaps he would gift Ella a kitten on some special occasion. A kitten that would be tamed and kept in the house, away from hungry animals and unable to damage the land itself. In the near three decades since the First Fleet arrived, many stowaway cats had gone feral and had an adverse impact on rodent populations. The doctor knew this was not a positive effect. Rodents, for all their trouble, had a place in the environment.

"What does Ngana mean? I assume it is a Dharug word," Ella guessed.

Dr Bennett grinned and replied: "It means *black*, and she is. She has one tiny white spot on her chin, like a droplet of milk."

The sound of a wagon in the driveway interrupted breakfast. Dr. Bennett was just rising from his chair when Mrs. Hughes rushed in.

"Doctor, it is one of the timbermen. He is badly cut on his leg."

Ella quickly followed Dr. Bennett outside where a man lay in the back of a wagon, bloody and agonized with pain. He was holding one thigh and moaning. The doctor shook hands with one of the two drivers.

"Miss Fielding, this is Carson McDougal, foreman of the Dixon timber operation some sixteen kilometers northwest of here. McDougal, Miss Fielding is my nurse, arrived from Canada not long ago."

The men looked Ella over with hungry eyes, even the injured man. Carson McDougal nodded a lascivious greeting, winking at Ella.

McDougal and the other driver, Benson, carried the bleeding man into the clinic and laid him on a table in the treatment room. Ella, without being asked, began cutting the heavy canvas pants away from the injury and cleaning the wound. She overheard McDougal telling the doctor there had been an accident with a large crosscut saw.

"Warner, here, he were on one en' da saw when it jump off da log and cut inta 'is leg. Gouged 'is leg pretta dip."

Dr. Bennett turned toward Ella, nodded with approval at her work, cutting away Warner's pantleg and cleaning the cut. He asked—

"Will you suture, Miss Fielding?"

"Yes, doctor."

"Good. We three will hold the patient while you suture and close the wound. Give him a generous shot of whisky first."

Carson McDougal turned to Dr. Bennett.

"She gonna do it? Uh girl?"

Dr. Bennett smiled. Ella sighed.

When would women be free of this outlandish male tyranny, she wondered.

"Yes. But she is no girl, McDougal; she is a woman, an educated, highly trained nurse, quite capable. Women have small hands and are adept at stitching things together, including…flesh."

Ella handed the man a brimming shot of whiskey. He slugged it down anxiously. She proceeded to pour peroxide on his wound, telling him that it would produce a burning, bubbling sensation. He remained still at first, then began to moan and writhe as the solution boiled on his raw skin.

"That goddamed shit hurts!"

Such a baby, Ella said to herself.

She paid no mind to the profanity. She doused the suturing thread in peroxide and threaded the needle.

"First stitch going in," she said.

As the needle pierced his skin, the patient grunted and yelled, "Bloody bitch!"

He drew air between his teeth as Ella punctured his skin again and began to sew a row of finely placed sutures, tying off each one perfectly. She apologized for the pain she caused, though her remorse was met with fury.

"Ouch! Fuggin' cunt!"

Ella paused before continuing her work.

"You, sir, appear to have a limited vocabulary."

"I charge extra for vulgarity," Dr. Bennett announced, "especially when directed at my nurse."

Carson McDougal told Warner to shut his mouth, though McDougal himself had been eyeing Ella as if she was a tasty morsel and thinking her virginal vagina was surely wet and tight. He liked what he saw. She was young and pretty.

"Sutures are finished," Ella announced. "I will put a dressing on the wound."

Dr. Bennett handed her a small can of eucalyptus salve and bandages.

"What is that fuggin' goo?" Warner groaned.

"I make a salve from eucalyptus leaves," the doctor explained. "You need it to prevent infection."

Within a few minutes Warner's leg was salved and covered in a sterile bandage. An outer, tougher bandage was wound about his thigh to complete the job. Still irritable, and muttering obscenities to himself, he was carried back to the wagon. The doctor had supplied him with extra salve and clean bandages, admonishing him to change the dressings every day for a week, then cut out the sutures on the tenth day.

McDougal paid the doctor his fee, then motioned for Ella to step aside and speak with him. She was careful not to step too near, for the foreman smelled like a mixture of rotten teeth, sweat, and repulsive body odor. She had smelled this sort of body odor before but could not place what it was. Sweat mixed with something else, but what?

"I be mighta impress'd by da sewin' job ye done on ole Warner," McDougal said. "Ye looks too pretta ta knows much 'bout medi-sin. Ye say ye a nurse, really? Ennaways, Miss Fields, Warner be vulgar ta ye. I be thinkin' p'raps I kin micks it ups ta ye by takin' ye ta suppa down 'n Parr'matta sum night. They be real goo' vittles at da inn do'n thar, Molly's Place. We cud dances a bit, drinks some, an' then bounce me sausage in ye basket...well, ye knows ma meanin'. I kin shows ye a real good time. Whatta ye say, pretta babe?"

He was staring right at her breasts as if they were two squeezy toys!

Ella stammered a moment, surprised at the man's audacity. His sausage in her basket? How obscene!

"No...no thank you. It would be most unprofessional of me, Mr. McDougal. I have no interest in such an evening. You have paid your bill. Good day."

She gathered her skirts and walked away quickly, glad to be separated from his strange odor and indecent talk. McDougal fumed as he climbed onto the seat of the wagon and took the reins.

"Sassy damn bitch. I were gonna mick Warner apolerjize, bu' no' now. She be ever-a-thing he sayed an' worst!"

Dr. Bennett took Ella by the arm the moment the men left. She seemed upset. She was shaking. He led her inside to his office and closed the door.

"Miss Fielding, sit here. I will fetch us each a shot of whiskey. You did an excellent job on that wound, by the way. I knew you would. But sometimes we get overwhelmed after treating patients. It passes."

He patted her shoulders lightly and went to the liquor cabinet.

"Did Carson McDougal say something improper to you? He can be intolerable at times."

He handed Ella the shot of whiskey and watched in disbelief as she drank it down in one large swallow.

"You *are* upset, Ella!"

He had called her Ella, not Miss Fielding. Ella.

She looked at him with pleased surprise. He took her glass and lowered his head for a moment.

"It is time we stopped the Miss and Doctor, Sir and Ma'am," he said softly. "I prefer Ella—a pretty name that suits you and is less school-marmy than Miss Fielding."

He smiled sweetly at Ella and slid one of his hands under one of hers.

"Please call me Thad. My mother named me for her brother. I have lived with Thaddeus for six-and-thirty years now. It is a good name. It means *courageous heart.*"

She managed a little smile.

"Thad, such a nice name. I like it, and you do have a courageous heart...Thad."

Ella ironed her skirt with her hands and looked at the floor of Thad's office.

"Thad, Mr. McDougal asked me out to dinner, a place in Parramatta called Molly's. He was demeaning about it, calling me 'babe' and telling me I was too pretty to be able to suture a wound. He wanted the dinner to be an apology for Warner's profanity...and afterward he wanted..."

Thad screwed up his face.

"Molly's? That is a...a...whorehouse that happens to serve food. You said 'no' I hope."

Ella nodded and began to giggle.

"What??" Thad uttered.

Ella shrugged and giggled more.

"What sort of food would a whorehouse serve, Thad?"

She broke into a full bout of laughter at his exasperated expression.

"You act as if I would know, Ella. I do not!"

He let out a loud sigh.

"If I needed congress with a woman, which I do not and will not until I am married, I surely would not go to Molly's Place. The whores there have every social disease known....and they are ignorant and smell disgusting."

Congress? Not a sausage bouncing in a basket? Such a fusty, moth-eaten word—congress. Could he not just say *sex*? She giggled, then was quiet.

Thad's mention of the whores' bad odor reminded her...

"Thad, McDougal had an odd smell about him. I recognized it, have smelled it in the past. But I cannot name it."

Thad stared at her and slowly broke into a smile. She was perceptive indeed. Immensely perceptive, and far more educated than he had expected her to be. He would tell her the truth, lay it out plain and simple.

"He has gonorrhea, Ella. I suspect you smelled it in your hospital work in Canada. The odor is unmistakable. McDougal used to come to me for treatment, but there was little I could do. Some doctors treat gonorrhea with mercury, but that is dangerous. Mercury causes other ills, including ulcers and madness."

He paused, looking down at his hands.

"I am sure he has infected many women, especially Aboriginal women. And then they infect their men. I have banned him from coming here except on business, and he is not permitted to visit the Bidjigal or Wangal camps on my property. No doubt, he goes to other camps."

"Ella, you are a brave woman," Thad continued, rubbing her hand, "an intelligent woman, and a solicitous soul. I am grateful to you for answering my advert for a nurse, and exceedingly happy to have you here, not only as a nurse and teacher but as a friend. Gregory was my sole source of good company before you arrived."

Acacia House was quiet for a few weeks after the timber-getters had been given medical help. In the meantime, Ella sat in the gardens and sketched the curious flora of Australia, wrote letters, and sewed new clothes for the children. She made a jaunty cloth hat for Mani which he promptly put on his head and refused to remove, even at bedtime.

"Missy Fieldin', she mick dis fo' me," he would tell anyone who asked about the hat. "If on head, no one steal."

He did promise Ella she could wash it once a month.

Toward the middle of November, Thad took Ella with him in the curricle to Turramurra to tend to a man with cancer. She had seen many types of cancer, but not this one. Skin cancer. Apparently, it was a serious problem in Australia and becoming worse.

"I believe it may be the fierce sun and heat here that causes it," Thad said as they rode slowly along a rocky, uphill road. "So many people work in the sun with their faces and other body parts exposed. They work until their skin blisters, then develop odd brown spots and moles. The Aboriginals' dark skin may protect them."

Axle, the buggy horse, came to a stop. He did not like the rocks and holes in the road, nor pulling the curricle uphill. Thad got out and led Axle for a few minutes before jumping back in with Ella.

"He is an old horse, content to stand in the barnyard shade and sleep. I think he has rheumatism, the equine version. A little exercise is good for him."

Ella smiled and adjusted her straw hat. The sun was, indeed, fierce.

"Mr. Byrne, our patient today, is an orchard worker, always in the sun," Thad continued. "I have told all the orchard workers they should wear cabbage hats and long sleeve shirts of lighter colors to protect them from the sun. It is hard to get them to listen."

They passed a *billabong* where the flowering gum trees were filled with squawking galahs. Ella spied several grey kangaroos drinking. They were jills, some with joeys. Thad slowed the curricle to let her take in the endemic scene. She sighed and asked if Thad desired to paint such an authentically Australian tableau.

"If there was time and I had my paints, yes. I think you know I am smitten with kangaroos. Nature certainly was having an imaginative day when she made them."

When they resumed their travel, they spoke again of disease.

"What I know of cancer is that it is duplicitous, Thad," Ella stated. "The damage happens now, but the payment for it comes later. I know almost nothing about skin cancer, but when I lived in Bytown, in Canada, I saw the lungs removed from an old chimney sweep after he died. They were black inside and full of small tumors. I cannot help but think his exposure to soot, the breathing of that black stuff, caused the cancer."

Thad put one arm around Ella and gave her a gentle hug. She was a thinker, a woman who could break down problems. Yet, when she looked in his eyes, he felt a shiver course down his back. She was so lovely, she smelled like fresh blooming roses, she seemed delicate and dainty. But he knew she was incredibly strong and smart.

"I am fortunate to have you as my nurse, Ella. You are far more capable than I thought you would be."

But as a woman? How did he feel about her as a woman, she wondered. He had put his arm around her. Was he thinking of kissing her?

Not just yet.

Thad retreated to his side of the curricle seat. They reached Turramurra by noon, no thanks to the dawdling Axle. Thad found a shady spot for the horse and slung one rein over a low tree limb. A bucket of water was fetched, and Axle quickly drank, cocked one back hoof, closed his big brown eyes, and went to sleep.

"He is one of the half-dozen horses that came here with me by ship," Thad said. "I fear I am a little too indulgent with him."

Thad led Ella through a labyrinth of bark-walled shacks and into a larger one, well-chinked with mud.

Kevin Byrne sat at a table sharpening a knife. He was a handsome Irishman of middle age, though his nose and one cheek were scarred from the doctor's healing handiwork.

He greeted Dr. Bennett warmly and insisted Thad and Ella have lunch. His wife had laid out a fine table with her wooden plates and pewter cutlery and was eager to serve them. Bread and cheese were the main fare, with a fruit mix and nuts as well. The beverage was ale. Ella had never tasted macadamia nuts. They were buttery and delicious.

After lunch, Byrne rolled up the sleeve on his right arm and showed it to Dr. Bennett. Ella could see several scars where Thad previously had removed pieces of diseased skin.

"I got two new ones, doc. I been wearin' long sleeves and a hat, but they still come. The missus, she makes a paste of flour and water and puts it on my nose."

He pointed to a misshapen dark brown spot on his left arm that was black in the middle and pinkish on its uneven edges.

"I bumped this one carrying water. My wife put salve on it and bandaged it, but it does not heal."

Thad put a hand on Kevin Byrne's shoulder.

"It will not heal, Mr. Byrne. I am sorry. The damage has been done…was done years ago. I can only remove it and hope I have taken all the cancer. I fear we will do battle with these cancer spots for the remainder of your life."

Thad asked Byrne a barrage of questions. Was he tired? Headachy? Nauseous? Did he feel himself growing weaker? Had he lost weight? Did he have night sweats? Was his appetite flagging? These were a few of the indicators of sickness inside his body, signs the cancer had moved from his skin to his internal organs.

"Kev bin so tir'd a' late, Doc-tor," Mrs. Byrne said.

Byrne waved her away and guzzled several shots of rum while Thad prepared to cut off the two cancer spots. Ella and Mrs. Byrne held her husband's arm while Thad made quick, deep cuts. They bled profusely.

"Miss Fielding will suture the cuts. She has steady, deft hands. Women often are better at sutures than men."

Kevin Byrne nodded and gripped the edge of the table with his hand while Ella sprinkled powdered yarrow on his cuts as a styptic to slow the bleeding. She then doused the cuts with peroxide and passed the needle in and out of his bloody skin. Thankfully, each cut needed only a few sutures.

Ella smiled sweetly at him when she was finished suturing and began bandaging his arm.

"The last man I sutured, a timber-getter, screamed and cried like a baby and called me profane names."

They laughed together for a few seconds.

"So those timber-cutters is not so tough after all?" Byrne said, chuckling.

"They are not!" Ella responded.

As Thad and Ella were packing up, Mrs. Byrne brought out a small crock sealed with paraffin.

"'Tis appabutta frum las' atum'. Tankee for helpin' me man."

They accepted the gift graciously. Ella hugged the woman, knowing how worried she was for her husband.

"Keep the wound clean and covered. Snip away the sutures in ten days. I shall come check on you again in a few months," Dr. Bennett told Byrne. "In the meantime, send someone should you need me."

Thad and Ella walked past the bark houses back to their curricle. They could hear coughing in one of the little houses.

"Consumption," Thad whispered. "I know that cough. There is no cure."

Axle reluctantly resumed his duties pulling the little buggy, walking as if his hooves were stepping on nails.

"His joints will loosen up shortly," Thad said. "Perhaps I will find some turmeric to sprinkle in his grain. In the meantime, I will ask Henry to massage his front knees and walk him a little more."

"Is that what you recommend to your human patients?"

Thad chuckled: "That and gentle walking and stretching. I have a few patients who come to me for rheumatism. Mr. and Mrs. MacArthur from down at Parramatta do. Perhaps you have heard of them. They are quite influential in the colony, although John manages to offend just about everyone he meets. I simply ignore his jabs. Elizabeth, on the other hand, is intelligent and sensible, albeit a bit opinionated. I like her all the same. I must take you to meet the MacArthurs soon."

Thad talked with Ella then about Kevin Byrne's cancer—

"Mr. Byrne looks wearier and paler each time I see him. He is thinner too, though he may not realize it. You heard his wife say he is tired. I am sad to say he will likely die soon, maybe within the year. The cancer has gone to his internal organs."

Axle stalled out again, requiring Thad to get out of the curricle and lead him for a way. Back in the little buggy, Thad continued the conversation.

"We will need to make arrangements for his wife and children to join us at Acacia House when she becomes a widow. The fruit company will evict her from that house, as crude as it is. I am sure I can find work for her. The two children can attend school with the orphans. If I do not extend a hand to Mrs. Byrnes, she may be snared by the circumstance of many widows in this colony—earning an income from prostitution."

Ella stared at Thad's beautiful profile, smiling to herself. She had decided he was the kindest man in New South Wales, and maybe the most judicious. He was handsome, well-liked, wealthy, and educated. A self-made man. She had worked for him for almost two months now and was growing fonder of him by the day.

Suddenly, he shot her a quick glance and caught her staring at him.

"Am I being inspected? I do hope I pass muster."

She giggled and pushed a stray curl under her bonnet.

"You pass, Dr. Thad. You pass easily. I was just thinking how thoughtful you are, assuring the Byrnes' well-being when Mr. Byrnes passes. They are nearly in poverty now. I am sure Mrs. Byrnes will be unable to earn enough money for those children and herself when her husband is gone, unless she turns to selling her charms."

Thad nodded and turned to look at Ella straight on.

"We both know what happens to women in those circumstances. Either they remarry in desperation, or they start selling their favors."

Ella thought how lucky she was to have an education and a job.

"Did you imagine you were doing a kindness for me when you sent me an offer of employment, Thad? You were, you know, and I must thank you for it."

He took her hand.

"And are you happy here, dear Ella? Dirty children, roaring male koalas raping their mates, big scary snakes, sick people's blood and pus and snot, and obscene patients yelling profanities at you—there is yet more fun to come!"

She squeezed his hand.

"I am happy, Thad. I feel appreciated and useful. And I am learning so much from you and Gregory."

Five

Spring passed into summer, and the intense heat arrived, heat such as Ella had never experienced in Canada or England. She had been warned about it by the maids. Emily brought her a flimsy, sleeveless nightgown to replace the heavy, high-necked, long-sleeved gown she had been wearing to bed. Still, she woke every morning sopping wet with perspiration.

"Ye will lose modesty in this season, ma'am," Emily said. "Even thee doctor and Father Gregory sheds clothes and wipes sweat frum they brows."

It was true. Ella recalled the first scorching day she came down to breakfast and found Thad with no waistcoat or jacket and the sleeves rolled up on his white shirt. The collar was open at the neck, enough to reveal the dark hair on his upper chest. His bare arms were hairy and muscled. Ella tried not to gawk. She had often wondered what he looked like under all his layers of clothes.

Did he wonder the same about her?

She wore a thin cotton dress with a low neckline and short, puffed sleeves. Emily had convinced her to shed a petticoat or two, as well as her stockings and long underdrawers. She was given a short pair and felt almost naked from her thighs down.

Father Gregory seldom appeared for meals now. Thad told her the heat bothered Gregory terribly. Mrs. Hughes had one of the maids take his meals to the small rectory attached to one side of the church, as it was much cooler in the south-facing edifice.

The children had the summer off from school, though they were still made to do chores, weed the gardens, keep their dormitory and themselves clean, and to say their prayers of gratitude. It was far too hot to sit in their classroom all day. They played outdoors, apparently unaffected by the heat. On the hottest days, they took refuge inside the church, with its doors open to admit the cross-breeze, and played games and sang. Often, the older children took the raft of orphans to Cockle Creek, about half-a-kilometer northwest of Acacia House, where they could splash and play and, one day a week, bathe.

The landscape of New South Wales soon became parched, with reddish-brown dust whirling about and kicking up small *willi willies*—dust devils—that laid down a patina on everything. The gardens cried for water. Blossoms wilted away. Every morning, Ella carried bucket after bucket of water to the thirsty plants. Mrs. Hughes thought this unladylike, but Thad allowed Ella to do as she wished so long as she did not injure herself or suffer from the heat.

The first evening after watering the gardens, she complained of sore arms as she and Thad sat on the front porch swing together conversing and drinking cold tea. Thad seemed to have an endless supply of tea, a memento of his past life in England.

"Let me see your arms," Thad said, taking each of them and softly kneading the sore muscles of first her upper arms and then her forearms. His large, slender hands were gentle.

"They have been overworked," he whispered to her, grinning.

As he continued kneading and rubbing, the pain began to subside. Thad and Ella looked into each other's eyes.

"Am I making you uncomfortable, Ella? I touch you uninvited, I take you alone in the buggy, and I sit close to you here on the swing. We speak of unspeakable things too, things germane to medicine. Back in England I would be scorned for my behavior. You would be considered a ruined woman."

Ella laughed, grateful Thad did not believe in strict rules of conduct between the sexes.

"Your hands are most skillful, doctor. My arms feel much better. Thank you. And…I do not feel ruined…rather, I feel cared for and appreciated. I am thankful you do not subscribe to the ridiculous rules of propriety forced upon us in England."

"Indeed," Thad agreed. "So many things in England are wrong, in my opinion. But we do not have the time to discuss them. I prefer to simply enjoy your company, Ella."

A rumble came from the south. Clouds had gathered, forming a dark line over the trees. Ella marveled at the approaching storm, its blues and purples bruising the sky.

"A thunderstorm," Thad said. "It will likely be violent. Usually is this time of year as the seasons change."

They watched the clouds rapidly advancing and the sky darkening all around them. Thunder and lightning grew in volume and intensity. Warrigal crawled under the swing and laid down next to Thad's feet.

A brisk wind fronted the rain, then became stronger. The porch's hanging ferns swung to and fro; a pillow was blown off a wicker settee; dust whirled. Yellow acacia blooms fluttered in the air like frightened butterflies and tumbled over the dry ground.

There was a flurry of staff heard putting down windows in the house. Mabarra ran to the clothesline and grabbed the sheets she had washed. At the barn, Henry was coaxing Wanyuwa, Axle, and the other horses into their stalls. Father Gregory could be seen shooing the children into their dormitory.

Within minutes tiny pellets of hail fell, then large droplets of rain began hitting the ground and the slate-shingled porch roof, thrumming like small drums. Some of the drops blew through the railings and fell on Thad, Ella, and Warrigal. Frightening ribbons of lightning were followed by the loudest thunder Ella had ever heard. She leaned close to Thad. He put one arm around her.

"There was a terrible storm at sea as I sailed here on the *Isabella*," she said. "It was so forceful I thought the ship would sink, and all of us aboard would drown—officers at the helm, crewman on deck and in the rigging, and the many convicts chained below, not to mention me cowering in my little cabin. The ship rolled like a toy boat in a bathtub, and waves washed over us. I need not tell you I was on my knees praying for deliverance."

Thad embraced her tightly.

"You are safe here on dry land, sweet Ella…dry land about to become wet land."

He chuckled low in his throat. This had become Ella's most loved sound.

The thunderstorm moved swiftly over Acacia House, flashing and cracking as it consumed and reduced the great heat of the day. Rain poured in sheets and drenched the landscape. Waterfalls fell from the roofs of all the buildings. Windborne rain tore into the trees, ripping away blossoms and loose bark. Falling branches smashed plants in the gardens.

For some ten minutes the rainstorm, like a river in the sky, saturated the atmosphere and everything below it. Then, as quickly as it had descended on Wahroonga, it left, moving north to drown the hills and valleys of Hawkesbury and Broken Bay.

Thad took Ella by the hand and walked with her through the flower gardens. The ground was riddled with small channels that had formed to carry away the surfeit of water. Small plants had been uprooted and others flattened. Flowers hung their wet heads, as if crying. Some had their delicate stems broken.

Behind the house, Cockle Creek was heard roaring as it overran its banks. Ella lifted her skirts and walked with Thad to see it. The rush of muddy water had risen nearly twice the original width of the creek and was causing a loud racket as it passed over rocks and around trees. As Thad and Ella watched the noisy spectacle, the drowned body of a wallaby rushed by on its way to who knew where.

They walked arm-in-arm to the church to check on the children and Gregory, sloshing as they went. Ella no longer cared about the hem of her dress or the mud on her shoes. On the back porch of the church, she slid off her soiled slippers and placed them beside Thad's muddy boots.

The children were huddled together in the church pews. Mani ran to Ella and hugged her.

"Ye safe, Missy Fieldin'! Ye safe! I worry fo' ye an' doc-tor. Dat *mungi* so scary!"

"Yes, we are safe," Ella told him, "and so are you and all the children. What is *mungi*, Mani?"

"Oh, it light-ning."

He proceeded to do his best impersonation of lightning—lurching, jerking, and pointing his fingers like arrows. Ella smiled at him and looked around the church.

"Where is Father Gregory?"

"He go see steeple and cross."

Thad guided Ella to the front pew and seated her.

"I will go see if there is trouble," he said.

Ella invited the children to huddle around her. She began reciting a little poem she knew about rain, friendly rain, not the torrent they had just experienced.

Summer brings the rain
To wash our forests clean,
Rain will shine the leaves
On all the pretty trees...

"We heard a crack of lightning over-top the church," Lucy said, her eyes huge. "There is a lightning rod, but Father Gregory is afraid the *mungi* might have hit the metal cross on the steeple."

Bubuk and Jiemba came into the church looking drenched. They sat on the floor and smiled sheepishly. Mani pointed at them and giggled.

"They go Lovers' Cave!" Yarran said. At sixteen, he was the oldest boy at the orphanage.

All the children laughed. Mani made a kissy mouth and smooched the air.

"Children!" Ella scolded. "Mocking is unkind!"

Mani pouted, sticking out his large lower lip.

"Buh, Missy Fieldin', they go *nganaba*! Cave! It too soon."

The children were snickering. Yarran grinned and said—

"Father Gregory call it Ridin' San George. Ha!"

Ella was flummoxed. She looked from child to child, feeling she was the only one uninformed about the cave and Bubuk and Jiemba. Had they gone there to kiss?

Gregory returned. He told Ella that Thad was checking on the glasshouse.

The children grew quiet and waited to hear about the steeple and cross.

"The cross is unharmed," Father Gregory told them. "God has spared us. He must know how good you children are."

Yarran pointed at Bubuk and Jiemba.

"Mayba not dose two."

Laughter erupted. Father Gregory held up his hands to indicate quiet.

"We must all keep to our own business," he said. "You may go outside now and play, but keep watch, especially on the ground. The storm has displaced many animals."

He signaled to Bubuk and Jiemba to remain. Miss Fielding too. After all the children were gone, he sat down on a pew opposite the two teenagers.

"Have you two been in the cave this afternoon?" he quietly asked.

They nodded. Jiemba's eyes filled with tears. She wrapped her arms tightly around Bubuk. The gesture told Ella what all the mocking and teasing had been about.

"You may not believe this, but I know what love is," Father Gregory told them. "I have experienced yearning and desire. I once loved a beautiful girl in France. I thought the sun rose and set on her, that the moon shone in her lovely blue eyes. I adored her and desired her. But she did not love me back. She did not want a life as a vicar's wife. My heart shattered in a thousand pieces. I cried for her; I was worthless with grief. The visiting cardinal told me as penance I would not be permitted to speak for a sennight."

The teenagers were wide-eyed. So was Ella.

"Only by coming here with Dr. Bennett, and building this church and orphanage, did I find solace."

Gregory's confession dumbfounded Ella. She had thought him passionately devoted to his calling, so much that he could not fall in love or marry. Now, she realized he and Thad had both come to Australia with broken hearts.

Bubuk whispered to Father Gregory—

"Father, do you not love Annie Gray-Face? She loves you with all her heart. Do you not see how she looks at you on Sundays?"

Father Gregory lowered his head.

"I do love her, Bubuk. I love her as I love all my parishioners. But I believe she is far too young for me. I am on the far side of forty. She is but sixteen."

"But Father, Annie hears the call of God to do His work," Jiemba added. "Would it not be a blessing for her to be your helpmate, your wife? You have said, yourself, that there is so much work to do here."

Gregory glanced at Ella and sighed.

"I shall consider it. But for now, we must talk of you, Bubuk and Jiemba. You are both so young, and though I know you are promised to each other, I feel you should wait to go to the cave until you are older and married."

He turned to Ella.

"Miss Fielding, perhaps you have an opinion on this matter."

Ella looked from Gregory to the two children. And they were children, she thought. They could be no more than thirteen or fourteen.

"I believe the act of loving is beautiful, but it belongs inside marriage," she began. "I think of marriage as a blanket of safety where two people protect each other and promise to be true to one another. It is God's will that we marry first, then join our bodies in love."

Father Gregory smiled and nodded to Ella. She had said the right thing.

"I agree with Miss Fielding. I ask you both to wait. We can talk about marriage soon, I promise. Go now and keep watch on the little ones."

After they had gone, Gregory sighed and took Ella's hands.

"Ah, to be so young again and in love. It is hard for them," he said. "Were you ever in love, Ella?"

She thought back to Bytown, where her late mother, Suzanna Fielding, had moved when Ella was only twelve. There was a tall, handsome boy—

"He was a hawker who brought us potatoes and turnips and carrots. Oh, the way he would look at me! He could undress me with his eyes. But…diphtheria came through our area of Canada. He was so sick. I took him soups and juices and tea. Sat by his bedside and read to him, prayed for him. One day I went to see him, and his mother told me he had died that morning."

Gregory had tears in his eyes. He reached for Ella and pulled her into a hug. She noticed his hands were shaking.

"It must have sorely tested your faith, dear Ella. I am sorry you suffered so. Has Thad told you about Edith Fullerton? She is the reason we came here."

He released her and looked into her entrancing blue eyes. She had eyes like the girl he had loved so long ago.

"Gregory, please tell me about Annie Gray-Face, the one who loves you. Denying yourself and her because of age difference is foolish. If you love her…"

He shook his head.

"I am quite fond of her, but I believe she is more in love with the thought of serving God in this church than with being my wife. She is Bidjigal. If I married a native, I would lose most of my white congregation. This is how it is in our society, Ella."

Thad appeared at the door. He looked at Ella and Gregory almost with an expression of suspicion. Ella pulled her hands away and stepped back from Gregory.

"Not to worry, my friend," Gregory said, smiling at Thad. "We were just discussing two children who seem to have discovered the wonder and excitement of love. Bubuk and Jiemba."

Thad cleared his throat.

"Ah, yes. They are of that age."

Thad paused, fumbling with his waistcoat pocket watch. Ella had not seen him dressed so finely, except for church, since summer began.

"I came to tell you I am going down to Sydney for a few days, likely a week if I can contract with some businesses for work on our property. A letter has come from England via an arriving ship. My Great-Uncle Frederick Bennett in Sussex has passed at age one-and-ninety. A ripe old age to be sure. I am his closest heir. My barrister in Sydney is in contact with the Bennett family barrister in Northampton, the man who is handling the will."

"We will take care of everything here, Thad. Safe travels," Gregory said. His jaw was quivering slightly. Ella thought he must be cold from climbing on the wet roof of the church.

"This is more good fortune, my friend," Thad said to Gregory. "Shall I ask the glassworks to send up a man to take measurements for stained-glass windows in the church?"

Ella's eyes lit up.

"Oh, Gregory, you so deserve that! Think of the activities we could do with the children—stories, art, arithmetic, ciphering, poems. Just the beauty of the windows would be a blessing."

Gregory chortled and wrung his shaky hands.

"Of course, Thad, if you wish."

"I do wish," Thad said smiling. "No vicar deserves those windows more."

Ella went to the door and took Thad's hands. The gesture was meant to reassure him.

"Thad, be careful," she said. "You know the road gangs are active around Wahroonga and Parramatta. There are those new footpads riding the roads too, bushrangers I believe they are called."

"I will take care. I always take a pistol when I travel to Sydney. May I bring you anything, Ella," he whispered.

"I need nothing…only you safely back at Acacia House."

He was deeply touched by her words.

All the way to Sydney, Thad thought about Ella Fielding and her sweet farewell. He could no longer deny his feelings for her. She was like no woman he had ever known. How brave she was to travel from the top of the world to the bottom to serve a doctor and a priest she had never met, to love and care for the children of the orphanage, to dauntlessly face the blood and gore of medicine and the oddities and dangers of Australia.

Only a few days earlier, she had helped him amputate a timberman's mangled foot, holding both of the man's hands in hers and giving him strength to endure the pain of the doctor's saw. She had prayed with him and told him she thought Dr. Bennett's carpenter might be able to fashion a false foot from wood.

A week before that, Ella had spent hours with the young orphan, Gimbawali, helping her cope with her first menses. The girl, whose name meant "stars," was only ten, an early age for puberty, Ella thought. Gimbawali was sure she was dying of a strange disease. She had run away and hidden in the forest beyond the church. It was Ella's soft, reassuring words that had drawn her back.

Ella had decided to sleep beside Gimbawali that night to whisper secrets to her of strong women whose bleeding was a signal they might someday bear children.

"Men cannot do that," she reminded the girl. "Men may give us the children, but we women carry the future in our wombs."

"No, Missy Fieldin', it be da spirits of da dead what gives us child'n."

Ella nodded. She had forgotten about the Dharug belief in the power of spirits.

Thad resolved to buy Ella something special in Sydney. After all, he was inheriting a bankroll from his uncle. She deserved something nice, a gift that would convey his feelings. A jeweled necklace? Perfume? A music box? She was not a woman much beguiled by trinkets and charms. A book was a better gift. Still the idea of a trinket attracted him. He could imagine a sparkling gem lying at her neck, a neck he longed to cover with kisses.

As Thad and his old horse, Wanyuwa, rode away, Ella walked back to Acacia House. Barring some medical emergency, she would have a few peaceful days to rest and read, sew, and play games with the children. There would be time to learn more Dharug from Mabarra too.

Ella had grown fond of Mabarra and was fascinated by her stories of Aboriginal life. Mabarra had been cast out of the Bidjigal clan at age three for fear that her strange blue-green eyes made her a sorceress. Relations with her clan were better now, due to Dr. Bennett's talking with the Bidjigal about unusual body features, such as rare eye colors and how they came to be. He convinced the Bidjigal that having such differences among them was an honor, a gift bestowed by the spirits.

During one of Ella's conversations with Mabarra, Ella told her about Carson McDougal's asking her to go to dinner at Molly's Place.

"He acted as if it was a favor to me! He said he wanted to put his sausage in...in my basket!"

Mabarra put a hand to her mouth, giggling.

"He is a devil, Missy Fielding! He tried to have his way with me one evening when I was returning from the Bidjigal camp!"

Ella gasped a shocked "no!" and grabbed Mabarra by the arm.

"He got me on the ground," Mabarra continued, "but I was able to kick his bollox as hard as I could. He rolled off me, calling me horrible names as I ran from him. Dr. Bennett was so angry. He wanted me to press charges with the constable in Parramatta, but I knew no one would believe a half-Aboriginal woman."

"Mabarra, I hope you now ask one of the men here to escort you to the Bidjigal camp. McDougal is likely not the only man in the timber camp who chases skirts. And there are bad men loose on the roads."

Ella paused, thinking what Thad had told her about McDougal.

"Mabarra, Dr. Bennett told me McDougal has a disease of his private parts. It is called gonorrhea. Do you know about it?"

Mabarra nodded and said the doctor had told her.

"He said I should suspect that disease in any strange man who approaches me," Mabarra whispered. "It is everywhere in the colony. Syphilis too."

Of course, it would be that way, Ella thought. The colony was overrun with convicts and whores. It was a lawless place in many ways, especially regarding the treatment of Aboriginals. Perhaps Governor Macquarie could clean up the colony, as he had promised. Thad had told Ella that Mrs. Elizabeth Macquarie had devoted herself to improving the lives of women in the colony. Had someone told her about the rapes and disease?

"Dr. Bennett said I must always carry a knife," Mabarra interrupted Ella's thoughts. "You should too, Miss Fielding. If not to fight off rapists, then to kill dangerous animals. We have venomous snakes and lizards, you know. Learn to throw the knife. Protect yourself."

The conversation disturbed Ella and lingered in her thoughts for a long time after she and Mabarra had spoken. She had felt safe at Acacia House when she first arrived. Now, she was worried. Dr. Bennett could not return home soon enough.

Two days after Thad left for Sydney, a guest arrived. The woman introduced herself as Mrs. Elizabeth Macarthur of Elizabeth Farm at a place called the Cow Pastures, south of Acacia House near Parramatta. For a few seconds, Ella confused her with Mrs. Elizabeth Macquarie, the Governor's wife. Then she remembered Thad telling about the Macarthurs.

Oh God! It is her, Ella thought, the woman Thad praised and admired and whose husband had made trouble in the colony.

"I know Dr. Bennett well," Mrs. Macarthur said after Ella had made her welcome in the drawing room. "He occasionally stops by my place to give me medicine for my headaches and stiff knees and hips. Handsome and kindly man, and a wonderful conversationist. He is quite knowledgeable."

Ella was in awe of Elizabeth Macarthur. The woman was tall and carried herself with confidence. Her face, while no longer beautiful, was delicately furrowed with age, and her hair was streaked with silver. Yet, she was handsome. And despite her many years in New South Wales, she still spoke with the Devonshire accent of her early years in England.

Ella had been told that John Macarthur, formerly an officer in the New South Wales Corps, had instigated no small amount of trouble during his time in the colony. His self-interest had led to many disputes and even duels. He had been sent back to England and tried for sedition, but the trial came to nothing. Macarthur had returned to New South Wales to resume his privileged life. Thad had mentioned that John Macarthur had gout and other infirmities that often consigned him to his bed.

The aggravation he had caused was eased, however, by the work of his intelligent and capable wife. Elizabeth Macarthur had made wise choices about the work at Elizabeth Farm and on the couple's large grant of land. Years before, her husband had obtained a few fine merino sheep from England. It was Elizabeth who oversaw the breeding of them into a vast flock. The prized wool from the sheep sold not only in New South Wales but also in England. The Macarthurs grew wealthier and wealthier, and John grew more incorrigible and foolish.

"For years now, I have promised Dr. Bennett a few merino sheep to start his own flock," Elizabeth Macarthur said as she and Ella talked and drank tea in the drawing room. "In fact, I believe my husband, John, made this promise as payment for the doctor's medical services quite some time ago, possibly when we were all sick with dysentery or my daughter was bedridden with weak legs, something Dr. Bennett said was called infantile paralysis. Thus, I am here to inquire as to where I should have Antony put the sheep."

Where to put the sheep? She had brought them with her? Who was Antony?

Ella was unsure what to say. Thad had told her Elizabeth Macarthur was opinionated, hot-tempered, even forceful in getting her way. And now, she had arrived uninvited with a load of merino sheep.

"Mrs. Macarthur, the doctor is in Sydney on business. I expect him back in a few days. Might you wait until then to speak with him?"

"Humph."

Mrs. Macarthur rose from her seat on the plush drawing room sofa, opened a curio cabinet, and began examining some samples of rocks, shells, and gems the doctor had collected. She turned to Ella.

"He has been fossicking, I see. When, on God's good earth, has he time for that?"

"Oh, I believe he brought those from England. He collected them as a boy," Ella said.

Mrs. Macarthur went to the window and looked out. The sheep in her wagon might be getting restless.

"Bennett has always been an odd one, casting off his aristocratic birthright and living like a commoner. He is a viscount you know! A true blueblood. But he never acts like it. I daresay next to my husband, Bennett is the richest man in these parts."

She picked up a carving of a mermaid from a table and examined it. A man's kind of dream.

"My husband does not care for the good doctor," she continued. "I am not sure John cares for anyone, aside from himself—but I...I find Bennett fascinating...and attractive, very attractive. God's hand, but I wish I was younger like you Miss Fielding. I would show him what a woman can be."

She muttered something about having seduced the handsome and pliable Lieutenant Dawes, the First Fleet astronomer, then turned to Ella with eyebrows raised.

"Have you, Miss Fielding? Shown Dr. Bennett your feminine wiles? You best not dally, as there are plenty of women ready to do so. Did you say he is in Sydney right now? The place is rife with dainty, porcelain-faced women in their fancy, flimsy garb, just ready to land on their backs in a rich, handsome man's bed."

Ella thought of what Thad had said about not needing sex until marriage. A proper gentleman, he had called it 'congress.' Even so, Ella was now quite uncomfortable with the direction the conversation was going. Elizabeth Macarthur might be one of the colony's richest and most influential women, here to gift the doctor merino sheep, but she lacked grace and good manners.

"I was once in love with Lieutenant William Dawes," Elizabeth confessed in a soft voice. "Do you know of him? He was a good-looking bachelor officer who gave me astronomy lessons at night. We fell into each other's arms more than once. I was quite sad when he was sent back to England."

Ella had no comment. She had read about Lieutenant William Dawes and hoped to someday visit the point in Sydney where he had lived in a bark shack, bereft of company, taking measurements of the Southern Hemisphere night sky and charting its stars and constellations. He likely could not resist a woman like Elizabeth Macarthur who had surely been extremely beautiful in her youth.

"Well, all that said," Elizabeth continued, giving Ella a sideways look, "I have brought a dozen merinos in my wagon today, and I intend to leave them here. Do you wish to provide me guidance on where to put them?"

Flustered, Ella stood up and rang for a maid. Mabarra arrived quickly.

"Yes, Miss Fielding?"

A look of disgust crossed Elizabeth Macarthur's face at the arrival of Mabarra.

"Mabarra, please find Henry and tell him I need him."

She motioned for Mrs. Macarthur to follow her outside.

"I believe Henry will know what to do."

"You mean that useless half-breed Bennett found lying in a ditch? The doctor seems to have a fondness for half-breeds...and for the tar-black ones too. I do hope he has not lain with any of the Aboriginal women. They are all so ugly, so primitive and stupid. Savages, all of them."

Ella turned to Elizabeth Macarthur in surprise. She blinked a few times, searching for the right words.

"Mrs. Macarthur, I beg your pardon! We do not consider our half-castes to be savages, nor primitive, nor stupid, and certainly not ugly. We endeavor to educate them and help them save their culture and lands. And as for the full bloods..."

"Humph."

Ella had not noticed the handsome young man standing next to the wagonload of sheep, but he had noticed her. His eyes roved over her like those of a dingo that had not eaten in weeks. He stepped forward into Ella's view.

"Miss Fielding, is it? I have been looking forward to making your acquaintance. The talk in this locality has you pegged a great beauty, an angel to the sick, and the most educated woman in New South Wales. I can see for myself how lovely you are."

Where had this overdressed, outspoken man ridden in from? And what was all this talk of angels and educated women?

Mrs. Macarthur was quick to explain.

"Please meet Antony Lambe, the overseer of my wool operations at Elizabeth Farm. I had him shipped down from England with the sheep. Ha! Lambe…an appropriate name, yes?"

She laughed. Antony Lambe executed a flamboyant bow, took Ella's hand, and kissed it.

"My lady, I am honored."

"Oh…uh…my pleasure to meet you, Mr. Lambe," Ella said.

Henry appeared just as Ella and Elizabeth were making introductions by the sheep wagon. There was much *baaaing* and shuffling in the cart.

"Two rams and ten ewes, all healthy. They should give the doctor a good start on his flock," Elizabeth Macarthur said.

A few chooks were scratching about in the dusty lane. Ella shooed them away. Mrs. Macarthur turned to Henry.

"Well, do not just stand there like a blockhead! Unload the sheep. Antony has them all tethered on one line."

Henry obediently climbed into the cart and began untangling the merinos from each other.

"Damned dullard!" Elizabeth spat. "He might be the worst of them. Thad decided to try and educate him. What foolishness was that?"

"Please, Mrs. Macarthur. I am sure Dr. Bennett will be glad for the gift of sheep, but do not demean our servants. They are loyal, good people, especially Mr. Douglas. The colonists have taken so much from the Aboriginals, sickened them, even killed many of them. We have no right…"

"Oh hush, girl. Enough of your Good Samaritan rubbish. I will say no more."

Mrs. Macarthur went to her wagon and took a basket from the seat. It was full of clothes she had made for the orphans. She handed it to Ella.

"I am sure Father Gregory can use these at the orphanage."

Ella saw the conflict in Elizabeth's face. It was obvious she despised the Aboriginals; yet she brought clothes for the half-caste children of the orphanage.

"Yes, thank you, Mrs. Macarthur. The children grow so fast we cannot keep them in clothes. I will take these to Father Gregory as soon as he wakes. He is resting. The heat bothers him. He seems to tire so easily these days."

Elizabeth gave Ella a simpering smile.

"Humph. I suppose the doctor has not told you what ails Gregory? The shaking of his hands and the way he shuffles."

Again, Ella registered a look of surprise.

"I…I believe Father Gregory simply works too hard," Ella replied. "He is so devoted to the children and the church."

Elizabeth had climbed onto the seat of her wagon.

"Indeed, he is, dear girl. Do give my regards to Dr. Bennett when he returns…and to Father Gregory when he wakes."

As Elizabeth Macarthur's wagon pulled away, Ella stood in confusion. She had met the legendary woman of Elizabeth Farm, a forceful and opinionated lady, indeed, and gruff. Ella had accepted the gift of a small flock of merinos, whether Thad wanted them or not.

Her eyes wandered to the handsome young man named Lambe. He had not left with Mrs. Macarthur. He was standing by the gate that opened into the farmyard, next to his high-spirited horse, and he was smiling. Ella was relieved Elizabeth Macarthur had departed, but what to do with Mr. Lambe?

Well, he was handsome enough, and he seemed well-mannered.

"While you and Mrs. Macarthur were visiting," the young man said, "your man, Henry, helped me cardon off an area of the field behind the goat pasture to keep the sheep…for now. I would be pleased to return and help fence a larger pasture for them. They are heavy grazers and will need much space."

Antony Lambe seemed a bit of a dandy, hardly a herd manager. He was dressed in fine clothes with a Coach Knot in his neckerchief and polished Hessian boots. His smile was pleasingly crooked. His brown eyes devoured Ella from head to toe.

"I am grateful for your kindness, Mr. Lambe, but I should wait until the doctor returns to commit to any plans for the sheep. Mrs. Macarthur is most thoughtful in gifting them."

Antony bowed again but made no effort to leave. As it was now mid-afternoon, Ella felt it necessary to invite him in the house for refreshments. He tethered his horse to a gum tree and followed her, eyes glued to the sensual swagger of her hips.

They seated themselves in the drawing room while Mabarra fetched tea and cream cakes. Ella tried to make light conversation. But at every turn, Antony interjected with flattering remarks about Ella's beauty and intelligence. He complimented her dress and hair, her large, ice-blue eyes, her delicate hands—the "loveliest" he had ever kissed.

"Miss Fielding, uh…may I call you Ella?"

What audacity!

"I think it too familiar, Mr. Lambe. Would you care for some cakes to eat on your journey home?"

Or perhaps a kick in the ass to hasten you on your departure? She made several other nuanced overtures to hint to Antony Lambe that he should leave.

"Well, before I go, Miss Fielding, might you agree to a pleasant buggy ride with me this Sunday afternoon? There is a lovely and serene waterfall at Lovers Jump Creek I would like to show you. We could picnic. Oh, did you know I am building a house for myself southwest of here at Emu Plains? It is a beautiful area along the Nepean River, quite secluded and cool, with many shade trees."

"Emu Plains? I am sorry, Mr. Lambe, but I have not traveled much in these parts since my arrival in October."

"Ah, well, you should see this beautiful land. I shall have to take you to the waterfall. About that buggy ride then. I am an excellent tour guide!"

His invitation, delivered with gentlemanly manners, had taken Ella by surprise.

"Oh, uh," she stammered, looking for an excuse to decline. "I really should help Father Gregory with the children on Sunday after church. I believe we are planning to cut fingernails and toenails."

Antony grinned, thinking how quaint her excuse was—the trimming of children's nails.

"Miss Fielding, I am certain Father Gregory would prefer you spend a pleasant afternoon with me than labor over children's hands and feet."

She paused, unable to conjure another excuse, then relented, nodding her head.

"Perfect!" Antony crooned. "I shall fetch you shortly before the noon meal. Do bring a sun hat. I shall bring the picnic and lemonade. Mrs. Macarthur has lemon trees, you know!"

Antony Lambe bowed and kissed Ella's hand again. He was barely out of the house before Mabarra met Ella in the front hall, taking her elbow urgently.

"Miss Fielding, I hope you deflected Mr. Lambe's advances. He is a notorious womanizer!"

Ella turned, her face a mix of drollness and concern.

"Well, I...I did agree to take a buggy ride with him on Sunday afternoon. I made excuses, but he was so persistent. And he is quite handsome and well-mannered. I see no issues with his invitation."

Mabarra threw her arms in the air.

"Oh yes, handsome and well-mannered—he is all of that and more. Handsome, well-mannered, and ready to rut like a Brahma bull. I believe Dr. Bennett may be opposed to your buggy ride. He dislikes Mr. Lambe."

Ella hesitated, then lifted her chin obstinately.

Why do I need Thad's permission for everything, she asked herself. Secretly, she thought this just might be the thing to cause a little jealousy. If Thad was attracted to her, surely he would react.

"Mabarra, I can take care of myself. I have not been off this property since I arrived, other than to accompany Thad, I mean the doctor, to Turramurra to treat a patient. Mr. Lambe has kindly offered to show me a waterfall. His intentions seem most honorable."

Mabarra stared in disbelief.

"Suit yourself, Miss Fielding, but be prepared to ward off his advances."

Ella passed some of the time until Thad's return by organizing her bedchamber bookshelf. The room remained moderately cool in the mornings, and she could get a few hours of work done. But by noon, it was stifling.

Heat-fatigued after her bedchamber work, Ella decided to go downstairs and take refuge on the south porch, a small and less luxurious addition than the front porch but treasured for its shade and cool summer breezes. It proved more pleasant than the house, with cool fresh air coursing through its railings and roof posts.

Thad would be home from Sydney today. Ella was anxious to tell him about Mrs. Macarthur's visit and the delivery of sheep. She hoped he would not be cross with her for allowing Elizabeth MacArthur to leave the sheep at Acacia House. She also wanted to ask about the woman's obvious bias against the Aboriginals. Ella had grown to love the orphans and Thad's half-caste employees. She felt ashamed that she had not been firmer with Mrs. MacArthur about both the sheep and her harsh words.

There was Anthony Lambe too. Mabarra had said Thad knew the man and disapproved of him. Ella would tell the doctor about her agreement to take a Sunday buggy ride with Lambe. She would say he seemed gentlemanly enough and she was anxious to see some of the countryside surrounding Wahroonga, even more of Wahroonga itself. She had been at Acacia House almost three months and had seen practically nothing of the lands around it.

As she sat comfortably on a settee on the south porch, sewing a birthday dress for one of the orphan girls, she heard a commotion on the opposite side of the house. She had barely put down her sewing and left the settee when one of the maids came running.

"Missy Fieldin', comes quick! Dural...his wife need ye!"

Ella took off running. It was the young, pregnant Bidjigal girl, Keira, she was sure. The girl's time had probably come, but there likely was trouble with the birth. Thad had warned her about it.

Mrs. Hughes was standing at the door to Dr. Bennett's medical office when Ella arrived. Dural stood outside holding Keira in his arms. The girl was moaning softly and clutching her large belly. Mabarra was talking with Dural. She pointed to Ella.

"I am telling him you can deliver Keira's baby. He is unconvinced. He wants Dr. Bennett. I will remind him of the dire consequences if his wife does not get immediate medical help."

Ella was nervous. She had never delivered a baby, though she had observed many deliveries. Could she do this? She hoped she was skilled enough. It would not be a normal birth. Thad had said the baby was upside-down. She turned back to Mabarra.

"Do you think the delivery might wait until Dr. Bennett is home? He is expected soon."

Mabarra shook her head.

"I am sure this cannot wait, Miss Fielding."

Ella stepped outside and looked at Keira. The girl's eyes were pleading for help. Ella took Keira's hand.

"Tell him I can do it," Ella told Mabarra. "You will help me, I am sure."

Father Gregory appeared behind the Bidjigal couple and asked if there was trouble. Mabarra explained the situation as she tried to get Dural to bring Keira into the clinic.

"I will help too," Gregory said. "I have participated in a few births."

He spoke in Dharug with Dural, pointing to Ella and Mabarra and emphasizing his words. Suddenly, Keira cried out loudly. Dural tried to comfort her, then looked intently at Ella, sizing her up. He nodded and walked forward and up the steps into the clinic.

Ella guided him to the surgery and quickly put a clean white sheet on the operating table. Dural laid his wife on the table. She immediately rolled on her side and drew up her knees to her chin.

Mabarra and Ella washed their hands thoroughly. Mabarra fetched a pillow and put it under Keira's shoulders and head.

"Mabarra, please tell Keira she needs to stretch out on her back and open her legs. We need to wash her, and then I must examine her."

As Mabarra tried to get Keira positioned, Ella made up the soapy water. She stepped to the table and began gently scrubbing Keira.

I feel odd doing this in front of her husband, Ella thought. The men usually disappear for births. I suppose he deserves to be here, though, and he may be able to help Keira cooperate.

"Ask Dural how long she has been in labor."

The answer was "since yesterday afternoon." Twenty hours at least by Ella's calculation. The many hours made her worry about the baby.

Ella cleaned her hands again and told Mabarra she was going to reach inside the birth canal and find out what was happening.

Keira flinched at first, as Ella's small fingers began examining her, then relaxed. Ella felt for the baby's head but instead found a tiny foot. The baby was breech.

She told Mabarra the news.

"What will you do, Ella?"

"I have no choice except to try to turn the baby head down. It will hurt, but delivery in a breech position is dangerous, perhaps impossible with a woman Keira's size. Do your best to reassure Dural and Keira. Tell them the baby cannot be born feet first."

Ella waited as Mabarra explained what needed to be done. Then, as carefully as possible, she inserted her hand into Keira, squeezed open the girl's cervix, and pushed on the baby's foot. Keira screamed, as her small cervix rebelled. Ella kept to her task, slowly moving the baby in its slippery orbit.

Keira moaned and whimpered. Her legs began to shake.

"Tell Dural the shaking is normal," Ella instructed Mabarra.

The message was relayed, and Dural responded with a long answer.

"A baby born breech is a bad thing in Dharug clans, Dural says to tell you. They are superstitious about it," Mabarra said.

"Well, then, Dural and Keira should be glad I am trying to turn the baby."

After a few minutes, Ella felt the baby's bottom and then its back. Finally, the back of its head touched her hand. She carefully grasped the small, hairy head and moved it over the cervix. With the next contraction she hoped Keira could push it through.

Throughout the turning process, Keira cried softly and squeezed Dural's hands.

Now began a long period of screaming and weakly pushing, as Ella had Mabarra give instructions and encouragement. After some dozen pushes, Ella felt the top of the baby's head lodge in the cervix. A few more pushes, and it would move through. She knew Keira was in terrible pain. She hoped the pressure of the baby's head would numb the mother's cervix.

Sweat ran down Ella's cheeks and dripped on the table. The bodice of her dress was wet with blood and sweat. Mabarra grabbed the escaped tendrils of Ella's hair and tucked them behind her ears. Father Gregory had fetched a small towel and was fanning Ella.

Keira screeched in agony, while Dural tried to comfort her. Mabarra massaged Keira's belly and praised her with each contraction. But the extreme pain made Keira pull back. Her cervix seemed too small for the task. Ella feared that Keira would faint.

"Tell Dural she must push, as hard as she can, or the baby will not be born. Both she and her child will die."

Ella managed to get two fingers around the back of the baby's neck. She held the infant and waited for a contraction. When it came, she pulled gently as Keira screamed and pushed. After five contractions, the head slid through the cervix. Ella told Mabarra to applaud Keira for her effort.

Now, to make the shoulders less broad, Ella would need to turn the baby sideways and pull the shoulders one at a time through the cervix. She now felt sure she could do this. There was progress.

I hope it is not too late, Ella thought.

Carefully, she pushed one baby shoulder back and tugged forward on the other. She had to be careful not to pull too hard, lest she injure the infant. All this time, Keira screamed and cried.

But suddenly, the young girl had a surge of energy and pushed hard, sitting up on her elbows and grunting and growling with the effort. She gave one final ear-splitting scream.

Seconds later, the tiny baby slid out of the birth canal into Ella's hands.

"A girl! Tell them they have a little daughter!" Ella cried.

Mabarra clapped her hands and gave Dural and Keira the news.

"She is so little and sweet. Maybe four or five pounds," Ella said.

The infant's hands and feet were doll size. Her fingernails were like miniscule, opaque seashells. And like some Aboriginal newborns, she had blondish wisps of hair on her head.

But she was not breathing.

Ella turned the baby face-down and patted her small back. She swabbed out the baby's mouth with a finger and patted more energetically. Lightly wrapping the baby in a towel, she massaged her vigorously.

"She is not going to breathe on her own!" Ella shouted. "Mabarra, take her while I cut the umbilicus."

After the cut, Ella took the little girl and laid her on another table. She wiped the baby's face with a clean, wet cloth and then put her lips over the tiny mouth. Father Gregory raised his eyebrows at this. Dural was surprised too and gave out a small gasp. Mabarra smiled.

Ella breathed in and out ever so lightly, as if trying to revive a kitten. She gently pressed several times on the baby's chest. This was a stand-in for the Bellows Method she had read about, a method for those who had drowned. Over and over, she breathed and patted. Over and over.

"I am not giving up! We have not come this far to let her die!"

Dural was becoming annoyed. He spat out several threats. If his baby died, he would kidnap Ella and torture her!

Father Gregory tried to settle him down.

"Look now, Dural," he said in Dharug, "she is giving her own breath to your child! She will breathe her own life into the child. What doctor do you know who would do this?"

Ella was determined, breathing into the baby's small lungs and pressing on her chest. Finally, there came a barely audible sputter. Then a small cough and fluid dribbled from her tiny lungs. Ella turned her face down. The baby's chest began to rise and fall on its own. Her tongue moved. Her head turned slightly.

Ella took the child's feet and hands in hers and vigorously massaged and wiggled them. She slid the baby into Keira's grateful arms. The newborn made a horrible face and then wailed loudly.

Dural looked at Ella in amazement. This woman had given her own breath of life to his child. She had saved his daughter.

"*Didjargura, dyin*," he said, reaching for Ella's arm.

Ella paused her work of tying the baby's cord at the naval. She smiled and nodded to Dural.

"He is thanking you, Ella," Mabarra said. "You should know the Bidjigal do not thank *whitefella*...but he is thanking you."

"Tell him I did my best."

After a few minutes, Keira and the swaddled baby were moved to another room in the clinic with a comfortable bed. Dural crouched beside the bed. He rubbed his wife's arm and murmured "*dadyibalung* Keira" over and over.

"Good Keira. Good Keira."

Thad arrived home some two hours later, tired and dusty and eager to see Ella. He had purchased something special for her and was anxious to find a private moment to give it to her.

By this time, the surgery was cleaned up and Ella was in her bedchamber reading. Henry took Wanyuwa to the barn and assured Thad he would give the old horse a good rubdown and dinner.

Old Betty, Mabarra, and Mrs. Hughes were in the kitchen preparing dinner. Mabarra was peeling turnips. Mrs. Hughes was chopping onions. Old Betty was stirring a large pot on the stove.

Thad stood in the kitchen doorway.

"Have I enough time to get a tub wash before dinner, ladies? I am so hot and dusty from the road."

Mrs. Hughes turned, mouth agape.

"Yes…yes you have time, Sir. But I must say you missed quite an event here earlier in the day."

"Indeed, you did," offered Old Betty.

Mabarra only smiled.

Thad waited for more to be said, but Mrs. Hughes stood with her mouth hanging open.

"I should let Father Gregory tell you," Mrs. Hughes finally said. "Perhaps he will join you and Miss Fielding for dinner. She is in her room getting ready for dinner."

The housekeeper turned and yelled for one of the footmen, instructing him to draw Dr. Bennett a cool bath and then bring Father Gregory to the house for dinner.

All through his bath and dressing himself, Thad wondered what sort of event had occurred. He didn't like secrets, but he knew it was better to hear things from Gregory's point of view than Mrs. Hughes'.

As dinner convened a short time later, Thad was the first to arrive in the dining room. He stood waiting for Gregory and Ella. The priest walked in next, so bothered by the heat he had shed his clerical robes and collar and stood in the doorway wearing only a thin cotton shirt and loose pants.

"Such a hot and humid day, Thad. I have a notion to go roll in Cockle Creek!"

Thad chuckled: "I may join you."

"How did your business in Sydney go?"

Thad cleared his throat and finished rolling up one sleeve of his shirt. He began rolling the opposite sleeve.

"As expected, there were letters to read from disinherited family members. Even my great-uncle's housekeeper raised a quarrel, saying she had served him for nearly fifty years and got nothing. I had my lawyer send her £30. My nephew, Jarod, and his wife are to live in Uncle's house and pay me an annual rent. I shall not balk if it goes unpaid. They are good people."

"Anyway," Thad continued, "it was tedious, tiring business. I signed all the papers and had my inheritance deposited in the Bank of New South Wales. I kept out a portion for myself, a portion to repair the church roof, and I bought a gift for Ella. Oh, and I met with the glassmaker, Mr. Welton. He will be up to meet with you about the church windows at the end of next week."

Gregory smiled and studied the beautiful red and beige Aubusson rug on the dining room floor.

"Ella is certainly deserving of a gift, Thad, especially after today."

Thad turned, and the two men looked intently at one another.

"I heard there was some sort of 'event' here today, as Mrs. Hughes called it. Would you care to enlighten me, Gregory?"

The story of the miraculous birth of Dural's and Keira's baby girl slowly unwound, richly embellished with all the details Father Gregory could recall. Thad listened half in disbelief as the priest revealed how Ella had given her breath to the child.

As his recollection ended, Gregory wrinkled his eyebrows.

"I must admit, Thad, that I have never seen such a thing in my entire life, not just the method Ella used to save that tiny baby, but her passionate effort. She was determined that the child should live. I cannot help but wonder if there is any other doctor or nurse in all New South Wales who would lay their mouth on an Aboriginal child's mouth and give breath to its lungs."

Thad wished he had been there to see Ella's rescue of the tiny baby, but if he had, mayhap Ella would have acquiesced, leaving the task to him. Ella seemed to hear the call of medicine clearly, no matter the patient, no matter the problem. She was not afraid to try any means to save a life. He wondered…would he have gone to such ends to save an Aboriginal baby?

At that moment, Ella breezed into the dining room, Henry's ornate fan in one hand cooling her face. Her light as air chiffon-over-satin dress fell down her shapely body in swirls of yellow. An orange sash separated the bodice and skirt and was tied in an elegant knot at one hip. She had regained a little weight and looked ravishing.

Thad was speechless, unable to take his eyes off her. Had she grown more beautiful just since he had been gone?

Gregory, who also was mesmerized, was not at a loss for words.

"Ella, you are a spectral beauty of the sunset in yellow and orange. And the gold threads of your hair only add to your allure! Seeing you now, it is hard for me to remember you sweating and bloody as you worked this afternoon to save an infant's life."

Ella stopped fanning abruptly. Did Thad know what had happened today, she wondered. The birth of Keira's baby?

She looked at Thad in question. He crossed the room, took her fan-less hand, and softly kissed it.

"Father Gregory told me how you not only worked to deliver Keira's baby but gave your breath to the child. I could not be prouder of you, Ella. You have earned a badge of trust and merit with the Bidjigal, and with everyone here."

Ella smiled humbly.

"Dr. Bennett, I only did what I thought you expected of me…and what I knew you would do. A life is a life, no matter, yes? Dural and Keira and their tiny newborn girl are in the clinic, if you wish to see them."

"Yes, I do wish to see them. Mabarra, tell the kitchen to hold up serving dinner for a few minutes, please."

He offered his arm to Ella. Gregory took her other arm, though his hand was shaky. The three went to the clinic and to the room where Keira was resting with the baby. Dural turned as they entered. He smiled and shook the doctor's hand excitedly.

"My daughter!" he said in Dharug, motioning to the small bundle in Keira's arms. "She lives because of the breath of the beautiful one."

It was Ella he looked at now. He took her hand and bowed down on one knee.

"Please, Dural," Ella said, pulling him up to face her. "I had to do everything I could to save your little girl. It was my duty."

Gregory translated into Dharug.

Keira held up the bundle and offered the newborn to Thad. The baby seemed barely larger than one of Thad's big hands.

"She is so tiny," he said to Ella. "Your small hands were just what was needed."

Keira held out her arms to Ella.

"*Ngubadi dyin!*" she said, as Ella enveloped her in a hug.

Ella turned her head to Father Gregory and raised her eyebrows in question.

"She is saying she loves you, Ella."

Ella put her cheek against Keira's. "*Ngubadi*," she whispered. As she pulled away, she asked, "What have you named her?"

Dural spoke then, blowing out a small puff of air and pretending it went from Ella to the baby.

"Ella-*Buwa*."

Father Gregory laughed and clapped his hands. Dural clapped too. Thad smiled, looking at the small face in the bundle before him. Ella was about to ask the name's meaning when Gregory said:

"Her name is Breath of Ella."

"Breath of Ella," she repeated. "How lovely, how thoughtful of Dural and Keira. Please thank them on my behalf."

Later, over dinner, Thad asked Ella how she knew to give her breath to the baby.

"I read about it. A book I found when I lived in Bytown told the history of England's Royal Humane Society and how they resuscitated the drowned from shipwrecks. It was a procedure developed by a Scottish surgeon in the 1730s. I was not sure it would work on so small a babe, but it did."

Over dessert, Ella mentioned that she told Keira and Dural they could return home if they wished.

"Once I saw the baby suckling, I felt sure the little one would be fine. However, Keira said she liked the comfortable bed here better than her sleeping place in the camp. I believe she wishes to stay tonight."

The next morning when Dural came to fetch his wife and baby, he had a dead flying fox and a dead possum slung over one shoulder, as well as a woven mat in one hand and a beautifully inscribed and painted spear in the other. He motioned to Ella.

"*Mana. Mana.*"

Thad smiled:

"These are gifts for you, Ella. Dural is giving you gifts as a thank you for saving his wife and baby. The possum is his wife's totem, the female totem, and the flying fox is his totem."

Ella stepped up to Dural and nodded her head, smiling. He flipped the flying fox and possum onto her shoulders and placed the mat and spear in her hands.

"*Bulbuwul dyin.*"

"He calls you a strong woman," Thad said.

Ella was a bit repulsed by the smelly, dead animals, but she said nothing, knowing they were Bidjigal tribute. Trying to recall Dural's words of thanks the day before, she stumbled through—

"*Didjurigura,* Dural."

He grinned and began walking backwards toward the door to the clinic. As he reached the end of the path, he turned and walked quickly inside to fetch Keira and the baby.

"At least he smiles," Ella observed, "which is more than I can say of his father."

Ella shrugged off the dead animals and gave them to Mabarra with instructions to do as she pleased with them.

"I am not keen to dine on a bat or possum, but I would like to taste wallaby. Henry brought in one this morning, did he not?"

Mabarra assured Ella she would enjoy a wallaby steak.

"It is delicious with yams and beet roots. I believe we are using the last of our beet roots now."

Ella studied the beautiful spear and the woven mat, still in her hands. Both were obviously precious items.

"Well," she said, shaking the spear, "Smelly old Mr. McDougal best not come around here again, asking me to go to Molly's Place!"

Six

The following day, Medang came in the afternoon and spoke to Thad. The Bidjigal were having a *corroboree* that night to celebrate the new baby's arrival and Ella's work of helping birth the child and breathing life into her tiny lungs. Come at dark, Medang instructed.

"It is like a party, Ella," Thad said when she questioned him. "There will be food and dancing, and you will be honored. We must go, or the clan will be offended."

Ella wondered what she would be asked to do. No matter. If Thad said it was important to attend, she would go without argument.

Near to sunset she stood in her bedchamber dressed in a muslin gown the shade of gray-green, gum bark. Her day shoes were on her feet so she could walk to the Bidjigal camp. Her hair hung loose about her shoulders and tumbled down her back nearly to her waist. Mabarra was brushing it.

"Mabarra, are you sure I should wear my hair down? My mother used to tell me it inflamed men's desires, that only women of the night wore their hair down."

Mabarra laughed.

"Ma'am, you inflame men no matter how you wear your hair, or what dress you wear, or what jewelry adorns your neck. You are a beautiful woman. All men want you—Mr. McDougal, Mr. Lambe, maybe not Father Gregory, but certainly Dr. Bennett. He adores you!"

Ella blushed and turned away from Mabarra.

"He does not!"

"He does. He is a hot-blooded, handsome, bachelor in his prime. I have seen how he looks at you. I know a man in love when I see one."

Ella turned and stared at Mabarra.

"Are you sure?"

Mabarra nodded.

"I have not seen him like this, ever before. He is a changed man since you arrived. He bathes and shaves every day, he wears cologne, he dresses nicely, he reads poetry. He has painted a portrait of you, did you know that?"

Ella covered her mouth with both hands before speaking again.

"Where? Where is such a painting?"

Mabarra motioned toward the doctor's bedchamber.

"It hangs over his bed, replacing Edith Fullerton."

"I must see it!" Ella declared.

Mabarra peeked out Ella's bedchamber door. The doctor's door was closed. She knocked, thinking of some mundane question she would ask if he opened the door, but he did not answer. He had gone downstairs already. Carefully, she eased open his door and motioned to Ella to follow.

Once Ella was inside, Mabarra pointed to the wall above the doctor's bed. There, with her hair done up elegantly, her icy blue eyes shining, cheeks glowing a soft pink, and wearing the dress she had worn her first night at Acacia House, was the portrait. It looked so much like Ella it almost frightened her.

"Could a man not in love with a woman paint like that? I think not," Mabarra said.

Suddenly, Ella felt guilty for accepting Antony Lambe's invitation for a buggy ride to Lovers Leap Creek and its waterfall. She meant to make Thad jealous, but it was a cruel plan. Did he care for her? Of course, he did, and she was wrong to toy with his feelings.

Seconds later, they heard the doctor call up the stairs—

"Ella, Mabarra, are you two ready to go? We are expected to arrive shortly after sunset."

"We are coming!" Ella called.

Both women rushed from the doctor's room and down the stairs. Thad smiled when he saw Ella. Her hair was glorious cascading over her shoulders and down her back. He longed to run his fingers through it but knew it would be improper. She was smiling at him in a special way. Was she up to something? He hoped so.

Gregory, who stood beside Thad in his clerical garb, chuckled at the two lovebirds. How long would it be until Thad and Ella confessed their feelings for each other? Acacia House needed a married couple and laughing children running here and there.

The vicar turned to Mrs. Hughes, who waited by the door, dressed in her finery.

"It has been a long time since I have attended a *corroboree*, Millie. Shall I escort you?"

Mrs. Hughes was holding a bag full of damper, the bread the Bidjigal loved. She handed it to the vicar and looped her arm through his. Gregory thought she was a fine-looking woman for her age, late sixty-something. She had been young and married to the elder Dr. Bennett's footman when Thad was born. She was the boy's nursemaid until he outgrew the need for one. And when Thad decided to come to New South Wales, she volunteered to come with him. She was a widow by then, looking for a change of scenery.

The group, including Henry, walked nearly four miles to the Bidjigal camp, Wibung, the children's dog, accompanying them. The moon, almost full, had risen in the gloaming eastern sky.

"The Bidjigal call the moon *yanada*," Gregory whispered to Ella. "A star is *birrung*."

Ella looked up at the dark sky, its stars shining down through the canopy of tall eucalypts.

"Thad has shown me the Southern Cross and the emu in the Milky Way where the Coal Sack lies," she said. "He says sometimes the emu appears to lie down and at other times it is running, depending on the season."

"Indeed," Gregory replied. "When running the people know it is time to hunt the emu. When sitting, it is time to collect the eggs. They are quite tasty. Perhaps we will have some this evening. The emu are laying eggs now. They are light green, and the males are the ones who sit on the eggs!"

Ella giggled: "Father Gregory, you are a fount of knowledge!"

Long before they neared the Bidjigal camp, high-pitched singing and clacking sticks were heard. Young scouts along the path saw them coming and took off running to pass the message that the honored guest was approaching. Soon, a group of young boys and girls appeared and flanked the party to escort them into the camp.

A great bonfire shone through the eucalypt forest, and smells of food wafted to Ella's nose. There also was smoke, fragranced by the smoldering of plants. Thad said the plants were sacred to Bidjigal.

Ella was excited but also worried. She clung to Thad's arm more tightly with each step.

"This is all so different, Thad. You will stay with me, yes?"

He put one arm around her.

"Ella, there is nothing to fear. These people are our friends. They only wish to thank you for saving the baby. Little Breath of Ella will likely marry a clan leader someday and pass down to her children the story of Ella Fielding, who gave her her first breath. It will be part of a women's *songline*."

"*Songline?*"

"Rather like a story and map combined. Aboriginals use *songlines* to find their way. Often, *songlines* show the way to sacred places."

As they entered the camp, Ella saw a large overhang of rock, perhaps thirty meters high, protecting the Bidjigal *wolli*. A small waterfall cascaded down into a rocky stream. Wildflowers were in bloom almost every place the firelight illuminated. Bark huts, called Humpies by the British, served as small homes for the clan.

Wibung found a quiet, cool spot and flopped down, ready to sleep unless he was called.

Medang shouted to his people that the honored one had arrived. Dural rushed forward and bent low before Ella. His body was painted in white patterns so that Ella barely recognized him.

The camp grew quiet. Ella was confused. Was she supposed to do something? Without thinking, she held out a hand to Dural. Carefully, he took her fingertips and pressed them gently against his forehead.

"He is acknowledging you as greater than himself," Thad whispered. "It is the ultimate tribute."

Dural stepped back and began what seemed to be a long sermon accompanied by much gesticulating.

"He is telling the story of Breath of Ella's birth and your part in it. The story must be told again and again so it is not forgotten."

Keira came forward with the baby, still wrapped in the small blanket from the day she was born. The blanket was dirty now, which gave Ella pause, but she knew the child would not sicken. The baby had her mother's milk and thousands of years of inherited strength as an Aboriginal. Keira placed the child in Ella's arms and led Ella to a tree stump covered in soft skins. She gestured for her to sit.

This is like a throne, Ella thought. Am I to be a queen among the Bidjigal?

As she sat humming and rocking the baby, the clan's women laid gifts at her feet, things that held value for them but to Ella looked like simple items—possum and wallaby skins, animal bones, pretty rocks, shells, a fish skeleton, a long snakeskin that made Ella shiver. Keira's mother brought a large piece of bark on which many colorful shells had been hooked with twine made from plant fiber. The woman proceeded to speak in Dharug.

"She has created the story of Breath of Ella's birth on the bark of a red gum," Gregory told Ella. "They write nothing down. Do not read. Instead, they do shell art, paint, sing, dance, and keep an oral tradition of stories. They will tell this story for a long time."

Thad touched the baby's face gently.

"It is possible, even likely, this place will become sacred because of what you have done, Ella."

The Bidjigal men began to beat drums and clack sticks. Each one went to the smoking plants and inhaled deeply. Some stepped around the bonfire in a circle and began to sing. Others joined the circle and danced, lifting one leg and then the other, shuffling back and forth. This was followed by an open leg stance. It seemed to Ella as if the dance recreated Keira's long labor.

Henry pointed at the performance with excitement.

"*Whitefella* use-ly mo' bad in Bidjigal story den good. Dis time, *whitefella* good. Missy Fieldin' good!"

The dancing went on for some time, then stopped abruptly. Had the baby been born in the dance?

Medang announced it was time to eat. A bark platter was brought to Ella by the women. Gregory heard their Dharug chatter as they explained to Ella what delicacies they had prepared. He hesitated to tell her what some of the Bidjigal foods were. Let her try them and judge for herself.

He watched as she fingered bits of meat, such as kangaroo, emu, and wallaby. She nodded at their taste and raised her eyebrows with surprise. She seemed to like the crocodile and turtle too. Yams were offered to her and Bush Bread. Sandpaper figs were eaten, along with tart *lilli pilli* berries. There was *barramundi*, which she liked very much. Thad told her it was a fish and that its name meant just that, "large-scaled river fish."

Ella resisted the various grubs at first, suspicious of their shape. Were they worms? Thad relieved her hesitation by popping several in his mouth. She tried one, the smallest one, rather reluctantly and found the taste buttery and like almonds.

"Did I really eat a worm…and like it?"

Thad nodded, chuckling.

"You must imagine you are eating a bite of chicken or pork, Ella. Then it will go down with ease."

A special bark slab of smoked eels was brought to Ella. Gregory told her what they were. He emphasized the importance of trying a few bites, as the eel was the master totem of the Bidjigal. Ella carefully pulled loose some cooked eel meat with her fingertips and slid it into her mouth. It was surprisingly good.

"When the acacia trees begin to bloom in spring, the eel run also begins," Gregory said. "The Parramatta River was a place where our Bidjigal trapped eels. In fact, Parramatta means 'place where the eel lies down.' The eel spirit is believed to reside there. But the presence of so many soldiers and colonials at the Parramatta village these days has ended most of the Bidjigal fishing. They get chased away."

Thad joined the conversation.

"They find eels at other places now. It is sad, as I believe Parramatta belonged to the Bidjigal for eons before the British soldiers chased them out."

Ella turned to Thad and offered him some eel meat from her fingers. He leaned in and accepted it, being sure to let his tongue rub over her thumb.

"You seem to be enjoying all this Bush Tucker, Ella," he said. "It pleases the Bidjigal that you like, or at least try to like, their food. Thank you for your gastronomic bravery."

Ella smiled and fed him another bite. Gregory chortled.

"When a woman feeds a man from her fingers, it is surely a sign of extreme ardor!" he said, grinning ear to ear.

Ella blushed, and Thad waved off Gregory.

"Annie Grey-Face is anxious to see you. Perhaps the two of you could feed each other," Thad smirked.

Ella tried to signal to the Bidjigal women that she had had enough to eat. Thad told them in Dharug. They walked away confused. Why had this honorable woman eaten like a tiny fairy wren? She should eat until her stomach bulged. This was a party!

"I am so full. How can they eat so much?" Ella whispered to Thad.

More singing and dancing erupted. More smoke inhalation.

"Why do they do that," Ella asked, "inhale the smoke I mean?"

Gregory patiently told Ella how the smoke was thought to cleanse a person. The situation dictated the type of green foliage that was burned.

"But they do not choke," Ella noted.

"No. They have grown accustomed to it. Smoke ceremonies are important in their culture. It appears they have chosen to burn hawthorn tonight. I am not sure what that means."

Thad and Gregory were invited to dance. Gregory declined, but Thad jumped in the dance circle and began imitating the male dancers. Ella enjoyed watching his jumps, kicks, and gyrations. Soon, the men began clapping their hands rhythmically around Thad, giving him a solo. Watching him, Ella, Mabarra, and Mrs. Hughes laughed so hard they had to hold their stomachs.

When a ritual women's dance began, Keira's mother approached Ella and took the baby from her arms. She pointed to the circle of women dancers, their breasts bare except for large designs around their nipples in white paint.

Djurumin…dangura.

"She calls you daughter and invites you to dance," Thad whispered after tucking Ella's long, radiant hair behind her ears. "You need not bare your breasts. I have told them that in our culture only married women bare their breasts, and only in the presence of their husbands."

Ella was embarrassed but also much relieved!

She found herself in the dancing circle before she could resist. Someone had taken her shawl and led her among the Bidjigal women. She began moving her feet side-to-side and swinging her hips. Following the others, she turned in a circle and threw her arms high. She waved her high arms from side-to-side, like a casuarina tree swaying in the wind. She shook her shoulders. This made her breasts and hips swing.

She looked outside the circle and saw Thad watching. He smiled and nodded at her. She was sure he was pleased that she was joining in with the Bidjigal women dancers.

Now, the women grabbed the wraps on their legs and lifted them. Ella complied, lifting her skirt to show her legs. Thad got a quick glimpse of her stockings held up with lacy garters above her knees. As she bent over and shook her hands over her feet, like the other women, Thad could see her breasts hanging enticingly inside her bodice.

He was feeling a bit unsettled by Ella's lack of propriety but also aroused. Perhaps women were meant to dance this way...to please their men. Thad knew the Bidjigal men would take their women to bed tonight. Thad, on the other hand, would take Ella home, and they would go to their separate rooms.

The dance ended, and there was more eating. Ella nibbled from the bark tray brought to her, but only to please Dural and Keira. Then, there was more dancing and singing. Finally, Ella looked at Thad and asked—

"Would it be ill-mannered if we said farewell to them? I am tired from all the excitement."

"They will understand, as do I. I am tired myself, and I am sure Gregory is exhausted."

He went to Medang and spoke at length. Suddenly the old clan leader held up his arms and gave a shout. Everything stopped. Medang spoke to his people, who then looked at Ella and crouched down with respect. She felt as if she were on display. In truth, she had been all night.

Medang came to her and bowed low. He reached up a hand without looking at her. Ella put her hand in his.

"*Djuguru*," he said.

"He calls you sister," Thad said. "He also wishes you a good night."

"How do I say 'brother' in Dharug?"

Thad whispered the word *babana*. Ella grasped Medang's hand tighter.

"*Didjurigura, Babana.*"

Medang was astonished, and for the first time he smiled at Ella.

She stood and waved to the encampment.

"*Didjurigura! Didjurigura!*" she shouted, smiling.

She looped her arm through Thad's. Their party of six, including the loyal Wibung, began walking home, escorted by six Bidjigal men with spears and torches.

It had been an amazing evening. Ella knew she was now revered by the Bidjigal. Most of all, Thad was pleased with her, even admired her. Was he beginning to love her? She leaned close and clasped his arm tightly as he guided her home in the dark. She resolved not to tell him about Antony Lambe and the Sunday buggy ride. She would send Antony a note on the morrow and cancel their Sunday date.

About halfway home, Gregory stumbled and fell. Thad and Ella went to him immediately, as did Wibung.

"It has been a wonderful evening, old friend," he said to Thad, "but I am so tired."

Thad helped him stand, and Ella dusted him off. Two of the Bidjigal men handed others their spears and torches and came forward, making a chair with their arms. Gregory allowed them to carry him home.

That night, Ella crawled into her bed happily exhausted. She had not stayed out past midnight in her entire life. What would her mother have thought had she seen her daughter dancing with Aboriginals? Indeed, what would her mother think of her coming to Australia? As strange as it was, with dangers lurking in so many places, Australia was beginning to feel like home, her home. And the so-called savages were not savage at all, but friends.

The *corroboree* had been eye-opening. She'd had a chance to see how the natives lived, to dispel some of her false beliefs about them. Their village was impressive, quite tidy and organized. The dancing was fun, and the food was exotic. Her stomach growled and snarled at the new things she had eaten. The Bidjigal obviously tolerated such food better than *whitefellas!*

As she lay in the dark waiting to fall asleep, she thought of Thad. He had enjoyed the food and the dancing, and best of all he had kissed her cheek as they said good night at her bedchamber door.

"You were incredible tonight," he had whispered. "Thank you for being so kind to the Bidjigal."

Did he mean she had secured his reputation with the Bidjigal, she wondered, or she secured his heart forever?

She rubbed her hands down across her breasts, her belly and hips. He had been looking at her of late. Looking differently than when she had first arrived. Mabarra was right. Thad felt affection for her. Was it love? That remained to be seen.

In his bedchamber, Thad sat on the chaise with whiskey. He had not bothered to pour a glass but held an open bottle in his hand, taking a gulp every few minutes. He wore only his trousers and his shirt, unbuttoned, to admit the cool breeze coming in the bedchamber windows.

He could not get the image of Ella out of his head, dancing, smiling, laughing. She was captivating. She was complete in every way. He desired her. He needed her. He had to tell her how he felt. He thought he would die for the want of her.

"Thad, I would love a tour of your glasshouse," Ella entreated at breakfast a few mornings after the *corroboree*. "I had only a short peek inside when Mabarra gave me a tour of the property. I want to see some of Australia's exotic plants and learn about them."

He looked tired. She wondered if he had slept last night or lain awake thinking…of her.

"Of course, Ella. I am sorry we have not toured the glasshouse yet. Life has been so busy since you arrived."

He reached across the table and took one of her hands.

"Do you have a swim dress?"

Ella wrinkled her eyebrows.

"Well, yes, an under-slip I could use. But why do I need it?"

Thad chuckled his low tones of amusement.

"The glasshouse will be terribly hot and muggy. We will want to go to the creek afterward for a cool splash."

After breakfast, Ella went to her bedchamber and found her under-slip in the chest of drawers. It was filmier, more transparent, more revealing than she remembered. It was too late to back out of going to the creek, so she shed all her summer day clothes and slipped on the white cotton under-slip.

She went to the cheval mirror and surveyed her appearance. Her ankles and a few inches of her calves were easily seen. If she looked very hard, she could see the outline of her nipples and her triangular patch of pubic hair. Was this too risqué? Yes. But this was for Thad—the maverick, the man she desired. She would put a light robe over herself so no one else could see her brazen swim garb. She slipped on old shoes to hike to the glass house and then the creek. Neither place was far.

Ella met Thad outside her room. He was just emerging from his bedchamber. He wore a light robe and old slippers. They sized up each other, and Thad smiled.

"I do not feel the necessity to take towels," he said in a low voice. "The air is so hot we will dry quickly, including our swim garb."

She nodded cheerfully and took Thad's arm.

"This is going to be fun," she said. "I will get to see your glasshouse flora and have a summer dip in the creek too."

The glasshouse was a short walk from Acacia House. Ella surveyed its iron architectural beauty, including a cupola with a kangaroo weathervane. Thad was so fond of kangaroos.

"Mr. Floyd, who made the framework for the glasshouse, fashioned that kangaroo for me. Floyd is quite the metal worker."

Ella agreed, giggling at the iron kangaroo dizzily spinning around in the breeze.

"You know, Thaddeus Bennett, I am surprised you have not tamed a kangaroo for a pet."

He made a face, then said, laughing: "There is still time, Ella Fielding!"

As the glasshouse door opened, Ella felt the hot, humid air hit her face. Thad grinned.

"I think you now understand why we should go to the creek after the tour."

The glasshouse, despite being uncomfortable from its heat and humidity, was filled with fascinating blooms and green plants. Thad gave a fabulous tour as Ella walked slowly through the little center path.

A tall Wonga Vine, not yet in bloom, curved down one side of the entrance door. On the opposite side, yellow Rough Guinea Flowers were in bloom. A Bower of Beauty Climber trailed up a tripod behind them.

All manner of grasses and ferns were interspersed among the flowers and vines. Ella loved the Rough Tree Fern and the fluffy white Velvet Cushions growing under it. The leaves of the Urn Heath were prickly but beautiful. Thad had several exotic Banksia and Grevillea varieties too, one with fuzzy, curly blooms that looked like worms and another with blooms that resembled torches.

At the far end of the glasshouse were flowers Thad had ordered from England. His favorites. There were peonies, irises, tulips, dahlias, lamb's ears, pinks, and fuchsias. A skylight over this portion of the glasshouse allowed some of the heat to escape, as these plants did not need it.

"We love having vases of fresh flowers in the house," Thad said, "especially at Christmas."

Christmas! Ella had not even thought of it. Yes, it was December, but Australia was so hot. Did they truly celebrate Christmas in this ungodly heat?

As they left the glasshouse, Ella sighed.

"I must confess I am not a pretty flower. The heat and clamminess are a trifle too much for me."

Thad chuckled, offered his arm, and turned toward the creek. They had not gone far into the wet eucalypt forest when a litter of juvenile tiger quolls scurried in all directions in search of their mother. Ella squealed with delight.

"Oh Thad, how cute! What are they? Do they bite?"

Thad squeezed her arm tightly.

"Tiger quolls. They bite, even as young as they are. Cute yes, but vicious little creatures. Do not try to catch one. Their mother will be cross with you. We normally do not see them in the daytime, but these pups, I suppose, are confused without their mother in the den. Rest assured she will return, and she will not like us disturbing her young. We had best move on, and quickly."

Near the creek a garden skink took off, giving Ella a brief fright. Thad remarked that watching her discover the wildlife of New South Wales was as much fun as sitting close with her on the front porch swing in the evenings.

"I especially like your fragrance, Ella. You smell so delicious when I am near you."

Delicious? My word, she thought, but that sounded almost carnal! Yet, she resolved to continue bathing with rose soap. She desperately wished to know the things Thad liked about her.

"Thad, you mentioned Christmas. How do you celebrate it here? In this heat, I cannot imagine singing Christmas hymns and giving gifts to the children."

"Ah, well...we do keep Christmas. While I was in Sydney, I bought candy for the children. Mr. Blenham, our carpenter, is making Jacob's Ladders for them. The staff get coins and candy. I usually give Gregory a bottle of good French wine. He is a Mayhew, you know, a Norman and proud of it."

Ella was relieved to hear there were gifts for the staff and the children. Perhaps she would ask to decorate the house during Christmas week. The children would enjoy decorating their dormitory and the church.

They arrived at the creek. The air around it was blessedly cool.

"Thank the Lord for Cockle Creek! So cool and refreshing on a hot day, just out of the glasshouse," Thad blurted. "It has another name, you know. The natives call it *Gibberagong* Creek. It means 'plenty of rocks,' and you will soon see that as fact."

Both were a little shy about shedding their robes. Ella turned her back to Thad and took off her robe and shoes. She checked the buttons at the shoulders of her under-slip to be sure they were secure. When she turned to face Thad, he was standing on a large rock at the edge of the creek in only his under drawers.

"Come and take my hand, Ella. The rocks along the creek are slippery. It earns its native name."

She obeyed, feeling modest to be wearing so little. Thad seemed not to care that only his mid-section was covered. She made quick glances at his hairy, muscled chest, at the hair under his arms as he reached for her. He had long, muscled legs.

They stepped gingerly into the water and slowly waded out to a deeper part of the creek. Ella giggled at the coolness of the water on her legs. She felt her nipples pucker. The bottom of her swim dress had ballooned with air as she waded deeper.

Thad let go of her arm and submerged himself for a short time.

She thought he was looking at her legs underwater.

Her dress was like an umbrella, revealing all of her legs...and perhaps more. She turned away from him. A moment later he surfaced with a huge splash, throwing his arms high. Ella turned back and caught a look at his wet swim drawers, which were sticking to his body. She looked away quickly so as not to think about what she saw—the outline of his private parts.

She had seen these things in her work as a nurse, but never on a man she liked…loved. She wanted to look at him; yet she did not.

"I highly recommend a good dunk, Ella. It is so cooling!"

Ella turned full on then.

"Well, why not?" she said laughing.

She pinched her nose shut with her fingers and went under, head and all. When she opened her eyes, she saw how clear the creek water was. Little fish were swimming about. A green Banjo frog hopped in the water and swam by. There was something on the bottom that looked like a tiny lobster.

She surfaced with a jump.

"Oh, Thad, what a wonderland of creatures, and the water is delightfully clear and cool!"

Thad was nodding, but she saw that his focus was clearly on her chest. Her wet swim dress was glued to her body, and her perky nipples were easy to see, along with the soft roundness of her breasts. Feeling embarrassed, she crossed her arms over her chest.

Thad cocked his head in question.

"Ella, please do not cover yourself. You are beautiful, incredibly so. I hope you are not ashamed of your body."

He waded to her, uncrossed her arms, and wrapped his arms around her.

"One thing I have learned from the Bidjigal is that there should be no shame about the human body. I am slowly accepting that for myself."

Ella looked up into his soft, golden-brown eyes and felt herself tremble. He was smiling at her, but in a special way she had not seen before.

"If I were as beautiful as you, Ella Fielding, I would never feel ashamed about anything."

He pulled her up into his arms and pressed his mouth on hers. She was stunned for a moment, then opened her lips. His kiss felt so wonderful as his mouth roved over hers, gently at first and then hungrily.

Ella had never been kissed on her mouth in all her six-and-twenty years. Not once.

How have I survived this long without a man's kisses, she pondered as Thad continued showering her with his affection, kissing her cheeks, her nose, her forehead, and the sides of her neck.

His embrace was comfortable…perfect, so right. She felt as if she was meant to be in his arms. She let her tongue trail over his lower lip. He trembled and pulled her closer.

"Ella, my sweet, I have wanted to kiss you since that first night when you arrived for dinner. I was expecting a much different woman, a matron, I suppose. When you appeared, it was like a dream."

Ella let her nose trail over Thad's neck. His skin smelled wonderfully masculine.

"It was the same for me, Thad. I thought you and Gregory would be old men, bald and grizzled. I was so surprised to find you both handsome, especially you. I must confess I have never known such a beautiful man as you."

Thad kissed her again, this time deeper and then urgently, his arms going around her and lifting her up until her breasts pressed against his chest. He held her thus with one hand clutching her soft, bare bottom. The under-slip had slid upwards to her waist.

"You must know how I feel, Ella. I can think of nothing but you, even when it is imperative that I concentrate on other things. Please…tell me you care for me, that there is no one else in your heart."

Ella looked into his imploring eyes.

"I do, Thad. I care deeply for you."

Realizing the impropriety of his grip on her bare backside, he gently lowered her onto a rock in the creek. They stood mesmerized for a few moments. Then Ella playfully kicked water on him and ran. It ignited a sensual game of splashing, laughing, kissing, and touching.

"You are a bit naughty, Ella Fielding! And…I love it, your fun-loving side."

He caught her and pulled her into another kiss. She went willingly, moaning as his mouth consumed hers. He pulled down her wet hair and ran his fingers through it.

"Here I am, ruining you even more, Miss Fielding. I cannot help myself. You are a goddess, perfection. Everything I could want in a woman."

He kissed her longingly, then they walked to the creek bank and climbed onto the shore. They slid on their shoes and robes. Thad kissed her all over her face and ears and neck. His mouth tasted wonderful on hers. She wanted his kiss to go forever.

"Your beautiful tresses will be dry before we get back to the house," he said, nuzzling her hair.

As they walked arm-in-arm from the creek to home, Thad told her how lonely he had been before her arrival—

"I went to dinners and parties and even a few balls. I truly wished to find someone. But always the women, the ladies…they all seemed so silly, interested in the most frivolous things. Conversations were mundane, even ridiculous. We talked about dresses and hairstyles and jewelry. They told me who was seen walking arm-in-arm in the parks of Sydney. Who planned to marry. I heard all the local gossip. The women were like dressed up China dolls, empty and expensive."

He stopped and turned Ella to face him.

"You are so different, Ella Fielding—genuine, warm, companionable. Your education is not about trivial matters but things that are important. Yet, you present yourself as a refined and graceful woman, one any man would be proud to claim as his own."

He took both of her hands and kissed them.

"I have seen you in a day dress sopping wet at a washtub, bathing children and dogs. I have seen you garbed in satin and lace, sitting across from me at dinner. I have seen you dancing, your hips swaying provocatively. And I have seen you dealing with sickness and injury, working to save lives. Never have I met anyone like you."

They kissed again and again as they walked. Ella was in a daze of ardor when they entered the house, wrapped in damp robes, arms around each other.

Mabarra was rolling pie crust on the kitchen counter. She grinned.

"You both look refreshed!"

"We are, indeed, refreshed," Thad answered. "But I have a thirst for cold tea."

He looked down into Ella's eyes, smiling.

"Will you meet me on the back porch for cold tea, say in a quarter of an hour?"

Ella agreed.

She and Mabarra watched him go up the back stairs to his room, then their eyes met. Mabarra began to giggle.

"Need I ask what the two of you have been doing?" she laughed.

Ella leaned close and whispered.

"I think we are…in love."

Mabarra nodded, smiling.

"Everyone here knows it. We just wondered when the two of you would realize it."

A moment later, Mabarra took Ella's arm.

"I think you had better cancel that buggy ride you have been putting off with Mr. Lusty Lambe."

With their friendship evolved into love, Ella frequently went to Thad's bed chamber to fetch books. His collection was varied, much more than hers, and she absolutely loved the masculine smell and feel of his things. His books were an extension of him.

It was a Sunday afternoon—the Sunday she was supposed to take a buggy ride with Antony Lambe, but she had sent a note canceling it. Antony was incensed, of course. He seemed fixated with Ella and had a short temper. She mollified him with a promise of an invitation to dinner yet set no date for it. She hoped he would forget.

She intended to laze away this Sunday afternoon reading in her chamber. Thad was in his office working on his ledger book and answering correspondence. They would catch up at dinner and afterward enjoy the front porch swing.

The door was ajar to Thad's chamber, as always, to allow Warrigal to come and go. Ella pushed it open softly and rounded the bed to reach the bookshelves. A canine foot and tail stuck out from under the bed. The dog usually slept on the rug by the door, but he had crawled under the bed, perhaps to lay on the cooler acacia floor.

"Snoozer! Are you more comfortable under the bed?"

Ella scanned the book titles until she found a good choice to read. Elizabeth Thomas' *The Vindictive Spirit* sounded interesting. Ella slid it off the shelf and turned to leave. Warrigal had not moved, but then he was nearly deaf, she knew. He had not heard her come into the room, nor thumped his tail in answer when she spoke to him. She bent down and tickled the pads on his back feet.

"Hello, Boy. Is it cooler under Thad's bed?"

There was no response. Ella jiggled his back feet; still nothing. She got on her knees and looked under the bed. She patted his backside. But Warrigal was quiet.

"Oh, no!" she whispered. "No! Not yet!"

She rose and went to the other side of the bed. On her knees again, she reached for the dog and pulled him from under the mattress. His eyes were partly open and glassy. His body had begun to stiffen.

"Warrigal…dear old boy, please wake. Thad will be devastated. You have been with him all the years he has lived here."

She lifted the dog and hugged him to her. She jiggled his ears and kissed his nose, but there was no response. He was gone. She prayed he had not suffered in his last hours. Thinking back, she recalled Warrigal had not come downstairs to be let outside that morning and then to lay under the dining room table at breakfast. Had he died before morning?

Ella gulped and looked at the ceiling. How was she to tell Thad his beloved dog was dead? It was one of the cruelest duties, the delivering of such a sad message. Slowly, she carried Warrigal downstairs and into the kitchen. Mabarra put a hand to her mouth when she saw Ella holding the lifeless dog. Tears streamed down Ella's face.

"Mabarra, dear old Warrigal has died. My heart is broken, for I must now tell Thad."

The kitchen staff gathered around, and more tears began. Mrs. Hughes puckered her mouth in a hard line so as not to cry.

"I shall take him to the doctor if you wish, my lady," she said.

Ella shook her head no.

"Thank you, Mrs. Hughes, but I must do it. I found him. He crawled under Thad's bed to die."

Like a funeral procession, the women followed Ella to the back of the kitchen and through the doors of the clinic. Thad was at his desk writing.

"Darling," Ella called tenderly.

He held up one finger asking her to wait a moment, then turned. He stared for a long time, gulped, and rose from his chair.

"I am so sorry, dearest Thad, so sorry. I found him under your bed when I went to your chamber for a book."

Carefully, Thad took the dog from Ella and cradled him as if he held a baby in his arms. It was quiet in the room, except for the soft sniffles of Ella and the kitchen girls.

"Thad, you gave him such a good life, loved him unconditionally. He was fortunate to have you as his master," Ella offered, sobbing.

Thad turned away from the women and held Warrigal lovingly against his chest. He rubbed the dog's head. Ella saw him begin to shake and knew he was wracked with grief.

"Dear old Warrigal," he whispered. "The best dog a man could have. You were such a loyal companion, a good hunter, an excellent watchdog. And now we must part with you…much too soon."

Mrs. Hughes fetched an old bed sheet and brought it to Thad.

"Sir, mayhap we can wrap him in this."

She took the dog from Thad and neatly encased him in the sheet, leaving only his face uncovered. Ella wiped Thad's cheeks with her handkerchief.

"Mabarra, please get Henry and tell him what has happened," Mrs. Hughes instructed. "He will dig a grave for Warrigal."

The beloved first dog to reside in Acacia House was buried in the little cemetery beyond the church. Father Gregory fought back tears as he recalled to everyone how Warrigal had jumped in the Parramatta River in July 1806 and swum after the boat conveying Thad and his entourage to their new home. He thanked God for giving humanity gifts such as dogs and cats and horses. Mani and Lucy stepped forward and laid wildflowers on the small grave. There was not a dry eye among the staff as Warrigal's inert body was interred, and the sheet was wrapped over his face. Everyone cried for the dog, yes, but more for his master, a man everyone dearly loved.

Thad fashioned a wooden cross for the grave using two sticks. Ella tearfully watched him pound it into the ground at Warrigal's head, then fall against it weeping. She went to him and put her arms around his back.

"My heart breaks for you, darling."

One of the masons whispered to Thad that he would make a gravestone with the words, *Warrigal, a Fine Dog, 1806 – 1818* chiseled into its face.

Ella had argued with Antony Lambe several times after canceling the buggy ride. Her refusal to go had fallen on deaf ears. The man continued to believe she wanted him, and he pursued her relentlessly as the Christmas holiday approached.

How did he know when Thad was gone? It was as if Antony had posted spies around Acacia House. He always showed up when Thad was away with a lame excuse to visit.

How were the sheep getting on?

Would Ella like to attend a dance down in Parramatta?

Mrs. Macarthur had sent him with a brandy cake.

There was a stomach ailment making the rounds at the Female Factory in Parramatta. Had Dr. Bennett been notified?

One day near Christmas, Thad was on a call at the new little settlement of Rogan's Hill, southwest of Wahroonga. John Rogan was starting a farm there, and he'd had an accident. A messenger had come to Acacia House mid-morning asking for help. It was a fall from high on the wood-framed house Rogan was building, and possibly a broken back.

Ella did not accompany Thad, as she was miserable with cramps that morning, the kind that preceded heavy courses. Emily had brought her fennel to sniff, cinnamon myrtle tea, and a headache powder. She also had drawn the curtains in Ella's room. A cool cloth on Ella's forehead helped ease the discomfort of the hot morning.

Thad knocked on her chamber door before he left for Rogan's Hill and kissed Ella softly as she lay prone on her bed.

"I have never understood why God burdens women so," he whispered to her, "to bleed painfully once a month and to suffer while giving birth. I know the female anatomy and understand how it works, but the misery seems unfair."

Ella held Thad's hands in hers. He was so handsome that morning, ready to go on his medical call. She truly wished she could go with him, but the bright sun and heat of the day were the worst things for her headache. Even the fragrance of Thad's shaving soap seemed overpowering, though on a normal day she loved his masculine smell.

She fondled his muttonchops affectionately. A few of the whiskers in them were white.

"Well, I hope you plan to speak to God about the burdens women bear, when you get to heaven that is. Surely, you will be let in by Saint Peter for all the good deeds you have done. I am not sure I could stand the bright light of heaven today."

She smiled half-heartedly and grasped her aching head.

"Be safe, my darling Thad. I hope you will be home by dinner."

Thad kissed Ella again, his lips lingering on hers. He kissed each of her cheeks and the very tip of her pretty nose, then every fingertip on each of her hands.

"These dreadful headaches pass after a few hours, sweetheart. Rest, and remember that you are my sunshine and moonlight, and that every star in my sky shines for you."

She smiled and squeezed Thad's large hand.

"I adore you, Dr. Thaddeus Bennett," she whispered.

After Thad left, she felt drowsy and slipped off to sleep. She woke a short time later to Emily gently touching her left shoulder.

"Ma'am, Mr. Lambe be here. He says he knows ye home and he will not leave 'til he sees ye."

Ella rolled on her side and groaned.

"You must tell him I am unwell and in my bedchamber. I cannot see him."

"I told him, but he be stubborn, ma'am."

A voice called up to Ella's open windows. It was Antony, standing outside under her chamber. How did he know which windows were hers?

"Miss Fielding! I hear you are sick in bed. Is that true, or have you the idea to be rid of me?"

Ella dragged herself from the bed and looked out the nearest window. Antony stood below, smiling happily when he saw her, only a silk night-rail clinging to her shapely body. Ella felt Emily's hands sliding her arms into a night rail.

"Antony, I am in no shape for a visit. I have been in bed sick all morning. Please go home."

"Shall I ride to the herbalist in Warrawee for a tonic? Tell me what ails you, so that I might bring back the right medicine."

He was so exasperating! And nosey! Did he not remember Thad was a doctor? Ella sighed and took a drink of the water Emily handed her.

"Antony, my ills are private. Please go away now. I cannot take guests today."

She left the window, shed the robe, and climbed back in bed. Still, she could hear Antony calling to her, persistently.

"Emily, please go down and tell him to leave at once. If necessary, get some of the men down at the barn to force him to go."

"Of course, ma'am. Is there anything ye needs?"

"No thank you. Just get rid of Antony Lambe."

She had hoped to go in the forest today with Henry and cut greens to decorate for Christmas. But she could not go in this condition. Woman's woes!

"Oh, and would you please tell Henry I am too ill to go fetch evergreens?"

"Ma'am, I am sorry to wake you again, but Henry needs you."

It was Mabarra this time, trying to wake Ella as gently as possible. She must have slept for several hours after Lambe left, hastened on his way by several of the Barn Boys.

"A cow accidentally kicked Henry in the back of his head a short time ago during the afternoon milking. He is in terrible pain and is a bit senseless. He needs someone with medical knowledge to examine him."

Ella threw back the sheet that had covered her and put her legs over the side of the bed. She was dizzy and a little nauseous. Mabarra helped her into a light summer dress as Emily twisted her hair into a basic bun. She slid into a scruffy pair of old shoes and headed for the men's bunkroom, Mabarra at her side.

Henry lay on his bed groaning. Mabarra had placed a cool wet rag over his brow. Ella knelt beside him and ran her fingers through his coppery hair.

"Dearest Henry, tell me about your pain. Where is it and how severe?"

Henry pushed the rag aside and pointed to the back of his head.

"It hur' realla bad, Missy Fieldin'. Wors' pain I evva hab."

"I am sorry, Henry. Does it throb, or is it a constant pain?"

Henry simply nodded.

"I think he means it is both," Mabarra put in.

Ella asked Henry if she might examine the injury to his head. He nodded, but when she lay her fingers on the bloody backside of his skull he cried out. She could see a half-circle of skull bone, about the size of the rim of a teacup, caved in at the base of his head. Blood oozed around the edges of the sunken bone.

Ella turned to Mabarra.

"Have Emily make up a strong headache powder and bring it...quickly! Also, something for nausea. I am sure his stomach is upset."

No sooner had she said this than Henry rolled away from her and vomited over the opposite side of his bed. The other men in the dormitory rushed to clean up the mess. They were glad to have something to do for their friend.

Ella wracked her brain for a diagnosis. Injuries to the head often caused a lackadaisical state—inability to be upright, sleepiness, nausea, vertigo, and severe pain at the injury site. A doctor in Canada once told her the back of the head was the most dangerous spot for an injury.

She absolutely could not give Henry laudanum for the pain, else he might slide into unconsciousness. He was senseless enough already.

Emily brought the medicines. Ella gently administered them to Henry. He thanked her and rolled back on his side. Ella fetched a second pillow and placed it behind his back. She would need Thad's help on this. Meanwhile, she sat at Henry's bedside listening for any change in his breathing and checking his pulse every few minutes.

Her female ills suddenly took a back shelf to her beloved Henry's issues. He was the most important person in her world at this moment. She rubbed his arm and hummed. The tune was one of Henry's favorites, "Three Ravens," an English ballad he had learned to sing with Ella.

Thad returned from Rogans Hill shortly before dinner. The kitchen girls told him what had happened to Henry and that Ella was by his bedside waiting for the doctor's return. Thad ran to the men's dormitory. He found Henry breathing lightly with Ella holding his hand.

"Oh, Thad, I am so glad you are here. I fear Henry is badly injured. I gave him something for head pain and nausea, but I know nothing else to do. He is sleeping deeply."

Thad pulled up Henry's eyelids and checked his pupils. He listened to the man's heart and lungs, then looked at the contusion on the back of his head.

"He is not sleeping deeply, Ella. He is in a coma."

Ella's hands flew to her face as she mouthed, "No!"

"We can do nothing but keep him comfortable and wait…and pray…and hope."

Thad ordered several of the men in the dormitory to carefully carry Henry into the medical clinic and put him in one of the beds. They were smart enough to grasp the pallet of blankets Henry lay upon so as not to jostle him too much. Thad stripped Henry to his underwear, as the heat was unbearable, and placed a clean, cool sheet over him. Henry was extra warm to the touch, likely suffering from a fever.

"I will have the staff take turns sitting with him, swabbing him with cool wet towels," Thad said.

At dinner, Ella was silent. She nibbled at her food, excused herself, and rushed to Henry's bedside. She needed to keep watch on him. Thad understood. He came to Henry's bedside periodically to check on the man, but there seemed to be no improvement.

As the hours passed, Ella thought Henry was traveling farther and farther away from consciousness. His breathing grew shallower. His heartbeat slowed and slowed. He made no response when Ella took his hand or whispered to him.

"Dearest Henry, please wake. You are so special to all of us. You have helped me through many trials since my arrival."

She thought back to the first moment she had met Henry. He was waiting near the bottom of the *Isabella's* brow as Ella disembarked the ship after her long voyage from England to New South Wales. He smiled at her, and she was transfixed. Was this what an Aboriginal man was like?

"Ye uh be Missy Fieldln', ma'am?" he had asked. "I nose ye is. Ye looks so fine. I uh here a' take ye hum now. I wooks fo' dockta Bennuh."

Home. How much his smile and that word had meant to her. She had been traveling so many months and never quite feeling completely well. Seeing her discomfort at making landfall, Henry gave her a chunk of ginger, telling her it would make an uneasy stomach feel better.

"Henry, we had quite a trip together up from Sydney, did we not? You drove those draught horses expertly. And I loved their names—Yuwin and Biyal. You told me the names meant 'yes' and 'no' in Dharug…and it made me laugh and laugh."

She giggled at the memory and stroked his arm affectionately. Thad stood quietly in the doorway watching and listening. His eyes filled with tears.

"You must wake now, Henry. You are a sweet, beautiful man. All of us love you, but me especially…and Thad and Gregory. We love you the most."

Two days later, on Christmas Eve, Henry stopped breathing, his big heart ceased beating, and he went to his just reward among the stars in Aboriginal heaven. A great cry went up in Acacia House and the orphanage at the loss of this dear man. Gregory and Thad were broken, especially Thad, who felt he had failed Henry as his doctor. Though Ella cried for Henry, she cried more for these two kindhearted men who had rescued Henry and given him a good life.

Later that day, as Ella sat on the south porch sewing a silk cover for Henry's death pillow, she heard the saws and hammers of the carpenters fashioning Henry's coffin. Mabarra washed and dressed Henry in his finest clothes. His body was laid in a piece of yellow silk that lined the coffin, and his hands were crossed holding the small wooden crucifix he had made when Father Gregory baptized him.

Thad believed him to be about age five-and-thirty. He had been Thad's steadfast assistant and companion for some twelve years.

Henry was laid to rest the next day after a heart-rending service in the church, led by Father Gregory. The orphans cried and hummed a sad dirge throughout the service. Some of them, remembering their Aboriginal roots, sang a death song and pattered their feet on the floor of the pews to imitate a death dance. Ella observed the grief sorrowfully. How could God allow such unfair things to happen?

Many people filled the chapel and spilled out through its doors. Though Henry was not Bidjigal, the entire Bidjigal clan came to his funeral, even Keira carrying her tiny baby. The Wangals who camped on Thad's southern lands came too. There were nearly ninety Aboriginals attending. Many of them had painted their bodies with death symbols and had cut themselves to show their grief. They sang songs of loss over Henry and placed things in his coffin they felt he would need in the hereafter.

Paperbark was slid under and around his body as protection. He was given a spear and a *womera* to launch it. He wore no shoes, for he would need to walk the earth barefoot with the spirits of the land before finding the pathway to heaven. Streaks of white ochre were painted on his face, symbols of the sky and stars where the Aboriginal ancestors lived.

In the middle of the service, Elizabeth Macarthur entered the church and stood in the back. Everyone turned to look at her. Ella was surprised, remembering how dreadfully Mrs. Macarthur had treated Henry on her visit to Acacia House. Had it all been an act, or had she come to know how special the Aboriginals were?

Father Gregory cried through much of the sermon he attempted to recite, praising Henry's innocence as an abandoned child, his fortitude, his eagerness to learn, and the good things he had done for the orphanage and the church.

"Let his spirit go to his birthplace at Jilling so that he might be reborn there."

The priest bowed his head to pray but could no longer speak. Thad finished for Gregory, who was too overwrought to continue. The doctor choked up himself. Mabarra could not sing the tribute she had written for Henry without tears.

People filed by the coffin and said their good-byes. Ella was surprised to see the Byrnes family and a number of timber-getters pass by. Elizabeth Macarthur came forward, placing a yellow rose on Henry's chest.

"Go to your maker, Henry Douglas," she whispered. "I am told you were a good man given a good life by another good man."

Mani captured everyone's sentiments as he bid farewell to Henry. Placing his small hand on one of Henry's cheeks, he slid a sprig of fragrant frangipani into Henry's hair and said—

"I gibs yo' favrit flower, Henfry Doug-less. You wuz a goo', goo' man. I be sure God an' de spirits gonna takes you ta hebben. *Yanu*—goo-by."

Four Bidjigal stepped forward after all the tributes were said to place the cover on Henry's coffin, but not before Thad laid a copy of *Gulliver's Travels* under Henry's folded hands. It was a book Henry had loved. Thad had read it to him and told him how the land of Lilliput was 30° South latitude—the same latitude as the center of Australia in Never-Never. Eventually, Henry learned to read well enough that he could read the book himself.

"Safe travels to the next world, dear old friend," Thad whispered. "Here is something to take with you on your journey to the spirit world."

Seven

It had not been the autumn Ella had imagined. The trees in Wahroonga did not change color as in Canada and England. They were mostly evergreens—casuarina, Norfolk pine, white cypress pine, hoop pine, offering only cones. There were many, many gums, so many Ella could not learn all their names. They were evergreen eucalypts that, rather than popping autumn color and shedding leaves, sloughed their bark, dropping it in thin gray-brown strips or large grey chunks.

Summer had been no better, hot and sultry, with violent rainstorms upending drought and intense heat and sunlight bearing down on everything. She felt the New South Wales seasons had betrayed her in a cruel joke of reversal.

A pall had lain over Acacia House after the death of Henry. The staff went through the motions of their daily work but without pleasure. Christmas Day, the day of Henry's funeral, had passed unnoticed, even by the children and Father Gregory. No stockings were hung, no Wassail bowl was filled, no Yule Log burned. Old Betty forgot about the plum pudding and eggnog she always made for Christmas.

No parishioners arrived for a Christmas Eve or Christmas Day service at the church, sympathetic to the grief at Acacia House. The vicar forgot about Christingle and Boxing Day. Worst of all, there was no singing, the most joyful part of the holiday.

When the 1819 New Year arrived, and the doctor realized everyone, even the orphans, had forgotten Christmas, he passed out his gifts to the children and staff.

"He would so have enjoyed this," Thad told Ella, hinting of Henry, yet reminding her that Aboriginal custom forbade anyone to say the names of the dead. "He loved to give gifts to the children. He especially loved singing with them. *The Coventry Carol* was his favorite."

"Yes," she agreed, "and he would have been a wonderful father himself. For a time, I thought he and Mabarra might…"

As a Christmas gift, Thad gave Ella a new copy of Jane Austin's *Emma*, complete with a pink ribbon bookmark attached to the spine. He had intended to gift it to her when he had returned from Sydney in November, but in all the excitement surrounding the birth of Ella-*Buwa*, the *corroboree* afterwards, and the sadness at the loss of his dog and then his beloved friend, it had slipped his mind.

A velvet box, inside which lay a beautiful brooch of diamonds and pearls, was his other gift to Ella. He kissed her tenderly as he placed the box in her hands—

"I know you are not a woman much beguiled by jewels, but I believe you deserve this brooch. It comes to you with all my love, forever and always, sweetest Ella. You are, indeed, an extraordinary woman…*my* extraordinary woman."

He carefully pinned the brooch on her dark blue dress, centered on the tight bodice just below where her breasts were pushed together by her corset. Gently, he leaned down and kissed the hollow place of her neck where her pulse throbbed.

"Perhaps we should set a date for our wedding to cheer up this unhappy place," he said.

Ella smiled and put her arms around his neck.

"Is this a marriage proposal, Thaddeus Bennett?"

He chuckled low in his throat and answered with a deep long kiss.

"It goes without saying, but I will say it just the same. Be my wife, sweet Ella. I cannot live without you."

She whispered a tearful *yes* and laid her head against his broad chest, listening to the regular and strong beat of his heart. He was in his prime, full of healthy masculinity.

I am to marry this wonderful man, she thought. I cannot believe such happiness is mine…especially after the sorrows we have endured.

She hoped their wedding would return Acacia House to gladness again. Marrying Thad would certainly bring her immeasurable happiness. And they would have children, lots of them. Little feet pattering about the house.

"Yes, we should set a wedding date."

Ella stared at the ceiling of her chamber as she lay in bed that night. She had said *yes* to Thad. She was going to be his wife. It gave her such contentment to consider it, to think about the future. A secure future. Would she be a good wife? A good mother? Dear God, but she had never envisioned such a fine future for herself.

She thought then of the nuisance Antony Lambe had been until the day of Henry's passing. He did not attend Henry's funeral but came by a week later, lecturing her about women who taunt men, renege on promises and play with tender hearts. When she chased him away a final time, he was livid but did not lose his temper. She had told him she was in love with Thad and was going to marry him. Period. But Antony refused to believe it, calling Thad boring and singular-minded.

"You desire him only for his money and status," Antony rudely accused, his arm clutching Ella's waist. "I am certain you would gladly trade riches and reputation for a life of passion and unending adoration from me. I shall be rich someday too, but for now I can give you so much more love than the dull Dr. Bennett."

Antony had turned up at Acacia House at unexpected times after the New Year of 1819, always when Thad was away, asking to see Ella and saying he had come to help now that Henry was gone. He put flowers on Henry's grave. Ella warned him not to say the dead Aboriginal man's name. Antony offered to bring her a new sheepdog to replace Warrigal, one from a valuable litter of pups newly born at Elizabeth Farm.

Ella had made excuses for not wanting to see Antony, many excuses. But he was beyond persistent. Gifts were left for her—flowers, candy, fancy handkerchiefs, ribbons and a shell comb for her hair, poems he had written in her honor, sketches of her and scenes he imagined if they would marry, even a sweet striped kitten in a basket.

Ella adored the kitten, which she named Hestia for the Greek goddess of the hearth but sent Antony a note telling him to send no more gifts, that to court her was useless. She detailed her plans for a June wedding and her future with Thad, hoping to show Antony how much she loved the doctor. She told him she would never leave Thad, that they would have a family, that they would remain together for all eternity.

"How can you be in love with me when you have spent so little time in my presence?" she insisted. "I am not in love with you, Antony Lambe. I can never be! You must stop pursuing me."

Her entreaty seemed to bring an end to Antony's persistent, romantic overtures, or so she thought…until one raw night in late May of 1819. The wedding banns had been posted for Ella and Thad, with a notice in the *Sydney Gazette.* They planned to be married in early June. Word of the betrothal had reached the Macarthurs, and then Antony.

No one heard hoofbeats that night, or the jingle of a horse's bridle. A drowsing nightjar flapped its wings and chirruped an alert. A horse whinnied in the barn. But there was no response from a sleeping Acacia House.

Thad did not stir in his bed, so exhausted was he from attending the birth that day of twins for a woman in distant Castle Hill.

Perhaps the creak of the kitchen door was only the wind, Mrs. Hughes thought, nestling deeper under her blankets and returning to her slumbers.

Wibung lay asleep on the porch at the back of the church. The dog was growing old now and was nearly deaf. He heard nothing that night.

Ella, also, was fast asleep as cunning footfall came slowly up the stairs, down the hall, and to her door. The knob turned softly, almost soundlessly. A faraway voice in her dreams seemed to say, "You are mine, beauty."

She awoke as a hand with a damp cloth covered her mouth and nose. She struggled for some twenty seconds, falling to the floor as she kicked and hit her assailant. Strangely, no one in the sleeping household heard. Ella's fight soon gave out and she succumbed to the deep darkness engulfing her.

She did not feel herself being carried the distance, out of the house and across the gravel to the end of the driveway. She was unaware of being lifted over a horse's neck and yanked upright into the arms of her kidnapper. A blanket went around her.

The horse, called Zeus, jolted forward, and Antony Lambe uttered an almost evil snicker. Ella Fielding would be his, no matter how he obtained her.

As Zeus bounded over the many miles toward his master's house at the edge of Emu Plains, Antony imagined Ella in a checkered dress, standing at the iron stove in his cabin, frying rashers and flipping pikelets for his breakfast. He saw her hanging wash on the line and cleaning dishes in a metal tub outside the kitchen door.

In another reverie, she was chopping wood and then bending over, weeding a vegetable garden, her sweet, round backside facing him enticingly.

Last, he allowed himself to imagine her naked on his bed, gesturing seductively for him to join her.

The miles and small villages passed as Antony's loyal horse galloped over the moonlit nightscape and up into the Pennant Hills. The equine knew his way now and located the shallow ford across the Nepean River. He picked a path among the rocks and bounded up the opposite bank, then headed south along the rugged riverbank road. Near the river's weir, Zeus turned inland on a barely cleared track.

A small cabin came into view with a pasture and lean-to shelter next to it. Zeus halted outside the door, grateful to be home. Antony carried his listless prize inside the house and placed her on his bed. He went back outside, hobbled Zeus, threw down some hay from the lean-to, and turned the tired beast loose. Back in the cabin, he stared hungrily at Ella, excited he had pulled off her abduction.

"This is where you belong, Ella Fielding," he said out loud. "The two of us will bring civilization to Emu Plains. We will marry, have children, and leave behind our legacy of love and family."

Acacia House awoke the next morning as usual. At 8:00 a.m., without the bell yet sounding to summon Emily, the maid went up to Ella's room. It was late. Was Ella sick? Had she lain in? The mistress should have rung by now.

Emily knocked softly at Ella's door. No answer. She knocked again, but there was still no response. Emily quietly entered and immediately saw there had been a struggle. The covers were kicked off the bed, a chair was cast backward. Ella's pillows were strewn, one under the bed and the other beneath a window. The potted fern in the wicker plant stand had been overturned.

Emily rushed downstairs to the doctor and priest, who had finished breakfast and were waiting for Ella to join them.

"Sirs!! Come an' see Miss Fieldin's room. She be gone, an' thee place is a mess!"

Thad rushed upstairs, knocking over a table outside the dining room as he went.

"My God!" was all Thad could say when he saw Ella's room. It looked as if a fight had taken place.

Gregory stood on the bottom step of the stairs, unable to climb to the second floor. Thad rushed to his friend—

"Someone has abducted her, and she struggled with her captor."

Gregory's face vexed.

"Who would take dear Ella?"

Thad slowly turned. His face was red with anger.

"Can you not guess?"

He went to his room and fetched his pistols. Gregory blanched at this.

"Thad, please do not do anything you will be sorry for. We should get the constable and go about this the right way."

Thad paused, loading his pistols, and looked squarely down the stairs at Gregory.

"Fetch the constable, then, and meet me at the Macarthur's' place."

Gregory had not ridden a horse in some time, perhaps years. His body was often wracked with pain, especially in the morning. His arms and legs were stiff and shaky, and of late he had suffered vertigo. His rusty riding skills were tested as he and Constable Martin Wells tore across the countryside to Parramatta, home of the Macarthurs and their ovine overseer, Antony Lambe. Gregory sorely hoped Ella was there, safe in the care of Elizabeth Macarthur. He dared not think what Thad would do if she was harmed.

Young William Macarthur was standing by the hitching post at the Macarthur's vast Elizabeth Farm when the priest and constable arrived, as if waiting for them.

"Everyone is in the house, Sirs. They are waiting for you."

Gregory quickly scanned the room as they entered the house, a much smaller and more rustic place than Acacia House. He recognized several faces, including Thad's, but nowhere did he see Ella or Mr. Lambe.

John Macarthur offered them both a glass of rum, but they declined.

"Tell me what you have learned," Gregory said to Thad.

John Macarthur interrupted—

"We have not seen either Mr. Lambe or Miss Fielding. We have no idea where they are."

Elizabeth Macarthur stepped forward then.

"But we were just discussing the fact that Antony—Mr. Lambe—has been building himself a house on the wooded edge of Emu Plains, beyond the Pennant Hills. Perhaps he has taken Miss Fielding there…if indeed, he is her abductor."

"Of course, he took her!" Thad shouted. "He has been improperly badgering her for months now!"

Gregory leaned against Thad and took his arm.

"Easy, my friend," he whispered. "I know you are upset, but we must keep our wits about us."

Gregory nodded toward the Macarthurs.

"I have informed the constable of all that has transpired with Mr. Lambe. The man is, no doubt, utterly smitten with Miss Fielding, to the point of madness. He has continued to visit Acacia House uninvited and has sent all manner of notes and gifts to the lady, despite her having discouraged and refused him. I am sure Dr. Bennett has told you he and Miss Fielding are betrothed. I believe this news may have sent Mr. Lambe over the edge."

Constable Wells turned to Thad.

"It is my understanding that you brought your pistols, Dr. Bennett. Thus, I believe it best for you to accompany me to Emu Plains. We will start our search at North Pennant and follow the shore of the Nepean River. You will keep your pistols sheathed until I call for them. Understood?"

Thad nodded, a bit irked to be ordered about by Martin Wells, a drinker and laggard who happened to wear a badge of authority.

"As it is now past noon, we should not expect to reach Emu Plains by dark," Wells continued. "Thus, we will need to camp for the night. Are you prepared for that, Dr. Bennett?"

Thad hesitated, but John Macarthur stepped forward, tottering on his cane and wearing a ragged robe and slippers.

"Elizabeth, fetch camping gear for Dr. Bennett and Father Mayhew!"

He turned to Thad and Martin Wells.

"You may need a few extra men. My sons, James and William are both good guns. It is imperative you have cover if you head into Antony's property. He is a crack shot."

Martin Wells nodded. The Macarthur boys went to fetch their camp gear and guns.

"I will come too," Elizabeth said rather flatly. "Antony will listen to me."

The horses thundered over the dry, compact earth separating Elizabeth Farm from Emu Plains. Elizabeth Macarthur had said she knew approximately where Lambe's cabin was located, but when the group arrived at the Nepean River ahead of schedule, she was unsure which direction to ride.

As it was still daylight, they searched the east side of the river, finding nothing but many cube-shaped turds scattered about the ground. Wombats had burrows there, conveniently located along the river. Their droppings were curiously geometric, as if produced by machine.

Finally, in the descending darkness, the weary posse picked a campsite. The Macarthurs bedded down near one another, while Constable Wells found a spot off to himself. Gregory, who had not slept on the ground in years, made sure no wombat shit lay on his chosen spot. He eased his saddle-sore body onto the dirt under a tree next to Thad.

"My friend," Thad began. "I do not want you injured if there is a fray tomorrow morning. The illness that plagues your joints and hands in such a grievous manner prevents you from fighting. Please, promise me you will stand off if violence begins. I can hold my own."

Gregory chuckled. Thad put an extra blanket over him, knowing the cold night ahead would likely cause the priest much pain.

"I cannot fight despite wanting to, Thad. My hands are stiff and shaky from holding reins, and my legs may be permanently bowed by the saddle so that I forever walk with a drover's waddle. I am grateful to God that I did not fall off my horse today."

He laughed and threw up his arms, exasperated.

"Nor can I see well anymore, Thad. I have not told you, but my hands and arms and legs have begun to tremor more of late. My vision grows poor as well. Whatever assaults my body seems to grow worse."

Thad asked for more details, but Gregory feigned the need for sleep.

"Let us speak of these things at a later time, Thad. I am exhausted tonight."

Thad laid back and listened to his friend fall off to sleep with quirky snorts and gurgles. He felt helpless as a doctor, unable to diagnose Gregory's troubles. It had begun much like rheumatism, or so Thad thought. Gregory had told him about the spells of dizziness and the occasional problems with sight. Now, the priest had revealed more, speaking of worsening tremors.

Thad resolved to research the symptoms again once he was back home and Ella was safely at his side. He tried to fall asleep, but thoughts of Ella being held captive, perhaps being hurt or violated, filled him with enormous fear and anger. He hoped he could hold back from beating the life out of Antony Lambe.

Ella awoke with a terrible pounding in her head. She tried to reach for her forehead but could not. Upon further examination, she realized she was tied to a bedstead by her hands. As her vision began to clear, she saw a man sitting by the bed. He was drinking coffee. She could smell the pleasant aroma of the ground beans.

"Wh…where am I? Who are you and why am I tied up?"

"Ah, sweet Ella, you do not recall our midnight ride from Acacia House to my house last night? Despite your stupor, you clung to me like a new bride!"

Antony. Antony Lambe. She recognized his smarmy voice.

His hand reached out and touched her cheek. His fingers traced a line down to her neck and then her chest, where he fondled her bare breasts.

"Do not trouble yourself, Ella. The vicar from Parramatta is on his way. He will join us in marriage, and then I will cast away your dull doctor in a duel, the wealthy Dr. Bennett. He will have no say over you, as you will be mine."

It all came back to Ella, the months of Antony's annoying kindnesses, his gifts, his crafty notes and letters promising marital paradise, if only Ella would run away with him. Now, he had lost patience and kidnapped her.

Of course, Thad and Gregory and all the men of Acacia House were on their way, but to where? Where was she?

She turned her head to the window on the opposite side of the room. Outside was only the thick eucalypt forest of New South Wales' natural landscape, a tangle of dense limbs, assorted marsupials, and venomous snakes. How would anyone find her?

Surely, the Macarthurs knew where she was, where this cabin lay on their vast properties. Someone had to be coming.

"Antony, do you not think this a stupid way to gain a wife? To kidnap me in the night, take me to your cabin, and tie me up? What have you done with my clothes?"

He laughed.

"Such extreme measures would have been unnecessary had you come willingly, my love. I shall credit woman's ignorance for your mistake. The feminine sex often lacks sense."

Ella was infuriated, but she knew better than to argue with Antony, not as she was now, tied to his bed naked and helpless, her whereabouts unknown.

"Do not worry your pretty head, Ella. Vicar Samuel Marsden is on his way from St. John's Church in Parramatta. I sent him a note last evening asking that he come this morning and marry us. And I paid him handsomely for his services. As you know, he is the Parramatta magistrate, as well as the priest. He will not want a sullied woman like yourself left unwed."

Ella's face contorted in a commingled expression of shock and anger.

"I am not sullied, Antony Lambe! How dare you claim such a falsehood??!!"

I am not, am I, she wondered with second thoughts. It…the marriage act…could have already happened, but how would she know?

Antony grinned, stroking her sun-kissed tresses.

"You have lain asleep over a day now, Ella. Can you account for what has happened to you in that time? Might we have consummated our love by now?"

Within minutes, hoofbeats sounded outside. Zeus whinnied a warning from his paddock. Antony rose with a smile, seeing Vicar Marsden and a companion arriving on horseback. He turned to Ella and began untying her from the bedposts.

"My darling Ella, you will behave yourself now and marry me, else your silly Dr. Bennett will suffer and die. I have set a trap for him at Acacia House and will order it armed if you do not cooperate. Stand beside me woman, when Marsden enters, and say your vows."

He threw a dress at her. It was unfamiliar, checkered, not hers.

How had Antony armed a trap for Thad? He must have found friends at Acacia House to help him. And what sort of trap was it?

Antony stepped outside and welcomed the vicar and the assistant. Ella could hear them talking as she put on the dress Antony had given her. The three men stepped inside the cabin. The vicar admired Ella's pretty, blue and white checkered dress and her thick hair tumbling over her shoulders.

"Good morning, Miss Fielding! I am pleased to make your acquaintance," the vicar said brightly. "And I am happier still to be told you desire to join in wedlock with this fine man."

Ella winced. But in that moment, Antony reached in a pocket and took out a marriage license, the three-day type that was often used when a couple had to marry in a hurry. He handed the license to the vicar.

"I regret that some of my amorous actions have sullied Miss Fielding. She, too, has sinned and is ruined. Thus, we wish to be married immediately."

Ella opened her mouth to protest, but Antony squeezed her arm painfully. Vicar Marsden studied the license, then looked at Ella.

"Do not despair, my child. God understands these things so long as the offending couple marries at the earliest convenience. Mr. Williams from Parramatta is here to serve as a witness."

Marsden called to Williams to bring his Bible.

"The service will be quick, as I believe rain is due shortly. I need to return to Parramatta promptly."

Ella, still anchored beside Antony in disbelief, was yanked forward. Vicar Marsden immediately began the service for the sacrament of marriage. She heard the words enter her ears as if in a dream. She had not completely recovered from whatever sleeping elixir Antony had given her.

Did she take Antony as her beloved husband, in sickness and in health…

"I…I…uh…"

Antony squeezed one of her buttocks painfully, pinching the softest part.

"Say it," he whispered into her hair, "or Bennett will suffer a most painful death."

"Oh…I…I…yes. I do," Ella stammered.

Antony said his vows quickly. A ring appeared. Antony placed a beautiful gold band on Ella's marriage finger. She was shaking. Her eyes filled with tears—

"I fear my bride is nervous, Vicar Marsden. Perhaps you will finish quickly. Rain clouds loom nearer."

Marsden glanced out the door, then quickly pronounced Antony and Ella, "man and wife."

"I wish you both much happiness. Mr. Williams will sign as your witness," he said as he rushed out the door to his horse. "I look forward to seeing you both in church on Sunday. Your new husband is most loyal about church attendance, Mrs. Lambe."

Mrs. Lambe? Ella began shivering uncontrollably.

It had all happened so fast! Like a nightmare. Was she having a bad dream?

Antony slammed the door shut and bolted it with a slab of wood. He turned slowly to face Ella, removing his suit jacket.

"You are mine, Ella Fielding, all mine. Take off that dress and lie down on the bed. We will now begin our life as husband and wife."

Eight

A dusky light appeared on the eastern horizon. Thad lay awake waiting for dawn. He had not slept the entire night for thinking of Ella and the terrible experience she must be having. If Antony Lambe had so much as harmed a hair on dear Ella's head, Thad was certain he would kill him. The man was an animal.

The camp finally roused as the sun's uppermost arc appeared in the east. It was a beautiful sunrise, but no one noticed. The group was intent on finding Lambe's cabin and rescuing Ella. Not one of them doubted Antony Lambe was her abductor.

"Lambe is mad for Ella Fielding, Mother," James Macarthur said quietly to Elizabeth Macarthur as the group-turned-posse headed out on their horses, this time to find a place to ford the Nepean River. "He told us she is meant to be his wife, and he would see that it happens."

Elizabeth gave James an angry look.

"Did you know of this too, William?" she asked her younger son.

William nodded and tried to steer his horse away from his mother's.

"Well, the both of you should be punished for not saying anything. Dr. Bennett is not one to be trifled with. I am certain he will kill Antony if given the chance, and by law he has every right to. He is betrothed to the woman. You must keep quiet about your knowledge of Antony's extreme desire for Ella Fielding, else Bennett may call you to duel."

Toward mid-morning, the group crossed the Nepean at Emu Ford and headed south along the river's west shore. Young William Macarthur had confided to his mother that he had been to Lambe's cabin and knew where it was. Elizabeth Macarthur, protecting her sons, announced to the group that the location of the cabin had come to her in the night. She took the lead and led the group to the narrow, weedy track that accessed Lambe's cabin.

On the way, they crossed paths with Vicar Marsden and his assistant, Mr. Williams. It had begun to rain by then, and the vicar was in no mood to dally. He quickly told Elizabeth that he had been to visit Antony to perform a wedding and then hurried on his way. She wisely did not share this news with the constable or Thad or Gregory.

"The fool has married Ella Fielding!" Elizabeth quietly hissed to her sons. "There will be a shootout at the cabin, I am sure. Stay out of it. Let Bennett do the damage as the constable looks on. We will swear we had no knowledge of any of it."

As the group arrived at Lambe's cabin, everyone heard a scream. Thad knew immediately it was Ella. He leaped off his horse, pulling out his pistols.

"Stand off, Dr. Bennett!" yelled the constable. "I will handle this. Think before you act, man."

Thad reluctantly lowered his pistols. Gregory was suddenly at his side.

"Thad, let the constable deal with Lambe. Please."

Constable Wells knocked hard on the cabin door. The screams continued, causing Thad to shake with fury. What was happening to Ella?

"Antony Lambe, show yourself, or I shall be forced to break down this door and come inside shooting," Wells yelled.

Seconds passed, perhaps a minute. The constable stepped back, ready to crash through the door, when it opened, and Antony Lambe appeared. He wore only his breeches, one side of the placket buttons undone. His chest was bare, and it had several scratches and teeth marks. He stepped outside and crossed his arms defiantly.

"Antony Lambe," Wells growled, "I am here to collect Miss Ella Fielding. If you have harmed her, you will suffer the consequences."

Lambe's laugh began as a chuckle and then grew into a full-blown belly laugh.

"Harmed her? Why, she is my wife. Why would I harm her, and what business is it of yours, constable? A man may do with his wife as he pleases."

Thad started toward the door, only to be repelled by Constable Wells' outstretched arm.

Antony pretended to dust off his arms and chest, as if to clean away any evidence of Ella's fingernails and teeth. He stepped outside and turned his eyes to Thad, wearing an amused expression.

"She is a wild one, doctor, a she-cat who likes to scratch and bite. A woman on fire…"

Thad growled: "If you have touched her, Lambe…"

"Miss Fielding?" called the constable. "Are you unharmed?"

A faint reply came from inside the cabin—

"I am naked and tied up, Sir," she answered. "Antony Lambe forced me to marry him against my will!"

Thad pushed the constable aside and rushed into the cabin. Ella lay bare on the bed, only a small blanket covering her femininity. Her hands were tied to the bed. She struggled against the ropes the moment she saw Thad.

"Oh God! Thad, I thought you might not come in time. He forced me to marry him not an hour ago and has tried repeatedly to force himself upon me. I fought him off, Thad, but I am exhausted…and frightened. Oh, please take me home!"

Thad quickly untied Ella's hands and hugged her. He tossed her a dress that lay on the floor, then turned and went to the door.

"I will kill the son-of-a-bitch!" he yelled.

Gregory was quick to step in front of the affronted Antony.

"I care nothing for you, filthy beast," the vicar said to Antony. "But I will not see my friend go to prison for killing you."

Constable Wells grabbed Thad's pistols and shoved him away from the doorway.

"Antony Lambe" said the constable, "you are under arrest for the kidnapping and violation of Ella Fielding, the betrothed of Dr. Thad Bennett."

Wells approached Lambe, brandishing handcuffs, but Lambe stepped back.

"You cannot arrest me, you poor fucking excuse for a lawman! Ella Fielding is my wife. A man cannot be arrested for kidnapping his wife."

Wells shook his head in confusion.

"She was not your wife when you kidnapped her, Lambe. And kidnapping is a crime, wife or not."

Wells motioned to the Macarthur boys to grab Lambe. They tried, pulling him away from the constable, but Lambe easily fought himself free. He quickly proved himself a capable fist-fighter, putting both Macarthur boys on the ground and turning on Wells. The two exchanged punches. Wells went down, clutching his jaw.

"He is a trained pugilist," James Macarthur whispered to his mother after he was upright. "He could easily kill a man with his fists."

Lambe was now seething with anger. He turned to Thad.

"Dr. Bennett, you sorry excuse for a man, it is your turn. Fight me if you believe she is yours."

Lambe was heaving air, his fists tight. He went at Thad in a rush and punched the doctor's face hard. Thad went down, grabbing his bloody nose and mouth.

"Get up, you lousy bastard! Fight like a man!"

Thad got to his feet, blood running down his chin and neck, and took a hard swing at Antony. His fist connected with Antony's jaw, but the blow hardly fazed the man. Lambe was running on adrenalin. Before Thad could recover, another punch landed square in his gut. He doubled over and fell to the ground.

"Just as I thought," Antony said, gasping. "No competence at fighting. A pathetic, powerless fool. Is this what you want, Mrs. Lambe?"

Antony turned to the doorway. Ella stood on the sill dressed and holding his Baker flintlock rifle. It was aimed directly at Antony.

"I am not and will never be Mrs. Lambe," she uttered low in her throat. "You will never have me. I belong to Thad."

"Miss Fielding, no!" yelled Constable Wells.

But Ella had raised the rifle sight to her right eye. As Wells lunged to grab the rifle, she fired, hitting Antony in his neck. It was a clean shot to the left carotid artery. Antony fell to the ground, blood pumping out his neck with each remaining heartbeat, like a small fountain.

"Ella, I love…" were his last words.

Thad got to his feet and looked, first at Antony on the ground, then at Ella, the rifle still pointed at Lambe.

He walked to her and gently took the rifle. He put his arm around her.

"You saved my life, darling. I would have fought to the death for you."

Constable Wells went to Lambe and checked for a pulse. It was barely perceptible, then it was gone. The man was dead. Wells turned to Thad.

"Are you alright, Sir?"

Thad nodded and motioned to Ella.

"Yes. My betrothed saved me."

Ella burst into tears.

Gregory went to Antony, crossed himself, and spoke some words over the man's dead body. Then he turned to the constable.

"Constable Wells, Miss Fielding had every right to shoot this fiend of a man. Lambe kidnapped her, and who knows what else he did? The man was an animal with no self-control. The women in our household at Acacia House can tell you that. He tried to rape several of them. The Bidjigal and Wangals complained about him taking their women."

Wells nodded his head and threw a horse blanket over Lambe's dead body. He turned to the Macarthur boys.

"You both knew him well. Were you aware of this kind of criminal conduct?"

Both boys meekly denied any knowledge of Lambe's behavior. Their mother looked at Wells and shrugged.

"I had no idea either," she added. "You can never really know a person, Constable."

Wells dusted off his clothes and retrieved his rifle before walking to Ella. He put a hand on her shoulder and patted softly.

"Miss Fielding, I did not know about this side of Antony Lambe, the animal in him. I am disappointed in myself for not recognizing this sooner."

Wells swabbed beads of sweat from his forehead and sighed.

"I believe you have suffered enough disgrace and humiliation already…abducted, forced to marry Lambe against your will, and then abused by him. I will not ask for the details, nor will I bring charges against you. I believe you have undergone enormous pain and grief at Lambe's hands. His death will be recorded as an accident."

Ella dropped her head in relief.

"I am so sorry, sweetheart," Thad whispered to Ella. "If only I knew what madness he intended, I could have stopped him. You are such a brave woman, a strong woman."

Constable Wells fetched Zeus, unhobbled and bridled him, and led him to where Antony lay. He instructed the Macarthur boys to haul Antony onto Zeus and cover his dead body.

He turned to Thad and Ella.

"You can take Miss Fielding home now, Dr. Bennett. I will be up to Acacia House tomorrow to take a statement from you both, nothing detailed of course. Procedural doings."

Thad mounted his old horse, Wanuywa, and pulled Ella up in front of him, cradling her like a child. He tipped his hat to the constable and the Macarthurs. Ella pulled a handkerchief from his waistcoat and wiped his bloody nose. He, Ella, and Gregory rode off at a slow pace, back to Acacia House.

Despite all that had happened, Ella was keen to wait a few months for her marriage to Thad. His nose was healing slowly, and his blackened eyes too. Ella knew he would not want to stand in front of the church to be married with such a bruised face.

"I am ashamed I could not fight him more ably, Ella. He was a brute," Thad confessed.

"Dearest Thad, you are a doctor, and a bloody good one! You were never meant to be a fighter."

"But I swore to protect you, Ella…"

"Darling, please, let us speak of this no more. Antony is dead. We are together and to be married. I wish to forget what has happened."

Unfortunately, Ella's terrifying experience at the hands of Antony Lambe, and the lingering pain over the death of Henry, had left her with a dreadful case of melancholia. About a week after Thad brought her home from the cabin at Emu Plains, she took to her bed in a state of terrible misery. She ate little and cried incessantly. She could not sleep, yet would not leave her bedchamber. And when she did sleep, dreadful nightmares tormented her.

Thad was at a loss for what to do. In fact, the entire household felt helpless.

Gregory, however, had seen this sort of illness of the heart. His older sister, Sandrine, had fallen ill this way after the death of their father. She had been bedridden for months.

"Ella has suffered a mental breakdown, Thad," the priest said. "Her kidnapping and the shooting of Antony Lambe has so overwhelmed her she is unable to function day-to-day...for now. I suspect she will heal, but it may take time, perhaps months. Women are much more susceptible to emotional trauma than men. Perhaps it is from the manner in which they are raised, to be delicate, to behave as the weaker sex."

Thad felt mental trauma as well, but he feared expressing it. Men of his pedigree were stoic. He took walks and talked to himself to ease his sadness. He had nearly lost Ella, and now she was in a dreadful slump.

He read everything he could find about melancholia. He knew it affected some people for much of their life, but in Ella's case it seemed to be an accrual of difficult and painful experiences. A colleague, Dr. Herbert Manning of Strathfield, who was older and more familiar with the malady, advised Thad to be patient—

"I have seen this mostly in highly intelligent and extremely sensitive patients. Their minds seem more prone to sickness, perhaps because they are such profound thinkers with easily distressed moods. She will likely work this out on her own, but in the meantime, your household should be cheerful and encouraging, and you must be gentle, caring, and reassuring. Show her all the love you possibly can. Yet, be aware that sometimes love is not enough. She may fall deeper into sadness, even hopelessness. In such a case, she may try to take her own life."

Take her own life! Thad could not bear to think of such an outcome. The moment he returned from the consultation with Dr. Manning, he ran to Ella's chamber and pulled her into his embrace—

"You are my everything, Ella Fielding, my soulmate, my rock, my reason for living. You must fight this affliction and return to me. We are to be married, my love. We will have children! So much joy lies before us. Reach for it, my darling."

Gregory began giving short little uplifting sermons by Ella's bedside. She loved these, as Gregory was a master storyteller and adept at finding tales that fit her daily concerns.

When Ella confessed that her mind was reeling and would not stop bringing up images of sad and traumatic events, Gregory told her about his time in France at Chartres Cathedral when he had to walk the labyrinth as punishment for a sin.

"I had told one of the other priests about my experience as an impoverished youth, robbing my local church kitchen in Auxerre to survive. It was pilfer food or starve! Unfortunately, my story was overheard by a bishop. He forgave me, but when I told him the theft played over and over in my head, that it would not stop, he assigned me to walk the circular labyrinth outside the cathedral for hours, until the sin expunged itself from my heart."

"But I cannot go to Chartres and walk in circles, Gregory," Ella said.

He took her small hand and kissed the tips of her fingers.

"You must do it in your mind, dear Ella. I will describe the labyrinth for you so that you may picture it and put yourself in the picture. You must visualize walking 'round and 'round. The dreadful images in your brain will soon disappear, replaced by your footsteps."

To Ella's surprise, walking the imagined labyrinth made her feel better, but it did not eliminate all her anxiety. Day after day, the sad scenes of loss and pain replayed in her head—finding sweet Warrigal dead, being unable to save Henry, the kidnapping and shootout at Antony's cabin, plus the enormous change she had undergone coming to live in Australia.

When Ella seemed unable to stop crying, Gregory told her about a curious object his mother had owned.

"It was many years ago when I was barely twelve. My father died suddenly from paralysis of his heart. Mother and Sandrine were grief-stricken. They cried day after day, and my brother and I could do nothing to mend their hearts. A friend brought my mother a Lachrymal Bottle and told her to capture some of her tears of grief in it and seal it up. She did so and put the bottle on a windowsill in the sun. Her friend said when the tears inside the bottle dried up, she would stop grieving."

Ella sat up in her bed and looked at Gregory.

"Did it work?"

"Yes, I believe it did. I suppose my mother needed a trinket to convince her the time for grief had ended."

He helped Ella lie back down on her pillows. He refrained from telling her his poor sister, Sandrine, continued to suffer for many months.

"But you, sweet Ella, are too clever for such a ruse as a Lachrymal bottle to work. For you, I can only recommend a handkerchief."

He grinned mischievously and bid her good night.

Winter came on, and the short periods of daylight increased Ella's sadness. She was sure there was nothing so dark and unsettling as an Australian night. She confided to Thad that night was the worst time for a despondent person. It magnified fears. She could not fall asleep or remain asleep without candles glowing.

Thad began bringing Ella's little moggie, Hestia, into her room and sitting with her each night until she fell asleep. Hestia's rubs and purrs seemed to ease Ella's torment. Just petting the cat's velvety fur was soothing. Hestia embodied all that was happy and loving. Somehow, the feline knew her mistress was hurting and curled against her each evening for company in the darkness.

"I know she was gifted to me by someone I despised, Thad, but I love her so much. She is the only good thing to come from his hand."

Many nights Ella lay stroking Hestia while Gregory told stories, or Thad read to her. Time passed almost unnoticed by Ella until the days began growing longer. Her spirits slowly lifted, knowing spring was soon to arrive. There would be less darkness.

One morning Thad rushed northeast to Cowan Creek to help a Walkaloa man. A British farmer working the land at Broken Bay, the estuary of the Hawkesbury River, had accused the Aboriginal man of stealing a hoe. As punishment, the farmer cut off one of the man's hands.

When Thad told Ella where he was going and why, she buried her face in her pillow. The atrocities inflicted on the Aboriginals turned her stomach and broke her heart. She swallowed back vomit.

"Oh, Thad, I am in such a bleak place, and now this. How could anyone do such a thing?"

Thad held her, kissing her hair and one ear.

"Perhaps I should not have told you about this…but you are my nurse, soon to be my wife. We must tell each other everything. It burdens my heart too."

He held her close and kissed her forehead.

"I do my best to fight the inequality and crimes against the native people, Ella. I am but one man though, a man ashamed of my neighbors who commit these wrongs. Let us pray the future of Australia will be better for all of us, black and white."

He held her until she stopped crying.

"Perhaps I will bring the Aboriginal man here, let him heal where he will be treated kindly. We can find work for him."

The third week of September arrived, warm and promising. It was Sunday, and Ella was staring from her bed at the curtains in her chamber, soothingly undulating in the breeze. She could hear the congregation of the church singing—

> *How free the fountain flows,*
>   *Of endless life and joy;*
> *That spring which no confinement knows,*
>   *Whose waters never cloy.*

She sensed a ray of hope. Was she beginning to feel like herself?

An hour later, a knock came at her door, and she invited in the caller. It was Thad with a vase full of red and yellow flowers and one centered purple bloom.

"Spring has arrived, my darling! The acacia and waratah are early to bloom. I even tiptoed into Mrs. Hughes' garden and plucked a sprig of Happy Wanderer."

Ella buried her nose in the vase and wafted the subtle perfume of the acacia. It reminded her of the day she had arrived at Acacia House and why she had come to Australia—to work as a nurse and teacher in a place that desperately needed her compassion and skills.

And here she was lying abed, sobbing and feeling sorry for herself.

"Thank you, dearest husband-to-be. Perhaps all this color and the warmth of the days will rouse me from my stupor."

Thad kissed her forehead: "I am patient, my sweet. I know little about emotional illness, but I feel sure you will recover. My books advise me to let you rest, cheer you as much as possible, and assure you of my love."

He pressed his lips against hers and held her in a long kiss, a kiss infused with passion for the woman he adored. It made a tiny fire in her belly ignite.

After Thad went downstairs, Ella got out of bed and rang for Emily.

"Please fill my tub with bathwater and help me wash my hair. I have work to do and a wedding to plan."

Thad needed her…Gregory and the children too.

Emily clapped her hands with excitement.

"You be feeling better, me Lady?"

Ella grinned and began looking through her wardrobe for a dinner dress.

"I am done with this bed, Emily, and done with being sick of heart. It has been months that I have malingered in this room, thinking myself unable to face my hardships. Truly, I am thankful for my life here and the people who make it wonderful, especially my dear husband-to-be. Help me bathe, dress, and do my hair. I intend to surprise Dr. Bennett and Father Gregory with my appearance at dinner."

Thad and Gregory were speechless when Ella appeared in the dining room that evening. She wore a soft pink gown overlaid with a layer of sheer white tulle. Tiny pink flowers were embroidered on the edges of the bodice, the sash, and the hem. Their centers were seed pearls. She wore her jeweled brooch too, to remind Thad of her love for him.

But loveliest of all was her hair, twisted into a croissant-shaped chignon of burnished blonde. A stem of beribboned acacia flowers from Thad's morning bouquet was pushed into it.

"My darling Ella!" Thad gasped, unable to believe her transition from ill health to extraordinary beauty. Had she not been too ill to eat or rise from her bed just yesterday?

He rose from his chair and went to her, placing a kiss on her forehead. Carefully, he took her hand and led her to the dining chair beside his. She thanked him and let her gaze fall on the sundry dishes on the table. Everything smelled delicious. Gregory smiled at her knowingly.

"We are both so delighted to see you at dinner," Thad said. "Might you like some soup, my love. Your stomach must yet be queasy."

"Or warm milk and toasts," Gregory put in.

Ella smiled at both attentive men, then pointed to a bowl of creamed rice.

"I believe I can begin with the rice."

The rice was dished up by Gregory, and Ella began eating small spoonfuls.

"Oh, I did not realize how hungry I am," she admitted. "Perhaps I may also have some mushy yams…and those toasts you mentioned, dear Father Gregory!"

Thad filled her plate but cautioned her to have small portions.

"We should start modestly, my dear." He followed this advice with a kiss on her cheek that trailed across her face and down to her neck.

Gregory, seeing that the couple might fare better without him, gathered his plate and utensils.

"It seems a little hot in here," he said, grinning. "I shall take my meal to the cool rectory and leave the two of you to eat and converse."

Thad rose and went to open the outside door for Gregory, whispering a "thank you, friend."

Back at the table, Thad asked Ella's indulgence of the interruption and sat down next to her. They ate quietly for a few minutes before Thad softly asked:

"Might I know what caused your sudden recovery, darling?"

Ella laid down her spoon and dabbed at her mouth with her serviette. She turned to Thad and smiled. Her left hand slid gently onto his right thigh. Immediately, he wrapped his right hand around it.

"It was your kiss and the bouquet, sweet husband-to-be. I saw the acacia flowers and remembered why I came here. I am to be your assistant...and soon your wife. I have a wonderful life ahead with you."

He squeezed her hand and leaned close, placing a tiny, soft kiss on the tip of her nose.

"I love you so much, Ella. Acacia House would be lackluster without you. Your beauty and charm fill it with joy for everyone."

After dinner, Thad fetched a warm shawl and blanket for Ella. They settled side-by-side on the front porch swing. The blanket was placed over Ella's legs and the shawl was snuggled about her shoulders. She was thrilled to be outdoors. The scents of the flowers and the farm came to her and exhumed good memories of her time in Wahroonga. The front porch was one of her favorite places.

"Thad, I have been thinking that we should call this place Acacia Farm...all of it. You have built far more than a house here."

Thad looked around him and then down at his beloved, smiling. He pressed her to him and kissed her hair.

"I very much like that idea, my sweet. We can move the Acacia House sign closer to the house and put an Acacia Farm sign at the end of the long driveway. I hope you will allow me to keep my doctor-chemist sign in place."

Ella giggled and laid her head on Thad's shoulder.

"Of course. Your medical sign must stay where it is. But I might ask one of the men to repaint it. Would you like a caduceus put under your name?"

Thad thought for a moment.

"I doubt any of our patients will know the meaning behind it. But I would like your name to go on it—Ella Bennett, Nurse."

Bennett? Ella giggled even more.

"Well, then, we had better get married soon. I am still Ella Fielding, you know!"

Nine

The organ suddenly swelled in volume, and everyone stood up and turned their eyes to the back of the church...

Thad felt a shiver course through his body as he looked down the center aisle of the church and saw Ella slowly walking toward him. She was enchanting, a confection dressed in pale lavender silk-organza with a darker lavender bobbinet over her bodice. The brooch he had given her shone at her cleavage, and she held a bouquet of moonlight Grevilleas, cascading Australian roses, and one large pink spider flower in the center. She wore a crown of native and garden flowers in her hair with a silk train attached behind it.

Mabarra was singing from the choir loft, "Abide with Me." The orphans behind her were humming along and smiling to see their beloved nurse and teacher well and happy and marrying their favorite doctor.

Gregory shakily held the book containing the Sacrament of Marriage. His eyes were misty as Ella arrived at the altar. He had come to love her dearly and thought her the perfect wife for his best friend. She turned to Thad and smiled, her eyes fixed on his. Gregory leaned forward and whispered with levity—

"It is about time you were married!"

Though it was still spring, the late November day was unseasonably hot. Attendees in the pews were using the paper wedding announcements to fan themselves. Beads of sweat shone on Father Gregory's face.

The orphans sang "O Heaven, See before You Two Hearts" for the bride and groom and then cheered their own performance. The Bidjigal attendees followed with a tribal wedding song, complete with clacking sticks, jumps, and loud calls. Mabarra, who also was serving as a witness, stood off to the side ready to take the bride's bouquet.

For Ella, the service passed in a blur. Thad was so handsome, happy, and gentle when he took her hands to say his vows and place the ring on her marriage finger. Somehow, she managed to get through her vows and place his ring. Had she not done this very service only a few months prior...with Antony...and almost immediately become a widow at her own hands? The thought sent a shiver down her spine. She pushed it from her mind.

Suddenly, Bidjigal drums pounded and the organ, played by an inept but willing Mrs. Hughes, roared to life. The wedding ceremony was complete. Thad kissed Ella tenderly, lifted her into his arms, and headed for the back of the church. The congregation cheered and followed, anxious that the newlyweds not escape before congratulations could be offered.

A shower of flower petals—a tradition dating back to Ancient Rome—settled on the couple. Thad shook hands with the men and kisses were placed on Ella's cheeks. Elizabeth Macarthur stepped up to Ella and gave her a kiss. She was smiling as if she knew a secret.

"I am so glad to see you happy now and wed to the handsomest, kindest man in New South Wales. He will treat you as you deserve to be, I am sure. Love him as much as you can, dear. Have a joyful, prosperous life together."

Ella thanked Elizabeth and reminded her to come visit…in a few weeks, of course, after Ella and Thad had settled into married life.

As Mrs. Macarthur hugged Thad, Ella wondered if the woman had the stamina to make it through the wedding breakfast, which awaited on tables set up in the grassy field beside the church. Elizabeth Macarthur was heavy with perspiration and leaning on a cane to ease the painful rheumatism in her hips and knees. The morning had grown even hotter. Ella was counting the minutes until all the pomp ended, the guests departed, and she could be alone with her new husband.

Seats were taken at the tables, toasts were made, and plates were filled. Ella ate some of her meal, but her eyes kept turning to Thad. He looked happy beyond description. He had never asked her if Antony had hurt her, violated her. It mattered little now that the beastly man was dead. Thad was determined to love Ella as much as he could and make her happy.

It was well past noon when the wedding breakfast ended, and the many guests went home. Ella was on the verge of collapse. Her perceptive new husband sensed this and quickly lifted her into his arms and whisked her into the house and upstairs to his bedchamber. There was giggling and hooting among the staff, who all thought Thad could not wait another minute to make love to his lovely wife.

Instead, he was determined to make her comfortable, to ease the stress of the day. He laid her on his spacious bed, removed her dainty shoes, and loosened the sash on her dress.

"Rest for a while, Ella. I know it has been a difficult morning for you, what with the heat and all the clamor. You are still a bit melancholy, but I have a cure for that!"

His eyebrows bobbed up and down, and he grinned impishly at Ella. She grinned back, relishi8ng the thought.

"I'll get you a book. Dinner will be brought here to our room this evening, so there is no need for you to go downstairs."

Ella lay back in the soft bedding and smiled at Thad.

"Dearest husband, might you get this uncomfortable corset off me? I assure you the Spanish Inquisition could not have designed a more tortuous contraption!"

Thad chuckled and leaned down to kiss Ella.

"Shall I bring your night rail, and you may cast off all your wedding garb? I daresay you would be much more comfortable. I plan to do the same."

Within minutes, they lay beside each other comfortably dressed in only light, silk robes. The windows were open, admitting a light breeze. Thad pulled his new wife into his arms and kissed her deeply, rubbing his hands over her soft bottom. He peppered her face and neck with tiny kisses.

"Rest, my sweet. I know it has been an exhausting morning for you. We have all evening to share our love."

He yanked the bell pull, and minutes later Emily knocked softly. Thad went to the door and asked her to bring glasses of cool water and a bottle of claret. The girl was back in a flash with the requested items. She had even placed a tiny vase on the tray with two everlasting daisies, symbolizing the married couple.

Ella drank some sips of claret, and after a time, her eyelids grew heavy, and she fell asleep. Thad gently took her book, marked her place, and laid the novel on the night table. He wondered if she had noticed the portrait of Edith Fullerton was gone from over his bed, replaced by his vision of Ella.

Satisfied to simply be next to her, he nestled into her side and fell asleep.

Ella felt an arm around her and soft breath against her right ear. She turned toward it and caught the marvelous male fragrance of Thad—his shaving soap, the lightly-scented cologne he had worn to the wedding, and his natural male scent. Her husband. He was now her precious husband.

How long had she been asleep? It was dark outside the bedchamber windows, but a candelabra still burned in the chamber. Had she disappointed Thad on their wedding night with her exhaustion? Should she have been amorous?

She snuggled closer to him and placed a soft kiss on his lips. He moaned. She kissed him again, this time draping one of her long slender legs over his hip.

"Sweet husband, are you going to sleep away our wedding night?"

He raised his head dreamily and touched her bare leg. He realized she had wriggled out of her robe and was naked beside him.

"Ella, darling, you are…are exquisite, the most beautiful woman I have ever seen! God, but I am the luckiest man anywhere. I am so sorry I fell asleep."

"No, it was I who fell asleep. I am the one who needs to apologize."

Thad pulled her close, into a tight embrace.

"We were both so tired. The heat was oppressive, and the people…my hand is still numb from handshakes."

He rolled her onto her back and removed his robe. She gasped to see him completely naked, head to toe.

He, too, was beautiful. And he was hers, all hers, she thought.

His left arm went beneath her neck while he gently positioned her long hair in a fan-shape over the pillow. He paused to admire her before his fingers traced her cheeks, her nose, her mouth, her neck, and down her chest to one breast. He thumbed the nipple lightly. Ella drew in a breath at the sensation.

"Mrs. Bennett, you are absolutely the most enchanting woman I know. A goddess! From now on, you are my wife…mine alone. I shall cherish you and love you and give you as much happiness as I can."

"You already have," she whispered, her eyes glowing with a mischief he had never seen until now.

He kissed her lips over and over and then kissed her body worshipfully. She rubbed his back and his muscled arms, then allowed her hands to reach lower and stroke his buttocks. She could feel his male parts against her left thigh. He was fully aroused. His bare skin was hot.

He reached down and separated the folds between her legs, his fingers lingering to enjoy the wetness of her. He eased into her carefully, slowly. She gasped softly and clutched his arms as he took her virginity.

"I am so sorry to give you discomfort, sweet wife. I assure you this will be the only time."

"I know," she murmured. "Mrs. Hughes gave me a booklet about the wedding night. It was most informative."

She was grinning. Thad murmured his husky laugh and replied: "My father gave me a similar book when I was sixteen. It had diagrams."

The minutes that followed were a misty rush of kisses, pleasurable sensations, and his voice whispering his love for her. She responded with sighs and moans and pledges of her own.

"Thad, I love you with all my heart! I love you now and forever!"

"I adore you, my darling; I love you to the stars and…"

Suddenly, he grasped her tightly, buried his face in her neck, and groaned over and over. Though he sounded as if the worst pain had overtaken him, she knew he had found indescribable bliss in joining his body with hers. And she was inexpressibly happy. There was nothing she wanted more than to be with this extraordinary man for the rest of her life.

Breakfast was exceptional the following morning. Old Betty made special foods for the newlyweds and served them in pretty dishes with edible flower garnishes to celebrate the marriage of her master and his beloved. Ella ate until she could hold no more. Thad finished by rubbing his stomach in gratitude. He put one arm around Ella and kissed her sweetly over and over.

Polly, Thad's new dog, had been snoozing under the table. She stood up and placed her nose on his thigh, whining. She wondered at the sudden demonstrative affection between these two.

"Oh, Thad…she is jealous. You were all hers until I intruded. Did you not see her watching us in the bed chamber last night?"

Ella giggled. Thad scratched Polly's head and gave her a piece of egg.

"She will survive, darling. She knows how I feel about you."

To seal the deal, Ella reached for a slice of rasher and fed it to the dog. Polly wisely switched position, lying her head on Ella's thigh. The change made the couple laugh.

"Well, Polly," Thad said. "I see where your loyalty lies now!"

It was Ella's first day as Mrs. Thaddeus Bennett. She was blissful, dreamy, ecstatic beyond words. Rather than sitting across from Thad, she had taken the chair beside him.

"Sweetheart, I desire to whisk you away so that we might be alone together for a few days."

"I would love that, Thad. The wedding preparations were so hectic. It would be wonderful to share some quiet days together. Will it be a bridal tour?"

He smiled, nodding slowly.

"It will, my love, but I must warn you, bridal tour possibilities are slim in New South Wales. I am thinking you might wish a few days in Sydney at James Dempsey's new Lord Nelson Hotel. It is modern and perfect for newlyweds. We could make some day trips from there. I know you would like to see Dawes Point where the First Fleet's astronomer worked in the 1790s."

Dawes Point? Yes, she wanted to go there, if only to see the place where Elizabeth Macarthur claimed to have trysted with the handsome astronomer. It would also further whet her interest in the Southern Hemisphere's night sky, which she had already begun to study on her own.

"We will be assured of many hours of privacy at the hotel, my love," he whispered, "and I shall…"

Thad was unable to finish his sensual plans, for Gregory arrived, joking about the two lovebirds billing and cooing over each other at the breakfast table.

"Perhaps I should leave the two of you alone this morning. I can see your bridal tour already has begun!"

Ella giggled—

"We were just speaking of that. Thad has suggested a few days at the new Lord Nelson Hotel in Sydney. And he has offered to take me to see Dawes Point. How delightful, do you not think so Gregory?"

The cleric wore a light sweater, as the spring morning was much cooler than the morning before when Ella and Thad took their vows. Ella thought Gregory looked odd with a sweater pulled over his clerical robes. He was rubbing his hands together repeatedly and blinking his eyes.

"You might also enjoy a visit to the new lighthouse on South Head, Australia's first," Gregory added. "There is something truly symbolic about a lighthouse."

"Oh, Thad, I would love to see it!" Ella gasped, turning to her husband. "A lighthouse, how amazing, and how fortunate for Sydney."

Father Gregory attempted to speak but seemed unable. He looked down at his breakfast plate. Ella knew something was amiss with the priest. Had Elizabeth Macarthur not hinted there was? Gregory withdrew a handkerchief from one sleeve of his sweater. He had one very watery eye he needed to swab.

He tried to deflect Ella's interest in his ailing eye with a funny fact. Not thinking of her traumatic kidnapping by Antony Lambe earlier in the year, the always-comical priest proceeded to tell a joke about marriage.

"Ella, dear, did you know the bridal tour is a relic of the ancient practice of Bride Capture? 'Tis true! In olden times, if a man kidnapped his bride, he took her into hiding until she became pregnant, or until her relatives grew less angry with him. Gradually, the trip into hiding evolved into the expected and much-anticipated bridal tour."

Thad gave Gregory a dark look, while Ella stared at her plate of eggs. Gregory seemed confused for a few seconds before mildly convulsing, as if a shiver was coursing down his back, and uttering the beginning of an apology.

"Oh, oh my. I have done it. I have made a joke of a horrible situation. Ella, dear…"

His right hand and arm were tremoring. He closed his eyes to halt the mad attack of blinking. Ella made a mental note to ask Thad about the priest's ills as soon as they were alone.

"Ella, please forgive me," Gregory said, almost in a whisper. "I thought to make you laugh, but instead I have exhumed an unspeakable memory. I am so sorry."

Ella looked up and reached a hand across the table to him.

"Dearest Gregory, it *is* an unspeakable memory, yes, but it no longer hurts me. I have Thad now, and I am completely happy for the first time in my life."

Gregory's tremors eased as he held Ella's hand, and his blinking slowed. He smiled, glad to be forgiven. Still, Ella felt something strange in his grasp, a wicked suffering he did not deserve. Was there a dangerous undiscovered disease in Australia that afflicted his body?

The phaeton was loaded with luggage and a picnic basket and hitched to Wanyuwa and Axle. The hood was lifted to protect Thad and Ella from the intense Australian sun. The couple seated themselves close together under the hood—Thad in a three-piece lightweight suit and top hat, and Ella in a light green silk dress with yellow rosebuds and green leaves sewn around the hem and bodice. Her mother's pearls encircled her neck; the diamond and pearl brooch was pinned to her bodice. A dark green shawl lay over her shoulders, and a straw bonnet with yellow ribbon ties lay on the seat beside her.

Everyone at Acacia House, and even from the barns and fields, had turned out to see them off. As Ella waved farewell, Thad gently flicked the reins to tell the horses to get moving. Wanyuwa and Axle were not keen to be tasked with the bridal tour, though the children of the orphanage had polished their hooves, braided their manes and tails, and put flowers in their bridles. They moved forward slowly.

Thad turned to his new wife smiling and proud.

"I hope you do not mind a slow pace, darling. These two old boys are not apt to trot the entire way to Sydney. We have no reason to rush, do we?"

Ella hugged Thad's right arm.

"Of course not, sweet husband. I shall enjoy the scenery and the nice weather. Wanyuwa and Axle can take their time."

Polly barked and followed the Phaeton to the end of the driveway. She might have trotted all the way to Sydney with the couple had Mabarra not called her back to the house. Everyone at the newly named Acacia Farm shouted their congratulations to Thad and Ella and waved good-bye.

As the couple made progress toward Sydney, the conversation was light and happy. They made plans to rearrange their bedchamber at home, making it more comfortable for two people. Ella also wished to move her books to Thad's chamber and rearrange his bookshelves using a university method she had learned.

"I have them arranged according to fiction and nonfiction, all by author," Thad said.

"Are they alphabetized?" Ella asked.

Thad made a face.

"Well, they were in the beginning, when I first unpacked and shelved them. I suspect they are out of order now."

He put an arm around Ella and hugged her.

"Perhaps you can tidy up the shelves for us, darling. We are both such avid readers."

Ella talked about providing more equitable activities in the orphanage classroom so that girls could learn some traditionally male skills and the boys could learn some female skills. She thought they might begin with macramé, which seemed to her to be a non-gender handicraft.

"I learned it from a friend in England at the Montague in Bloomsbury. You will recall you were kind enough to rent me a room at the Montague until the *Isabella* sailed. My friend had been to the Middle East, and that is where she learned macramé. It is such a fun and lovely craft, somewhat like sailors' knots. But we will need lots of heavy cord. Perhaps I can find the right gauge in Sydney."

Thad leaned over and kissed her again.

"You may shop for anything you want in Sydney, my beauty. We are wealthy, you know. We can buy whatever we wish. I thought you might want to purchase some new shoes or fancy hats, some fashionable dresses, or even a few unmentionables."

He leaned close to whisper: "The corsets I have seen on you seem a bit worn. I should not like my wife's lovely breasts held up with raggedy corsets."

Ella was struck with a fit of giggling. She had never heard Thad talk so forthright about her body or her intimate apparel.

"Well then, I might take a peek at the new style of dresses," she tittered. "Mrs. Hughes' cousin told her in a recent letter that waistlines are coming down in England…at last! Coming down nearer to the natural waist. I do not like the Regency style with the skirt flouncing from just under the…the…breasts."

She giggled again, and Thad nodded, chuckling low in his throat.

"I must agree. In fact, I recall the pushed-up Regency style going to extremes shortly before I relocated from England to New South Wales. Women were putting rigid wooden shelves under their bosoms to hoist their breasts high. Rather ridiculous. I believe nature gave the bosom a wonderful shape and location on a woman's chest. There is no need to attempt to improve what is already perfect."

Ella stared at Thad a moment. He was smiling with all this talk of breasts.

"Darling, would you prefer I not wear a corset…just let everything fall where it will?"

He thought for a few seconds.

"Indeed, I would be happy if you wore no corset. Such an apparatus must be terribly uncomfortable to wear in the heat and what with all the squeezing and pushing it does. Unhealthful. Perhaps a light chemise would be better."

Ella smiled to herself. She would like nothing more than to liberate her body from the infernal corset.

"Alright then. I shall model a corseted and non-corseted Ella in our hotel room in Sydney. You may decide what looks better."

"What a fun idea, Mrs. Bennett! A bosomy fashion show from my favorite model!"

As they made their way through a small forest of blue gum trees, Ella marveled at some of the older, taller trees that had taken on peculiar shapes, almost as if they had many arms. Their bark appeared blue and tan under a season of peelings.

"I suppose those many branches provide resting places for koalas," Ella said.

Thad nodded: "You might see them asleep on the branches this time of day. They are more active at night."

As they moved deeper into the trees, Ella noticed marks on the trunks and asked Thad what they might be.

"Koala scratch marks, I suppose" he said, grinning. "They have sharp claws. If you look closely, you might also see a flying fox. Some of the branches have their spring flowers, a delicacy for the big bats."

Ella kept her eyes peeled, but no flying foxes or koalas were seen.

The track they followed was soft, almost wet, and meandered through the forest. The horses' hooves made mushy sounds on the bark and leaf litter.

"Where are we now, Thad?"

"Near Castle Hill, north of Parramatta. It is where our Bidjigal people originally lived. They were among the Aboriginals the First Fleet encountered when they arrived in 1788. Mabarra can tell you much about this place. Her mother lived here and knew Pemulway, the Bidjigal warrior hero. I should not utter his name; you know it is forbidden in Aboriginal tradition to say the names of the dead. But I do not know how else to explain his importance in Bidjigal history. He fought back against the intrusion of whites onto Aboriginal lands. He was easily identifiable by a blemish in his left eye."

Ella looked surprised: "That would have meant his death…for having a defect, would it not?"

"Fortunately for him, it did not. The clan considered him a shaman of sorts. Sadly, he was shot dead by a British soldier in June of 1802, and worse, his head was cut off and sent to England to Sir Joseph Banks, a novelty. You might recall from our history that Banks was a naturalist who sailed with Captain Cook. He convinced the British Parliament that New South Wales should be turned into a penal colony. Many plants, such as Banksia, and places, such as Bankstown, are named for him."

Ella made a face of disgust thinking of Pemulway's death. New South Wales certainly had a ghastly beginning, she thought. What sense did it make to send an Aboriginal head to England? And address it to Sir Joseph Banks, a man who spoke loudly against the abolition of slavery!

"We will drive the phaeton onto a river barge when we reach the Parramatta River and then glide down to Sydney with the river current," Thad told his new wife. "I thought you might enjoy that. Parramatta itself is a rather vulgar town. We will not get out of our carriage, but from the river you will see Rosehill where the Macarthurs live."

They arrived in Parramatta an hour later, just as Thad had said, and queued to board the next barge. As they waited, Thad watered and fed the horses and checked their hooves. Axle had seemed to limp as they arrived in Parramatta. After finding no issues with Axle's legs and feet, Thad decided the old horse was faking. Axle was certainly smart enough to do so.

Ella opened the lunch basket the Acacia House maids had packed and offered Thad some food and drink. It was a pleasant little picnic on the landing beside the river.

Thad talked about having received a copy of René Laënnec's brand new treatise called "On Mediate Auscultation."

"Laënnec is a French physician in Paris," he told Ella. "He invented our stethoscope and has been recording and analyzing the body sounds he hears with it. He is particularly interested in the heart and lungs. His treatise describes the sounds he has heard and what he thinks they mean."

Ella was fascinated—

"Might you allow me to listen to your heart and lungs as practice?" she asked.

He raised his eyebrows in question, then wiggled them up and down suggestively. Ella jabbed him playfully with an elbow.

"We can practice on all our staff, and even the horses, sheep, pigs, and goats. Hestia, Polly, and old Wibung too. We have no one to look after the animals should they become sick. We should learn more about them."

"You know, Thad, speaking of hearts and lungs, I have noticed Gregory is unwell. He has been shaking terribly, and his eyes often are watery and irritated. Please tell me about him. I *do* love him, you know, and I want to be able to help him."

Thad looked off down the river. The barge was coming. He thought for a few moments about how to explain Gregory's mysterious illness.

"Sweetheart, I wish I knew what afflicts Gregory. I have read countless books and articles regarding his symptoms and wracked my brain, even consulted with Dr. William Redfern in Sydney, who is much read on the shaking diseases. But I have found nothing definitive. All I can be sure of is that his ailment seems to be affecting his nervous system. That would explain the tremors and numbness in his hands, the vertigo, and the way he has taken to shuffling when he walks. Problems with his eyes? I cannot say what they might be."

Ella's face grew sad.

They were quiet now, watching the barge approaching. It landed, and passengers, buggies, and wagons began disembarking. The barge master wasted no time before reloading. Thad woke the horses from their equine slumbers and reined them toward the barge. Axle, ever the challenge, balked about boarding, then went cautiously as one of the barge workers led him to a safe spot and placed wooden chucks behind the front wheels of the phaeton.

"I am sorry, Ella, but there is no good news about Gregory. I believe his symptoms will continue to flare up from time to time, and he will slowly worsen and lose certain abilities. In fact, one of the errands I must do in Sydney is to meet with a furniture maker who fashions rolling chairs. I intend to buy one, though I am sure Gregory will say he does not need it. When the time comes, the carpenters at Acacia House can build ramps so that he may access the house for meals and visits and also the church and school. We will make as many adjustments as possible to help him feel comfortable."

It was difficult for Ella to imagine Gregory in a rolling chair. He had been so vigorous when she had first arrived at Acacia House. She smiled to herself thinking of the fun they'd had bathing the children and doing their wash and playing wild games with them. She remembered Gregory standing before the congregation every Sunday speaking his messages of love, kindness, and hope. He was no fire and brimstone preacher; rather, he spread the word of God inclusively and gently.

She would need to accustom herself to the infirmities that were about to assail the beloved priest. Thinking of it, she hugged Thad's right arm close to her side. Her eyes misted for a moment.

"Thad, he is not going to die soon, is he?"

Thad put both arms around her and hugged her, kissing the hair on top of her head.

"I do not believe so, darling. Some diseases infirm the body and perhaps weaken the mind, but not all of them cause an early death. Gregory is in no immediate danger of dying. I have kept a close eye on his vital signs, and they are all normal. His mind is as sharp as ever."

Ten

Ella was delighted when they disembarked from the barge in Iron Cove and turned the phaeton onto the lower Parramatta Road heading into Sydney. The route was winding and dusty, going from Balmain south around Blackwater Bay, then north past Darling Harbour toward The Rocks. Ella thought the buildings along the way were beautiful, all painted properly and adorned with pots of spring flowers. The city was headlong into gentrifying itself under the direction of Governor Lachlan Macquarie.

Thad narrated the drive as best he could, having visited Sydney on many occasions. They began to see Aboriginals fishing at Barangaroo, and ahead they glimpsed soldiers' barracks. Thad reined Wanyuwa and Axle along Kent Street. They passed the hilltop where Fort Phillip was located, named for the third governor of the colony, Phillip Gidney, and the hospital staffed by the Colonial Surgeons.

At the corner of Kent and Argyle streets stood the Regency-style Lord Nelson Hotel.

"Oh, Thad, it is wonderful. So new! I have never stayed at a hotel like this one."

The horses and phaeton were taken by hotel staff to the livery a half-block down Argyle Street. Thad proudly entered the hotel with Ella on his arm, porters behind them bringing their trunk. They received a warm welcome from the desk clerk who offered Ella a bouquet of flowers.

"We are pleased you chose the Lord Nelson Hotel for your bridal tour, my Lord and Lady. We shall do everything we can to make your stay comfortable."

As they climbed the stairs to their room, Ella whispered—

"Lord and Lady?"

Thad chuckled and hugged her around the waist.

"Have I not told you, Ella? I am a viscount. Dr. Thaddeus Michael Thurston Bennett, Third Viscount of Roselawn Manor, Northampton, England & Acacia Farm, New South Wales. Most of Sydney considers me a nobleman."

"Ah! Mrs. Macarthur mentioned this when she brought the sheep. She told me you are a viscount but that you do not really act like one."

Thad chuckled: "Elizabeth would say that!"

"Then I am an aristocratic woman?"

Thad smiled and nodded.

"Yes, in addition to being the world's most beautiful woman, you are an aristocrat. But mind you, Lady Ella, we are not condescending or snobbish. I refuse to behave like the arrogant lords of England. Part of my reason for coming to this colony was to escape the pompous elitism of my title. I despise an overbearing, showoff of an egotist."

"Indeed, you do," Ella replied, squeezing Thad's arm. "You are the kindest, most generous, and least self-aggrandizing man I know."

The bridal suite was elegant and luxurious. Ella was delighted the moment the door to the rooms opened. She threw her arms around Thad's neck after the porter had gone. They kissed tenderly before Thad invited Ella to have some of the champagne he had ordered for their room. He toasted their marriage.

"Mrs. Bennett, you are everything I dreamed of and more."

"And you, Dr. Bennett, are much more than I ever dreamed of for a husband."

Their glasses clinked together. Thad suggested they shed their traveling clothes and rest for an hour or so before dinner. But they never made it down to the supper room. Within minutes after their clothing was removed, they were in each other's arms.

After a hearty breakfast the next morning, Thad and Ella took a short walk to Dawes Point where Lieutenant William Dawes, a marine officer with England's First Fleet had set up his telescope and observed the southern hemisphere sky. Sydney had been but a small village back then, primitive and **unsophisticated.**

The point was a quiet spot beyond The Rocks on a ledge facing Sydney Harbour.[3] Thad escorted Ella to the place where Dawes had worked some two decades earlier. To Ella, it had seemed a holy place and Dawes a cosmic priest...that is until Elizabeth Macarthur confessed her affair with him. Now it seemed tarnished, dirtied. Had it really happened, or had Mrs. Macarthur been bragging?

Ella thought about the history she knew of the place—

---

[3] The place where Lieutenant Dawes camped is today situated where the Sydney Bridge is anchored on the west shore of the harbour.

Dawes Point was originally called *Tar-Ra* and was Eora Aboriginal land when the First Fleet arrived in 1788. As the eleven British ships slowly made their way along the twisting course into Sydney Cove, the Cadigal, Cammeraygal, Gadigal, Bidjigal, and other clans watched sailors climbing the rigging and thought them to be possums. The men with white faces and elaborate red and gold costumes appeared to be ancestral spirits. Dawes, who was surely at the rails on the HMS *Sirius*, would become one of the few trusted friends of the Aboriginals.

"He was a somewhat shy man and incredibly intelligent, educated, and refined," Thad told Ella. "His assignment as astronomer to the First Fleet was perfect for him. He was in his late twenties, and by the time the Fleet reached New South Wales, Dawes had established himself as a navigational expert, using the sun, moon, and stars to find the ship's position each day. He was also a gifted mapmaker and enormously organized, recording all manner of information in notebooks."

Ella studied the sandstone rocks of the point, backed by a stand of red gums and wispy casuarinas, which were sometimes called she-oaks by the British. The silken wind here, murmuring in the trees, seemed to carry memories.

Am I standing where his telescope sat…or he, himself, stood many times, Ella wondered. Or, where he and Elizabeth Macarthur lay together and fornicated? I sorely hope she lied about that.

"I read that he lived out here alone, except for the visits from the Aboriginals. Is that true?" she asked Thad.

"Yes. He built a small house, rather like an Aboriginal humpie, back in the protection of the trees. Alone? He was so busy with his observations and notebooks, he may not have felt lonesome. He affirmed many of the things we already knew about the austral sky and added more to our knowledge. He had friendships with the Gadigal, so mayhap he was not so lonely."

Could she find the nerve to tell Thad what Elizabeth had told her?

"Darling, you once told me we must tell each other everything."

"I did. Is something on your mind?"

Ella paused for a moment, looking out over the glorious harbour. Sunlight was shattered into thousands of shimmering pieces on its frothy surface.

"Well…it is a secret, Thad. You must promise to keep it just between us."

Thad chuckled: "I promise, darling. Now, what can be so serious as to be such a profound secret?"

"It is a secret I was told by Elizabeth Macarthur the day she brought the merino sheep. And it concerns Lieutenant Dawes."

Thad turned Ella to face him. He did a quick calculation and realized Elizabeth Macarthur was old enough to not only remember Lieutenant Dawes but possibly to have known him personally.

"What? What did she tell you about him?"

Ella paused, still wondering if it was right to tell Elizabeth's secret. But Thad had said they should share everything.

"She told me she went to Dawes for astronomy lessons, and that it led to a romantic affair with him. She said they made love on these very rocks."

Thad's expression went from surprise to amazement to amusement.

"My God! She told you that?"

Ella nodded, wondering if Thad was a little cross with her.

"I seriously doubt it happened, Ella. Dawes was…well, as I have heard it, he was a confirmed bachelor. Not really interested in women, though he did marry years after he left New South Wales. His wife was a childhood friend, I think, possibly even a spinster. Yet…I would not put it past Elizabeth Macarthur to force herself on Dawes. She tried to woo me not long after I arrived here. Of course, I spurned her advances. She is much older than me and not my type. Of course, she was married at the time, too."

Ella's mouth fell open. Had Elizabeth not encouraged Ella to pursue Thad? Had she not expressed her own interest in him by using the phrase, 'if I was much younger'?

"Why would she do this, try to have affairs with men like you and Dawes?"

"She has a dreadfully unhappy marriage, Ella. John Macarthur is not only impossible for his peers to deal with, he also treats Elizabeth disrespectfully. Gregory knows of this, for she came to him years ago for help. He prayed with her and gave her some advice. Neither of the Macarthurs are easy to get along with. It must be a marriage made in hell."

"Well then, let us keep this to ourselves. I wish to try to like Elizabeth if I can. I feel it is the neighborly thing to do. After all, she has not really offended me. Not much anyway, and I believe she truly likes me."

Thad hugged Ella close: "You are a kind and generous woman, dear wife. This is why you are such a fine nurse and teacher, and part of the reason I love you insanely!"

Insanely? Ella would not have applied that word to her love for Thad, but she grasped his meaning. Had he not gone a bit insane at Antony Lambe's cabin when he thought the man had harmed her?

Thad had already acquainted Ella with the stars, constellations, and peculiar features of the Southern Hemisphere night. Lieutenant Dawes would be proud of her, for she could find the Southern Cross and from it estimate the location of the South Celestial Pole, which had no star like the North Star in the Northern Hemisphere. Ella had seen the Milky Way over New South Wales as well as the Coal Sack, a dark place in the ethereal milk that was within what the Aboriginals called the Emu Constellation.

Then, there were the strange white smudges in the heavens, called the Large Cloud and the Small Cloud, below the star Canopus. They were first described in the year 889 by an Islamic scholar and in 1519 named the Magellanic Clouds for the Portuguese captain, Ferdinand Magellan, by the crew of his ship *Victoria* as it circumnavigated the globe. Astronomers were not sure what these were, but dubbed them nebulae, a term at the time for any of numerous unidentified celestial objects.[4]

Returning to their conversation about Dawes and women, Thad said:

"We will not discuss Dawes' morality, for we have no way of knowing the truth. People love good gossip. I have little taste for it."

He pinched her cheeks and kissed her nose.

"Most important to consider was Dawes' friendship with the Cammeraygal. As you already know, he befriended a group of them, especially a young woman named Patyegarang, or *Grey Kangaroo*. Some people believe he took her as a lover, but I am inclined to think that is pure gossip. They were only close friends. She was, after all, quite young."

"He was interested in communicating with the natives and establishing good relations with them," Thad added. "Patyegarang taught him her people's language, and he, in turn, taught her some English. He learned a great deal from her and she from him."

Ella loved the warm wind blowing onto Dawes Point from the Sydney foreshore, tousling her hair and the ribbons of her bonnet and pressing her dress against her legs. She closed her eyes and imagined William Dawes sitting on the rocks in front of her, next to Patyegarang, perhaps his arm around her in friendship.

---

[4] Today, we know they are small galaxies.

"You know, Dawes never became accustomed to the colonial attitude about Aboriginals," Thad continued, grasping Ella around her tiny waist. "He returned to England in 1791 after being harshly censured by the governor for his criticism of the handling of the killing of a British gamekeeper by an Aboriginal. Dawes thought the killing was self-defense and disagreed with the governor's harsh retaliation against the Aboriginals."

"His legacy is memorable, though," Thad affirmed, "including his notebooks on the sky and the Dharug language. I find his life especially meaningful, since he went on to work as an abolitionist. You know it is my personal hope that oppression of native people here and elsewhere in the world will end someday."

Dinner that night was extraordinary. Thad had arranged for an evening tour of the harbour on board a sloop owned by one of his Sydney friends. A meal of king prawns and orange roughy was prepared and served on-board, along with rice and grilled fruits. Thad had asked a violinist to play.

After dinner, as he and Ella held each other under a warm blanket, they enjoyed the incredible views of the night sky William Dawes had seen from Sydney Harbour.

"There, Ella, can you see the Clouds under Canopus? Those little smudges? The Aboriginals call them the Old Man and Old Woman. I read that Dawes aimed his telescope at them and thought he saw tiny stars inside them. I wonder? A smokey smudge in the heavens containing little stars…might they be growing, maturing stars? Do you think stars are born, mature, age, and die, like us?"

She turned and put one soft hand against his cheek.

"Such deep thinking, Thad! No wonder you are a doctor."

Later, back at their hotel, they cuddled together in bed after making love and talked about their future. It lay in front of them with great promise.

"Shall I always be your nurse, Thad, as well as your wife?"

He held her close.

"Always, dearest Ella, unless you desire to simply be my wife and the mother of our children. I suppose I could find another nurse and bring her to the colony."

"No need, my darling, But Thad, how many children do you suppose we will have?"

He was a little surprised at this question.

"My sweet wife, I believe that is up to nature and, to a lesser degree, God. But I do hope we have at least two. I would enjoy bringing up a boy and a girl."

"And what about Lucy? Do you wish to bring her into the house now that we are married and raise her as our own?"

Thad raised on his elbows and looked at Ella with concern. She was rubbi8ng her hands over the hair on his chest.

"That was never my intention, especially after you came into my life. Lucy has grown accustomed to living with the other orphans. I have never promised her a place in my house. Yet, I do hope she will become a teacher of our orphans when she is grown. She is an intelligent child."

Ella was satisfied. She loved Lucy, but she also believed the child belonged with the other orphans. Lucy was a good influence on the children and added to the diversity of the orphanage. If only the colony would send them more white orphans. It seemed too soon for attitudes about the mixing of whites and blacks to change. She made a vow to help Lucy work toward a career of teaching. There was a shortage of capable teachers in the colony.

Thad helped Ella get dressed the next morning so that they could board a hired carriage for a trip, as Gregory had suggested, to South Head to see Australia's new, first lighthouse. He kissed her neck tenderly as he buttoned the back of her lavender silk dress. She had forsaken her corset yet looked wonderfully feminine and youthful without it. Her pert breasts pressed against her chemise and fitted perfectly over the darts of the dress' bodice. She was much more comfortable without "the infernal corset."

Without Emily to do up her hair, Ella relied on Thad. He braided her long tresses and wrapped them attractively around her head. Ella managed to pin the braids securely before having Thad push a purple beaded comb into the mass to give it extra hold. The dark violet sash of her dress was tied in a big bow at her back. Finally, after kissing her toes and legs, Thad helped her put on her silk stockings and garters and slid her small feet into the white, kitten-heeled shoes.

The hired carriage was waiting for them outside the hotel. Thad had opted to leave Wanyuwa and Axle in the stable for a rest that day. The old horses would not like the hilly and rocky surface of the road leading out to the point, nor the heat of the day. As Thad took the reins of the hired carriage, he leaned toward Ella and kissed her cheek.

"Touring is such fun with you, my love. You have so many good questions and such playful thoughts on everything."

Ella grinned and returned his kiss. She was a man's finest daydream in her lavender dress. Thad was immeasurably proud of her. He hied the horses and steered them south to wend their way through Paddington and Woollahra to South Head Road. The road was rough in places though it had recently been repaired. As they bumped along, Ella wondered what the road had been like *before* repairs.

Ella spotted pink and grey cockatoos in the trees, their feathered headgear flared with excitement.

"Oh, galahs! How lovely they are, Thad!"

"Lovely, yes, but terribly noisy. We call a group of galahs a gabble. Perhaps a cacophony of galahs would better suit them. But then," he added, winking at Ella, "they are monogamous, forming lifelong bonds with their mates. I admire them for their fidelity."

Minutes later, a kookaburra flew up in front of the carriage with a wriggling snake in its beak. A willie wagtail chased the kookaburra, hoping to steal the prize. Ella pressed herself against Thad, hoping the bird would not drop the furious snake in their carriage as it flew over them.

"He will let it drop on something hard or bash it against a tree to break its spine," Thad told Ella, grinning. "Like us, he is not fond of a wriggling meal."

He knew she was disgusted by such things. But he boyishly loved to see her reaction, an adorable face of fright and revulsion. Plus, she snuggled close to him when she was afraid.

"And what kind of snake is it? Can you tell?"

"I can," Thad replied, pleased with himself. "'Tis a small, red-bellied black snake. Can you see its red belly?"

Ella glimpsed quickly, saw the snake's coloring, and murmured an assent to her amused husband. How lovely, she thought facetiously. She was glad to see the reptile from a distance.

Leaving the kookaburra and his catch behind, they reached a turn in the road where much of the harbour below was in view. Ella sighed with appreciation at the magnificent panorama. Her husband told her it was a grand view of Sydney Harbour and across the water to Booragee and Gooragai on the harbour's northern shore.

Thad shared what he knew about the imposing Sydney Heads that guarded the way into Sydney Harbour. He asked Ella to think back to the *Isabella's* arrival when she had traveled past the Heads. What had they looked like to her?

"I remember the great hissing and sighing lungs of the sea as the *Isabella* slowed and entered The Heads," Ella recalled. "Waves were smashing against the rocky cliffs and climbing high on their walls. I was much relieved to finally be almost at my journey's end."

"There are several heads jutting toward the sea, Ella. North Head guards the upper entrance while South Head, the loftiest at some 150-meters, is where we are going. Farther inside the harbour entrance are more heads. The First Fleet certainly chose a protected place to establish the colony."

"Tell me about the lighthouse, Thad. I have never seen one."

Thad was surprised. Ella had traveled by ship from Halifax to Liverpool, then to London by carriage. Her trip to Australia had given her several opportunities to see lighthouses.

"You must have been below deck for much of your travels, sweetheart."

"I was. The ship and the great open sea frightened me. I was terribly seasick for most of the voyage to New South Wales. The captain told me I would grow accustomed to the rolling and yawing of the vessel, but I never did. I stayed below for most of the journey."

Their carriage turned a corner, and the sandstone light tower came into view. Ella squealed, thrilled to see it. Banksia scrub was in bloom and heathland surrounded them. The view over the immense Tasman Sea was splendid.

"Thad, it is so tall! To think our colony now has its own lighthouse is amazing. What a feat of construction!"

"Indeed, it is," Thad agreed. "The lightkeeper, Robert Watson, will be giving us a tour. I sent a courier yesterday to arrange it. Watson is a former pilot and harbour master at Sydney. If you wish, we can climb to the lantern for a spectacular view of the Sydney Heads and the Tasman Sea."

Ella looked at Thad, astonished.

"He knows we are coming? You arranged a tour for us??!! Darling, you are so thoughtful."

Thad chuckled and delighted in the kisses she placed on his cheek.

She was an adventurous sort, else she never would have come to New South Wales in the first place. She rued her sickness and fears at sea, but nothing on land seemed to worry her, other than snakes, of course. Climbing to the top of the tall lighthouse on lofty South Head was an exciting proposition.

Ahead, Thad and Ella saw a man waving a greeting as their carriage pulled up to the lighthouse. He wore brown breeches with boots, a tan shirt, and a dark blue fisherman's cap. The colony had not yet designed a uniform for lighthouse keepers. Robert Watson was the first man to hold the occupation in Australia.

"Welcome friends! You must be Dr. and Mrs. Thad Bennett, the Viscount and Viscountess."

Ella smiled shyly to be called Viscountess.

Thad hopped from the carriage and carefully lifted his lovely new bride to the ground. He shook hands with Robert Watson.

"Mr. Watson, please meet my beautiful new wife, Ella. We are both so happy to make your acquaintance and see the marvelous new lighthouse. Thank you for hosting us."

"Of course," he offered as he knelt to kiss Ella's hand. "It is my pleasure, especially since you chose to visit my lighthouse as newlyweds. Edward, my son, will tend to your horse and carriage. My daughter, Rebecca, has prepared a small meal and hopes you will join us."

Rebecca was flying about the kitchen and said hello as she dished up the lunch fare. The food was a hodgepodge of fried fish, mashed yams, boiled onions, stewed tomatoes, and pickled beetroot. A fresh brown bread sat on the table as well, still warm from the oven. For dessert, Rebecca had baked an Illawarra plum tart. The plums had been harvested in July by the Dharawal people of the Wollongong area, she told Thad and Ella, and were preserved by Rebecca using a new process called canning.

"This is hardly a small meal, Rebecca," Thad said. "Tiffin is usually just tea and cakes!"

"'Tis my pleasure to cook for you and Mrs. Bennett, Sir."

Ella was interested in Rebecca's canning process.

"It was the Frenchman, Nicholas Appert who came up with canning in 1809," Rebecca told Ella. "He was looking for a safe way to preserve food for the French army. I am ever in his debt! Otherwise, we would go without vegetables and fruit for much of the year."

"I did not know the backstory," Ella replied. "Our kitchen cans foods from our orchards and gardens. One of the cooks told me it is still difficult to get glass jars here in the colony."

"Indeed, it is," Rebecca agreed. "They must be brought from England. While it is possible to obtain them locally, usually second-hand, they are quickly sold. I have been told windows are now the most sought-after glass items."

Ella helped Rebecca serve the meal. Thad and Robert Watson and his son, Edward, were deep in conversation when the food went on the table.

"We have been here in the lightkeeper's house only a matter of weeks," Robert announced, as they all sat down to eat. "Perhaps you smell the whitewash still drying on the walls. Certainly, our quarters remain in disarray, but I am sure you will indulge us, as we have had little time to organize the house."

"Of course," Thad replied. "I am sure your lightkeeping duties require much of your time, and they are, if I am not mistaken, your first priority."

"True," Robert affirmed. "We must never allow the light to fail. Everything else is second to that, even sleep and sickness."

Watson went on to praise architect Francis Greenway who had built the light tower and its adjoining quarters and installed the lantern and optic. Greenway was, in fact, a convict found guilty of forgery in England and transported to the penal colony. Yet, he was trusted by Governor Macquarie to erect the lighthouse, the most challenging structure Greenway had built to date. Watson noted that Greenway received his emancipation papers on the day the lighthouse went into service.

"Most people here call this the South Head Lighthouse, even Convict Lighthouse in honor of Greenway, but I am in favor of Macquarie Lighthouse, for without the vision and insistence of Governor Lachlan Macquarie it would not have been built. He is a man who does not let the petty machinations of British politics hold back progress. You may have heard he proceeded with construction of the lighthouse without approval by the British Secretary of State."

Thad clasped his hands in agreement—

"I do like a politician who moves forward with necessary work without undue argument and formal consent. It is easier, sometimes, to act with immediacy and ask for absolution later."

After the meal, Watson invited Thad and Ella to climb the nineteen-meter tower for a view of the area. The conical, sandstone lighthouse had wooden stairs and a rope railing winding to its top. The final steps—a steep ladder—led to the lantern where a series of specialized lamps were mounted on a revolving platform. They were fueled by whale oil and were fitted in a circular array in front of parabolic reflectors meant to amplify and concentrate the light. A clockwork mechanism that Watson wound up every few hours turned the platform, allowing the lamps to emit a bright flash. The light was said to shine many kilometers at sea due to its bright lamps and high elevation on the South Head.

"I did not realize whale oil carried such a stench," Ella observed after Watson had allowed Ella and Thad to smell the fuel.

Robert Watson chuckled.

"Indeed, it does, but it is one of the finest oils we have for the purpose of lighting a sentinel. It is most reliable and burns brightly, though it does soot up the glass globes on the lamps and the ceiling of the lantern room. We clean away the soot daily."

Thad was proud of Ella, for she asked good questions, made interesting observations, and she had not been squeamish about climbing either the tower or its steep ladder into the lantern, nor about smelling the whale oil. She had lifted her skirts and charged up the stairway and ladder, then poked her nose in the oil can!

Back on the ground, Thad and the lightkeeper continued their conversation about the lighthouse on a technical level while Ella wandered into the quarters and began helping Rebecca with the dishes.

"I am guessing storms here are terrifying," Ella said, drying a pretty China plate.

"They can be, but I am accustomed to storms," Rebecca assured Ella. "My father worked for a few years at the Signal Station farther south on the Head, so I learned to endure the storms. The worst of them happen mostly in winter."

"Signal Station?"

Rebecca smiled, realizing Ella probably knew little about seaside life.

"Yes, a place where men keep watch for ships and send up signals not only to aid the ships but also to notify the harbour master in Sydney that a ship is incoming. They also watch for unwanted vessels. Years ago, it was the French. The Governor feared the French would attack the colony and try to claim this land for themselves."

"Such an interesting life you have, Rebecca!"

"Well, and you too, Mrs. Bennett."

"Oh, do call me Ella. I believe you and I are about the same age."

They chatted for a time about running a household, Ella's voyage from England, and Rebecca's life by the sea. Then, Rebecca surprised Ella by asking a medical question.

"Forgive my cheekiness, please, but I have a problem I need a nurse or doctor to solve."

Ella's eyes lit up.

"Rebecca, my husband and I would be pleased to help you."

She waited, giving Rebecca time to muster the nerve to tell about her problem.

"Mrs. Ben…I mean Ella, this is odd, but I have constant foul breath and a slight soreness in my throat when I swallow. I have been coughing more than is normal too."

"Hmmm. May I look inside your mouth, Rebecca?"

"Of course."

The woman did indeed have rotten breath, but her teeth seemed clean and her tongue was clear and pink. Ella thought for a moment before a light went off in her brain.

"Might you have a blunt-end instrument, perhaps a small jam spoon or a crochet hook? This might be a problem with your tonsils since you also experience discomfort when swallowing."

Rebecca fetched a small spoon and gave it to Ella.

Ella asked Rebecca to open her mouth wide. she inserted the spoon and jiggled one tonsil. Instantly, a white object appeared behind the tonsil and then receded.

"Rebecca, you have a tonsil stone on this side of your mouth. It is of no danger to you, but it does aggravate the throat and cause coughing and trouble swallowing. And it will grow larger as time passes. If you like, I can remove it. There will be no pain."

Rebecca readily agreed but wondered what a tonsil stone was.

"Tonsil stones form when snot and phlegm and other goo gets trapped inside the wall between the tonsil and the skin of the palate. After a time, the stuff calcifies, or hardens, and forms a stone. It is likely the cause of your foul breath too."

"The stones take a long time to form," Ella added. "Repeated colds and illnesses of the nose and throat can cause them."

"Ella, my nose runs almost constantly! My father says something offends it, like lime or dust or flowers."

"He could be right about that, but a runny nose is also a tonsil stone symptom. Now, shall we remove that nasty stone?"

Ella eased the spoon into Rebecca's mouth and pushed on the tonsil. The stone came into view. The more Ella pressed, the more of the stone appeared. It was large, about the size of a pea. Suddenly, it popped out and onto Rebecca's tongue. Ella quickly grabbed it with her fingers. She showed it to Rebecca.

"Lord but it smells bad!" Rebecca said, covering her nose.

"It is all that nasty goo put down in layers. I will toss it over the cliff if you wish, but first may I check the other tonsil?"

A minute later, Ella had popped out a second stone from the other tonsil, a bit smaller than the first.

"I believe your foul breath and discomfort will be gone now," she told Rebecca.

"Oh, swallowing is easier already. Ella, you have cured me. I thank you so very much."

Robert and Thad returned to the house a few minutes later. Rebecca ran to her father and told how Ella had healed her ailing throat. She showed him the tonsil stones.

"I am so glad I asked her about my throat, father! She took a quick look and immediately knew what the problem was."

Robert Watson thanked Ella profusely.

"Aye, she has been complaining of it for many months now. What a strange thing—tonsil stones. We both thank you for your wisdom and your skilled hands. Your wife is a wonder, Dr. Bennett."

Thad was beaming. He knew how special Ella was, in so many ways.

"Would you take some plum jelly as payment, Ella?"

Rebecca ran to the pantry and returned with two jars of the jelly.

"You need not pay me, Rebecca, but I *am* fond of the jelly. It will taste wonderful on our cook's scones. Perhaps just one jar."

"Oh no, Mrs. Bennett. There were two tonsil stones, which means you should take two jars of jelly."

Ella giggled and accepted both jars of jelly. The odorous stones lay on the kitchen windowsill, ready to be thrown away.

"And I shall have fun flinging those smelly things over the cliff," Rebecca added.

Ella asked Rebecca to promise to come visit Acacia House.

"I shall knit you a warm scarf to ward off the cold winter winds here on South Head," Ella said. "You must come visit to claim it."

On the carriage ride back to the Lord Nelson Hotel, Ella was full of talk. The visit to the lighthouse and the family who maintained it had inspired her.

"I so enjoyed meeting the Watsons, Thad. It was wonderful to converse with a woman my age. Rebecca Watson is going to make some gentleman a delightful wife."

"Yes, I agree, but as she lives so far from society, it may be difficult for her to circulate among eligible bachelors."

Ella lifted the skirt of her dress and allowed some cool air under it. The day had grown quite warm. Thad glanced at her petite feet under a lacy petticoat.

"Is that petticoat new? I have forgotten what clothes we bought for you at the mercantile."

Ella knew Thad was elated to buy her new clothes and a few trinkets.

"Yes, love. New shoes, new petticoats, new chemise, and best of all no corset!"

Thad turned to look at Ella's chest. He looked pleased and kissed her hand lovingly.

"I can deny you nothing, my sweet Ella. I must say your figure is divine without a corset."

They rode in silence for a way, enjoying the scenery as the road from South Head dipped down toward Sydney. Cicadas sang. Ella caught a glimpse of two black swans in the water below, accompanied by their fluffy, grey cygnets. Thad had told her black swans were thought to be nonexistent before they were discovered in Australia by the Dutch explorer Willem de Vlamingh in 1697. In fact, before that time the term 'Black Swan" meant something that was "impossible."

"Rebecca Watson said there is talk of building a second lighthouse on the North Head at Lady Bay and perhaps one on the shores of Van Diemen's Land," Ella said, resuming a conversation with her husband.

"Both of those sites need lighthouses," Thad replied. "The question is money, my darling. England is not keen to funnel money into projects here in New South Wales, and I doubt the colony can raise such funds."

"Perhaps the colony can charge a small toll on entering ships. I believe that is being done in the United States at New York Harbour. They have some twenty lighthouses in The States, you know. Sandy Hook, I read, is the one leading to the port at New York."

Thad smiled: "It is a worthwhile idea, my love. Yet, I expect our governor does not wish to discourage any ships from coming here, so he may not be keen on charging a toll, even a small one."

He paused. Ella was thinking again. He could tell by her expression.

"Rebecca Watson said South Head had a tripod with a fire basket at first, before the lighthouse was built. Might those be erected at important places along the coast?"

Thad grinned. His sweet little wife was always on the hunt for better ways to do things.

"They could. I am not sure fire baskets are useful, however. A ship might run up onto the rocks trying to find such a small beacon. It is counterproductive for a ship to wreck looking for a light."

"True," Ella conceded. "I suppose I am enamored of lighthouses now that I have seen one. They are such humanitarian structures. And beautiful too. Should we not endeavor to build as many as we can on our coast?"[5]

"I should think so," Thad responded. "They signify civility. We need better roads too, bridges, dams, hospitals, and more constables with assistants. After all, we do live in a colony of many convicts. I believe there are some 12,000 inhabitants here at present, over half of them transported for crimes."

Ella was quiet for a few minutes, thinking of the cans of water paints that had been given to the orphanage as a gift, along with some children's books, all from a Newcastle family. The books were recycled, as were the paint pots, but that did not matter to Ella or the children. They did not mind using second-hand things.

"Perhaps I will sketch the South Head Lighthouse from memory," she told Thad. "The children will love sketching light towers and painting them. Lighthouses seem easy to draw."

"I have no doubt the children will enjoy sketching and painting the lighthouse. I believe Gregory will too. He fancies himself a bit of an artist!"

Thad pulled the carriage into the livery where an ostler was waiting to take the horses. He turned to Ella and smiled.

---

[5] Ella's wish eventually came true! Today, Australia has over 350 lighthouses.

"Ah, I must say I am deuced tired after our busy day. Climbing the lighthouse and taking in the brisk sea air has me feeling spent. Shall we go to our hotel room for tea and a rest before dinner?"

Ella grinned, knowing Thad's true intent.

The bridal tour days passed blissfully. Ella saw much of Sydney and was treated to a tour of the harbour by boat so she could see the lofty Heads from the water. But the most fascinating event was having tea with Governor Lachlan Macquarie and his wife, Elizabeth. The Macquaries admired Thad and were anxious to meet his new wife.

Their elegant residence, called Government House, was grand and spacious, with a long front veranda from which Sydney Harbor was visible. The Macquaries, both from Scotland, laid a beautiful tea table that day with flowers in a vase, biscuits and cakes and chocolates, and several kinds of tea. Mrs. Macquarie was coaxed to play her harp, brought to the colony by ship when the couple arrived in 1810.

"So, Dr. Bennett," the Governor began, "you enticed this beautiful lady to Australia to become your nurse, and then you charmed her into marrying you!"

Thad lowered his head, a bit embarrassed by the fact.

"I did, indeed, Governor. She is the most extraordinary woman I have ever known."

Thad leaned close to Ella and took her hand, kissing it softly. Mrs. Macquarie clapped her hands.

"Well done, Dr. Bennett! Well done!"

She turned to Ella.

"There are few women in Australia like you, Mrs. Bennett. Your husband was, for years, one of the colony's most eligible bachelors. Now, he is off the list."

While Thad and the Governor talked politics, Mrs. Macquarie took Ella to her sewing room to show her some swatches of extra fabric she had.

"I am sure the orphanage could use fabric. Children grow so fast and wear out clothes so quickly. It is such a fine effort the doctor and priest are about with the orphanage, raising those poor unwanted Aboriginal children. I commend them."

Ella smiled. Did Mrs. Macquarie know Ella's part in the improvement of the orphanage? She had cleaned up everything and impressed upon the children the importance of caring for their bodies, the temples of life God had given them. She had also begun teaching them about the greater world.

"I commend you and the Governor as well," Ella put in, "for your good work on behalf of the Aboriginals. Thad and I desire peace between the whites and blacks. It is a slow process though. I wish we might see our way to respect Aboriginal culture and lands while learning to live together."

Mrs. Macquarie stared at Ella a moment before commenting—

"Yes, I somewhat agree. But I am lax to accept their nakedness and unchristian behavior. I do want them to dress sensibly, attend school, obey our laws, accept Christianity, and respect land now owned by whites."

Ella held back from a response. She wished to tell the Governor's wife that those white-owned lands really belonged to the Aboriginals and had been taken forcibly. She wanted to remind Elizabeth Macquarie that Australia belonged to the Aboriginals, that they had lived here for thousands of years, and they did not need Christianity forced upon them. They had their own religion. But it was clear that the Macquaries still held strong racial biases.

As Thad and Ella bid farewell to the Macquaries and departed Government House in their phaeton, Ella mentioned her conversation with Mrs. Macquarie.

"She and the Governor have strange ideas about Christianizing the Aboriginals, dressing them in British clothes, and forcing them to attend British schools, not the friendly sort of school we have for them. The Macquaries see their work as progressive; yet their only progress in my opinion has been fewer murders of the natives."

Thad patted her knee.

"Even that is questionable," he said. "Only a few years ago there occurred the Appin Massacre and then the Hawkesbury and Nepean War. Many Aboriginals were slaughtered under order from the Governor. He even strung up the dead natives in trees to discourage others from rebelling."

"So, he is not as peaceable as I thought."

"No. His prejudice likely stems from the life he had after marrying his first wife. Lachlan MacQuarrie's fortune was earned on the scarred backs of African slaves who worked a family sugar plantation in Antigua."

Ella winced! "Are you certain of that, Thad?"

"Indeed, I am. There were about 300 slaves on the Jarvis plantation when Lachlan Macquarie married Jane Jarvis in 1793. She was sickly, though, and died of consumption only three years after their wedding. Her father gave Lachlan her inheritance of £6,000. Lachlan did not personally oversee the slaves, but he profited mightily from their labor. Mind you, I like the governor, but his past is discolored."

"Wealth earned through slavery." Ella declared, eyes wide. Thad nodded.

"Here I am gossiping, dear Ella!" Thad laughed. "But it sits between you and me. We shall not speak of it to others. I believe the good things Lachlan Macquarie has done for New South Wales outweigh any misstep by him."

"But there is one more thing I will tell you," Thad added, "largely because I believe it to be a plague upon this colony. Lachlan Macquarie contracted syphilis in Egypt during the Napoleonic wars. In 1807, he married Elizabeth, who is his first cousin. As you know syphilis is highly transmissible and never cured, only potshot remedies tried. I have no doubt his wife has contracted it."

Secrets. There seemed to be so many of them to keep. Ella knew by now that New South Wales was not so far afield from London. It may lay on the opposite side of the globe, but it had its own drama.

Before Thad and Ella departed for home, they visited a furniture dealer in Sydney Town. Albert Janson custom built almost all his pieces, only importing a few from England. Thad told Ella that in 1809 Jansen had built their bedchamber furniture and the formal dining room pieces.

"Before that, we dined atop stumps, and I slept on an upside-down set of crates softened with blankets on top. The crates kept me elevated above the small floods that sometimes came with summer rainstorms."

Ella giggled: "I am so glad we now have a proper bed, darling…and a lovely house in which to put it."

Did Albert Jansen have any rolling chairs on hand? He did. Four models. Thad examined all four at great length and chose the most expensive because he felt its wheels turned the smoothest and its seat was the most comfortable on his backside. Ella was amused watching him roll about the store, testing all the chairs.

While Thad investigated the rolling chairs, Ella perused the store with Albert Jansen.

"What is that odd seat in the corner, Mr. Jansen? The chair perched on spring coils?"

Albert Jansen chuckled.

"Ah! It is a chamber horse, Viscountess. It is designed to build muscles in the arms. Men sit on the leather chair and push it up and down. The coils under the chair resist the pushing, thus working arm muscles."

Ella looked at Jansen in disbelief, wondering what man would need such a gadget.

Jansen chuckled.

"I totally agree, Viscountess. It is a ridiculous invention aimed at men who get no regular exercise, who mayhap sit at a desk all day. Certainly, the Viscount does not need a chamber horse."

"Indeed, not," Ella replied, as they watched Thad testing the rolling chairs. He was a man with muscles and boundless energy.

Thad paid Jansen in cash for the rolling chair and had a store clerk securely strap it to the back of the phaeton, along with a tea table he had purchased for Ella for the south porch of Acacia House where she liked to sit to sew or knit. The livery up the street from the hotel kept the little buggy, the purchases, and the horses one last night.

Ten days after their arrival in Sydney, the couple had Wanyuwa and Axle harnessed to the phaeton and their trunk strapped below the rolling chair and tea table.

"We look like runaways!" Ella laughed as they rode out of town with so many things strapped to the back of the buggy. Axle whickered to another pair of carriage horses. They both answered with loud whinnies. It made Ella giggle.

"Horse conversation! I wonder what they are saying."

Thad chuckled: "You do keep me amused Ella. Yet I, too, have wondered on occasion if animals talk between themselves."

"Will the old horses be taxed pulling the extra weight?"

Thad laughed aloud and grabbed Ella's hand, kissing it.

"My darling, these old boys are tricksters. They would have you believe they are weak and lame. Horses are smarter than you think. And like us, they dislike work. Do not worry your pretty head about them. They can pull much more weight than this."

They rounded the city to the west at Iron Cove and once again boarded the barge for the easy trip up the Parramatta River. The tide was coming in and rushing into the river. A tow-path for oxen ran alongside the river to help if the barge grew lethargic in the eastbound river current when the tide ebbed.

"Thad, darling, thank you for the lovely purchases you made for me in Sydney. I feel it is all a bit of butter upon bacon, as I am so well kept and loved. I really needed nothing, you know...except you at my side."

Thad put his arm around Ella and kissed her forehead. He would buy her the moon and stars if she asked for them. But she had asked nothing of him other than books and his love.

At Parramatta, they disembarked and began the journey home over the crude roads northeast to Wahroonga. The sky was dark to the east, but Thad did not think the clouds were moving toward them. He kept his eye on them, nonetheless, as he had a large oilcloth at the ready to protect them and their purchases if there was rain.

They pulled into their dusty driveway shortly before dinnertime. Polly barked a greeting and wagged her tail wildly. Old Wibung did not even look up from his sleeping place on the porch behind the church.

Ella sighed, admiring the many flowers and trees that had burst into bloom in less than a fortnight. The acacias were showing off, and many of the eucalypts wispy, exotic flowers had begun to appear. Waratah flirted in bright red. Waxflowers sported pink and white petals. Grevilleas held a variety of colors and shapes. Emu Bush boasted purple stems. Early December was warm, yes, but lovely.

"Dearest Thad, I so enjoyed our bridal tour, but I am also glad to be home. Thank you, my sweet husband, for touring me all over Sydney."

Thad kissed Ella as they walked from the driveway to the house: "I enjoyed it too, my darling. Now, we can settle into a happy married life."

The Barn Boys already had Wanyuwa and Axle unharnessed and were leading them to the barn for food and water and to be curried. Two men were unloading the couple's trunk, the tea table, and Gregory's rolling chair. Thad had ordered the chair taken into the house until the time was right for it to be given to Gregory. His order came just in time, for Gregory emerged from the rectory, swabbing his head. It had been a hot day. He waved and shouted that he would join them for dinner.

"Hoo-way!" Mani shouted when he spied the couple from the spotted gum treehouse. "Dok-tor Benna and Missy Fieldin" back!"

The boy paused and then comically smacked his forehead—

"I be dinbin! She Missa Benna now!"

Eleven

The happy newlyweds did settle into normal married life. Ella rose each day eager to make small changes to the house and do things to please her husband. She reorganized their bed chamber library and had Mabarra dust all the books as they were put in their proper places. She even added small, alphabetized tags to the shelves to help in locating books.

Thad's medical office was painted a soft light green. Ella thought his mood was buoyed by his favorite color. She had a new tablecloth made for the dining room table and placemats and serviettes to match. The piles of fabric sent from Mrs. Macquarie soon were cut into patterns for little boy shirts and breeches and dresses for the little girls. There was even some silk which Ella made into cravats for Thad.

Ella's chamber was designated as a sick room and a birthing room, in hopes the couple had children in their future. Ella often wondered about that. Mrs. Hughes had told her that as a married woman, she now possessed the look of motherhood in her bright peachy complexion.

"Why, Mrs. Bennett, I even think your breasts look different and those slim hips of yours are widening a little, ready to bring forth a babe when necessary."

This embarrassed Ella and sent her to the bed chamber she shared with Thad to appraise herself in the mirror. The comment about her breasts surely came as a result of her not wearing a corset. But her hips widening?

When Thad walked in and asked what she was about, her answer amused him.

"Mrs. Hughes says my face has a maternal glow and my figure is enlarging!"

"Darling, if your figure is changing, it is only for the better. I, myself, have noticed your hips and bosom increasing a bit, while your waist remains small. What man would have grievance with that?"

He pulled her into his arms and kissed her, softly at first, then deeply, and finally ravenously. When he lifted her and began carrying her to the bed, she resisted.

"Sweetheart, I have chores to do. Can your ardor not wait until we come to bed?"

He looked at her, perplexed and a little crestfallen. All this talk of hips and bosoms and tiny waists had inflamed him. Ella could feel his pants swelling under her hip.

"I do not think it can be delayed, dearest wife. I must confess I waited until age six-and-thirty to know the joy of a beautiful and sensuous wife, mine to love whenever and wherever I desire. My ardor needs to be satisfied now…and perhaps tonight as well."

The house staff whispered all afternoon about the door to the master chamber being closed and the laughter and sighs and moans coming from the other side of it. Mabarra and Emily tittered in the kitchen, eavesdropping while making bread and scones. Mrs. Hughes eyed them and grinned.

"My guess is there might be a little one on the way before long," she giggled.

"I agrees," Emily said. "He can no' keep his hands off her!"

"Nor she keep her hands off him," Mabarra added.

The happiness at Acacia Farm, as the house and land was newly dubbed, lasted only until the winter of 1820. Word came north from Sydney in June that there was sickness. Rubeola. Measles. It reached Acacia House at the end of July.

By mid-August, the sick lay everywhere at the farm, in the aisles of the church, in the barns and the men's bunkroom, in the house, and saddest of all in the orphanage. Thad worked day and night to tend to the sick, determined to save every one of them. Ella was worn out from tending to so many patients. The afflicted cried with sore throats. Some vomited or developed flux, and all had extensive rashes. Others suffered from chills and went from feeling cold to hot and back to cold again. A few lay inert, unable to take much of the water or bone broth offered to them.

Measles had arrived in Sydney by ship and spread to all parts of New South Wales, including Wahroonga. Thad, Gregory, and Ella were run ragged in those first weeks. Almost all the sick were Aboriginals or half-castes, or young white children who had never had the disease. Thad scraped the rash of an ill adult and placed a smear under his microscope, a gift from his doctor father. The insidious little red dots he saw were numerous. How could things so small make people so sick? What had his father written about this? He rummaged through his notebooks to find his father's precious notes.

"By no means," his father had penned, "should patients be bled or cupped, bathed in salts, or treated with mercury. Nothing should be applied to the pustules. They will eventually scab, dry, and disappear. Patients should rest and be given plenty of fluids to fight fever. A cool bath will help. The disease will run its course."

Ella cautioned the children to cover their mouths when they coughed or sneezed, hoping to stem the transmission of the disease. She made sure they drank copious amounts of water. The stockpile of eucalyptus candies the kitchen had made to soothe sore throats and coughs was quickly used up.

Mabarra had trimmed all the children's fingernails short so they could not scratch open the tiny pustules of their rashes. Clothing was removed for comfort, replaced by blankets to ward off the winter chill. Cold rags provided mild relief from the intense fevers and itching. Mrs. Hughes ran shifts of maids washing diapers to deal with the flux. Emily carried cups of nutritious broth to the children.

Ella and Thad took turns grabbing precious moments of sleep. The kitchen sent them plates of food and hot tea to help them keep up their energy. Both were run ragged.

Ella had just finished her rounds among the children one afternoon and had assigned special caregivers to the sickest. She wiped her brow with her forearm and stepped out onto the porch at the back of the church. The cold air felt good. She sat down on a crate and sighed, letting her head fall.

Thad appeared and called to her.

"Ella, I know you are exhausted, but we need to see to Yarrin. He is extremely sick. Mrs. Hughes got him into a bed in the clinic and is comforting him now. Would you check on him soon?"

Thad's voice finally registered in Ella's ears. He seemed far away. Ella rose unsteadily to her feet and turned to him.

"What did you say, Thad?"

She was slumping and wobbly, with sleepy eyes and a drawn face. Right away Thad saw a hint of rash on her face and neck. He touched her cheek. It was flaming hot.

"Dearest Ella, how long have you been like this?"

She stepped to the edge of the porch and vomited violently, then reeled, and Thad caught her in his arms before she hit the wood planks.

Gregory passed by with a large bucket of rags to rinse at the pump. He stopped when he saw Ella in Thad's arms.

"She has it," Thad said. "My God, Gregory, she is sick with measles!"

Gregory staggered back to the deck and looked at Ella.

"Lord save her," he said, "she *does* have it. She must never have caught it as a small child, as we did. She has no resistance to it."

Thad was shaking his head no. He had not thought to ask her.

"I must get her in the house and to bed. Measles is especially hard on adults."

"Of course," Gregory said. "I can manage here. I have several helpers."

Ella had felt so tired, as if she could not lift her feet to walk. The hot interior of the orphanage had slowly become a blur. She felt herself going through motions but wondering what she had accomplished. Her throat was on fire, hurting so badly she could barely swallow. Perhaps she should get to the house and tell Thad. Yet, all she wanted was to lie down and sleep.

She remembered that she had stepped outside, just for a minute, wiping her forehead on one arm. She could barely stand upright. She found a crate, turned it over, and sat down, dropping her head low. Sleep beckoned; she needed so much to lie down and sleep. But a voice in the distance called her name. *Ella!*

Who's there? Let me rest please.

Dr. Bennett. Thad. Were they the same person? She saw him indistinctly. Her mind seemed weak.

Ella!

She mustered all her energy and got to her feet.

"How long have you been like this," he was asking?

She did not know. Suddenly, her stomach heaved and emptied over the edge of the porch. She was falling then, so sleepy, feet crumpling under her. Arms went around her…she was lifted in his strong arms. Distant voices again, something about a rash. Her head rolled toward his chest.

She felt herself carried a long way. She was undressed and placed in bed. A sheet was laid over her and a blanket. A cold compress was placed on her head. The distant voice came again.

"Ella, my darling wife, rest now. I will get you through this, I promise. Rest, sleep."

The last thing she remembered was a kiss on her forehead.

"She cannot die from this, Gregory! Please, pray to God with all your might that she will not die!"

Father Gregory rubbed Thad's back as his upper body lay over Ella's chest clutching her. She had been comatose for more than three days, her fever raging and her body peppered with the tiny red pustules of measles. Emily had been relentlessly carrying cold cloths to Ella's room and had helped Thad put her in a cool bath each day to keep her fever down and ease the itching. Still, Ella did not improve or wake.

Gregory signaled to Emily that they should leave Thad and Ella alone for a while.

"There is naught we can do, Emily," he whispered. "Only God can help."

When Gregory returned downstairs, he was greeted by Mabarra and Mrs. Hughes.

"A few of the Bidjigal have come—those not yet sick. They have come to cry for Mrs. Bennett's recovery," Mrs. Hughes said. "They are gathered by the church. Shall I send out some food?"

"They will not eat," Mabarra informed Mrs. Hughes. "They only mourn for the sick and the dead."

Gregory opened the door and stepped outside. Mabarra followed him.

Madang and the remainder of his followers stood in the space between the gardens and the church. Their skin was painted in white designs, but they had cut themselves on their arms and legs and blood ran into the designs and onto the ground. They danced and cried out.

"They cry for Mrs. Bennett to throw off her illness," Mabarra said. "They wound themselves to experience her pain and suffering."

Father Gregory joined the Bidjigal, opened his arms to heaven, and began to pray out loud in Dharug, so loud his words silenced the crying and dancing.

"Dear Lord in Heaven, take into thy arms those who have died here and in the Bidjigal camp. Raise the others from their beds so that they might continue their lives. We ask forgiveness if we have offended You, dear Lord, and we offer our blood as shame. We are but your children who sometimes sin. Take the red spot disease from us and return us to our happy lives. We ask this in the name of Jesus, our Lord and Savior, who bled for us so that we might live. Amen."

A chorus of "amens" arose from the Bidjigal. They understood *amen*. Most of them attended church regularly, if only to hear the miraculous music of the organ, the singing, and to partake of the food handed out afterward. Each one stepped forward to receive a blessing from Father Gregory. It consisted of the laying of the crucifix on his belt against their foreheads and his words, "Go with God."

Thad appeared before the group, a trace of tear tracks on his cheeks. He raised his voice to thank the Bidjigal for their kindness and reassure them that their dance and blood would take away pain and save many lives, perhaps even Ella's life.

Mrs. Hughes handed out damper and cheese for them to take back to their *wolli*.

As the Aboriginals departed, Thad and Gregory could not help but notice how their number had decreased. Many of the clan had contracted measles and died. Others lay dying in the camp.

"Madang," Thad called.

The Bidjigal leader turned, his face solemn.

"What of Dural, Keira, and Breath of Ella?"

Medang looked off into the distance, then stepped closer.

"The baby lives. We mourn her parents."

Thad lowered his head, his eyes welling with tears again.

"We mourn for all the people who have died," Gregory said, "but especially Dural and Keira. If it pleases you, we will take Breath of Ella into our orphanage."

Medang thought for a moment, then nodded.

"It would please me. I will bring the child to you."

Thad was sure he had clung to Ella for hours. She cried out softly, as she had been doing since she had fallen ill. He sat up and looked at her sick face and body. She even had measles under her fingernails and on her scalp. For the umpteenth time that day he lifted her eyelids to appraise her pupils and peered inside her mouth at the angry red color on her throat.

How could this happen? They had been married only a few months before she had fallen so ill. What had he done to displease God? Could he not have a few years of happiness with this lovely woman? Did he not deserve it after a life of service to the sick?

He took Ella's hand in his and kissed it. He picked up the book of poems he had been reading aloud to her and resumed his heartfelt rendering of Percy Shelley's latest poem, "Ozymandias."

*I met a traveler from an antique land
Who said: "Two vast and trunkless legs of stone
Stand in the desert...Near them, on the sand,
Half sunk, a shattered visage lies, whose frown,
And wrinkled lip, and sneer of cold command,
Tell that its sculptor well those passions read...*

He put aside the book and dropped his head in his hands. He felt alone, deserted, without the energy or know-how to move forward. He could do nothing for Ella but pray. He left her bedchamber, closing the door softly, and walked to the orphanage.

He heard wailing long before he arrived. Voices of the Aboriginal children were fraught with sadness. Mani had died, a favorite with everyone. The boy's Aboriginal half had no defense against measles. It was a completely foreign illness. Thad had been much concerned for Mani after he began having seizures the prior day.

As Thad knelt at the boy's side, he noticed Mani still wore the hat Ella had made for him. His favorite blanket was tucked about his shoulders. Hardly a spot on his face was not measled, though with death the spots had begun to pale. Was he nine or ten? Thad could not recall. So young to leave the world of the living. The boy's expression was frozen in eternal repose, eyes shut and the smallest of smiles on his lips. Had he gone to meet his ancestors, as the Aboriginals all believed they would when death took them? Thad hoped so.

Gregory came and knelt with Thad. They cried together...for Mani, for Ella, and for all the sick and dying.

"I believe," Thad said, his voice a choked whisper, "Mani has suffered a swelling of the brain. I read about this a few days ago. It happens to some measles patients...those with little or no resistance to the disease. I suspect Mani had the swelling when his seizures began."

"My friend," Gregory finally said, "there is a baby you must check...little Bouddi. She came to us only last week from the Darkinyung people. Her family have all passed. I fear..."

He could not finish. Both men knew how bad the disease was among the full-caste Aboriginals, especially the infants. So many were dead or dying. Thad had made numerous trips to the native camps, but there was little he could do.

Jiemba lifted tiny, exanthem-peppered Bouddi from her cradle and handed her to Thad.

"Dr. Benna, she no longer cry. Jus' quiet and staring. I thin' Bunyip com' fo' her. He wan' steal her from us. I sing to her, bu'..."

Jiemba was superstitious. The Bunyip was the Aboriginal equivalent of the boogey-man. Normally, Thad discouraged such beliefs. But he could not do so on this day. Like himself, Jiemba was at a loss to explain the sickness and death that had overtaken New South Wales. He would not chastise her.

Thad took the infant, Bouddi, and nestled her in the crook of his left arm. He pulled Jiemba to him with his other arm, hugging her affectionately. She seemed immune to the disease, for she had not become ill. Thad wished he knew why, as it would help him understand the sickness and perhaps find better treatments.

Jiemba had worked tirelessly to care for the sick.

"Your singing is likely the best medicine for her, Jiemba. Babies love a soft song. Thank you for your caring heart. God sees your goodness."

He felt the infant's cheeks and reached inside her blanket to feel her chest. Her little heart was beating normally. She was not as hot as he expected.

"Has she had a wet napkin recently?" he asked. "Has she nursed?"

Jiemba tilted her head curiously.

"I chan'e nappy dis moanin', Dr. Benna. I not showa if Kalina noose her."

Kalina was another Aboriginal unaffected by measles. She had a baby about four months old and plenty of breast milk. She had been feeding several young ones, including Bouddi.

Thad checked the baby's napkin and found it wet. He grinned. It seemed the worries over little Bouddi might be over. If she wet her diaper, she had surely nursed that morning. Both were signs of improvement.

"Tell Kalina to keep offering milk to the baby. You can offer Bouddi water from one of the syringes in the clinic. No crying means she is content. I believe the infant will recover."

Jiemba laughed with joy. She had dealt with so much death and sadness that one small babe's improvement meant everything. As if to confirm the doctor's optimism, Bouddi looked at him with her chocolate brown eyes, crinkled up her sweet round face, and smiled.

The pounding of hammers echoed through the eucalypt forest around Acacia Farm, bouncing back sorrowful news. The carpenter and his helper were fashioning coffins of all sizes, and they were unable to keep up with the demand. Thad went to them, soberly nodding his head in thanks and offering drinking water from a bucket.

Beyond them, he turned onto a *bidi*—a trail—to the burial ground. The cemetery had been established in 1808 when the first of Thad's people had died, an elderly house maid who suffered a stroke in the intense heat of the Australian summer. Second to be buried was a field worker who had died of snakebite. Others had followed—women lost in childbirth, victims of the 1813 influenza epidemic, babies born dead or too soon to survive.

There was Henry too, lying peacefully beside a comely blue gum, his feet facing the rising sun. Thad stopped next to Henry's small headstone and removed his hat. The inscription, intended to preserve Henry's goodness but not his name, read: *A Dear Friend to All.* The half-caste man would be forever imprinted on Thad's memory and heart.

Behind the gravestone was an emu nest with nine fresh-laid eggs. They had not yet turned the dark green color of incubating eggs, and there was no cock emu sitting on them. The activity of the gravediggers had likely frightened away the parent emus. Thad thought of bringing the eggs to the kitchen but reconsidered. Perhaps their location had something to do with Henry's beliefs about death and the afterlife.

Thad walked to the far end of the cemetery and retrieved the bucket of drinking water he had brought with him. His eyes roved over the piles of fresh earth beside rectangular holes. The sobering scene suddenly caught him off guard, as he imagined Ella in a wooden box being lowered into one of the graves.

His eyes filled with tears. He gasped in grief, rushed out of the burial ground, and broke into a run back to Acacia House. As he entered the kitchen, Mrs. Hughes met him. She noticed his face wet with tears. Dared she tell him more bad news?

"Oh, Dr. Bennett, I am so glad you are here. It is Yarrin. You must go to him immediately!"

Thad reluctantly changed his original plan to check on Ella and instead went to the clinic.

Yarrin lay inert on a bed with Mabarra alternately pressing his chest and blowing air into his mouth.

"His heartbeat is gone, Dr. Bennett. I saw Ella do this to Keira's baby."

Thad pressed one ear to Yarrin's chest. Nothing. He nodded to Mabarra to continue her life-saving effort. But after several minutes with no resumption of the boy's heartbeat, Thad put his arms around Mabarra and held her.

"You did all you could, Mabarra. I am sorry. Yarrin is gone."

She put one hand over her mouth and teared up. Shuddering, she clung to Thad. He patted her back softly.

"I feel guilty so many have died while I have suffered nothing," Mabarra cried. "Why am I spared this disease?"

Thad had no explanation. He could only hold Mabarra and reassure her.

"Death is difficult enough to accept with strangers," Thad said, "much less dear friends and loved ones. I think Yarrin is climbing into the stars now to meet his ancestors, yes?"

Mabarra nodded, sniffling. Thad handed her his handkerchief.

"Tell me how Ella fares since I last saw her."

He turned Mabarra away from the dead Yarrin and steered her toward the stairs.

"Shall we go see my sweet wife?"

Mabarra nodded. They climbed the stairs together and quietly entered Ella's bedchamber.

Ella resembled a sleeping princess from a fairy tale as she lay in the sick room, hands folded, eyes closed, and her glorious, blonde-streaked hair arranged on her pillow. Thad put one hand on her forehead. She felt cooler…or was he only wishing she did. He lifted each of her eyelids. Was the redness gone from her eyes? Was her rash a little paler?

Mabarra replaced the cloth on Ella's head with a cooler one. She dabbed softly at Ella's neck and chest with another cloth. Thad took Ella's hands in his.

"My darling, it is time to wake now. Open your lovely eyes," Thad entreated.

He stroked and squeezed her hands. She gave no response. Dear God, had her brain swelled like Mani's brain had done?

"I know she will wake, Sir," Mabarra assured him. "She is a strong woman. She needs you."

I need her more, Thad thought. I cannot live without her.

From one of the windows in Ella's chamber, Mabarra glimpsed one of the burly farmhands carrying the limp, thin, speckled body of Yarrin. She gulped to hold back more tears. The boy was being taken to the carpenter to be put in a coffin.

All this death! She felt she could not endure any more of it. Two of her young friends in the household had died. Yarrin was gone. Seven orphans. Six field workers. More Aboriginals than she could count. And she had yet to be told about Mani, dear sweet Mani, whom everyone had dearly loved.

She turned to the bed where Thad still held Ella's hands and was whispering sweet words to her. She could not live if the doctor lost his beautiful, beloved wife. Her friend and confidant. A kind, loving, and hardworking woman.

"I will sit with her, Dr. Bennett. I shall call to you if she so much as twitches her nose."

◦◦◦

Medang came early the next morning with Breath of Ella in his arms. She was eighteen months old now and knew Thad, Gregory, and Ella by sight, as well as many of the Acacia Farm staff. She went into Gregory's arms eagerly and tugged on his sandy-colored hair.

"Fa-Fa," she called the priest, presenting herself for a kiss.

Father Gregory kissed her chubby cheek.

"She will be much loved here," he assured Medang. "She will grow to womanhood and honor the Bidjigal as her people."

The aging Bidjigal leader nodded and turned to go. He had not taken two steps when he stopped, turned back, and laid his head on Breath of Ella's chubby thighs. She twirled her fingers in his hair, gurgled happily, and repeated, *Gumang, Gumang*--Grandfather, Grandfather.

"*Ngubadi, ngyini gurung.*"

"*Gumang* Medang says he loves you, Breath of Ella," Father Gregory said. "I know he will come visit you. We will give you the best of care and much love."

By dinner time, Breath of Ella was chasing Wibung and running about the orphanage naked, playing with all the children who were not sick. When Thad arrived, she was beating on the floor of the children's classroom with sticks and putting on her own singing and dancing performance.

"She is certainly energetic and healthy," Gregory commented. "I grow weary just watching her."

Thad chuckled. This was a child who would have died without Ella's interventions. It seemed a miracle to see the little one now so strong and spirited. She'd had a mild case of measles and had recovered rapidly. Why? Thad wondered. Was it her special status among her people? A wisp of sacredness?

"Yes, she is remarkable," Thad quietly replied. "From such a frail beginning, she has grown so strong. She appears partially immune to measles. Some children are…but I am at a loss to know the reason."

As Thad observed Breath of Ella's unabashed Bidjigal recital, her dancing and singing, her chubby baby arms and legs flailing, the huge brown eyes and sweet rosette mouth of her round face…a thought began to take shape in his mind.

What if he could somehow communicate to Ella that her little namesake needed her?

Needed a mother, a father, and all the love they could give her.

Needed siblings.

What if…

Thad swung Breath of Ella up into his arms, making her laugh joyfully. She turned her face to his and puckered her lips affectionately.

"Elwa-Boowah kiss whi-fella, dokker. Gib lub."

She snugged her arms around Thad's neck and smeared a messy kiss against his cheek. She held him close for only a few seconds before clapping her hands in satisfaction.

"Elwa-*Boowah* lub dokker Bent-et!"

Thad's eyes misted. He returned her kiss and said softly—

"Dr. Bennett loves you too, sweet Ella-*Buwa*."

He patted his chest and made a heart shape with his fingers. Ella-*Buwa* imitated the gesture and smiled, revealing a dozen white baby teeth.

"Shall we go and wake Miss Ella from her long sleep? She also needs a kiss from you. In fact, all of us do."

Twelve

Acacia Farm
Wahroonga, October 1829

Three-year-old Suzannah toddled along the gravel driveway, gripping her mother's hand and clutching a toy pademelon Mabarra had sewn for her. Eight-year-old Gregory ran ahead, trying to catch up to his stepsister, Breath of Ella.

"Papa, Papa!" the boy yelled, seeing his father riding a new horse toward Acacia House. "May I ride?"

Thad slowed the big horse to a stop and dismounted. True to her name, Guwayana's long cream-colored mane, fetlocks, and tail were tousled by the wind. "Wind" was the perfect name for a horse, Thad thought. Guwayana meant "wind" in Dharug.

"Come. I will lift you onto her broad saddle. You, too, Ella-*Buwa*."

Guwayana stood quietly as Thad lifted his young son and adopted Bidjigal daughter onto the horse's back.

"So high up!" Gregory cried with pleasure. "Please, Papa, lead her to the end of the lane and back!"

Thad grasped Guwayana's bridle and urged her to walk with him. Ella-*Buwa* made a clicking sound with her tongue to encourage the horse. Guwayana's huge feet clopped softly and sent up small puffs of dust from the dry ground. She neighed a greeting to the other horses below the house in the spacious barnyard. Her belly jiggled as she nickered, making the children laugh.

Guwayana was a Clydesdale draft horse crossed with the Shire breed, among the largest of the working draught horses. She stood seventeen hands at her back, was incredibly strong, and carried herself regally. Her temperament, as with most draught breeds, was gentle and sweet. Thad had purchased her, along with her large saddle, from a farmer at The Ponds, near Reverend Samuel Marsden's Dundas Farm. She was a replacement for the Belgians, Yuwin and Biyal, that had died months earlier.

"Big horsey! Big horsey! I wide too, Papa!" Suzannah cried, pulling on her mum's hand. The little girl's hand—the one not holding her toy pademelon—was sticky from a hardened chunk of sweet *mulga* sap she was sucking.

Thad walked Guwayana out the driveway and back, then lifted Suzannah up with her sister and brother.

"Paddy wide too!" Suzannah shouted with exasperation, pointing to the treasured stuffed toy her mother was holding. "Paddy not ebba wide a big, big horsey like Gwana!"

Thad chuckled and took the toy from Ella, placing it in his little daughter's arms. Suzannah handed him the wet and sticky *mulga* candy.

"You are such a plucky little one, Sweet Suzie! Keep Paddy safe," he told her, "and hold tight to your big brother. We will walk Guwayana to the barnyard."

Ella, encumbered by a near term pregnancy, fell into step with the horse and riders, watching carefully lest little Suzannah, or any of her three children, tumbled. She smiled at twelve-year-old Ella-*Buwa*. The girl had Keira's lovely coffee-colored skin and long, thick hair, which Ella kept braided, and she was blessed with Dural's intelligence and prowess. Thad and Ella were raising her in both worlds, white and black, and hopeful the example they set as adoptive parents would ease racial tensions in New South Wales.

The Red Spot Disease—measles—along with a serious bout of influenza in the winter of 1822 had nearly decimated the dwindling population of Aboriginals in New South Wales. Unlawful murders of the natives also continued to reduce their numbers. The Bidjigal encampment was barely a quarter of the population it had been when Thad had moved onto Wahroonga lands in 1806.

Medang had survived the contagions but now was crippled badly with rheumatism. Thad estimated the old man to be in his late eighties. Few natives lived to such a ripe age. Illuka, the Bandajalong boy who had grown up at the orphanage, took care of Medang and sought to preserve the old man's stories so that they might be learned by Ella-*Buwa* and the few young Bidjigal remaining. Ella-*Buwa* visited her grandfather often and began to speak Dharug fluently.

Yet, a sickness of the mind plagued the adopted Bidjigal girl more and more as she grew older. Only a month earlier, Ella-*Buwa* had told Thad that she had had a dream in the night where she saw her grandfather walking up the Milky Way, using the stars in it as steps.

"He comes nearer the time when we will be forbidden to say his name," she had whispered to her stepfather.

From the porch behind the church, Father Gregory sat in his rolling chair watching the Bennett family and their new horse. The sight of them all together always made him smile. He had been present at the birth of Ella-*Buwa*, had performed the wedding of Ella and Thad, and had assisted Thad with the birth of the couple's biological children. And, he had baptized all of them. The children were true Australians, he thought, conceived, born, and being brought up in New South Wales.

Annie Grey-Face stepped onto the porch next to Gregory. She had insisted on moving into the rectory to care for the priest after his infirmities left him unable to walk on his own. She slept on the floor of his bedchamber, wishing only to be near him in case she was needed. Gregory turned a blind eye to her presence, telling Thad there was no congress between them…nothing more than friendship. Thad and Ella cared little about the arrangement. In fact, they hoped Annie might crawl in bed with Gregory some night and give him the carnal pleasures he had denied himself for so very long.

They wished the two might marry and assured Father Gregory and Annie that if they were wed, they could survive the taunts of society, for Ella and Thad had been able to turn their cheeks when rude and hateful people slung insults about their adoption of Ella-*Buwa*. A *whitefella* priest with an Aboriginal wife would make a strong statement about God's love for everyone and the need for change in Australian relationships with the natives.

Annie lovingly placed a blanket over Gregory's inert legs and tucked it under and around him.

"Apra affanoon cold. Fatha muss kip leg warm. Not git pa'n."

Gregory ignored her admonition to look after himself but took one of her hands.

"Look at them, Annie...are they not a beautiful family? Ah, but had I a painting of this scene—parents and children and a babe in Ella's belly, yet to be born! They are Australians through and through."

Annie nodded her agreement and continued fussing over the blanket she had placed on Gregory. Satisfied that it covered him sufficiently, she handed him a small bowl of nuts. Thad had read in one of his medical journals that nuts were good for the nervous system.

"'Et now. Nut goo' fo' you. Kittshen mak' rowst chook fo' dinna. Ol' Betta say appa pie too."

At the gate to the barnyard, the children were lifted down from Guwayana's broad back, and the huge horse was handed off to one of the ostlers. Thad and Ella chuckled at the three children bidding the draught mare farewell and throwing kisses her way. Little Suzannah took one of Paddy's stitched paws and waved it at Guwayana.

"Paddy say ta-ta, big horsey!"

Thad grabbed the little girl and lifted her onto his shoulders. She shook a reproving finger at her siblings and informed both that they were too big for shoulder rides.

"They are growing up loved," Thad whispered to Ella. "We are giving them the best life...and we will do so for the little one you carry," he added, patting her abdomen softly. "I believe the baby will come soon."

She squeezed his hand affectionately.

"Maybe by the end of this month, Thad. I am beginning to feel the baby drop lower. Perhaps you can check if it has turned."

Ella had delivered a fragile baby boy after birthing Gregory. The little boy lived but three days. Heartbroken, Ella feared having more children. But then, sweet Suzannah arrived healthy and lively. "Suzie," as Thad had nicknamed her, was a daddy's girl. Thad adored everything about his littlest child since she resembled her mother in nearly every way and imitated Ella's mannerisms. Thad loved that she called herself "Hoozie."

Ella was naturally worried about giving birth again, though Thad had assured her the unborn babe had a strong fetal heartbeat and was growing well. She hoped for another boy, though she knew Thad did not care which gender the next child was.

Days before this, rocking her little stepsister to sleep, Ella-*Buwa* had sagely told Thad: "This one—our sweet Suzannah—will someday give birth to the *Nagayin Gurung*, the one who will keep us walking on this land. Her words will preserve our songline forever."

Thad, confused, asked Ella-*Buwa* what she meant. But the young Aboriginal girl had trouble explaining her prediction.

"*Gemang* Medang tells me I am a seer. He says I must write down my dreams, for they speak truth."

On a warm night the first week of November 1829, baby Benjamin was born. As hoped, the birth was easy, and the baby was healthy. Thad and Mabarra delivered the child, while Gregory sat at Ella's bedside, holding her hand and cheering her effort. Two of the Barn Boys had made a hand chair with their arms and carried the priest upstairs to Ella's bed. He refused to miss the birth. He had attended all the others' and staunchly declared he would be at this one too.

"A little brother!" young Gregory yelled when Thad brought the news to his other three children.

"Yes," Ella-*Buwa* agreed. "Two boys, two girls. Our family numbers six now!"

"I see babee bruffer wite now!" Suzie insisted, jumping up and down.

Thad smiled: "Let me check that your mum is awake. She is tired, you know. Birthing a baby is hard work."

The children waited at the bottom of the stairs while Thad went up to see Ella.

"How birfa babee har' wouk?" Suzie asked her older sister. "Can no' jiss pull ou' mum bellwe?"

Ella-*Buwa* smiled and replied: "No. Babies do not get pulled out, Suzie. They get squeezed out...by the mum. She has a special tunnel for that inside her body. It takes time, many hours, and a lot of pushing to squeeze the baby out the birth tunnel."

Gregory made a face. He had never heard this explanation, but he had seen animals having babies. The family's dog, Bugi, Dharug for "bark," had given birth to a litter of puppies the year before, seven little squirming, squeaking bundles. Gregory had watched, helping his father wipe each puppy's face with a cloth before giving it to its mother for bonding. Thinking back, he remembered that Bugi had seemed to squeeze each puppy from her backside. Had his mum done this with him, his sister, and now the new baby brother? Had she licked each of them clean, as Bugi had done?

Ella giggled when Thad reported the anticipation of their three older children to see the new baby boy. Father Gregory sat beside the bed holding newborn Benjamin. The miracle of new life had never ceased to fascinate him.

"Bring them up, darling," Ella said. "They should meet their new sibling. He is barely an hour old."

As Thad led the three children to the birthing chamber, he cautioned them about being quiet and careful around their new little brother. "We will," they responded in unison. They began to tiptoe the moment they reached the top of the stairs. Each one first went to Ella and kissed her cheek, after which the three gathered about the priest to see their newborn brother.

Ella-*Buwa* sat down next to Father Gregory and looked at the tiny face of her sleeping stepbrother, Benjamin. He was red and wrinkled with miniscule white dots on his nose and forehead. A tuft of golden hair sat upon the top of his head. His little mouth was round and pink, and he made almost imperceptible sucking noises. One of his doll-sized hands had clasped the vicar's index finger.

Gently, Ella-*Buwa* slid one of her index fingers into the baby's other hand. He grasped her finger eagerly. She smiled.

"He is so strong for such a small one, Father Gregory."

"Indeed, he is. This grasping of fingers is a sign he is healthy."

Ella-Buwa smoothed the baby's swath of golden hair. Her mother was watching her.

"He looks like Suzie did when she was born," Ella-*Buwa* said.

"You had golden hair too, Ella-*Buwa*, but yours was very curly," her mum told her."

"Wha' 'bout mines?" Suzie whispered, remembering what her father had said about being quiet.

Ella ran her fingers through the horsetail Mabarra had made in Suzie's long blonde hair.

"Oh, your hair was as golden as the acacia flowers, Suzie! And Gregory's too. Flaxen. All of you were such beautiful babies."

Ella-*Buwa* hummed softly, a faraway expression on her lovely face.

"Father Gregory," she asked, "how far from Australia is India?"

The vicar looked at Ella-*Buwa*, wondering what had made her ask such an odd question.

"Let me see," he said. "I think it must be several thousand kilometers. It is north-by-northwest of here. Why do you ask?"

Ella-*Buwa* smiled to herself, remembering the dream she had awoken from three nights ago. A baby boy had risen from the morning mists of Acacia Farm and grown into a man. People called him Dr. Ben. He was exceedingly tall and handsome, with dark hair and amber eyes, like his father. She saw him standing at the rail of a ship and then riding an elephant in a land of flowers and temples. He had joined the Queen's Troops in India to serve as a doctor. Sadly, she also saw him die of malaria shortly after his marriage to a beautiful English woman.

"I was just dreaming of India a few nights back," Ella-*Buwa* explained to the priest.

After a minute, Ella-*Buwa* gave up her seat to Suzie and went to her mother's side, taking her hand.

"Do you feel well, Mum?"

Ella nodded and squeezed Ella-*Buwa's* hand.

"I know that expression, my sweet girl. What are you thinking?" her mother asked.

Ella-*Buwa* smiled, then looked at her mother's shrunken abdomen. She knew pregnancy and childbirth were difficult, and that some women died after giving birth. She also knew her stepparents would lay with each other for years to come and there would be many chances for more babies.

"Benjamin should be your last baby, Mum. You are almost nine-and-thirty now. We have the perfect family, I think. We need not have fourteen children like the McCurdys in Killara. Mrs. McCurdy is no better than a slave in that household, a brood mare, and her body is worn out."

Ella giggled: "Fourteen!! Oh, never! But you are correct. Four is a good number."

Ella-*Buwa* was wise beyond her years, for two years later, Ella lost another baby, this one only half term. Thad quietly buried the tiny, barely-formed, boy fetus next to the earlier lost baby boy, who had been named Michael and lived but three days. The couple did not name the half-term boy. Ella-*Buwa* told her stepparents the baby was not fully formed and so had been taken back into the earth by the spirits. This gave Thad pause, for he—and only he—had seen the fetus, and it was missing an arm.

Ella was weak and fevered for many days following that miscarriage. She lost much blood. Ella-*Buwa* tended to her diligently, lovingly. Thad worried Ella might have child-bed fever and treated her with every herb and medicine he knew for infection. But she was strong-willed and fought off the sickness just as she had done with measles.

"You must not have more children, Mum," Ella-*Buwa* gently warned again.

Ella shared this with Thad. After that, whenever Thad made love to Ella, he made sure to spend his seed in a handkerchief. Though this method was not a guarantee, it worked for the couple. There were no more Bennett children, no more dangerous miscarriages or difficult births. Thad and Ella had left their legacy to the colony of New South Wales in the parenting of four *first* Australians.

The wedding guests, including Ella, were dancing around a bonfire that shot skyward over the open space between Acacia House and the church. There had been ample rum and wine to imbibe…perhaps a little too much of the potent spirits. The Aboriginals did not hold their booze well, easily becoming inebriated. Ella was in her cups too.

Father Gregory and Annie had finally decided to quit "living in sin," as Gregory jokingly called it, and tie the knot. Reverend Armand Napoli, newly arrived from Spain as Gregory's young assistant, had given the sacrament of marriage inside St. Andrew's Anglican Church on June 9, 1833. He had blessed and given his stamp of approval to the interracial union. Like Gregory, Father Armand was a liberal thinker, and, as such…he was courting Mabarra.

"You are an inspiration to all of us," Thad said to Gregory and Annie when asked to speak at the wedding reception that evening. "You are two of God's most capable and sensible soldiers!"

Those not dancing were eating. The Bidjigal had brought their bush tucker, and Old Betty had made her best recipes, though she was barely able to get around anymore. She had turned eighty a few months before the wedding. Thad had reduced her duties. But with the help of the kitchen maids, she still could turn out excellent fare.

Armond Napoli taught the Bidjigal a lively reel. They loved it and began revising it with their own steps. Ella joined in. Thad watched with amusement as she flung her skirts high and kicked, showing her shapely legs. She had no idea what dance steps to do, so she followed Armand and Annie Grey-Face's lead. Annie whirled in circles and shook her hips. She whirled again and shook her breasts.

Then, to Ella's surprise, Annie shed her blouse and let her bare breasts show, like the other Bidjigal women who attended. Gregory cheered and laughed. Thad wished to turn away, as this woman was his best friend's new wife, but he could not move. The dance was mesmerizing. He stared at all the breasts with great regret.

Ella turned to Thad and teasingly began unfastening her bodice. He shook his head no, then shrugged.

"When in Rome, do as the Romans do!" Gregory laughed from his rolling chair.

Thad gave him a look of dismay.

"Ogle at your own wife!" he replied, jerking his head toward the half-naked Annie.

When he turned to look at Ella again, she had removed her bodice and danced wearing only her thin chemise. It left little to the imagination.

"She has bonded with the natives!" Gregory quipped.

He enjoyed watching Thad's alarm, as everyone looked at his beautiful wife's risqué dancing and jiggling breasts inside her chemise.

The dancers were jutting their hips enticingly now and mimicking the joining of a married couple. Suddenly, Mabarra appeared, wearing only a thin cloth below her waist. Thad gawked. Before Ella had arrived at Acacia House, Thad had thought he desired Mabarra. He had resisted, however, because of the mixed-race taboo at the time. Was she taunting him now? Her breasts were large chocolate globes. She had painted a star around each pointy nipple.

"They are enacting the wedding night," she whispered to Thad. "Perhaps you should turn your head, Dr. Bennett. There will be no modesty."

She scanned the crowd until she found Dr. Napoli. If nothing else convinced him to marry her, surely her dancing with a bare bosom would. Armand Napoli was hungrily staring at Mabarra as she joined the dancers. She was a goddess, he thought. But with sudden embarrassment, he turned to Gregory—

"Vicar, I daresay the Holy Father would greatly disapprove of our partaking in this lewd celebration with the Aboriginals."

Gregory made as if to push away the younger vicar's thoughts.

"They are my wife's people. We give them the light of faith. Thus, we must respect their traditions, even those that lack modesty. Were not Adam and Eve naked before they sinned?"

Ella swung by Thad, dancing a seductive circle around him as she snapped her fingers. She stumbled and fell against his chest.

"I feel so…so…free, my love," she moaned with wine breath, draping her arms about his neck.

Thad held her. The skirt of her dress had slipped to her hips, with no bodice to hold it. She pressed herself against him provocatively. She was drunk. Yet, a surge of desire overtook Thad, and he kissed her passionately.

"You are, perhaps, remembering your own wedding night?"

Dr. Napoli stood beside the couple, smiling as he said this.

"The Bidjigal have taught us the human body is beautiful and to have no shame about it," Ella said. "Thad told me so at Cockle Creek when we first kissed."

Seconds later, she whirled away and was back in the circle. Thad watched with ambivalence as she grasped the bottom of the chemise and lifted it over her head. A cheer went up, and well it should have. Thad thought her the most beautiful woman in all creation.

"You are a lucky man, Dr. Bennett," Napoli said. "She dances for you and you alone."

One-by-one, people slumped on the ground when the dance ended. Annie Grey-Face came to Gregory and sat on his lap. His rolling chair creaked with the weight. He chuckled and patted her bare back.

"Dr. Benna," she said to Thad. "We Bid-ji-gal canna hab da fire drink. We grows stu-pid quik."

"Yes," Thad agreed.

He turned to Gregory and Armand Napoli.

"We were foolish to allow alcohol at this celebration. They will all go home drunk."

Gregory put a hand on Thad's arm.

"It is no sin to celebrate this way. We have harmed no one. The Bidjigal…and our lovely wives…have no shame about their bodies, and there is no reason they should. But I agree we ought to curb the drinking a bit next time."

Thad retrieved Ella's chemise and bodice from the ground and brought them to her. She slid on the chemise looking sheepish.

"Are you ashamed of me, my dear husband?"

He wrapped his arms about her.

"Never," he replied, kissing her hair. It fell down her back in a golden cascade. "But you must promise to reserve any further immodesty only for me. You are mine, sweet Ella. It is not my wish to share you with others."

"I apologize if I was wanton," she whispered, leaning against his shoulder. "I am tired now. Will you put me to bed, darling?"

He gave her a light kiss on her mouth and swept her up in his arms.

"Gregory, my wife has exhausted herself with the drinking, eating, and dancing and wishes me to put her to bed. I bid you good night and wish you and your new wife, Annie, a happy life together."

"The timber-cutters are angry," fifteen-year-old Ella-*Buwa* told her father after he had put her mother to bed. "I saw them in the flames of the bonfire, riding their horses fast. I dreamed of them last night. I cannot stop them from coming here."

Was this another convoluted prediction from his adopted Aboriginal daughter, Thad wondered. He dearly loved her, but *Gumang*-Medang had filled her head with all sorts of ideas about seeing the future. The old man was gone now. He had walked up to the spirit world a year earlier, as Ella-*Buwa* had predicted. Thad was grateful for the Bidjigal stories and lessons Medang had taught Ella-*Buwa*, but Medang's insistence that the girl was gifted with a special sight—one that allowed her to see things about to happen—was not something Thad could abide. It was, in its simplest form, witchcraft, and he did not believe in it.

"The timbermen have no cause to be angry with us, Ella-*Buwa*. They mind their own business, as do we. I worry about your vivid dreams though. Perhaps you should take some valerian to help you sleep more soundly. I will get you some."

As Thad went to the clinic for the sleeping herb, Ella-*Buwa* walked out the lane and settled herself on a stump near the road so she could keep watch. The vestige of a brilliant, titian-colored sunset spread itself over the western sky. Darkness came quickly. Thad searched for some time before he found his adopted daughter.

"I have made you valerian tea, sweet girl. It will help you rest."

Ella-*Buwa* took the teacup and thanked her stepfather. She knew his intentions were good. But like so many people in her ken, he did not understand her second sight. He wished she could rest easy about things she dreamed of, but this was not her purpose. She was called by the spirits to see the future. Mabarra understood. She would tell Mabarra about the timber-cutters.

Ironically, some of Ella-*Buwa's* predictions had come true, such as the death of her grandfather and the loss of another Bennett baby in 1832. There were enough accurate prophesies to make Thad feel uneasy. Even Father Gregory was worried about Ella-*Buwa*. She had readily commingled her Christian beliefs with those of the Bidjigal; yet there was another level to the spiritual world she inhabited.

A week before his wedding, she had told the vicar she'd seen and spoken with his father, who had been dead many years. When Gregory challenged her on this, she provided an exceptionally precise description of the elder Mayhew, down to his mannerisms and the small scar on the left side of his neck. The vicar was sure she must have found the sketch he had made of his father, yet…

"Your father wishes you to know," Ella-*Buwa* had said, "he approves of your intended marriage to Annie Grey-Face. He is in a place now where bigotry does not exist."

Ella-*Buwa* wanted to tell Father Gregory about her vision of the timber cutters, but the night had come, and she had gone to bed, as her stepfather requested. Her vision was incomplete, however. Her dream did not indicate why the timbermen were angry. Maybe she would dream again this night, if the doctor's tea was ineffective.

Quiet finally descended on Acacia Farm around midnight. The valerian tea had done its trick. Ella-*Buwa* slept contentedly. Thad held Ella in his arms and dozed erratically, immersed in thoughts of his wife's lascivious dancing, of his best-friend finally getting married, and of his Aboriginal daughter plagued by dreams. More than once, he got up to check on all four of his children. They were precious gifts, his legacy to the world.

Nestled in their small bed in the rectory, newlyweds Father Gregory and Annie Grey-Face slumbered peacefully. Father Armand slept with the children in their bedroom-converted-orphanage. Their number had fallen to fifteen after the measles outbreak. Another died from a fall while trying to reach a kite stuck in a tall red gum tree. Illuka, who had cared for Medang until his death, had returned to the orphanage to help with the teaching. A month before Father Gregory's wedding, Illuka had died suddenly while playing ball with the remaining orphans. Dr. Bennett believed it might have been a weak heart, for the young man had grabbed his chest and cried out before falling dead on the grass.

Thad heard the tall clock chime 2:00 a.m. He fell deep asleep shortly thereafter, exhausted and satisfied all was well with his world. The thundering of horse's hooves he thought he heard an hour later seemed to be in a dream, for Ella did not rouse, and there was no one else moving about in the house. He slept on.

Bugi, the dog, awakened and sat up, his ears alert. He left young Gregory's chamber and walked into the upstairs hall. A low growl escaped his mouth...

Annie Grey-Face, whose ears were ultra-sensitive, heard the clamor. She carefully got out of bed so as not to disturb her sleeping husband and went outside. Voices...she could hear men talking in the distance. The talk drew nearer. The black night came alive with light.

"This'ill titch dat crip of a' ole priest 'bout nigger-lovin'."

A fiery torch landed on the roof of the wooden church. Then another. Within seconds, the dry casuarina shingles caught fire. Annie heard the men crashing against the church door to gain entry. More torches illuminated the interior of the church. She began to run back to the rectory to wake Gregory, but not before she heard—.

"Waddya says we grabs dat black bitch a' his an' shows her a goo' fuckin'?"

A round of "yeahs" followed.

Annie changed course, realizing the men would beat and rape her if they caught her. She circled around the orphanage and headed into the woods. Some distance back the road, she surreptitiously crossed and ran for the Bidjigal encampment. A few seconds later, two men appeared, one on each side of her. She screamed, but there was no one to hear her.

"Thad, what is that light outside our windows?" Ella asked, sleepily from their warm bed.

Thad woke and went to one of the windows.

"My God, Ella! The church is on fire! There are men on horses galloping around it."

He roused the house and ordered the staff to make a bucket brigade to fight the fire. By the time it assembled, the horsemen were gone, and the church was beyond saving. Flames licked the branches of a tall ironbark tree and set it afire. Embers rode the night breeze and landed in the grass field next to the church.

The orphans were rescued quickly by the women of the house. Father Gregory was carried outside in Thad's arms. All the while, the priest was crying and screaming for Annie. Where was she? Had the arsonists taken her? Would she burn alive? Unable to know for sure, everyone stood back, helpless, and watched St. Andrew's Anglican Church, its little rectory, and the attached orphanage burn to the ground.

The Barn Boys used blankets and fetched buckets of water from the house spigot to extinguish the field fire. They were able to save the large spotted gum that held the children's treehouse.

Ella-*Buwa* took her father's hand. Only hours earlier she had warned him about the angry timber-cutters.

"I dreamed again, Papa. The timbermen are angry that Father Gregory married a Bidjigal. They also are angry that you and Mum adopted me."

She looked at her stepfather with tears in her large brown eyes.

"I should go, Papa? I am old enough now. My dreams tell me I have work to do among my people. I must spare you and Acacia Farm further violence."

Thirteen

July 22, 1850
Acacia House, Wahroonga

Suzie sat with her mother in Ella's bed chamber, humming a soft song and knitting. Every few minutes she checked Ella's breathing and pulse and adjusted the blankets pulled high against her mother's neck. Ella Bennett was otherworldly, in the final hours of her life, horribly thin and pale and wracked with coughing and raspy breath from consumption. She could not keep down food and drank very little water or broth. She was suffering miserably, and Suzie knew—no, hoped—her mother's tortured life would end soon.

It seemed an unfair dénouement for such a brilliant woman, Suzie thought. How could God allow this kindhearted and compassionate woman to die in such undeserved agony?

In fact, many things had occurred at Acacia Farm in the previous two decades that Suzie could not fathom, things she felt truly were unfair—

Annie Grey-Face had never returned after the church fire in 1833. Her body was found a few weeks later north of Waitara. Her hair had been burned off, her fingernails pulled out, her breasts cut off, and an axe handle had been jammed up her vagina after she had been beaten with the blunt end. Thad had vomited when the constable told him the news.

No one in the timber camp was charged, though everyone in Wahroonga and its vicinity was certain the lumbermen were responsible. Had Ella-*Buwa* not tried to warn her stepfather? Had Annie not said her marriage to Father Gregory was highly unusual and might be perceived as an insult to whites and blacks?

How could men behave so brutally, Thad had thought as he wept for Annie, and worse, how could they not be held accountable? He had hoped Australia might be more civilized since his arrival nearly thirty years earlier. Could Governor George Arthur's modern theories of reform not quell the hatred that still plagued the colony? Thad never told Father Gregory what happened to Annie, only that she had vanished. The vicar assumed his young Aboriginal wife had suffered second thoughts about marrying him after the fire and had run away.

Father Gregory died six years after the fire, in 1839, badly crippled, bedridden, and in severe pain. Thad could do nothing for his friend beyond comforting him. Gregory had hesitantly accepted a room in Acacia House to live out his final months. Jiemba cared for him devotedly, bringing his meals, bathing and dressing him, writing out his stories and sermons for the farm staff, and reading to him. But one winter night, the vicar aspirated part of a meal and in subsequent days developed pneumonia. He died within a week, his own lungs smothering him to death. A miserable ending for such a vital and beloved man. Thad mourned his friend as he might have grieved for a brother.

Ella-*Buwa* had left Acacia Farm a few days after the fire, her whereabouts still unknown. Ella cried for days afterward, as did the other children. Thad felt guilty for allowing Ella-*Buwa* to go. Mabarra chided him, saying the girl was barely sixteen and a sure target for the bushrangers who roamed the countryside or the timbermen. Ella-*Buwa* had said she was going to live with her people, but when Thad went to the Bidjigal *wolli* to look for her, he was told she had already left, her destination a mystery.

Mrs. Hughes, so beloved by the staff at Acacia Farm, died in May 1836. She had been helping Mabarra hang out the wash when she suddenly cried out and grabbed her forehead. Seconds later, she fell to the ground. She was comatose by the time Dr. Bennett arrived. He tried in vain to wake her. That evening, as he clasped her hands at her bedside, her heartbeat slowed, and she exhaled a long, sorrowful, life-ending breath.

Thad dolefully ruled her cause of death as apoplexy. She had been with the Bennett family since she was thirteen, almost her entire life.

When Suzie was twenty in 1845, she married one of the Beckhams of Sydney, a wealthy barrister eleven years her senior. The wedding was a huge event that was covered in the society pages of Sydney newspapers. Two years after their marriage, the Beckhams had a child, a son they named Louis. He was Thad and Ella's first grandchild and a blonde like his grandmother, Ella. The Beckhams lived comfortably in Woolloomooloo in a fine house with staff. Suzie had married well, took naturally to motherhood, and was exceedingly happy. Her circumstances provided the only joy for the Bennett family in the years following the fire at St. Andrew's Anglican Church.

It was only three years after giving birth to Louis that Suzie returned to Acacia Farm to care for her mother in her last days of consumption. Suzie brought little Louis with her, hoping to bestow some gladness on her mother and father and her brother, Gregory, and his wife, Mattie—the only Bennetts besides Ella living at Acacia Farm then. Mattie Bennett was of little help in Ella's final days. Mattie was pregnant for the third time and suffering from constant nausea and headaches. Still, Gregory was hopeful. Everyone wished she could carry this baby full term, for she had lost two earlier babies.

However, only a week after Suzie arrived, she found herself caring for both her mother and Mattie, who had begun fainting and having seizures. One evening Mattie began to hemorrhage. As the hours passed, the bleeding increased. Thad delivered Mattie of a premature baby the next day. The infant, a little boy, lived only a few hours. His mother followed him in death two days later, taking her last breath in the aggrieved Gregory's arms. He asked that the two be buried together in the Acacia Farm cemetery.

Suzie had written to her younger brother, Benjamin Bennett, the moment she saw her mother's appearance, a mask of death on a skeletal body. Benjamin had sailed for England in 1847 to study medicine at the Royal College of Surgeons. Ella had been sick since before he left, so the news of her impending death was no surprise to Benjamin. In his most recent letter home, he had said he'd met a lovely woman, the daughter of an earl, and hoped they would marry when he finished medical school. He had applied and been accepted to work for the British army in India when he finished his medical studies. Suzie wondered how many years might pass before Benjamin would return to Australia.

Thad gradually grew morose. He felt as if he was failing everyone, for he could do nothing for Ella and had lost Mrs. Hughes and Mattie, along with her baby. He was guilt-ridden over the horrific murder of Annie Grey-Face, and he had watched helplessly as his dearest friend, the vicar, painfully died. Thad doubted his skill as a man of medicine. He suffered miserable regrets. His father would be embarrassed, he decided, and disappointed. So many people Thaddeus Bennett had loved were lost on his watch. He doubted he'd see Benjamin again. And now his wife lay dying.

A faint shadow fell over Ella's sickbed. Suzie paused her knitting and turned, thinking it was her father.

"She is sleeping, Papa..."

Her stepsister, Ella-*Buwa* Bennett was standing beside her. It had been seventeen years since Ella-*Buwa* had left Acacia Farm. The two women stared at each other, then Suzie spoke.

"I thought never to see you again, dearest sister."

She grasped Ella-*Buwa's* hand and kissed it. Ella-*Buwa*, much taller than Suzie, put her arms around her sister and kissed her head.

"I have seen you every day in my heart, sweet Suzie," she assured.

She wore a simple muslin dress the color of the deep orange sunsets at Acacia Farm. She was barefoot, having doffed her dirty boots downstairs, and held the strap of a kangaroo fur bag slung over one shoulder. There was a bouquet of dried banksia in her free hand, dried because there was little in bloom in July. Carefully, she laid the flowers on the table beside her stepmother's bed.

"I doubt Mum will wake. If she does, I do not think she will know you," Suzie said. "She has begun to lose her senses. She often does not know Papa or me. When her pain grows unbearable, she calls for her own mother. Papa gives her as much laudanum as he dare."

Ella-*Buwa* took one of her mother's frail hands and kissed it softly. She touched Ella's gray-streaked hair. Her stepmother was only nine-and-fifty, too young to depart this earth and walk up the river of stars into heaven. Ella-*Buwa* stared at the grim remains of her beautiful stepmother for a long time before speaking.

"I thank you, Mum," she whispered, "for giving me life, your breath and your heart. For teaching me how to love and to serve others, for faithfully granting me, my siblings, and my dear Papa your best years. I grieve that you will leave us tomorrow, yet I know your pain will remain here with us. You will climb into the heavens to be with the spirits. You will dance among them again, and they will honor you for all the good you have done. A new star will shine in the sky for you, and you will be called *Garadgi Dyin*, "doctor woman."

Ella-*Buwa* gently laid herself across her mother's chest and cried the tears of two minds—one that mourned the loss of a beloved mother, the other relieved to know her mother's pain would be left behind. When she stood up, Suzie wore a puzzled expression.

"Why do you come home now, when Mum is nearly gone? She cannot hear your words. She does not sense your presence. My God, where have you been all these years?!"

Ella-*Buwa* lowered her head, as if in shame. For a short time after she left Acacia Farm in 1833, she had lived with her people, the Bidjigal, in the *wolli* south of the farm, but she found no peace among them. The dreams and images that tortured her sleep continued, even intensified. She followed a *songline* into the mountains where she lived alone for a time, visited by the spirits of her true mother and father.

They told her she must use her gift of sight to help others. So, she began a *walkabout*, following streams and tracks until, after many months, she ended up at a Wiradjuri camp in Orange, east of the Blue Mountains. Though *walkabout* was traditionally reserved for boys and men, Ella-*Buwa* refused to follow such guidelines, telling the male leaders of the Wiradjuri that her gift of sight placed her above them in rank.

There, among this large mob of native people who also spoke Dharug, her strange prescience had been accepted, though many of the Wiradjuri clan stepped carefully around her and even avoided her presence for fear she might see something bad about their future. She had craved writing materials once the notebooks she carried in her kangaroo backpack were filled with stories, predictions, and sketches. A boy named Yalgu, meaning "jumper ant," befriended her and began making flat pages for writing and drawing from the shed, dry bark of grey gums. She taught him the English alphabet and some simple words. When she left on another *walkabout*, he went with her.

They traveled south to a village near the Tucoerah River where a clan of Gweagal accepted them, though they were made to camp outside the comfortable cave used by most of the people for sleeping. Ella-*Buwa* advanced her reputation almost immediately by predicting a flood and convincing the clan to move inland. They honored her by naming the abandoned, flooded cave for her. Yalgu learned to craft his own shield and bone-tipped spear. He kept himself and Ella-*Buwa* in fish and meat…until he left the humpie they shared and took a Gweagal wife.

In the early spring of 1850, Ella-*Buwa's* dreams had begun to take on a dark theme of death. Her stepmother, to whom she owed everything, was dying. Ella-*Buwa* could hear the agony, the persistent wheezing and coughing; she could smell the blood from dying lungs. She saw her stepmother's pale, thin form lying on a bed. Suzannah Fielding, her stepmother's long-deceased mother from Canada, appeared to Ella-*Buwa* one night and told her she must return to Acacia Farm to bid farewell to Ella.

Papa would come back any minute now to take up his sad vigil by Mum's side, Suzie thought. He had gone to his chamber to wash up and then to the kitchen for something to eat, although he ate little these days. He looked careworn, almost pitiful and shrunken. At nine-and-sixty, Suzie wondered how long he would live once Mum was gone. Ella was the center of his life, his companion, his passion and singular desire, the beat of his heart and his every breath. Their love was matchless.

He always opened his aggrieved heart at Ella's bedside, kneeling and drolly calling her Aphrodite of Acacia Farm and Empress Ella of Wahroonga. He said her beauty and proficiency in all things had for years frozen his tongue, rendering him unable to speak of how great his love was for her. He threaded her hair with his fingers, stroked her pale, sunken face, kissed all her fingers, and told her stories from their youth when love had first bloomed in their hearts. Did she remember sitting on the front porch swing with him? Would she gladly kiss him again at Cockle Creek? Had she aimed to arouse him to madness when she danced bare breasted around a Bidjigal fire? When did she first know she was in love with him? Did she realize he had fallen in love with her the first night they met?

He sang to her softly in his mellow baritone voice, a song they had sung to each other and their children—*All Things Love Thee, So Do I*. His chin trembled and teardrops dribbled down his cheeks as he recited poems to her from her favorites—Byron, Southey, Wordsworth, Hawthorne, Louisa Costello, and Robert Browning. Ancient Sappho was beloved as well, with her inflaming words: "Love shook my heart, like the wind in the mountain…You set me on fire!"

Almost comically, he danced around her bed holding her hands, laughing and tapping his bootheels on the floor. His handkerchief, fragrant with his masculinity, he tucked in her nightdress that she might sense him near, always. He brought her pretty stones from the creek and spent flower pods from the acacias.

"Darling Ella, I have always selfishly hoped it would be I who would leave this earth first, so that I might not grieve so if it were you instead. What kind of doctor am I that I cannot even heal my own sweet wife?"

It was almost more than Suzie could bear, this raw display of her father's grief. He would return at any moment now, with the too-personal spectacle of his anguish. It would not be her mother's suffering Suzie would remember, but her father's…

When Thad entered Ella's bed chamber with a cup of tea he hoped to coax Ella to taste, Ella-*Buwa* turned to face him. She smiled sweetly, the smile she had always reserved only for him.

"Hello, dearest Papa."

He stared for a long time before setting down the teacup and wrapping his arms around her. She was the manifestation of his dear wife's determination and energy…as much a part of Ella as any child born of her body. They shared a few moments in greeting, then Thad wiped a tear from her cheek and looked intently into her watery brown eyes.

"How did you know? We have heard nothing from you in years, have not known your whereabouts. How did you know your mother is dying?"

Ella-*Buwa* gave her stepfather a soft, understanding smile. He had never shown much confidence in her ability as a seer.

"Papa, I think you know the answer."

He slowly nodded. Perhaps it was time he embraced his stepdaughter's gift.

―――

On July 23, 1850, Ella Fielding Bennett drew her last breath lying in her devoted husband's arms, her children at her side, except for Benjamin who could not sail home from England to Wahroonga.

Thad held an elaborate funeral for Ella. The wooden church at Acacia Farm was gone, as was Father Gregory, so Father Napoli gave the service in the brick St. John's Cathedral in Parramatta. Ella looked elegant in repose, wearing a light blue dress and lace gloves, her hair in curls about her lovely face. Mabarra tinted her lips pink and rouged her cheeks to give some health to her appearance. Her mother's pearls encircled her neck and lay against her earlobes. Thad had wanted her to look as she did on that first evening they met at dinner.

Some hundred guests attended. Many came forward to speak, often telling of times Ella had been kindhearted toward their families or had treated their wounds or illnesses with tender care. They praised her beauty and elegance, her intelligence, her devotion to children, especially Aboriginal children, and lauded her love and affection for her husband and her own children. The most moving speaker, though, was Ella-*Buwa*, who recounted her birth in 1817 and the miracle of her stepmother's life-giving breath.

Not in attendance was Elizabeth Macarthur. She had died at age three-and-eighty in February 1850 of a stroke, having outlived her husband by many years and preceded Ella by almost six months. In later years, the two women had become close friends. They decided they had much in common and devoted themselves to writing their stories of life in the colony and working for philanthropic causes. After Elizabeth's health failed, she moved to Clovelly on Watsons Bay to live with her daughter, Emmeline. She and Ella often visited each other at the bay, sitting in The Gap, a rock bridge in the bay facing the sea, reminiscing.

Ella Fielding Bennett was taken from St. John's Cathedral after the funeral service and interred in the small cemetery at Acacia Farm. After that, never a day passed that Thad did not visit her grave to lay a flower or a note or a pretty shell or rock…until a wildfire consumed all of Acacia Farm in the summer of 1871, leaving behind only embers and ashes. Thad was never the same after that. His widowed son, Gregory, moved to Wareemba on the lower Parramatta River and opened a cargo shipping business. Thad, growing feebler by the day, went with him. He never practiced medicine again, but his reputation remained esteemed throughout New South Wales.

Dr. Thaddeus Bennett spent his last years sitting by the ferny banks of the Parramatta River and remembering the wonderful life he'd been given in Australia. He and sweet, lovely Ella had lived fully, completely, happily.

Ella-*Buwa* came to see her father one summer day in 1882. Thad was in his chair by the river, staring into its muddy shallows. Beside Ella-*Buwa* stood a tall, half-caste man. He was smiling. His skin was much darker than Ella-*Buwa's*. They both kissed Thad on each of his cheeks.

"Papa, this is my grandson, Mula Dhulay, the *big man*, because he is so tall and broad. I share him with a Wategoro husband at Liberty Plains, west of Sydney. We have two daughters. Wigay is his mother. Her name means *berry*."

Thad looked at his great-grandson up and down, then smiled.

"You are a handsome chap," he whispered, no longer in possession of his deep mellow voice. It was little more than a rasp by now. He took his great-grandson's large hands and squeezed them affectionately. He turned to Ella-*Buwa* and took one of her hands too.

"I knew you would come to see me, my daughter. Yet, I dread our reunion, as I know it means my time is short. I will die soon, yes?"

Ella-*Buwa* knelt, as did Mula Dhulay.

"We all must die, Papa. I believe you are ready to join Mum, that you find no purpose in living now. She waits gladly for you at the gate of heaven."

Thad nodded. It was true. He thought of Ella every day and longed to join her in death.

"There are Quakers in Liberty Plains who seek peace between the British and Aboriginals," Ella-*Buwa* said. "Mula Dhulay and I work with them. I would be pleased if we might achieve some semblance of tolerance, enough that my people no longer fear the British rifles and hangmen. Mayhap in my grandson's old age, true peace will exist."

Thad was pleased his stepdaughter was continuing his quest for tolerance between the blacks and whites of New South Wales. He had long dreamed of a world where people were equal.

He also was happy Ella-*Buwa* had a husband to protect her, though he knew she likely could protect herself. And she had daughters and a grandson, heirs to carry on her bloodline and tell her story.

"I have lived in both worlds here, Ella-*Buwa*. I am grateful to have been your stepfather. I am grateful you brought your grandson to me as well. He is a fine man, I see, and I know he had been raised to be wise."

Ella-*Buwa* and Mula Dhulay kissed Thad again. Ella-*Buwa* reached into her kangaroo fur bag and pulled out a harp shell, a rare find on the beaches of New South Wales. She turned it until Thad could see the inscription, she had made on one side. It was a small family tree with Thad and Ella on the trunk, then Ella-*Buwa* and Mula Yuindyu, her husband known as *tall man*, her daughter Wigay above, and finally Mula Dhulay on top. Thad fondled it with gratitude, for it said his story, Ella's story. The stories of Ella-*Buwa* and her family would carry on.

There was another name too, a name next to Mule Dhulay. It read Wugongga.

Mula Dhulay leaned down and pointed at the name, Wugongga.

"She is, how you say *dyinmang*? Wife. She my wife, grandfather Bennett. She wit' child, vera big wit' chil'."

Thad sighed, smiling. His work and his dynasty of heirs would prosper in Australia.

On a cool, breezy morning in March 1882, Suzie Beckham stopped by her brother's home in Wareemba with a plate of fresh-baked biscuits.

"Doctor Bennett be in his rocker on thee riverbank," Emily told Suzie.

Emily had been with the family for many years, having sailed to New South Wales in 1806 at age two with her mother, who served the doctor and vicar. Now at eight-and-seventy, she had grown a bit plump and grey but was hale for her years.

After Ella had died, Emily became the doctor's steadfast helper and confidant. She moved with him to Wareemba in 1871 after the fire destroyed Acacia Farm. They spent many hours talking of Ella and sharing memories of her. Emily had promised herself never to leave Dr. Bennett. Her heart went out to him in those decades he lived on without his beloved wife.

Suzie transferred three biscuits to a smaller plate, poured a cup of milk, and walked down to the river's edge to visit with her father. She spent time with him like this at least one day a week. If it was a Sunday, she brought her son, Louis, who was not long for New South Wales. He would sail to England in a few weeks to attend Oxford University, where, following the footsteps of his grandfather, he would study medicine.

Thad was in his usual place—his riverbank rocker—a book open on his quilt-covered lap. His eyes were closed, and his head lay comfortably against the back of the chair, which Emily carried down to the river for him every morning. At 91, he deserved to nap whenever he wished.

Suzie softly greeted him and put the plate of treats on one of his knees.

"Papa," she whispered, "I brought your favorite cinnamon biscuits. They are still warm."

He did not stir. She crouched at his feet and looked up into his furrowed face. His hair was completely white now, his body gaunt, and his hands gnarled with arthritis. Yet, he was still a handsome man in his fine suit and neatly tied cravat.

A sapphire dragonfly softly landed on his hand and was still. Suzie stared at it a moment, wondering why it was so tame.

"Papa?"

Epilogue

Fraser Park, North Wahroonga
March 29, 1987

Fraser Park was a favorite picnic destination for single, widowed mother, Kim Carterton, and her two daughters, Phoebe age 10 and Jenna age 12, along with their mixed breed but mostly German Shepherd dog, Jasper. The family lived in a double-story, gabled cottage on Boundary Road in North Wahroonga not far from the park.

"Mum, can we bring our fossicking tools please," Phoebe asked.

"Yes!" shouted Jenna. "Last time we took the tools we found a spearhead!"

How could Kim deny them? She had initiated and nourished their interest in fossicking with her stories of digs she had worked on as an archaeology student in the 1950s at Flinders University in Adelaide.

"Of course," Kim yelled from the laundry room where she was folding clothes.

It was Sunday, laundry day. This was the last load. She reached in the dryer searching for a stray sock that had divorced its partner.

"You know the drill about getting dressed for the picnic—long pants, socks, and hiking boots. I have bug spray and will pack the picnic. We'll take Jasper, but he must stay on a leash."

A half hour later they were on their way, the girls waving to people as they passed through a neighbor's backyard and onto Lister Street. A few hundred meters later, they turned west onto a crude path into Fraser Park.

Shed bark from the many stringy-bark gums and other peeling eucalypts matted the narrow path where they walked single file. If the girls saw any litter, they snatched it up and stowed it in a small trash bag they always brought with them. Kim had diligently taught them to respect the earth, as she knew her late husband, Russell, would have wanted. He'd been an environmental engineer and had died in a pedestrian accident in Ryde when the girls were toddlers.

Remembering the recent sighting of a tiger snake in the park, Kim warned the girls—

"Mind the rule about snakes. They aren't yet in their winter sleeping places. Rustle your walking sticks in the dry grass and bark mulch along the path so any reptiles who don't wish to meet you slither out of the way."

Phoebe giggled: "We don't want to meet them either!"

After about ten minutes, they came to the clearing where they liked to picnic. Kim walked the periphery of the clearing rustling her walking stick and eyeing the ground, then allowed the girls to sit down on the forest floor. Jasper was tethered to a nearby tree, as he had a penchant for chasing any other animals he saw.

Kim passed out sandwiches and opened a bag of crisps. She had treats for Jasper and a pack of caramel Tim Tams for dessert. When the girls had finished eating, they cleaned up their lunch and pulled out their fossicking tools, which amounted to several garden-sized shovels, picks, and trowels, plus old dry paintbrushes for cleaning their finds. Kim had gifted each of them magnifying glasses several Christmases earlier, simple instruments that opened up a miniature world in the dirt.

"Where should we go, Mum?" Jenna asked.

"Wait! Let's do what we did last time!" Phoebe said with her usual animation, gesticulating with her hands and walking stick. "One of us closes our eyes and turns in three circles. We go into the forest where the person who circled ends up facing."

"Mum, you close your eyes and do the circling," suggested Jenna. "You always seem to pick good places."

Kim laughed and did as instructed. She ended up facing northwest, at least according to the small compass attached to one of the beltloops on her pants. The three of them, along with Jasper on his leash, cautiously tramped off into the woods with Kim in the lead, banging her walking stick on the ground and rustling the mulch. They had gone about a half-kilometer when Phoebe indicated a place where they had discovered the spearhead.

"Here! This spot!"

They chose a section of the ground about a square meter in size and made a string grid over it. Meanwhile, Kim tethered Jasper to a tree and gave him a fresh soup bone to chew on to keep him happy. She had a clipboard with paper where Jenna had drawn a grid and numbered it. It was as sophisticated as she planned to get with her pre-teen daughters. She only wished to whet their appetites for archaeological field work.

"Okay, choose your grid squares and start digging…carefully. Let's see if we find anything interesting."

They conversed as they dug, finding rocks and roots and litter. Phoebe found a few cigarette butts and a chewing gum wrapper. Jenna unearthed two bottle caps and a plastic comb with several teeth missing.

"Nothing of value yet," Jenna said.

"Perhaps not to you girls," their mother explained, "but far in the future that comb would be an amazing find. It would tell many things about 1980s people: They cared about their appearance enough to groom their hair anyway."

"Future people might think it was an ancient body scratcher," Phoebe joked.

Her older sister made a face and rolled her eyes.

The mini archaeological dig went on for over ninety minutes before all the grids were dug and sifted. Jasper had fallen asleep. Their mother was laying on the ground nearby, almost asleep herself. The girls filled in the grids on the clipboard with information about their finds. When they had finished, they sat back on their haunches and sighed.

"No spearheads this time; not much of anything," Jenna said.

"Yeah, nothing to get excited about," echoed Phoebe.

Kim sat up and shrugged: "You know what I've told you. Archaeology is 99% digging and 1% finding. Shall we pack up and head home?"

They began gathering their tools and wiping off the dirt from them. Jasper awoke and yawned. He stood up and shook himself, making the metal ID charms on his collar jingle.

"Wait! Wait! What's that?" Phoebe shouted, pointing.

A small angular stone covered in cobalt blue lichens jutted up from the ground about five or six meters away from where they'd made the grid. Phoebe stood, looking at her mother. How had they not seen it until now? Kim smiled.

"Keen eyes, Phoeb! Go see if you wish."

Seconds later, Phoebe and Jenna were on their knees studying the stone. They pushed away the dried grass and shreds of bark around it.

"Mum, it's carved, and I think there's writing on it!" Jenna called.

Kim joined the girls and studied the stone.

"I think it could be a gravestone," Kim said. "Go get your tools, and let's find out."

After a few minutes of digging, they were able to unearth more of the stone and read some of the writing.

Phoebe was thrilled: "Mum, it says Bennett, someone's name!"

"Keep digging," Kim said, as intrigued as her daughters to find out whose gravestone this might be.

The stone lay somewhat flat to the ground, making excavation of its surface almost easy. Jenna used one of the old paintbrushes to clean away the excess dirt. Gently, Phoebe peeled off some lichens with the trowel and needle-nose pliers, but not too many, for Kim had told the girls that lichens could help date stones.

"Gregory Thomas Bennett, it says," Phoebe announced, trying to control her excitement. "Born—August 22, 1820, Acacia House, Died—November 17, 1889, Wareemba. Mum, it's way old!"

Kim bent down and rubbed her hand over the writing. It was old, all right. Bennett? Bennett? She tried to recall if she had heard that name from Wahroonga's history. She had taken a class about Wahroonga from the historical society, but it had been a few years ago.

"He was sixty-eight, Mum. Do you think he lived here in Wahroonga?"

Kim shrugged: "I assume so. People usually were buried near their homes back then."

Jenna stood and began looking around.

"Mum, here's another stone! I can tell by the smooth, flat surface of the ground."

They rushed to it and began clearing away the debris and dirt. It was broken off its original pedestal. Minutes later, the flat stone came into view and the name was revealed.

Ella Louise Fielding Bennett
Beloved Wife, Mother & Nurse
Born—August 3, 1791, Grimsby, England
Died—July 23, 1850, Acacia House

"I'd venture a guess Gregory Bennett was her son," Kim said. "She came here from England during the Colonial Period. Such an amazing find!"

The girls charged through the woods looking for more gravestones.

"Girls, stop! Remember the rules. Use your walking sticks to rustle the grass and tap the ground."

They halted, realizing the danger. Slowly, each girl went forward, tapping the ground and looking for other gravestones. Some five meters from Ella Bennett's grave, a third stone jutted up from the dirt. A blue gum root had unearthed part of it. The girls quickly used their tools to dig down and reveal it. As their mother watched, they cleaned the face of the stone—

Rose O'Reilly Martin
Devoted Maid
Born—April 3, 1752, Wexford, Ireland
Died—September 4, 1806, Wahroonga

Kim studied the dates on the gravestone. When had this woman arrived in Australia? Her date of death in 1806 and place of burial contradicted what Kim had learned about the settlement of Wahroonga. She had read that a man named Thomas Hyndes sent male convicts to cut timber here in 1822. They were believed to have been Wahroonga's first white inhabitants. How, then could a woman have died in 1806 and been buried here?

The gravestone discoveries continued—

Mildred Griffin Hughes
Chief Housekeeper
Born—June 11, 1751, Taunton, England
Died—May 13, 1836, Acacia Farm

Father Gregory Linnaeus Mayhew
Vicar, St. Andrew's Anglican Church
Born—July 26, 1766, Dieppe, France
Died—February 2, 1839, Acacia Farm

And then, of all things, a horse's grave! A horse!

Wanyuwa, the Finest Horse
Born—1804, Northampton, England
Died—January 30, 1829, Acacia Farm

"Mum! Come look; another one! Another Bennett…a really important person, I think!" Jenna yelled.

Dr. Thaddeus Bennett
2ⁿᵈ Viscount Lord Sommerfield
Beloved Husband & Father
Physician & Chemist
Born—October 12, 1781, Northampton, England
Died—March 8, 1882, Wareemba, Sydney

"He was a Viscount! Whoa! And a doctor too. I bet he was rich!" Phoebe shouted to her mother.

Kim smiled and tousled her youngest daughter's ponytail.

"There were a few aristocrats here in those days," she explained. "I'm guessing Dr. Bennett came here because the new colony needed doctors."

What had they found, Kim wondered. Were these people homesteading in Wahroonga before Thomas Hyndes' timber-getters? Surely, they were. The gravestones said as much.

"Do you think the Bennetts are a family, Mum?"

"They very well could be, Jenna. In fact, I'd say it's likely."

It was nearly dark when Kim and the girls were forced to give up their search, too dark to write on the clipboard, even with flashlights, which they always brought with them on these exploratory jaunts. But they went home jubilant. They had found many more graves. A story had begun to take shape of a doctor who was also a viscount, his wife, their children, a vicar, and many pets and unnamed people.

Clustered together were eight Bennett graves. There were others--women--with Bennett listed as a middle name...Bennett women who had married and come home to Wahroonga to be buried. One gravestone said only "A Dear Friend to All, birthdate unknown," and December 24, 1819 as the date of death. Was it a neighbor" A dog? No, the pets appeared to be named: "Axle, a Good Horse," "Warrigal, a Fine Dog," "Hestia, a Sweet Cat," "Sugar, a Tame Wallaby, "Elmer," a Good Mule. The "Dear Friend to All" was an enigma. So was "Breath of Ella." That one was most puzzling of all. There were others like it, graves that simply said: "A Special Boy," or "A Kind Lady," or "A Favorite Barn Worker." Most poignant were two tiny stones, both with small stone-carved lambs laying on top. One of the lambs had a broken ear--

Baby Michael Bennett
Born—October 4, 1823, Acacia House
Died—Aged 3 Days,

Stillborn Baby Bennett

January 12, 1832, Acacia House

The girls had carefully recorded all the names and dates from that day. They would study them and try to piece together the story of the cemetery. Kim planned to take Jenna and Phoebe to the Kur-in-gai Historical Society to report the discovery of the little cemetery in Fraser Park and try to identify the people buried there. How lucky they were to have such a genuine mystery to solve.

They returned to the old cemetery plot the next Saturday, though the weather had turned cold as autumn deepened. They exhumed more gravestones, lots of them with names other than Bennett. Two graves had survived the passage of time and remained upright, though debris had nearly buried them and one had "Mike Loves Amanda" crudely scratched into its top.

"How stupid," Phoebe said when she saw the graffiti. "People should have more respect."

Her mother and sister agreed.

It turned out the two upright stones belonged to "The Gardner's Wife" and "Emily Tate, Personal Maid."

The girls carefully recorded everything written on the gravestones and made a diagram of the cemetery on a large piece of foam core. Three weeks after their discovery of the cemetery, the foam core and their notes were taken to Mrs. Maria Stockwell at the historical society.

Mrs. Stockwell was nearing age ninety and beyond grandmotherly, the girls decided. She had far more wrinkles than their Gram, Kim's mother, and she used a cane to steady herself as she walked. She knew most everyone in Wahroonga and was the city's authority on its history.

It was mid-April, and the office inside the historical society was uncomfortably warm. The girls said so to their mother, in whispers of course. Kim responded by whispering back—

"Society members are mostly pensioners. Older people mind the cold."

Jenna nodded, shedding her jacket and sweater. Phoebe was admiring the elderly Mrs. Stockwell's earrings and necklace—lovely green stones surrounded by pearls—when Jenna began explaining why the three women had come to visit her.

"Mrs. Stockwell," Jenna began, "my mum and my sister and I have made an amazing discovery up in Fraser Park in North Wahroonga. You see, we are the Cartertons, amateur archaeologists, and we like to dig around in the park. Our mum studied archaeology at university. Mind you, we always clean up our digs and cover them over when we're finished. And we pick up litter in the park too. So, anyway…several weeks ago, we discovered an old cemetery in Fraser Park. All together, we have uncovered thirty-eight gravestones that were fallen and covered by dirt and plant material, many of them from a family named Bennett."

"That's right," Phoebe chimed in. "And the oldest grave appears to be dated 1806. That's only eighteen years after the British 'First Fleet' arrived in Sydney."

Mrs. Stockwell's eyes widened.

"You say the oldest is 1806? Really? I think you three ladies probably know Wahroonga wasn't officially settled until 1822 when timbering came to the area."

Kim stepped closer.

"We do know that, Mrs. Stockwell. But we can't seem to reconcile what we've found up in Fraser Park with the known history. Thus, we're hoping you might be able to tell us something about those graves."

Jenna showed Mrs. Stockwell the foam core diagram they had made of the cemetery. The old woman sat down at a table and began studying it. She "hmmed" to herself now and then. Her fingers traced the names and the words Acacia House and Acacia Farm.

Suddenly, she gasped!

"Ella Fielding Bennett! I have seen that name...on the back of a painting. Let me think now...where did I see it?"

She thought for a time, as Kim and her girls waited in suspense, then Mrs. Stockwell said she was going to call another member of the historical society, a Mrs. Barbara Hanson, who would know the answer. Mrs. Hanson arrived only a few minutes after being called. She greeted the Cartertons, then turned to Mrs. Stockwell.

"Maria, she's the woman in that lovely painting Estelle bought at an estate sale in Asquith a few years back. The blonde woman in the light blue dress. Her name, Ella Fielding, is written on the back of it."

Mrs. Stockwell threw up her hands in recognition: "Oh, yes! "Yes! And didn't Estelle buy a scrapbook of paintings too...by the man who painted Ella Fielding?"

"I believe so," Mrs. Hanson agreed.

Within minutes the five of them were in Mrs. Stockwell's old Range Rover heading for Estelle Ebbits home in Beecroft. Kim and the girls sat huddled together in the back seat, excited about a possible solid clue in the cemetery mystery.

Mrs. Ebbits, who lived in an old brick house, turned out to be a lovely octogenarian, much like Mrs. Stockwell, only spryer. She wore a polyester floral dress and white pantyhose, but with pink bedroom slippers. Her hair was completely white, which fascinated the girls. Their mother, now forty-one, was just beginning to get white hair above her temples.

Mrs. Ebbits insisted the group sit down for tea and biscuits before she took them to her attic and began rooting around among her antique finds.

"I love a good rummage sale," she told Phoebe, offering her Butter Danish biscuits. "Take several, my dear. And, you know, I love antique shops too!"

Kim, Jenna, and the other two women were admiring Estelle's old fireplace andirons with dragons on them. Over the mantle was a painting of Governor Brisbane, an original painting.

"This house is like a museum," Maria Stockwell whispered to the girls, followed by cackles.

"Now," Estelle began, "tell me about this Bennett cemetery."

Jenna took the lead and explained, in much detail, about the discovery the Cartertons had made in Fraser Park. She showed Mrs. Ebbits the foam core diagram of the cemetery.

"We've calculated it occupies over two hectares," Phoebe put in. "The graves are mostly buried under layers of soil and weeds, but we found two stones, under briars and vines, that are still upright. The cemetery plot is far off the main trails in the park. It's no wonder they haven't been discovered until now."

After studying the diagram for a few minutes, Mrs. Ebbits looked up, grinned, and said--

"I believe I know some of these people! Follow me, please."

She led them upstairs and into a hallway where a fold-down ladder was located in the ceiling. A rope pull hung down. Jenna immediately took charge and folded down the ladder. All three elderly women insisted on going up into the attic, even the ageing Mrs. Stockwell with her cane.

"You'll hand this up to me once I'm at the top of the ladder, won't you sweetie," she said to Phoebe with a smile.

Phoebe nodded and took the cane. She held the ladder tightly until Mrs. Stockwell had made her way to the attic. The other two women, who were already up the ladder, grabbed the old lady by her arms and hauled her the last couple of steps. The girls watched with amusement.

Kim shrugged and whispered to her daughters: "These are women who aren't going to let anything stand in their way!"

The attic was a jumble of boxes, trunks, wardrobes, and furniture, all covered in old dusty bedsheets. Mrs. Stockwell sneezed a few times, while Mrs. Ebbits poked about among her treasures for a few minutes before shouting: "Here! I've found the painting."

It was large, about the size of the window over Kim's kitchen sink. A cloth was wrapped neatly around it, and underneath that was brown paper. Mrs. Ebbits laid it down on an old oak leaf table and began carefully unwrapping it. The anticipation was killing the girls.

"Mum, I hope it's really her!"

"Me too," Kim replied.

"I think it is her," Mrs. Hanson stated confidently, folding her arms across her chest.

As the brown paper disappeared, the back of the painting came in view. In the lower right corner, in black script ink, was written—

Ella Fielding
Nurse & Teacher
Acacia House, 1818

"Mum, she was a nurse!" Jenna crooned. "She and the doctor fell in love."

Kim smiled, relishing each small discovery.

Mrs. Ebbits and Mrs. Stockwell carefully flipped over the painting. All five of them purred with delight.

The woman was breathtakingly beautiful, so realistic and joyful in appearance she seemed like she might lean out of the painting and hold a conversation with everyone.

"She is gorgeous," Kim announced. "It's amazing to think an elegant woman like her lived in Colonial Australia, maybe here in Wahroonga. According to her gravestone, she was born in 1791 in England. She must have sailed here sometime before 1818 when the doctor—the viscount!—painted her portrait."

Phoebe bent down to read the artist's signature.

Thaddeus Bennett

"Oh, look! Her husband…her future husband, signed the portrait."

It was Phoebe who spoke, following her proclamation with a squeal of delight.

"I was sure of it," Barbara Hanson said. "Estelle, you had that painting sitting against the wall in your dining room for the longest time. That's where I recall seeing it."

"Righto, Barb. I planned to bring it up here once it was wrapped up."

"I've got another treasure I bought the same day at the same place," Mrs. Ebbits went on. "It's a scrapbook of drawings and paintings. I think Thaddeus Bennett was the artist. Some of the drawings are signed with the initials, T.B."

She hemmed and hawed for almost a minute before going to a trunk under a window and extracting a scrapbook. She dusted it off.

"Yes, this is the one."

For the next half-hour, they sat at the big attic table with two flashlights to brighten the dim space and sifted through the worn, leather scrapbook, looking at excellent renderings of people, animals, and buildings. There was a receipt for payment of stained-glass windows for St. Andrew's Anglican Church, tucked in front of a watercolor of one of the windows. A small portrait near the back of the scrapbook was of a little blonde girl, "Suzie, age four." She was holding a rumpled stuffed doll made to look like a wallaby...or was it a pademelon?

Another sketch showed a man, dressed in a black robe, sitting at a desk reading a book, a quill pen in his hand. A shaft of sunshine shone down on his bent back, and a raggedy dog lay asleep at his feet. The caption read—"Wibung, the sheepdog, and Father Gregory reading his annotated Bible."

"Mum," asked Jenna, "what's an annotated Bible?"

Kim studied the sketch.

"Well, it must have had notes written in it explaining things. Annotations are notes."

There were several sketches of a woman's face and shoulders in various poses. Everyone agreed she was the lovely Ella Fielding. Kim commented that Thaddeus Bennett must have adored her.

"A few of the art works are dated," Mrs. Ebbits said. "Notice the sketch of the Aboriginal man named Wugan. He's Bidjigal, I think. The date is 1806--quite early. The Bidjigal lived in these parts back then. You may wish to go see Charles Dixon in La Perouse. He can tell you a lot about the Bidjigal and other clans from this area. I think he'd be very interested in the cemetery."

Acacia House was painted across two pages of the scrapbook, large and handsome, a welcoming place. The trees around it were in bloom. Ferns hung from the porch ceiling and a porch swing and chairs were sketched.

"Oh, Mum, I think we know these people from their graves!" Jenna cried. "Acacia House…maybe the Bennetts lived there. It probably was their house. It, or its footprint, has to be somewhere near the cemetery. You told us settlers buried their family members near their homes in rural areas."

"Possibly," Kim acknowledged. "And there is mention of a church inscribed on one of the stones, St. Andrew's, I think. It surely could not be our current St. Andrews. There may be a footprint of the old church."

Every sketch and painting held a tale yet to be unraveled.

"Oh, and there's this," Mrs. Ebbits added. "It looks like a receipt book Dr. Bennett kept."

She handed it to Kim. It was full of dated medical receipts, detailing pay for treatments and surgeries. Kim paged through the receipt book and paused on a page: "Staunched the bleeding on Aboriginal Walkiloa man with severed hand. Sutured radial artery and small bleeders. Salved and bandaged. Brought him home to prevent further violence. Payment from him, whittled kangaroo."

"Oh my gosh, Mum!" Phoebe said, looking over Kim's shoulder. "A severed hand? How would that happen, does it say?"

Kim shook her head no, but from what she had read about the local natives, it seemed likely the hand was cut off as some sort of punishment. How would the man have whittled with only one hand?

"Perhaps Mr. Dixon has information," Kim suggested. "We'll make arrangements to go see him."

Some loose papers attached to the receipt book listed employees in alpha-order and their monthly pay. The document was dated March 1, 1827. At the top was Beatrice Byrnes, kitchen maid, £1, 12 pence. Farther down the list, Jenna recognized Mildred Hughes, chief housekeeper, £2, 24 pence.

"Holy cow," Phoebe cried. "Is that all the money they made in a month?"

Kim reminded her of the time period—1820s.

"I'd say it was probably generous for that time. Those maids were housed and fed for free, I'm sure."

"Take the scrapbook and receipts and other papers with you," Mrs. Ebbits said. "I think they will be more meaningful to you than me. When you've learned more, bring them back and share with me."

Maria Stockwell stood and rubbed her back.

"Estelle, these are the most uncomfortable chairs!"

She laughed and hugged Estelle.

"My back is too riddled with arthritis to sit up here in the attic any longer," she explained, "and it's getting dark."

One-by-one, they made their way downstairs. Everyone helped Mrs. Stockwell navigate the ladder. Estelle and Barbara held on to her arms, the girls steadied her legs, and Kim ended up catching her as she descended. Phoebe handed the old lady her cane.

"Whew!" Mrs. Stockwell said, laughing. "Estelle is going to have to get a block and tackle installed to get me up in her attic next time!"

The girls doubled over with laughter. Old people making jokes was too funny.

Tea was cold in the dining room by the time they came down from the attic. The girls each grabbed some biscuits for the road and jammed them into their pockets. Jenna slid the scrapbook and other goodies Mrs. Ebbits had given them into her backpack, along with her notebook about the cemetery. Phoebe grabbed the foam core diagram and the map of Fraser Park Mrs. Stockwell had given her.

Kim offered effusive thanks to all three women, as did the girls. There were hugs…and more hugs.

"We are so proud of you girls for the work you've done here," Mrs. Ebbits said.

"Yes! And keep searching," Mrs. Hanson added. "Who knows what else you'll find?"

Mrs. Stockwell simply sighed and hugged the girls again: "What fun this has been, even the ride down the attic ladder."

They drove back to the historical society and said farewell to Mrs. Hanson and Mrs. Stockwell.

"I shall expect a presentation to the historical society soon," Mrs. Stockwell declared. "This is quite a discovery, one folks in Wahroonga will be excited to hear about."

"Of course," Kim promised. "We'd be delighted to give a presentation."

Jenna and Phoebe nodded excitedly. They suddenly felt like sleuths, important history detectives.

What they didn't know that day was that their lives were about to change in ways they had never imagined.

University of Technology, Sydney
November 29, 2011

Thirty-six-year-old Dr. Jenna Carterton waited offstage for her introduction. She was nervous, despite thorough preparation and a new dress that flattered her tall, willowy figure. Public speaking had never been her forte, nor her desire as a side hustle to teaching and writing. Yet, here she was, a speaker in demand. In a few minutes, she would be talking to a large audience at the Australian Center for Public History in Sydney.

Her doctorate in history had been conferred by the University of Adelaide seven years earlier. She had returned to New South Wales and promptly been hired as a professor of history at the University of Sydney. She rented a micro-apartment in Chippendale, an old mother-in-law space her landlady had told her hadn't been used for years. If Jenna was willing to clean it up and do some minor repairs, she could live there for a bargain rent.

The cause of Jenna's notoriety was her first book, written during her time at University of Adelaide and completed while she taught history courses at University of Sydney and pursued tenure. Her mother was amazed Jenna could write a book and a doctoral thesis at virtually the same time, not to mention fulfilling requirements for tenure. Jenna confessed her thesis had been easily turned into a book, with some minor changes and more of a storytelling style. She'd had help from several teaching assistants.

Titled *The Forgotten History of Acacia Farm*, it presented the known facts about the Bennetts, Father Mayhew, and their entourage of maids, farm workers, tradesmen, and the orphans the vicar raised. It was written in the style of an historical-biographical novel, which made it enormously readable and engaging. Jenna had done years of research and field work to learn the history of Acacia Farm and its people, from the time of the Carterton's discovery of the cemetery in 1987 until her book's publication in 2009. And she was still learning. She had a filing cabinet of notes and clippings, plus several important primary sources. Most important of all was the cemetery itself.

It had been cleared, restored, and enclosed with a Victorian-style iron fence and was now an important place, for it had altered Wahroonga's supposed history. The Cartertons had been honored at its dedication in 1996. Both Jenna and Phoebe spoke at the ceremony, making their mother more than proud.

Jenna's research led her down many avenues of local history—

A ship's manifest at Australia Emigration & Immigration confirmed that Dr. Thaddeus Bennett, Vicar Gregory Mayhew, and many of the names found in the cemetery in Fraser Park had, indeed, arrived in New South Wales in 1806 on the ship *Fortune*. Rose O'Reilly Martin, the house maid who died in 1806, only a short time after Dr. Bennett took possession of the land in Wahroonga, was listed as a *Fortune* passenger as well. Her husband, Cyrus Martin, came with her and survived the voyage from England, though he was not found in the Fraser Park Cemetery, and no further information about him was located. Jenna thought perhaps he had returned to England.

Ella Fielding was listed on the ship's manifest of the *Isabella* for 1817. In searching for a reason why she came to New South Wales, Jenna discovered on a microfilm of the *Sydney Gazette* a small notice about her arrival, answering an advert for a nurse placed by "the esteemed 2nd Viscount, Dr. Thaddeus Bennett of Wahroonga." The blurb said Ella Fielding had traveled from Canada to England and thence to New South Wales and finally Wahroonga. She was described as "an attractive Canadian-English woman of considerable education and refinement."

The Emigration & Immigration Department also had a Register of Land Grants and Leases for 1792–1867. Thomas Hyndes was there in 1822, but not Dr. Thaddeus Bennett. How had Bennett been deeded the land without record of it being done? Aboriginal and colonial history expert, Charles Dixon, had the answer. Jenna had interviewed him several times. He told her some land grants were made in the colonial period without applications. He suspected this was the case for Dr. Bennett's land. It was simply passed on to him without being recorded, a misstep by one of Governor King's administrators, or perhaps a deliberate oversight to circumvent land laws of the time. However, a land grant at Wareemba in 1871 was recorded as belonging to Dr. Thaddeus Bennett.

Equally puzzling was the lack of a record for St. Andrew's Anglican Church in the New South Wales Church Registers. Jenna was able to locate a marriage bann for Dr. Thaddeus Bennett and Miss Ella Fielding of Acacia House, Wahroonga, in the *Sydney Gazette* in the spring of 1819, and a birth certificate for one of their children, Benjamin Bennett, found in an old archival record book at St. Paul's Anglican Church in Wahroonga. Benjamin had been born in Acacia House in November 1829 and christened at St. Andrew's Anglican Church by Vicar Gregory Mayhew the following month. Benjamin's grave was not in the old Acacia Farm cemetery, however. Jenna could discover nothing more about him as an adult. He seemed to simply have vanished from Bennett history.

Mrs. Ebbits located the marriage license for the Bennetts in her attic, recording their nuptials in St. Andrews Anglican Church on November 30, 1819. After giving the attic a thorough scouring, she also found several birth certificates, including that of Gregory Thomas Bennett, born in 1824, and Suzannah Louise Bennett, born in 1826.

Charles Dixon had information about the Bidjigal who lived in and around Wahroonga. No names could be verified, since birth records were not kept for the Aboriginals in those years. Their traditional funeral traditions usually buried their story with them—no named graves or recordings of their deaths. Dixon told Jenna the nameless gravestones in the Fraser Park cemetery likely belonged to Bidjigal people who worked for the Bennetts, or Aboriginal children from the church orphanage.

Dixon told the girls: "Saying or writing the name of an Aboriginal who has died might disturb their spirit."

Thus, no records of who they were had been passed down.

Mrs. Ebbits again proved enormously helpful when she notified her network of antique shops, collectors, and libraries about the new cemetery discovered in Fraser Park. She found a diary from a collector at Hornsby that was kept by Suzannah Bennett when the girl was an adolescent. The woman who owned it had found it at a garage sale in Normanhurst but had not been able to identify the girl. The diary, though some of its pages were blank, was a trove of fascinating information for Jenna Carterton. Suzannah kept her diary diligently until she was fifteen. There was a long absence of writing afterward, but she took it up again in the late 1840s when she had returned to Acacia Farm to take care of her sick mother.

In her diary, Suzannah reported that her father affectionately called her 'Suzie.'

Papa loves me so much, and I love him. He frequently tells me how much I resemble Mum. I have her very blue eyes and blonde-streaked hair.

She noted that a young woman named Lucy, an orphan from Ireland, was her nanny and that she liked an older boy named Charles Byrnes, whose family had come to live at Acacia Farm after the death of his father from cancer. He had been a patient of Dr. Bennett's.

Suzannah's diary talked about the Bennett team of doctor and nurse and their work. Their daughter was adept at detailing her father and mother's medical calls and surgeries and the conversations they had at mealtimes. She even mentioned the day the family's old housecat, Hestia, died and wrote a poem for the cat. She told how the family always held funerals for their pets and buried them in the Acacia Farm cemetery.

One day, out of boredom, Suzannah Bennett described the entire house, Acacia House. This was a special gift for Jenna's research. Jenna compared Thaddeus Bennett's drawing of the house to Suzannah's description. They were strikingly similar. This is how Jenna learned the doctor had designed and installed running water in Acacia House, which was, perhaps, the first home in the colony to have it—

Mum allows me to bathe in her tub one day a week. I am thoroughly scrubbed, and my hair is washed with lavender soap. Mum says, 'cleanliness is next to Godliness.' Papa tells me I am very huggable and kissable after my bath!

There was information about Suzannah's older stepsister, a full-blood Bidjigal named Ella-*Buwa* her mother had delivered at birth and her parents had adopted. Suzannah described how "intelligent, perceptive, lithe, and athletic" Ella-*Buwa* was and how she taught Suzannah many things about the natural world. Her Aboriginal stepsister also made guesses about the future. One day she told Suzannah she would have a son someday who would be the "carrier heir." Suzannah had no clue what that meant.

But she was able to find out Ella-*Buwa* meant Breath of Ella. This delighted Jenna, as there was a gravestone in the Fraser Park Cemetery inscribed Breath of Ella.

The girl's blood grandfather, Medang, frighted Suzannah sometimes, but he was a good teacher too. Suzannah described how he caught a venomous brown snake one day and had his sister cook it for dinner. Suzannah did not care for the snake meat but ate it anyway because her father had taught her that open-mindedness was among the best qualities to nurture in oneself.

Suzannah wrote of playing with the children at the orphanage for half-caste and full Aboriginals, run by Father Mayhew, who Suzannah said had a strange disease that affected his nervous system and rendered him unable to walk. She wrote how she and her two brothers and stepsister liked to push the vicar around the property in his rolling chair while he told them fantastic stories. From the symptoms Suzannah described, Jenna surmised that Father Mayhew had either multiple sclerosis or Parkinson's, both diseases unknown to medicine by those names in the teens and twenties of the early nineteenth century.

Suzannah also reported that, after Father Mayhew married an Aboriginal woman named Annie-Grey Face in 1833, the timber-getters at Colah angrily set fire to the church. It burned to the ground, along with the tiny rectory and orphanage. It was a total loss, including her father's prized organ, the church's lovely stained-glass windows, and Father Gregory's extensive book collection and personal notebooks on the flora and fauna of New South Wales. Dr. Bennett offered to rebuild the church and orphanage, but the vicar begged off, saying he was too old and sick to be a priest any longer. He never got over the loss of his precious St. Andrew's and the disappearance of his beloved Bidjigal wife. He died in 1839.

Suzannah returned to Acacia House in 1849 when her mother, Ella Bennett, became sick with consumption. Mother and daughter talked a great deal, and Suzannah learned about her father's loyal half-caste Aboriginal friend, whose name Ella could not say aloud. Her mother told how the doctor had rescued the man and taken him to his camp at Wahroonga. Most delightful was Mum's recollection of the man fetching her from the *Isabella* to Acacia House.

He was the first Aboriginal person Mum had ever met, and she came to love him dearly. Even without telling her truths straight-on, he taught her that the Aboriginals were not savages, not inferior to whites. Mum told me how handsome this man was, even with smallpox blemishes on his body, scars from his clan initiation, and a missing front tooth. Mum said he had the most beautiful and genuine smile of anyone she knew in Wahroonga, except Papa, of course. Mum considered him the definition of handsome!

Suzannah's mother's voyage to New South Wales in 1817 and her love affair with Dr. Bennett was colorfully recounted in the diary. Ella even told Susannah about her first kiss with the doctor at Cockle Creek and then…a tale of a man named Antony who was obsessed with her and kidnapped her shortly before her planned wedding to the doctor. She noted that it was the stuff of adventure novels of the day. Jenna had to agree and eventually added all the drama Suzanna recounted about Acacia Farm to her book.

Ella Bennett succumbed to consumption in 1850. The funeral was briefly described in Susannah's diary, along with the family's enormous grief—

I am too young to lose my mother, an intelligent, beautiful, and vibrant woman whose hands have healed so many, brought up my siblings and me, and given Wahroonga health, guidance, and generations of Bennetts. I am at a loss for words. The hole in my heart is enormous. Papa, too, is inconsolable. He goes to Mum's grave every day and tells her of the activities at Acacia Farm. Such one-sided conversations seem to give him strength to go on without her.

The final important bit of information from Suzannah's diary was about a bushfire that swept through Acacia Farm in the summer of 1871. Susannah was forty-six by this time and lived in Woolloomooloo with her husband. Her older brother, Gregory and Dr. Bennett, lived on the farm. The *Sydney Gazette* published a story about the fire—

The bushfire was thought to have started at a small orchard in Waitara, just west of the present-day main road in North Wahroonga. Sparks from a small cooking fire near a horse-powered cider press landed in a pile of dry rags. The blaze came to life rapidly and moved east through the dry summer bush, pushed by the wind. It jumped Cockle Creek and proceeded through more bushland until it met and engulfed the wooden buildings at Acacia Farm.

Susannah wrote of Gregory, her father, and the staff, escaping to the main road passing Acacia Farm,[6] and watching helplessly as their home burned. Windows exploded in the doctor's beloved glass house. The intense heat melted its framework into gruesome shapes. Not even its kangaroo weathervane survived.

The barns burned quickly. Thad sobbed as the treehouse and its old spotted gum were destroyed. The beautiful house where he had lived for over sixty years, shared a life with his adored wife and children, and practiced medicine seemed to burn and collapse in minutes. In less than an hour, Acacia Farm was gone.

Suzannah wrote that no one was hurt, including the livestock that had been quickly set loose, but everything else was a total loss. Even the heavy foundation timbers of the buildings disappeared, sold by Gregory to a builder at Pymble. He sold most of his recovered livestock, except for a few horses, and relocated to a home just west of Sydney at Wareemba, near the Parramatta River. He invested his father's great wealth into a business running cargo vessels up the river to the city of Parramatta and beyond.

Jenna began uncovering a huge amount of material during her university years. Her sister, Phoebe, had enrolled in 1995 at the recently established Macquarie University south of Wahroonga. She matriculated as an archaeology major but spent countless hours in the university library scaring up information on the history of the area during the colonial period. She was especially interested in ancestry studies. Phoebe was able to trace some of the Bennett lineage from Thad and Ella to Susanna's son, Louis Bennett Beckham, who sailed to England in 1882 to study medicine. Had Louis married and had children? Had he returned to Australia at some point? Were these Beckhams related to her mother's family? Jenna was still working to find out.

---

[6] Later renamed Grosvenor Street.

Since publication of her book, Jenna had delivered many talks in and around Sydney and had appeared on news and talk shows. She installed an exhibit about Acacia Farm at the Kur-in-gai Historical Society, much to the pleasure of the society board. There was even chatter in Melbourne of making her book into a movie. The exceptionally handsome and charismatic James Purefoy was suggested to play Dr. Thaddeus Bennett alongside fetching Tamzin Merchant as Ella Fielding. The book had all the important elements for a transition to film—romance, action, grief, joy, and the reticent history of Colonial Australia.

Jenna had finished her PowerPoint talk at the Australian Center for Public History to a large, attentive and responsive audience that had given her a standing ovation. She had answered many questions and listened to comments, most of them intelligently put forth. She had sold and autographed many books. The evening was near its end, and she was thankful no one had kept her too long by droning on with a lengthy story. This sometimes happened—a person who was lonely or too talkative, holding her at the autograph table when she was tired and only wished to go home. Lingerers, she called such people.

She and her assigned assistant from the history center began packing up unsold books and stowing the projector and computer. There was also an easel with an enlarged image of her book sitting on it, with her picture in the lower right corner. She thought it was a good image of herself, though she felt she still possessed a girlish, twelve-year-old face. It seemed not to matter to audiences though. It was her accomplishment in routing out a heretofore unknown history that impressed people who attended her talks and book signings.

Soft footsteps sounded behind her, and she turned to see a tall, handsome, dark-haired man in a casual suit. He had a folder in his hands and was smiling.

"Oh no," she thought. "The dreaded lingerer! He'll talk for an hour about something boring and insignificant."

"I'll fetch a cart for the boxes," her assistant said, rushing off and leaving Jenna with the lingerer, the sole other person in the auditorium.

Jenna smiled at the man, who seemed to be staring at her in awe. He had thick black hair, a tanned complexion, and the most arresting and unusual bronze eyes. He also had two copies of her book in his hands. Two copies? Perhaps he was buying one for himself and a gift for someone else.

"Miss Carterton? I hope you will accept my highest compliments on your presentation. It was top drawer! You are an excellent speaker and a lovely and accomplished woman."

He had a polished British accent.

"Thank you. I'm glad you enjoyed the program."

Jenna avoided any reply about her being lovely and accomplished. Rather than make eye contact with the man for more than a couple of seconds, she looked toward the door of the auditorium, hoping the assistant would return soon. She disliked being alone with a strange man, even a handsome, well-dressed one with startling eyes.

"I bought this copy of your book from your assistant after the program," he said, still smiling and holding up a fresh, new hardcover. "I hope you'll autograph it for me."

He handed her a pen, an expensive pen such as a businessman would own.

"This one I purchased last year," he said, holding up the other copy, obviously well-used. "I have marked it up with information and would like to give it to you, as I think some of my notations will be helpful...even surprising. There also is some interesting research in this file folder that might fill in some gaps for you."

What could this man know about Acacia Farm, especially since he seemed to be from England? Jenna gave him his autographed copy. She was tired but took the notated copy and file folder with as much gratitude as she could muster. She displayed her best smile. And she glanced at the auditorium door again, wondering when her assistant would return and free her from this man's unwanted attention.

"I wonder if you might join me for tea or coffee," he offered. "I think we have much to discuss."

Jenna was not keen to go for tea or coffee with an unfamiliar man. She paused a long time before politely declining.

"I know this is an audacious and spur of the moment request, Miss Carterton, and I do apologize; but please trust me when I say you may wish to hear what I have to say."

He was, indeed, handsome and certainly well-mannered. Jenna giggled nervously.

"You haven't introduced yourself, sir. You seem to have a keen interest in Acacia Farm?"

"Forgive me…yes, I do have a great interest in the people of Acacia House & Farm. And I am so happy to have found you, Miss Carterton! It was only through an alumni publication from Cambridge that I received notice of this program. Naturally, as I was in search of you, I booked a flight from London to Sydney."

He made an effort at a formal bow, then stared at Jenna. She was growing uncomfortable with him. Yet…he had flown all the way from London to hear her talk. Why?

"I am…Thaddeus Michael Bennett. Thaddeus and Ella Bennett, of whom you have written much, were my 6th great grandparents on my father's side of the family. They also were your 6th great grandparents through your mother's lineage, the Beckhams, who descended from Suzannah Bennett Beckham's son, Louis Beckham.

He became a physician in England and returned to Australia in the 1890s. He married Amelia Graham of Sydney, the daughter of a shipbuilder. You are descended from their son, Gerald Beckman, your mother's great-grandfather."

"As for my lineage," he continued, "Louis and Amelia Beckham's daughter, Elsa Beckham, married the son of a doctor named Benjamin Bennett, who died in India. I am descended from that son, Albert Bennett, who was born and raised in England."

He paused, letting the information process in Jenna's brain.

Jenna's mouth fell open uncontrollably. She was descended from the Bennetts by way of her mother, Kim Beckham? Had she been researching her own family history all along?

"So, you see, Miss Carterton, we do have much in common."

He smiled at her and extended his hand in friendship. Suddenly, he appeared so much kinder and more virtuous. Not a lingerer at all.

"Miss Carterton," and here he paused for several seconds, holding Jenna in suspense, "we are…very distant cousins, distant family. We are the 9th generation of genuine Australians."

***

Sydney Sun-Herald, August 6th, 2013

Dr. Thaddeus Michael Bennett of Cambridge, England and Jenna Lynn Beckham of Annandale, Sydney, were joined in marriage on August 3rd, 2013 at St. Paul's Anglican Church, 1711 Pacific Highway, Wahroonga…

The End

Did you enjoy *Under the Acacia Trees*? Have a comment?
- lightkeeper0803@gmail.com

Other Books by Elinor DeWire
- www.ElinorDeWire.com

- www.amazon.com/stores/Elinor-De-Wire/author/B000APJJ0M?ref=ap_rdr&store_ref=ap_rdr&isDramIntegrated=true&shoppingPortalEnabled=true

Novels under the author's Pen Name, J. J. Scott
- www.amazon.com/stores/J.-J.Scott/author/B07QQ36XBT?ref=ap_rdr&store_ref=ap_rdr&isDramIntegrated=true&shoppingPortalEnabled=true

Made in United States
North Haven, CT
15 August 2023